Fantasy: An Anthology

Beyond Seduction

Beyond Innocence

Praise for
The Demon's Daughter

"Thoroughly engrossing . . . deeply sensual . . . a must-have for fans of more erotic romance."　　—*Booklist*

"A sensually erotic novel and one of Ms. Holly's most entertaining."　　—*The Best Reviews*

"An entertaining historical romantic suspense fantasy . . . What makes Emma Holly's tale so powerful is that fans from several genres will believe in this alternate Victorian world."　　—*Midwest Book Review*

"Holly has created another gripping story here . . . that gives the reader something to think about after the last page is turned."　　—*The Romance Reader*

"A wonderful, heartwarming book . . . fresh and detailed, impossible to put down."　　—*Romantic Times*

And for Emma Holly

"Emma Holly is a name to look out for."　　—Robin Schone

"[Holly] creates tantalizing tales."　　—*Rendezvous*

"One of the best writers of erotic fiction around."
　　—Susan Johnson

"Emma Holly never loses a firm grasp on what makes romance work."　　—*The Best Reviews*

continued . . .

Prince of Ice

A Tale of the Demon World

EMMA HOLLY

BERKLEY SENSATION, NEW YORK

THE BERKLEY PUBLISHING GROUP
Published by the Penguin Group
Penguin Group (USA) Inc.
375 Hudson Street, New York, New York 10014, USA
Penguin Group (Canada), 90 Eglinton Avenue East, Suite 700, Toronto, Ontario M4P 2Y3, Canada
(a division of Pearson Penguin Canada Inc.)
Penguin Books Ltd., 80 Strand, London WC2R 0RL, England
Penguin Group Ireland, 25 St. Stephen's Green, Dublin 2, Ireland (a division of Penguin Books Ltd.)
Penguin Group (Australia), 250 Camberwell Road, Camberwell, Victoria 3124, Australia
(a division of Pearson Australia Group Pty. Ltd.)
Penguin Books India Pvt. Ltd., 11 Community Centre, Panchsheel Park, New Delhi—110 017, India
Penguin Group (NZ), Cnr. Airborne and Rosedale Roads, Albany, Auckland 1310, New Zealand
(a division of Pearson New Zealand Ltd.)
Penguin Books (South Africa) (Pty.) Ltd., 24 Sturdee Avenue, Rosebank, Johannesburg 2196,
South Africa

Penguin Books Ltd., Registered Offices: 80 Strand, London WC2R 0RL, England

This is a work of fiction. Names, characters, places, and incidents either are the product of the author's imagination or are used fictitiously, and any resemblance to actual persons, living or dead, business establishments, events, or locales is entirely coincidental. The publisher does not have any control over and does not assume any responsibility for author or third-party websites or their content.

PRINCE OF ICE

A Berkley Sensation Book / published by arrangement with the author

PRINTING HISTORY
Berkley Sensation mass-market edition / November 2006

Copyright © 2006 by Emma Holly.
Excerpt from *Fairyville* copyright © 2006 by Emma Holly.
Cover illustration by Franco Accornero.
Cover design by George Long.

ISBN: 0-425-21259-9

BERKLEY SENSATION®
Berkley Sensation Books are published by The Berkley Publishing Group,
a division of Penguin Group (USA) Inc.,
375 Hudson Street, New York, New York 10014.
BERKLEY SENSATION is a registered trademark of Penguin Group (USA) Inc.
The "B" design is a trademark belonging to Penguin Group (USA) Inc.

PRINTED IN THE UNITED STATES OF AMERICA

10 9 8 7 6 5 4 3 2 1

Author's Note

For those who are new to my demon stories, the race humans term "demons" call themselves "yama." Up until their recent discovery by human explorers, the yama lived in scrupulous isolation. Now the races share an alternate Victorian Earth, but the yama are far more technologically advanced. Thanks to genetic tinkering, they are also stronger, more attractive, smarter, and longer lived. Their culture values emotional control above all else.

Naturally, yama view humans as inferior, though many can't help being fascinated by human passions. Complicating matters is the fact that human energy, or chi, is easily absorbed by yamishkind. The transfer produces a relaxed euphoria that is sweeter than any drug—and potentially addictive. Worst of all, human emotion accompanies the imbibing of human chi. As a result, the practice is frowned upon.

Xishi is conceived

Humans say the yama aren't like you or I. Allow me to assure you, however, that as different as the average yama is from the average human, they are not half so peculiar as the average yamish royal.

—Maxwell Philips, *The True and Irreverent History of Demonkind*

The emperor of the yama was coming into heat; he simply was too drunk to know it.

His humble maidservant, Xoushou, was the reason for both conditions. It was she who had slipped the pharmaceutic accelerator into his meals for the past two weeks, she who kept his silver goblet brimming tonight. Most importantly, she had timed everything so that his sexual cycle would reach its peak while the empress and her clique were unreachable. The emperor himself did not dare interrupt his wife when she was at her private mountain spa. She had made her feelings about that icily clear the first time he tried.

Theirs was not a love match—at least not on the empress's side. Xoushou had come to think the emperor had a yen for his wife, a yen the empress almost never gratified.

Xoushou hid her satisfaction under hooded eyes, fighting not to squirm on her embroidered pillow in the shadowed corner where she sat awaiting further orders. The empress's withholding nature was to the good. Her husband's signs of restlessness were rising, and Xoushou could not deny she was looking forward to enacting every aspect of her revenge. True, the emperor's father had been responsible for banishing Xoushou's family from its rightful place in the inner court, but like all the royal line, Emperor Songyam was a handsome man: tall, slender, and, when his rut was on him, virile as a bull.

His strength was apparent in his pacing, back and forth, back and forth, kicking his lavishly embroidered bed robes away from long, muscled calves. Whatever disadvantages came with the royals' peculiar, inbred genetics, the advantages were obvious. No other yama were as physically perfect, and none had minds as sharp. It took a finely honed intuition to survive among the intrigues of the court, never mind to hold the throne for as many generations as this dynasty had. The power Songyam's bloodline represented was an aphrodisiac even to one who had suffered at its ruthless hands. Fascinated, Xoushou watched the emperor's organ rise, the thickening arch of flesh pushing against his thin sleeping silks.

She wet her lips with anticipation, but he seemed not to notice the change in his body as he passed the deep-set windows. The Forbidden City's moonlit mansions comprised the view, none of them as high or huge as the emperor's. Below his aerie, the Silver River snaked through the large, walled complex of royal houses, its frozen surface powdered by recent snows. The swooping silver rooftops had been powdered, too—still as death, their scheming inhabitants presumably asleep within.

One lone aircar, the crest for a royal house glowing on its side, banked west to avoid the strict no-fly zone above the emperor's home.

Though warmer than the scene outside, the imperial apartments echoed it. Set in a marble palace on the highest of the city's hills, the emperor's rooms were furnished in the delicate blue and white of snow at dusk. Their floors were lacquered, also white, with scrolling patterns of platinum and gems inlaid into the shining surface. Wherever he stepped, the emperor trod upon his own riches. The gems, primarily sapphires and diamonds, twinkled in the candles Xoushou had lit.

She had chosen their illumination not for nostalgia or romance, but to prevent the emperor from noticing that his eyes had grown more sensitive to light. This was one of the first signs that a royal was going into heat. Had Xoushou not been born a daughter of the blood herself, she would not have known this; such secrets were closely held from the inferior ranks. But Xoushou *was* royal, despite her present lowly status, and she did not wish the emperor to realize what was happening until it was too late.

He stopped pacing, startling her as he turned to speak. "You are sure the empress will not return for another week?"

Xoushou was pleased to hear his words were slurred by drink. Her plan required that his powerful intellect be dulled.

"I am certain, Your Magnificence," she responded in the sweet, low voice she knew to be her greatest seduction. "The empress's chief of staff was very clear about her schedule."

The emperor pulled a face at his favorite pet, a yellow-tufted angelbird that was nibbling on a cricket in its silver cage. Never in a million years would he have shown his frown to Xoushou. To display so great a crack in his self-command, and before a supposed servant, would entail a loss of face no royal yama could recover from. Had he not had two bottles of strong provincial rice wine in his royal belly, he wouldn't have frowned at the bird, either.

"I don't see why Nala has to travel so much," he said with the slightest hint of petulance. "You'd think there was nothing to do here in the capital."

Empress Nala traveled so much because she liked to be alone with her lovers. Unlike her husband, she had no trouble reaching a satisfying climax without her biologically congenial mate.

Rather than share a breath of this awareness, Xoushou lifted the bottle that sat wrapped in its warmer by her side. "Would Your Magnificence like another glass of wine?"

"Had too much already." The emperor leaned his brow against the nearest window's winter-cool glass. "My head hurts. And I'm aroused. Not that *she* would care."

The last was muttered, but Xoushou knew she could respond.

"Does Your Magnificence need me to summon a pillow girl?"

Her choice of words—"need" rather than "wish"—guaranteed he would refuse. No emperor "needed" a bed partner when he wasn't, so far as he knew, in rut.

"It is nothing." He waved his slender hand dismissively, despite his erection being stiff enough to stick straight out.

"Perhaps you would like me to massage you," Xoushou suggested, "so that you may relax enough to sleep."

He looked at her, his pupils glittering in his rim-to-rim silver eyes. Despite his drunkenness, the glance was sharp . . . and perhaps suspicious, as if her offer had been too quick. Xoushou cursed herself and dropped her head respectfully, but her luck was still running gold. The emperor shifted from foot to foot in his beautiful embroidered slippers. His cock had begun to jerk against his robes at the thought of female hands close to it—never dreaming that the blood that ran through those hands was as blue as his. He rubbed his neck, thumb and fingers stroking idly down the strong tendons.

Or not so idly, as it happened. The glands that nestled beside those tendons, the two that signaled his kith was rising, showed streaks of red. Fortunately, he could not see the telltale sign, nor were the structures swollen yet. He thought what he felt was normal, inter-peak arousal. His cycle was not, after all, due to reach its height for twelve more days. If no self-respecting emperor would *need* a pillow girl outside of that time, neither would he stoop to the services of his own hand. Whatever part of him wanted massaging, Songyam had people to do that.

"You have the oil I like?" he asked, as if his answer truly depended on this, rather than the desire swelling in his loins. "The one that smells like oranges and cloves?"

"Always, Your Magnificence. I keep it ready in your cabinet."

"Good," he said, the word husky.

As Xoushou rose from her cushion on the floor, Songyam stumbled into a wide, throne-shaped chair. His knees sprawled to its white, silk-upholstered arms. The head of his cock poked unnoticed through his robes, as ripe and dark as a plum. He rubbed his palms up and down his thighs, his tongue flicking out to wet his upper lip. The gesture exposed the dark forked marking at its sharp red tip. The coloration, known as a lamril, was natural to all yama. The shape of the emperor's was especially elegant. Xoushou shivered. To bare one's lamril to a member of the other gender was a flirtatious act—though she suspected this was not intended by the emperor.

He was drunk indeed to show himself to her this way.

Xoushou turned before he could see the heat in her cheeks. Determinedly, she stepped to the carved teakwood cabinet that held his favorite oil. Xoushou had massaged her emperor many times before, though never with the intent to gratify him sexually. Theirs was a rigid society. Maidservants were for waiting on one hand and foot; pillow girls were for sex. Maidservants weren't supposed to know about heat and kith, but pillow girls had to. With little hands-on instruction behind her, Xoushou prayed her touch would please the emperor when employed like this.

Her hands shook as she removed an etched crystal flask filled with golden fluid. Within the flask shivered a concoction different from that she'd always used. Tonight, the orange-scented oil was spiked. Xoushou's cousin, who clerked at the Long Life Pharmacy outside the walls, had contrived to steal a vial of artificial female essence, the precise female essence that matched the empress's.

The substance was intended only for emergencies, when the emperor was in heat and the empress unavailable. Such things happened even in the closest marriages; women did have other things to do, but no emperor was expected to suffer the maddening, week-long effects of rut without release. To prevent this possibility, the royal physicians devised the artificial essence. To insure no one but the empress could claim the issue of her husband's seed, the essence always included a powerful spermicide.

Always, that is, except tonight.

Xoushou's sex blazed with longing, and not only at the thought of what she was about to do. Along with drugging the emperor, she had dosed herself to guarantee she'd come to him fertile. Hormones circulated in her body, double their normal strength. Xoushou pressed her thighs together, abruptly finding it hard to bear her desire.

She must not betray herself. She must lull the emperor into thinking he burned alone.

"Why do you linger there?" he demanded now. "I do not wish to wait tonight."

"Forgive me, Your Magnificence," she said, turning hurriedly. "I was contemplating how best to please you."

"You always please me," he said gruffly as she approached. She noticed he had covered his cock again with his robe, though the silk could hardly hide its huge, rampant state. "You may be rohn, Xoushou, but your hands have their own simple genius."

Xoushou gritted her teeth at being referred to as a member of the lower class. To her relief, the annoyance steadied her hands. She knelt in front of the emperor's throne-like chair, between his still sprawled thighs. Another wash of excitement threatened to overwhelm her. She could smell the musky scent of his arousal, could feel her heart thump faster in response. She looked into his handsome face with what she hoped was a shy expression. The emperor leaned toward her, probably unwittingly. She had never massaged him in this position. Before, he'd always lain on his front on a special table while she soothed his back.

"Is this what you wish?" she asked softly. "For me to start with your feet and legs?"

His eyes had darkened, their pupils swelling with anticipation. The black disks receded slightly when she specified what she meant.

"Yes," he said, remembering the face-saving pretense that he did not require a genital massage. "We will do that instead tonight. I am certain it will relax me sufficiently."

Breath held, she poured the oil into her palms, warmed it by rubbing them together, then removed his left foot from its pointed slipper and placed it on her thigh.

As she began to work the oil into his arch, a long, soft sigh escaped him. He sagged back in the white silk chair. When she glanced up, his eyes were closed. He appeared utterly blissful. Too blissful. Xoushou hoped her cousin had been right about what the vial of the empress's essence would do. Fortunately, she needn't have worried. By the time she lifted his second foot, the emperor was squirming, his buttocks tightening with discomfort on the chair cushion.

"Enough of that," he ordered, almost gasping it. "Proceed to my legs."

"Of course," she said, shifting her well-oiled strokes to his muscled calves. Her own body was alive with lust. This was really happening. After a lifetime of machinations to reach this place, after years of assuming a false identity, of slaving in the palace kitchens, of slowly working her way up the ranks and earning trust, Xoushou was finally where her mother had always meant her to be. Soon the House of Huon would have its revenge—mere minutes from now, to judge by the emperor's look of erotic strain.

He groaned as she squeezed a fresh palmful of oil over his knees. Very close to losing control completely, he crooned her name like an old-fashioned prayer. "Xoushou. Ah, Xoushou, your chi is always sweet, but tonight it is magnificent!"

She almost let go in shock. He had never mentioned that he liked the feel of her energy before. Yama were sensitive to chi. They could read and send emotions through their auras. The emperor's praise, however, seemed indecently fervent—as if her energy were not the ordinary sort, as if it were as pleasing as a human's.

Xoushou pushed the unthinkable suggestion away, unwilling to let it even form in her mind. She must not allow those old lies weaken her, because lies were all they were. This praise was just the emperor's rut talking, and perhaps the instruction her mother had given her in the royals' private bed arts. Her hands were simply more skilled than the emperor expected. She tightened her grip on his knees again, only to have him clamp his hands on hers.

"Thighs," he rasped, sitting now. "Rub the full length of my thighs."

She did as he asked, feeling the heavy muscles twitch and tense beneath her oily strokes. She put her weight behind each push, letting intuition lead her, the intensity of her own arousal precluding subtlety. The emperor was still leaning forward, and both their lips were parted, both their breaths shallow and fast. When her fingers slid up to his hip bones, his gaze locked onto hers.

It was said humans could not tell one yama's eyes from another's, but the emperor's were the soft, blurred silver of a coastal sky at dawn. His pupils were swollen with excitement, but had not swallowed his whole iris. Each eye matched the other, each slanting cheek, each chiseled side of his jaw—a crowning example of facial harmony. Instincts wired into Xoushou's genes responded helplessly to his perfection, joining the drugs she'd taken earlier. Hot, creamy fluid welled from her sex. Here, right in front of her, was an ideal sire for any female's child.

The emperor's nostrils flared at her scent. "You like this," he whispered, heat pouring off him in successive waves. "The little rohn likes touching her emperor."

"Yes," she admitted, because it could not be denied. "I would touch you more if Your Magnificence would deign to allow it."

Her strokes had pushed his robe off his cock and balls. She did not need to look to count its forceful pulsing, did not need to see to guess its raging height. She could not drop her gaze in any case. His fiery stare held her prisoner.

"You are not properly trained," he murmured—but as if he wished her to argue.

"No, Your Magnificence, but I am here and you could guide me. It is my duty to give you ease in any way I can."

The emperor's lips curved in a tiny smile. "Your words are as honeyed as your voice. I believe I could permit you to move your caresses to my testicles."

"More oil might make that better. In case I am awkward."

"Do it." He leaned back, pushing his thighs even wider to let her in.

Xoushou poured another measure of adulterated oil into her palm. Then she hesitated. She could not quite reach all she wanted to.

"Your Magnificence," she said in her humblest tone. "Do you suppose you could slide farther forward and sling one leg over the chair arm? To help your servant in her inexperience."

The emperor's grunt of acquiescence sounded suspiciously like a laugh, but if he doubted her artlessness, he forgot that doubt the instant she surrounded his testicles in her hands.

His groan was loud and heartfelt.

"Drunk," he muttered even as he tilted his pelvis closer. "Must be very, very drunk."

Unlike other yama, the royals' seed accumulated over their cycle, not being reabsorbed by their bodies when it built up. Xoushou knew the emperor must be tender from the swelling and heat she felt, but it wasn't more than a minute before he curled his hand over hers and urged her to squeeze harder.

"Pull, too," he said, his fingers hot, his voice nearly all breath. "Pull the sac as far as it will go and squeeze with plenty of pressure. You need to loosen the deep tension."

His head rolled from side to side against the chair back as she obeyed. Sensing his distraction, she dropped her pretense of awkwardness, letting her fingers be as clever as her mother's training allowed.

"Yes," he sighed. "*Yes.* Get those damn reservoirs of seed warmed up."

A thrill rolled up Xoushou's spine. He was forgetting who he was talking to, forgetting he wasn't supposed to be able to spill without his empress. She pulled his sac upward instead of down, kneading and squeezing with one hand while her second reached behind to his perineum. Here, where his penis rooted into his body, was a pressure-sensitive ridge of flesh. Beneath it was his final kith gland, the one they called the kingmaster. It was russet now, pushing out from the silky skin as if a walnut had been buried there.

Xoushou slid three oiled fingers over it hard, knowing that if his kith could be coaxed into his seminal vesicles, Songyam would grow too aroused to resist anything she did. Kith was an aphrodisiac to royals, male and female, a physiological guarantee that they'd never lack incentive to procreate with their genetically ideal partners.

"Harder," he gasped, his back arching violently as the oil sank in. "Rub me there harder." His hand had formed a fist on his bare hip bone. Xoushou knew he was longing to stroke his neglected stalk. A lifetime of arrogance was all that kept him from giving in.

"You need more oil," she said, releasing everything she held at once.

He blinked at her, glassy-eyed and shamefully flushed. "Yes," he said with dreamy impatience. "I need your oil on me. I need your hands hard and oiled all over me."

Without warning, he came out of the chair, looming over her and forcing her to shift back. The move alarmed her, but he simply tore off his robe and lay on his back unthreateningly, his body writhing naked on the cool white floor. Xoushou found this unabashed display of sensuality oddly exciting. Songyam seemed not to care that the sapphire and diamond inlay dug into his skin. Indeed, he seemed to enjoy the smooth friction.

"Kneel between my legs," he said. "I want you to—" He swallowed and licked his lips, his lamril flashing again. "I grant you leave to put your hands on my phallus."

She was glad he was too lost in rut to watch her face as she complied. She doubted her triumph was well hidden. She was so close now. A single hurdle remained to guide him over, and she'd have everything she and her mother had ever dreamed.

She poured one long stream of oil onto his cock, biting her lip as three rich runnels parted over the crimson head. The slit in its center appeared to gape, as if hungry to soak in its own downfall. With loving slowness, she fisted the oil down and up his rut-fattened shaft. The pumping motion had exactly the effect she'd hoped. His thighs tightened dramatically a second before the clear, warm fluid of his kith let loose a fountaining spurt.

The relief this entailed, along with the attendant aphrodisiac effect, at last alerted Songyam—if only dimly—to his danger. He was now much wetter than the oil alone could have made him.

"Wha—?" he murmured, his head coming off the floor.

"Oh, Your Magnificence, I am sorry," Xoushou said, already prepared for this. "I must have thinned this batch of oil too much, and now you are overly slippery. I fear it is difficult to maintain my grip."

She feigned a loosened hold, distracting him from whatever he suspected was happening.

"Need it . . . harder," he insisted. He tried to press her fingers closer, but being royal—and sober—she was as strong as he was.

"Perhaps I should stop," she said, letting the worry a rohn might have betrayed sound in her voice. "Perhaps it is wrong to continue an activity that cannot culminate in release."

"No, no," he protested through gritted teeth, clearly determined to have that release, even if he expected it to be dry. "What you're doing is perfectly pleasant. I believe I can reach a peak if you keep it up."

Had he truly been between heats, a dry climax would have relieved him. While he was in rut, it would only wind up his tension more. Xoushou was tempted to try to give him one, to guarantee her control over him, but feared any orgasm now would involve ejaculation and lots of it. Already his testicles were rucking up, swollen and twitching with their stored-up load. His hand crept toward his sac, instinctively wanting to knead it, but he held back and made a fist an inch away. Xoushou lightened her grip even more.

Frustration flashed in the emperor's eyes. His gaze slid from her face to her breasts, which were shaking with her efforts behind her traditional gray servant's robes. As he stared, mesmerized, a deepened flush crept into his face— perhaps because he was thinking what she hoped he was, or perhaps because he'd noticed how very pointed her nipples were.

Come on, Xoushou thought. *Don't make me suggest it. Let your body tell you what it wants to do.*

Xoushou knew he wanted to be inside her, between her legs and thrust in her sex. It was the strongest instinct royal males possessed. Songyam's conscious mind might not realize his seed was set to explode, but his body could have no doubt. His body knew it could impregnate someone tonight and wanted desperately to seize the chance, no matter if that someone was a lowly maid. The problem was, if Xoushou suggested they copulate, she was bound to make him suspicious. Worse, if she didn't suggest it and waited much longer for him to voice the idea, he'd spill his seed anyway. All her risks would be for nothing. She'd be charged with treason without having accomplished it.

Xoushou cursed him in her mind. She hadn't expected Songyam to be so responsive to her loosened grip. He was nearly thrashing now, grinding his teeth and straining for the ejaculation he didn't even know was coming. When his gaze slid yearningly from her bouncing breasts to the tie of her servants' robes, she knew she had to take a chance.

"I am sorry," she said, praying her low, mellow voice would work the magic it did on most men. She slowed her strokes a fraction more. "I am not doing this well enough. I am only a maidservant, untrained for sexual pleasures. If I were a pillow girl, I could . . . But I am only frustrating you."

"You are fine!" the emperor gritted out.

Pretending to be overcome with shame, Xoushou released his organ and covered her face.

Songyam swore with a coarseness she was surprised to hear him capable of. He sat up, winced at the discomfort this caused his genitals, and gripped her shoulders in both hands. She opened her eyes when he shook her. He was so far into heat only the slimmest rim of silver kept his eyes from being wholly black. Xoushou shivered deep inside, part fear, part unbridled thrill. She'd never seen a male this aroused.

"All right," he admitted. "Maybe I do need a tighter friction, but I wager I know where to find it." His gaze slid to her abdomen, and this time she couldn't contain her shiver. "Are you small, Xoushou? You look as if you would be."

"I do not know," she said, her trepidation unfeigned. "I am a virgin."

His eyes did go black then, the highest sign of excitement their kind could display. Apparently, taking a virgin sounded good to him.

"Lie back on the floor," he said, his voice like gravel. "You are not going to be one much longer."

He did not wait for her to spread her legs, but yanked them apart himself. He settled between her thighs without delay, grunting as he took his shaft in hand. As soon as he'd positioned the knoblike head against her gate, he shoved inside.

A streak of pain shot through her, but to her amazement, he was the one who cried out.

"Xoushou," he said, gripping her hip to wedge himself deeper. "I am sorry to hurt you. The chi in your pussy is so sweet. And you are tight. So, so hot and tight."

He began to move inside her, long, hard strokes he seemed unable to restrain. Xoushou clutched his broad shoulders. The pain was fading, and his kith was gushing inside her. His genetic profile must have been a near enough match to hers to spur a reaction. Her sex contracted hard around his cock and began to burn. The itch was both delicious and unbearable. Frantic to ease it, she pushed her hips to meet his.

"Yes," he said, his next stroke kicking in harder. "Yes, thrust with me."

Faster and faster they went, until Xoushou feared she would scream. The friction couldn't be enough for her, the heat, the impossible pleasure that rose and rose. She couldn't control herself. The strength with which she met him soon grew violent. Happy now that his body's needs were finally being met, the emperor gloated over her struggles.

"It's true what they say then," he said mockingly, between panting breaths. "The lower classes are more passionate."

Xoushou did scream then, partly in fury and partly because her orgasm was breaking in a wave of ecstasy so huge it seized her entire body and blanked her mind. She was lucky these rooms were soundproofed, or the other staff would have come running. Her only comfort in her disgrace was that a moment later the emperor was screaming, too, his pelvis slamming into hers so deeply she thought she felt his seed shooting to her throat.

Songyam's climax was massive, even more dramatic than her mother warned. Spume after spume of royal seed shot toward her womb as the emperor caught her to him with claws of steel. His groans of enjoyment could have been a beast's. Xoushou came through all of it, even when his eyes rolled up and his body—especially the part that was locked inside her—turned to stone.

He remained in this position for at least a minute, quivering with helpless pleasure while his pent-up seed overflowed her pussy and spilled out.

He collapsed then, not merely exhausted but actually passed out. Shaken, Xoushou took a moment to find the strength to squirm out from under him. She stood gaping down at his unconscious form. If he hadn't been breathing, she'd have feared she'd killed him. She knew the empress liked to deny him, but surely this reaction was extreme!

Telling herself it didn't matter, Xoushou covered her perspiring belly with a trembling hand. Thick, warm semen ran down her thighs. Though she knew it was too soon to tell, she fancied her chi had changed. Did it not hum through her stronger than before? And wasn't this increase in life force an auspicious sign?

One thing seemed certain. Soundly pleasured as he was, the emperor would not be complaining that his humble maid had mistreated him—assuming, of course, that he remembered it.

Either way, it did not matter. The empress had already approved Xoushou's transfer to one of their distant and rarely visited summer palaces. The empress liked the idea that the women who worked for her husband could not wait to leave. If Xoushou was pregnant, she would gestate far away, returning to the Forbidden City only after she'd delivered. The baby would enable her to enact the second phase of her plan. If she wasn't breeding, she and her mother would know they had done their best, but Xoushou doubted that was the case.

The emperor had taken her with such power a rock could have conceived.

Corum does not die

∞

"No one could be sorrier than I," Corynna's private physician said. The words scarcely ruffled his smooth, calm face. Whatever the dreadfulness of his news, whatever his long association with her family, he would never be less than professional. "Your Highness, I fear I must recommend termination of this pregnancy."

Corynna's heart stuttered in her chest, and her hand clenched protectively atop her abdomen. Though her trailing sleeve hid the telltale gesture, her spirit despaired. Had she not known from the very first that something was amiss? Was that not why she had delayed this examination for four whole months?

She fought to keep her voice as level as her old friend's. "You said the defect would not be visible."

"I said it would have no physical expression. It will be visible every time the child encounters stress." Dr. Rhang straightened his business tunic, a well-pressed physician's black with gold trim. "The constellation of genes that enhance our ability to restrain our emotions is not functioning properly. Were you to carry the fetus to term, your son wouldn't have even a rohn's ability to control himself."

Corynna's hand rose from her belly to her throat. "He could learn control. Do not studies show our traits depend on nurture as much as genes?"

"If he were anything but the son of a prince, my oath would not oblige me to object. He may rule Midarri House someday. Think what suffering this handicap would inflict on you and your husband, and on the baby. Is that the life you want a child of yours to lead?"

Corynna turned away, unable to school her face to stillness anymore. The examination had taken place in her private chambers, late at night, a favor from Dr. Rhang to her. They sat in matching green armchairs near her balcony window, a delicate red lacquer table with an untouched plate of sticky-rice treats between. Outside, in the Forbidden City, snow blew in sparkling, moonlit gusts from the curling eaves. Her old rohn nursemaid would have called it fairy dust.

"Come, Corynna." Dr. Rhang laid a gentle hand on her arm, his use of her given name expressive of their long affection. "You and the prince are young. This condition is a random mutation, not inherited. Chances are your next child will be healthy."

"If there is a next child," Corynna said, boldly meeting his eyes. "You know our marriage was a better political match than a genetic one. In seven years, despite all the drugs you have pumped me full of, this is the first time I have conceived."

"Your Highness, it was you for whom the prince's eyes went black. That means the match is close enough. I have faith—" He cleared his throat, for "faith" was not a subject lightly touched upon. "Both my experience and my training lead me to believe you and the prince will have a family."

Corynna dropped her gaze to her lap, just beginning to be overshadowed by her pregnancy. As close as they were, Dr. Rhang was ignorant of her secret shame. Her female essence had not, in seven years of coupling, spurred her husband to his final sexual development. Yes, Poll's kith rose for her. Yes, they shared passion when he spilled his seed. But that last bit of genital evolution, the one that made conception easier, evaded them. Poll said it did not matter, that caring about such things was for romantics.

If that was so, then Corynna was a romantic. She admitted—if only to herself—that she loved her husband. She wanted them to be a perfect match.

She also wanted this child.

The realization swept across her body in a prickling wave. The feeling was so strong it could have been fear, but Corynna knew it was not. She was attached to this small, flawed being. From the moment of his conception, she had felt a sweet, unnatural tug. Perhaps her son's genetic defect had twisted her emotions. Perhaps this urge to protect and love was no more than a biochemical imbalance. It made no difference to Corynna. She would do anything to save his life.

She pushed herself up from the lime green chair, already beginning to sway from the shift in the center of her body's weight. She turned to Dr. Rhang, who regarded her patiently, no doubt confident that his professional advice would be respected. Corynna squared her shoulders and raised her chin, drawing on every drop of royal dignity she had. Faintly, like a ghost glimpsed from the corner of the eye, she saw the doctor's aura shrink closer to his skin. The reaction was involuntary. Like her, he was daimyo, just not a royal aristocrat.

"I will teach my son control," she said. "From the moment he first draws breath, I will do whatever is required to turn him into all a prince must be."

The physician opened his mouth, but was too shocked to let anything out. Corynna continued. "You will not tell my husband what we discussed. If, by the time the boy reaches his majority, Poll finds him unacceptable, he will name another heir. This boy will have his chance, and you are not to stand in his way."

Dr. Rhang blinked twice before recovering. "My oath forbids discussing any information you do not wish, but

I really must inquire if you are sure. You do not know what you are getting into, if what you are proposing is even possible."

"I will make it possible," Corynna said, "and I thank you for your loyalty."

Dr. Rhang rose and bowed, hearing the dismissal in her words. With his usual grace, he gathered up his satchel of equipment—the intrauterine scanner, the probes and gentyping box. The only sign of his disapproval was the stiffness in his strides as he left the room.

Corynna released her breath in a gusty sigh. Now that she was alone, her hand crept back to her belly, gently stroking its curve as if the child inside could feel her petting it. Just then, it moved inside her, a feathery kick of recognition, and she truly could not help smiling.

"I love you," she whispered, savoring the dangerous words. "I love you, my little prince."

She wondered if this was what human women felt for their babies, this compulsion to cuddle and cherish. The possibility unnerved her. Corynna had never met a human. There had been some interaction between the races since human explorers stumbled into the yamish city of Narikerr, but in the four intervening decades no human had been admitted to the capital. She was both repelled and fascinated by those she saw on the evening vids. They had to be filmed surreptitiously, of course. Film was not a technology the yama had shared with these lesser beings; other technologies but not that. Corynna had always thought humans seemed colorful, what with their funny clothes and grimacing faces. Until now, they'd also seemed as foreign from her experience as they could be.

Restless, she opened the partitioned windows to her balcony, hoping the brisk night air would cool her heated face.

Thinking about humans reminded her of *The Terrible Scandal of Xasha Huon,* as it was billed by the repertory companies who spread the tale, each swearing their re-creation took no liberties with the truth. Naturally, the actors had to swear this. Presenting fiction on the stage was illegal.

Corynna had been a girl then, but she could still picture
Xasha Huon's rigid face as the doddering old emperor pronounced her sentence in the Plaza of Justice: banishment for
life to the provinces, and her entire family obliterated from
the Book of Honorable Names. From that day forward, the
Huons were not to be considered royal, or even upper class.

In one quavering imperial pronouncement, their fortunes had plunged from daimyo to rohn, from aristocrat to
servant—all because, twelve years earlier, while posted with
her husband to spy on a human lord, Xasha had taken a for-
eigner into her bed. To have enjoyed the sexual favors of
another race might be forgiven; yama were erotically adven-
turous, and human chi was reputed to be a sweeter drug than
opium. To have been found out, however, and to have the
tryst become a source of public titillation while the blood of
emperors ran in one's veins, could not be overlooked.

Then and there, with all the royal houses watching,
the Huons' proud, long hair was shorn to chin length by
the emperor's guards. Corynna remembered staring at the
daughter's locks—Xoushou, she thought she was called.
They had lain in a perfect sheaf across the marble pavers,
black with a touch of rubies in the noonday sun.

The color had matched the mother's hair, but Corynna
had looked into Xoushou's tearstained face, a girl scarcely
older than herself, and wondered if she could be what the
rumors said: a monstrous mix of yamish and human blood.
Corynna's father had sworn it was impossible for the races
to interbreed—they were close but not close enough.
According to him, any hints that the matter might be otherwise were a ploy to raise the scandal players' fees.
Nonetheless, the question rose in Corynna's mind. The
girl was weeping . . . and in public.

Of course, if Corynna's beautiful hair had lain on the
pavement, if *she* had been forced to leave her home and
live as a rohn, perhaps she would have cried as well.

Corynna shuddered, her own hair falling straight and cool
down her back, lifting at the edges in the open window's
breeze. Her hair had not been less than hip-length in twenty
years.

Maybe, considering the position she and her son were now in, it would be better not to dwell on that tragedy.

She looked out across Thousand Plum Tree Square, over the lower palaces and up the hill to the new emperor's home. Silver gilt glinted on the roof tiles beneath the snow, and Corynna saw she was not the only yama awake tonight. Candles burned behind the seventh-floor windows, shadows showing black against the muted gold. The moving shapes were obscured by the glass's privacy glazing, but to Corynna's eyes they looked like two eager lovers coupling on the floor.

Well, good for Songyam, Corynna thought. She liked the new emperor. He seemed more evenhanded than his father. Oh, some said he was weaker, but to her mind he deserved whatever comfort he could find—with or without his steely empress.

Corynna touched her belly lower down. Perhaps her own husband would want sex tonight. She had always respected Poll, but since this child had quickened within her, that respect had grown warmer. With warmth had come a heightening of her desires. She had taken care not to express her needs too frequently, lest her husband grow suspicious, but luckily Poll seemed to welcome her increased ardor. Then again, what royal male would not? No matter how many pillow girls they kept, they all liked to complain they were impossible to sate.

As if he'd heard her thoughts, the prince chose then to enter her chambers. He was dressed for bed, and had the sleepy look of one who'd recently been in it. Without warning, tears pricked her eyes. He had been waiting up for her news.

With an effort, Corynna tamped down an urge to run to him. His arms would have felt extremely comforting around her now. Instead, she waited for his approach.

"How was the examination?" he asked, his manner calm, his expression as always quiet.

Corynna wished she could confide in him, but she knew how conservative he could be, not to mention how protective. He would side with Dr. Rhang, if only to spare her pain.

Nearly Poll's match in height, she smoothed a length of blue-black tresses behind his ear. He hid his secret pleasure at the gesture with a hasty lowering of his eyelashes.

"The exam was fine," she said. "The child and I are strong. It is a boy, as you suspected. You were right to counsel me against worry."

"Good," he said, dipping his head to kiss her quickly on the mouth, something he did not usually do outside of intercourse. "I am glad to see you calm again."

Hoping her guilt did not stain her aura, Corynna slid her hands up the silk lapels of his dark green robe. She must be very careful now. The success of her plan to save the little prince depended on her husband's compliance. She spoke as lightly as she could. "I do have a favor I would like to ask."

"Do you?" Poll's dove gray eyes creased infinitesimally in a smile.

"I should like to ask Matreya back to the house."

"Your old nursemaid?" Her husband's eyes widened.

"I know you think she is superstitious, but I would feel more comfortable with her around. Certainly, you cannot doubt her loyalty. She would defend the life of our child with her own."

"I do not expect that to be necessary; we are too far from the line of succession." Her husband covered her hands with his, coaxing them into rubbing up and down his chest. Corynna held her breath as he appeared to think. "If you truly wish it," he finally conceded, "but you must promise not to let her use her folk remedies on you!"

"I promise," she said. "The only remedies I shall request are those we can employ in bed."

"In *bed*," he repeated with a hint of teasing, a humor that could only fill her with relief. "It is amusing you should mention that. I was thinking we might celebrate there tonight."

"Now?" Corynna asked, even as her body clenched and went hot. "Your cycle is not due to peak for another week."

Her husband drew her hands to his hips. "Since when have I only been interested in my wife when I am in heat?

Besides, I have noticed your own interest has been more marked of late."

"You do not mind?" she asked with a tremor she could not conceal.

"Never," Poll assured her, his fingers squeezing hers warmly. "If this is the effect a few extra hormones have, I wish I could have given you our little prince sooner. I value you, Corynna. You are more than the black of my eye; you are the wife I would have chosen for myself."

This was high praise among a people whose bodies chose mates for them. Corynna could offer Poll no less than her deepest bow of respect. He seemed pleased to receive it, and she was glad for that. Ruthlessly, she squelched her wish that—as she had heard the shameless humans did—she could have thrown her arms around him.

The dagger turns

A year had passed since Xoushou Huon seduced her emperor. She'd spent most of that time in self-imposed exile. Now, however, she was back in the Forbidden City. Delighted to have left the stultifying dullness of the provinces behind, she handed her ivory travel pass to the guard at the great North Gate. One could not leave the royal complex without this carved block of bone—no more than one could enter. The imperial guard, young and handsome in his uniform of crimson, blue, and green, scrutinized the pass more closely than an older soldier might, going so far as to key up the hologram to ensure it belonged to her.

The wait did not trouble her. She was bundled for winter in a cultured sealskin coat, a gift from her kindhearted new mistress. Her mistress's chief of staff, less kind, informed Xoushou that the princess had a soft spot for mothers, and the maid had better not dream *he'd* let her take advantage.

A smile threatened to rise at the memory. Had the chief of staff known half the advantages she planned to take, he would have struck her dead on the spot.

The House of Midarri was everything Xoushou had hoped. Its line often intermarried with that of the imperial house; for centuries their genetic profiles had been complements. Many imperial princes' eyes had gone black for Midarri daughters—and vice versa. Best of all, the House of Midarri had but one son, one precious male offspring who had to produce issue or their genetic legacy would die with him. Xoushou had drunk in the whispers that her new mistress could not conceive, that the match between her and her husband had been close but not perfect. The emperor would not wish to see that bloodline fail, no matter how low the Midarri son seemingly had to stoop for his mate.

Xoushou knew, simply *knew,* that mate would be her infant daughter. Her blood would be the strongest the future prince would come across. Xoushou had only to use her new position as Corynna Midarri's maid to maneuver them together while they were young. Proximity and the magic of royal genetics would do the rest. Should the emperor have a daughter—as yet there were only sons—she would not have the daily access three-month-old Xishi would. She would not have an entire childhood to send her pheromones up the prince's nose.

The House of Huon would resume its rightful place among the powerful. If the emperor's closest allies were humiliated in the process, all the better. The friends of those who had humiliated the House of Huon deserved a taste of their own medicine.

With thoroughly yamish pleasure, Xoushou anticipated many years savoring her triumph as it unfurled. Yamish males chose their mates on the cusp of sexual maturation, sometimes as late as twenty-one. After maturation, their eyes might flash black for other reasons besides encountering their ideal match, and thus the signal might not be honored.

Knowing how very likely success was, it was difficult to contain her glee as the handsome guard waved her on. She kept her walk as stolid as she could. She wouldn't have minded hiring an aircar, but rohn weren't allowed to fly. On this journey to tie up her last loose end, she didn't want to attract regard.

As she entered the outer city's northern end, she patted her fur coat's pocket. The vial was there, and she ordered herself not to check again. The streets swirled with a winter fog today, cold and damp, but smelling pleasantly of the snowcapped mountains from which the mist descended.

Those mountains formed a near impassable ring around the capital. Known as the Dragon's Teeth, they had allowed this city to be built more openly than other yamish settlements. Other cities were protected by ice and snow, by precipitous gorges and artificial climate patterns. The intent had been to keep the yama isolated from inferior beings. For millennia it had worked, until one small group of human explorers stumbled into the icebound city of Narikerr. To people like Xoushou's everlasting disappointment, the idiot prince who ruled it had been too intrigued by the strangers to stamp out the pestilence before it spread.

Now the emperor had "diplomatic relations" with humans. Now he sent envoys to their cities and kept that disgusting Queen Victoria secure on her throne by giving her technology no other humans had. Not their highest technology, of course, but to Xoushou's mind, any concession was too much. Let the humans kill each other with their backward little guns and swords. For that matter, she didn't understand why the emperor hadn't wiped them out long ago.

The supposed healthful deliciousness of human chi was no excuse, nor was the "entertainment value" of their dramas. What need had yama for entertainment? Tranquillity was their ideal—or should have been. Only the most jaded would see humans as anything but a blight. Xoushou had heard they liked to call themselves the empire on which the sun never set—as if her people had not been civilized while theirs scrabbled in the dirt. Humans even had the gall to call her kind demons!

Seeing Xoushou's unguarded glower, a fellow pedestrian crossed to the other side of the street, no doubt assuming she was unhinged.

Ignoring him, she stomped past a bookstore that, as luck

would have it, specialized in importing human fiction. "Latest translation from Mr. Dickens!" its sign declared. "Will Little Dorrit die?" To her disgust, a line of customers snaked into the street; aristocrats to judge by their lush, jeweled coats—though they did have the decency to muffle their identities in their hoods. Naturally, they would be high-born. Purchasing these books required a special license from the empress, who had decreed that reading human fiction was a means to strengthen emotional control. How strong, Empress Nala speciously reasoned, could daimyo be without obstacles to fight? Xoushou suspected the exorbitant price of each license, coupled with the empress's fondness for expensive toys of the male persuasion, had more to do with her leniency.

But this was not Xoushou's concern. Shaking her head, she smoothed every trace of anger from her face as she strode around the end of the bookseller's line. Her cousin's home was miles from here, and Xoushou needed to reach her and return in an innocuous amount of time. Her business there would be quick: Greet her cousin, break the vial, and wait for the noxious cloud that boiled out of it to do its work. Xoushou had swallowed the antidote already and would not be harmed. Once Jela Huon was dead, the last link between Xoushou and the trick she'd played on the emperor would be cut.

Through their secret communication channels, Xoushou's mother had reminded her that she must not omit this step. Little Xishi was safe and in place. Jela Huon would have years to dream up a thousand kinds of blackmail or, worse, a thousand attacks of conscience. This, of all possibilities, could not be allowed. Besides which, they didn't need Jela anymore.

It was fitting, Xoushou thought, that the woman who had betrayed her oath to the royal pharmacy would die from another of its products.

She found that she did not mind the thought of killing her relation. Jela had never been anything but a dupe. Xoushou's mother and little Xishi were the only family that mattered now.

An alley beckoned up ahead, a familiar shortcut to the residential area where Jela lived. As always, Xoushou peered down it before entering. This was the back of a row of restaurants, small but thriving rohn businesses. Clouds of garlic-roasted pork wafted out, causing her mouth to water. She could not see clearly through the mist and steam, but the lane appeared empty. Her ears caught only the sounds of city squirrels scrabbling at the compacted trash. Their teeth were so sharp they could survive by nibbling corners off the stone-like blocks, but Xoushou didn't fear them. They were used to people and not violent.

Satisfied, she slipped into the alley's shadows, pleased she could cut time from her trip. Her shoulders relaxed between the sheltering walls. She stood straighter and walked more freely, more like the royal she was born to be.

One day she would walk like this all the time.

Her attacker fell from the sky—or, rather, from a heavy steampipe hanging overhead—landing on her like a load of gold ingots. Xoushou pitched backward beneath him, his weight driving her breath from her without a chance to scream. Stars shot across her vision as her head hit the wall. His knees snapped her ribs a second before the pain stabbed in.

Despite her disadvantage, she tried to fight. To her dismay, the prick of a knife at her throat stole that option.

"What do you want?" she gasped, mortified to hear how scared she sounded.

The man bared his teeth like a wolf gloating over prey it was certain of. Her mind raced wildly. His was not a face she recognized. Had Jela somehow discovered what she meant to do? But, according to her intelligence, her cousin was unmarried and had no child. Xoushou had chosen her not only for where she worked, but because she had no strong family ties.

The man cut through her confusion by pressing down on his dagger. Blood welled from the pinching spot. His clothes suggested he was poor, but he would almost have to be to fight with a knife in this day and age. Xoushou didn't even think it was charged.

"Is it my coat?" she asked, still struggling to speak steadily. "I would happily give you that."

The man's face turned as cold as the Dragon's Teeth. "I imagine you would, but unfortunately for you I am no thief. I am a friend of Jela."

He gave the word "friend" the intonation that meant lover.

"I was just going to see her," Xoushou said eagerly. "To tell her how successful our plans have been."

"Do not waste your breath," said her attacker, his eyes disturbingly black with excitement. Clearly enjoying her predicament, he shifted until one knee compressed her broken ribs. Xoushou gasped in pain a moment before his second knee pinned her right arm.

"Do you think you're the only yama who employs spies?" he said with derision. "Do you think that because you put a few strangers between yourself and your recent purchase we cannot track where it ended up? I know what you carry in your pocket—and in your heart. I guess it wasn't bad enough to drag your cousin down with your family scandal. You Huons had to have her risk her life to help you, then reward her by murdering her."

"Who has uttered such lies?" Xoushou cried, trying to stretch her fingers into her pocket to reach the vial. It wasn't easy to smash, but if she could get her arm free enough to do it, she could kill her assassin. "Jela is the only ally I have!"

"Jela *was* your only ally," the man corrected. "Now you have none."

In one swift, grunting motion, he shoved the knife through her throat. The thrust was so forceful it severed her spinal cord. Xoushou had an instant for a final thought: that it did not matter if she died. Her kind new mistress would protect her daughter, for honor if nothing else.

In the grave or out, the House of Huon would have its revenge.

⌐⌐

For six nerve-racking months, Corynna Midarri had been listening to her baby cry. Squalls of indignation, wails of

misery, heartbreaking whimpers of unmet longing—
Corynna knew and dreaded them all.

Royal infants were expected to take some period to get
over their birthing shock, but six months truly was the outer
edge of what was normal. Corum should have been sleeping through the night by now, should have been enjoying
his babyhood, should have been calmly exploring his new
world!

Corynna was ready to tear her long royal hair out, and
Poll had begun to speak of calling in a specialist. If Corynna
didn't find a cure for her baby's strange condition soon, he
would be taken from her and consigned to a hospital.

Unfortunately, when she had spoken so determinedly to
Dr. Rhang of "training" her son's control, she had forgotten her pupil would be an infant.

"I am sorry, mistress," her old nurse, Matreya, said. "I
cannot seem to quiet him today."

She was walking the whimpering baby around Corynna's
chambers, bouncing him gently against her breasts. Baby
things lay scattered across the formerly elegant furniture, as
if a cyclone had deposited them. Not daring to let others in
on her secret, Corynna had not hired a wet nurse. Corynna,
Matreya, and occasionally his father were the only people
who saw the child. In the time since he had been born,
Corynna had watched her old retainer turn from a lovely
older-looking rohn to a haggard, overworked woman with
silver hair. Corynna had, rather fearfully, once offered to let
her go, but Matreya had refused.

"I love him, too," she had said. "He is a horrible screech-
ing beast, but he tugs at me. Who will protect him if we
don't?"

At the memory, gratitude burned behind Corynna's eyes.
Though the emotional volatility of her pregnancy had, thankfully, receded, she knew she wasn't wholly herself yet.

"It is my fault," she said now. "I think he senses I am
upset about the news of Xoushou."

"That's impossible," Matreya said. "You aren't even
holding him, and yama do not see auras until they are three
or four."

Corynna did not argue. The nurse knew as well as she did that her son was not a typical yama. "It shocked me to hear she was stabbed. Xoushou seemed like a sweet young girl when I hired her, so humble and well mannered. Not at all the sort to die violently. I wonder if it was the father, the one who abandoned her when she became pregnant."

Matreya muttered something about young maids that did not sound sympathetic, then sighed with relief when— between one whimper and the next—Corum subsided into sleep on her shoulder.

Corynna rose, immediately unable to resist touching him. His fat little cheek was squashed against his nurse's collar, his rosy mouth puckered, his warm back rising with his weary breaths.

Corynna laid her hand across his ribs. Her son's spiky black lashes were dewed with tears. "What a wonder that these small lungs should have such sound-propelling power! But at least we know he is healthy. He has even started gaining weight since we stopped putting my milk in bottles."

"He is a spoiled little prince," Matreya whispered, because few royals nursed their children at their own breasts. "But he is pretty when he's not squalling."

"He is that," Corynna agreed, a second before her throat choked up shamefully. "What am I going to do, Matreya? How am I going to teach an infant to see reason?"

"Sh-sh," Matreya crooned, rubbing Corynna's arm as if she were a child herself. "We will think of something. Maybe we could take him to the courtyard more often. He seemed to like being outside."

"But I am afraid he will stop liking it, and everyone in the house will hear his noise."

Matreya made a clucking sound. "There is one other thing we might try, though I doubt your husband will approve."

"Anything," Corynna said, actually wringing her hands.

"It is a folk remedy I read of, that the people of my class used to use. When a child is . . . born troubled, his family searches out an easy-natured child. The family pays the parents to keep him or her, and lets the two play and rest together. Supposedly, the energy of the quiet child calms the troubled one."

"Little Xishi," Corynna breathed, seeing where this was leading. "She *is* a quiet child. I remember feeling rather jealous when I watched Xoushou rocking her."

Matreya did not blink at the confession, having grown used to such oddities from her mistress. "She needs someone to care for her, Your Highness, now that she is orphaned. You would be doing both yourself and Xoushou a great service. And as long as you didn't tell your husband why you were doing it, I expect he'd think your actions honorable."

"I expect he would!" Corynna said, breaking into a smile Matreya was startled enough to return shyly.

"I'll get her now," the nurse said, thrusting Corum gently into her arms.

He grizzled once, but did not awaken at the change of arms. As soon as the nurse was gone, Corynna pressed her lips to his silken hair.

"We're bringing you a friend," she crooned. "A nice, calm friend who's going to set you a good example."

The child, Xishi, was awake when Matreya brought her from the servant's nursery. Though months younger than Corum, her eyes were bright as they looked about curiously. She had a round, pleasant face, and her dark hair was red-black rather than the more common blue. She burbled softly when she saw others in the room.

"Let's try laying them together in Corum's crib," Matreya suggested.

Xishi wriggled and jerked her arms as she was lowered, but she did not protest. Corynna gnawed her lips before doing the same with Corum. If there was one thing her son hated, it was being let go of for bed. He preferred being carried around the suite for hours.

Predictably, his eyelids fluttered open as he was settled. His unnaturally powerful lungs filled with a breath. Corynna braced herself for one of his wails, but midway into screwing up his little face, her son relaxed.

The other baby's fist had hit him. At once Corum's head turned toward her and, rather than a wail, an inquiring cheep left his rosebud mouth.

Seeming equally fascinated, Xishi stared back at him—though she was perfectly quiet. The little girl looked like an owl with her big, wise eyes.

"Ba-ba-ba!" babbled Corum, clearly a happy sound.

Corynna sank to her heels beside the crib to watch, thoroughly enchanted by this development. Corum was rolling over to get a better look at his companion, a trick he had learned a few weeks ago. His head wobbled upward. And then Corynna saw something she never had before, not even when he was nursing. Corum's silver eyes went completely black.

She knew this happened sometimes with babies, that it was a simple pleasure response and nothing to do with mating. It couldn't be that, in any case. This little girl was rohn, and rohn did not make matches in the upper class. The unease that shivered through Corynna was only the result of her hormones being out of whack.

"I think they like each other," Matreya murmured, kneeling down at her side.

Unimpressed by the miracle he was enjoying, Corum yawned and collapsed onto the mattress, his hand falling—accidentally, Corynna presumed—on top of the little girl's. His eyes were shut in sleep now, hiding whatever color they displayed. Xishi closed her eyes as well, apparently agreeable to a nap. Her soft, baby-sized sigh lifted her belly.

"Thank goodness," Corynna said, shaking off the final twitches of her concern. Sighing a good deal louder than the little girl, she rose to her feet and stretched her aching back.

"Thank goodness indeed," Matreya agreed. "Now all we have to do is pray this lasts!"

A parting of ways

❧

To eight-year-old Cor Midarri, his playmate Xishi was the most interesting being in the world. His other friends—if you could call them that—didn't understand his preference for a lowly rohn, but Cor couldn't have cared less. Xishi was a songbird from the land of fairy. He would never tire of listening to her tales.

Such was her attraction that, one morning during his lessons, when he spied her from a palace window in Thousand Plum Tree Square, he pleaded a stomachache to his tutor and immediately fled.

A sense of freedom filled him even as he bounded down the stairs. Spring in the Forbidden City tended to be quiet, for this was when many heads of house toured their concerns in the provinces, giving the capital an abandoned air. Cor's own father was away seeing to their family's cultured fur factory. As seldom as Cor saw him, Poll Midarri might have been a stranger. His mother said the prince would spend more time with him when he was older, but the promise seemed as distant as the man. And what did it matter when he had Xishi to play with?

She was sitting cross-legged under a flowering bough. Cor crept closer, one eye on her and one on any balconies from which his mother or nurse might spy his truancy. Xishi's eyes were closed, her body perfectly still. Her thumbs and forefingers formed relaxed circles where they rested on the knees of her servant-gray trousers. The rise and fall of her chest was slow.

"What are you doing?" he whispered, fully prepared to be entertained by her answer. Perhaps she was pretending to be a statue while she hid from an evil witch. Unlike other children, Xishi never obeyed when told to curb her fantasies. All she did was stop sharing them around adults.

To Cor's delight, her made-up stories were better than the few his nurse let slip.

At his whisper, Xishi cracked one eye. "I'm breathing in the Golden Cloud of Peace."

Because only she was near, Cor laughed and sat beside her beneath the plum tree. The marble pavers were scattered with fallen blossoms. The sun that warmed them was the only golden, peaceful thing he knew. He waited for his friend to explain herself.

"It's a true thing," she said. "Not made up. I read about it in a book Matreya hid in her cupboard. It said the Golden Cloud of Peace suffuses everything. It said the world is made of it and not of particles. It said if you get very quiet and breathe just right, you can feel it inside of you."

"That's religious stuff," Cor said, not sure if he was intrigued or horrified.

"I don't care. I've been trying this all morning, and I think I've begun to feel it. It's a sort of humming throughout my bones."

"That's your life force. Lots of people can feel that."

Xishi shook her head, her straight, chin-length hair flipping with the movement. Cor loved her hair. He thought it looked like garnets dipped in ink. It made his throat hurt to know she could not wear it long like royal girls.

"This hum is different," she insisted. "It's stronger than life force, and it's quieter than anything. It makes me feel as if nothing mattered but sitting here."

That, at least, Cor could not approve of. If Xishi decided to spend her life sitting in their palace's front court, who would play with him?

"I don't see why you need to be peaceful. You're not the one who cries when people tease."

"Oh, Cor," Xishi said, "you haven't done that in ages. I bet you've almost outgrown that."

Like his mother and Matreya, Xishi knew about Cor's "problem." Unlike them, she never took it seriously. She also seemed to think he'd be fine without her. She didn't understand how much he needed her, how he didn't feel quite whole when they were apart. A year ago, his mother had told them it was time to sleep in separate rooms. Cor hadn't told anyone, not even Xishi, but he'd cried himself to sleep for a week.

Xishi turned to him with the little smile no one else seemed to see was always on her face. She claimed her lips just curved that way, but Cor doubted that. Xishi had as many emotions in her as he did. She was simply better at hiding them.

"Maybe you should try this," she said. "Maybe if you felt the Golden Peace inside you, you would be calm enough for your mother."

Cor pulled a face. His mother was always so stern with him—not cruel like some mothers, but forever gently pointing out the thousand ways he fell short of what a prince should be. Matreya was little better, though she did occasionally praise him, too.

Seeing his reaction, Xishi took his hand. At once, a soft wave of comfort rolled through his body, the wonderful magic only she performed. "I shouldn't have mentioned your mother. Tell me what you'd like to speak about. Maybe algebra?"

Cor grimaced again at her teasing. "I wish Mother would let you take classes with me. That tutor is so boring."

"How can he be boring? He's teaching you to calculate all the money you'll have someday."

The reminder that he was royal and Xishi wasn't didn't improve his mood. He fought to keep his shoulders from slumping. "I shall hire you when I am prince," he said. "I'll put you in charge of every coin."

"And I will steal at least a third of them," Xishi promised. "As every good chief of treasury should."

Though her lips didn't curve any more than usual when she said this, her eyes twinkled so merrily Cor couldn't help smiling. Her hand still gripped his, a little sweaty in the noonday heat. In that moment, his heart felt too large for his chest, as if the sun itself were trying to burst out.

"Cor—" Xishi said, her expression suddenly startled. "Your eyes . . ."

Which was when his mother's fingers latched like pincers onto his ear. "What did I tell you," she hissed, "about holding hands in public?"

Still gripping him by the earlobe, she pulled him so swiftly across the square and up their palace steps that he stumbled to keep up. Then, because he had begun to cry, she yanked him into one of the empty first-floor reception chambers. It was an ugly room, with dull black floors and dusty, mustard-colored furniture. Cor bit his lower lip and stared through wavering, tear-blurred eyes at a hideous dragon-shaped divan. The dragon's mouth had a dull brass pearl in it, which the dragon looked as if it longed to cough out.

Cor was trying not to look at his mother, trying to control himself, but despite his efforts, a tear escaped.

"Stop it!" his mother snapped, and lashed her hand across his cheekbone.

Cor swallowed his emotion back in shock. In all his life, his mother had never struck him. For a moment, she appeared rather shocked herself, but then she pressed her lips together with great firmness.

"I am only trying to help you," she said in a more moderate tone. "To protect the future that should be yours."

Cor nodded unsurely. He had heard this before, though the jagged leaping of the colors in his mother's aura was new. Royals weren't the best readers of energy and, usually, it was too dim for him to see. When she sagged onto the hideous divan, as if she were too tired to stand, the back of his neck tightened.

"It is time," she said, which sounded ominous. "I have tried to wean you of your dependence on that girl, but I see the cut must be cleaner. I can put it off no longer. Xishi must be sent away today."

"No-o," Cor moaned, horror like a storm brewing in his chest. "Xishi is my friend!"

"Xishi is an eccentric servant girl who makes it easier for you to cling to your bad habits."

"Xishi is my *friend*," Cor repeated, thinking perhaps his mother hadn't understood. "The only friend I care about."

"She is bad for you."

"She is nice to me—nicer to me than you!"

His mother paled as if he had returned her blow. When she spoke, her voice was rough. "You are too young to know what is best, Corum. You must trust me to protect you."

"I will be better," he swore desperately, despite being very much afraid he was going to cry again. "From now on, I will try ten times harder. But please, please, do not send Xishi away!"

His mother did not remind him princes do not beg. "It is decided," she said. "It is time for you to grow up."

Her eyes almost looked sorry as she put her hand on his shoulder, but Cor took no comfort in the rare contact. Instead, he shook it off.

"I hate you," he hissed as venomously as she had minutes ago. "I shall never, *ever* forget what you've done today."

Then, to prove that he could do it, he stalked stony-faced from the room.

Xishi's sleeping room was a tiny, windowless closet opening onto a back hall. It was lacquered pale blue inside, which was pretty, but its only furniture was a pallet and pegs for clothes. The closet beside hers held floating palanquins used to transport stately folks around the royal complex, "stately" being—as far as she could tell—a euphemism for very old royals. Her lack of neighbors made it quiet. Xishi had not liked moving here from Cor's room, but she was glad for her isolation now.

If one had to cry, better to do so in privacy.

She wiped her sleeve across her dripping eyes, finally understanding what Cor fought against all the time. Xishi knew she was different from most yama. They wore masks of contentment, while she usually felt it. To her, it had always seemed easier to look for the pleasant side of a situation. The world might not be perfect, but it was interesting. It had Cor in it, after all, and any world that had him couldn't be all bad. Sadly, the world without Cor wasn't looking very nice at all.

The creaking of her closet's door informed her that her muffled sobs had been heard.

Since the sleeping room was child-sized, Matreya had to bend to lean under the low lintel. Neither Princess Midarri nor Matreya had ever seemed like a real mother, but of the two, Matreya was closer. She *tsked* at Xishi's weeping, then handed her a hot, steamed washcloth.

"Come, come," she said as Xishi buried her face in it gratefully. "This is not like you, though I suppose I should be thankful you have already heard Her Highness's decision."

"Cor's tutor overheard her." Cor's tutor had been spying, wanting to be sure his runaway charge was punished. His poorly suppressed glee to share what he'd heard had been obvious. With the washcloth pressed to her throbbing face, Xishi waved at a little bundle sitting on her bed. "I packed my things."

"Well." With a soft popping of her knees, Matreya knelt halfway in the door. "It was good of you to think of that. I see you're not a baby anymore. We may now speak woman to woman and rohn to rohn."

This unusual prospect interested Xishi enough to slow her tears, but not enough to silence her confession. "I don't want to be sent away," she whispered.

"Of course you don't," Matreya said, "but you must know the prince depends on you too much. I'm sure you never meant to harm him, but your presence allows him to avoid growing into the proud royal yama he was meant to be. He has you for company, and thus need not conform to what his peers expect."

"They tease him."

"They will stop as soon as he toughens up. I'm sure a clever girl like you can see that."

"Maybe," Xishi admitted.

"*Maybe*, she says," Matreya repeated to the ceiling, as she sometimes did when speaking to her ancestors. Ancestor worship was not approved of, but she was only rohn, and no one scolded her. She turned her age-creased eyes back to Xishi. "You care for Corum, don't you?"

"I love Cor," Xishi said, not caring how that sounded.

Matreya's eyes went round, but she recovered. "Well, if you love him, Xishi—and who am I to say you do not?—you must do what is best for him, even if it hurts. You must leave this house without a tear."

"What does it matter if people see me crying?"

"Perhaps 'people' do not matter, but Corum does. If he sees you pining for him, he will pine for you. Wouldn't you rather he be calm and strong?"

Xishi was not convinced the nurse's reasoning was sound, but she nodded grudgingly. She knew Cor being calm and strong was what she ought to want.

"Good girl," Matreya praised, forgetting they'd been talking woman to woman. "Your courage does you proud. The Infinite Mercy Orphanage will be honored to have you."

Having some experience with what adults considered an "honor," Xishi was less sure of this. Nonetheless, she mopped her face clean of its last tears and gave the nurse her hand. Though Xishi was eight, and no longer a baby, Matreya accepted it.

All the way out of the palace the nurse held on, only letting go when she passed Xishi into the care of the tall, young guard who would escort her to her new home. This soldier might slow his pace for her, but his hands were reserved for his plasma pistol. Knowing this, Xishi walked beside him as straight and steady as she could, never once looking back for the heart she had left behind.

Madame Fagin

~

As Xishi feared, Infinite Mercy Orphanage didn't live up to its name. Oh, there was mercy there—food and shelter, certainly—but that mercy had limits. Girls with fanciful imaginations, girls who had been tossed out of palaces, girls whose mothers were infamous victims of unsolved crimes could not expect to be adopted—no matter how appealing visitors found them. The orphanage's staff had an obligation to warn prospective parents what they might be in for. For that matter, the other orphans deserved warnings, too. If they desired to find families, they had best steer clear of dubious playmates.

More than once, Xishi overheard the staff's whispered cautions. "Don't get too close to that one," they would say. "Don't let her give you one of her hugs." That the children in their care might be desperate for comfort was beside the point. To have parents again was their deepest hunger, and most came to believe that Xishi was a threat to that.

She grew used to the sight of four-year-olds shrinking back against the wall when she walked by.

Ironically, Xishi was often chosen by prospective parents when she was still new to the orphanage. Something in her seemed to call to them. They'd squeeze her rounded face and declare her a "darling child." "Look at that aristocratic little nose" was the commonest refrain. As a rule, the upper classes did not adopt, and Xishi understood her pleasing appearance counted high to rohn. It counted less as she grew older, when it became apparent that her nose was the only wellborn trait she would carry into adulthood. In many ways, she wasn't even up to the standard of servant stock, but the staff would never know how hard she worked not to care.

In the nine years she spent at Infinite Mercy, she did her best to avoid anger and despair, knowing these emotions wouldn't hurt anyone but her. On the other hand, sheer, ornery stubbornness became her friend. She did her chores without complaining, but she also continued being kind to new orphans—even after they were taught to stay away from her. In whatever way they let her, she consoled the young ones who were left unchosen on Viewing Day. If they would listen, she entertained them with her made-up stories. Most of all, she never stopped dreaming that her life would be better in years ahead.

She vowed to remain the optimist she'd been as a child. What matter if that shield had a ding or two? Better to cling to it against all reason than to give it up. At least, that's what Xishi thought.

On the morning she turned seventeen, an event marked— so far as she could tell—by no one but herself, it seemed a change for the better might be in the works. Now past the age of lessons, she was overseeing the carpet sterilizer's progress down the upstairs hall when the matron motioned her to shut it off.

The matron was a tall, ordinarily pretty woman of perhaps fifty. Her prettiness would have been greater had her mouth not borne a constant pinch—but perhaps this was a grimace she saved for Xishi.

"You're wanted downstairs," she said. "You've a visitor, though I don't know why. Anyone can see you're never going to grow out of that baby fat."

This cryptic message delivered, the matron turned away, leaving Xishi to guess whether she ought to spruce up. She was too old for her visitor to be a hopeful parent. She had, however, despite the staff's efforts to prevent it, made a few friends among Infinite Mercy's former residents. Over time, they had been forgetting her in their new lives, but, conceivably, it was one of them.

Deciding the possibility warranted that her hair be combed, she descended to the receiving parlor somewhat less mussed than she might have been.

To her disappointment, no friend awaited—though the person who did looked as if she might lend interest to the morning. Amid the repressively elegant black and cream parlor furniture stood a truly extraordinary female. She was taller than the matron, which was tall indeed, and her lithe and perfect figure was wrapped from throat to ankle in a scarlet stretchsilk gown. The garment was tight enough to reveal the shape of every body part beneath, and the skirt portion was so narrow, Xishi wondered that her guest could walk. Her nails were lacquered silver, her fingers bristling with diamonds.

If this weren't enough to awe Xishi's unworldly eye, her long, crimped hair was the color of winter wheat. Fair hair was extremely rare among the yama, and regarded with such suspicion that those who had it usually dyed it black. These unusual locks made no apologies for themselves, but were decorated with a number of tiny jeweled insects, as if the creatures had landed there in admiration and could not force themselves aloft again.

Struck speechless by this vision, Xishi didn't quite manage to shut her mouth before the woman turned around. The woman's face was painted, yet another unfamiliar fashion choice. Watching Xishi attempt to recover her manners caused the woman's shining, scarlet mouth to purse, precisely as if she wished smiling were allowed.

Xishi knew the gesture well, having used it enough herself.

"Please come closer," said the woman. "I want to get a good look at you."

Xishi's eyebrows lifted, but she stepped into the parlor, onto the center of its gray carpet.

The woman circled her, her long legs stretching her gown with each feline stride.

"*Excellent* figure," she said, a compliment Xishi hadn't heard even once before. She was curvier than most yama, and shorter, too—hence the "babyfat" comments. Obviously suffering no doubts about her own opinion, the woman continued. "Good hair, though that touch of red will show better when it's long. Lovely skin. Perfect symmetry in your face. Shoulders fine. Waist good. Your feet are rather more acceptable than I expected, though you do need to learn to stand gracefully."

Having reached Xishi's front again, the woman ran her assessing gaze up and down. "Those breasts could be your fortune if someone got you out of that ugly gray uniform. Of course, none of your assets matter a whit without good hands. Give them here, my dear, and we'll see what your future holds."

The woman thrust out her own hands, palms up. Not seeing how to refuse politely, Xishi laid her own on top. It had been so long since she'd been touched by anyone willingly that the contact sent an unwitting jerk of shock through her limbs. The woman's metallic green eyelids fluttered closed and stayed down.

"*My*," she said, the word a sigh. "What *beautiful* energy you have. It's positively delicious. My dear, you were born for this!"

"Forgive me for asking," Xishi said, feeling her cheeks grow hot, "but what exactly do you think I was born for?"

The woman drew her hands back reluctantly. "To be a pillow girl, of course. Why else would I come to this dreary drabhouse tricked out like this? Goodness, I can hardly wait to start training you!"

"Don't I—" Discovering she had lost her breath, Xishi tried again. "Don't I have a say?"

"Oh, *really*," scolded the woman. Her voice was considerably more inflected than was common, though Xishi found the affectation appealing. "You're seventeen. Infinite Mercy won't take care of you forever, unless you *want* to spend your life working as their drudge. I wager what little schooling they've given you won't prepare you for much. You have a reputation for being queer, which means your marital prospects are slim. Finally, to put it bluntly, you're too alluring to waste on other jobs. It would be absolutely criminal for me to leave you here!"

Xishi opened her mouth to protest, but a gasp of confusion was all that came out. It was more than a little disconcerting to hear this stranger rattle off her personal business.

"You could set yourself up for life," the woman went on soothingly. "Not right away, of course. You'd have to compensate me for my investment first, but in seven or eight years if you're careful, you'll be able to work for yourself. Or not at all, if you prefer. Imagine the freedom, Xishi. Imagine the security."

Xishi could imagine it—though not that she might get it by being a pillow girl. Pillow girls were courtesans, and that seemed far too glamorous for her. "How . . . long does your training take?"

"Four years, give or take." The woman's painted face had settled into creamily satisfied contentment. "You're welcome to investigate me. In fact, I insist. I'm Violet Fagin, madame of the Purple Crane Pillow House. We're very exclusive. Nothing less than daimyo for my boys and girls. It's all spelled out on our site on the yamaweb."

"We don't have yamaweb access at the orphanage."

"Well, there you have it," said Madame Fagin. "That travesty alone is reason to work for me."

Xishi forgot herself enough to rub her temples, her brain feeling oddly numb. "Four years . . . ," she repeated slowly.

"And seven or eight more to pay off your debt and build a nest egg. I'll even grant you right of refusal, if that makes deciding easier. Princes will line up for a girl like you. I expect you'll be able to pick and choose without either of our purses suffering. Mind you, I don't usually grant refusal rights, so for *goodness*' sake don't tell the other girls I did."

Her manner of speaking was so strange, Xishi wasn't certain she believed her. Like most rohn, she had a knack for reading auras. The upper classes' gift lay in manipulating the messages they sent—generally variations on the theme of *I'm better than you*. Madame Fagin was no daimyo, and her aura's colors didn't suggest deception, but Xishi knew some yama had good control.

"You really think a . . . a prince would like the way I look?"

"Oh, honey!" Madame Fagin exclaimed. "Half the time, men don't admit what they're craving even to themselves. But when everyone around you is vanilla, what can you want but a taste of spice? I've made a fortune—no, I've made *ten* fortunes by being a little different. And you, you're both beautiful and ever-so-slightly off. Trust me, dear, those poor, bored sons of the royal houses will eat you up."

Xishi was uncomfortable with this praise, especially because it concerned princes. She hadn't heard from Cor—or anyone else at Midarri House—since she'd been sent away. Now and then, she saw the family on a viewscreen in a shop when she ran errands. The Midarri were close to the emperor and newsworthy. She watched Cor win a martial arts competition once this way, which cost her a scolding from the matron for returning late.

The prince had grown up very handsome, and the acrobatic brilliance of his leaps and kicks had dragged her breath from her more than once. That aside, she knew it was foolish to think of him as hers, or to wonder if he remembered her. He had shown none of his old emotion during the bouts. Matreya must have been right about the benefit of her absence. He had overcome his old problem. In more ways than one, the days when they'd been each other's closest friend were ancient history.

Struggling not to show how hungry she was for compliments, Xishi informed the madame that she would investigate her pillow house, and would come to a decision within a week.

"Excellent!" said Madame Fagin in her emphatic way. "I look forward to signing you!"

⟿

Madame Fagin's reputation proved to be as impeccable as her manner of claiming it was strange. Xishi inquired after her in every way she could—mostly through shopkeepers and old friends, one of whom obligingly looked her up on the yamaweb. Every source said the same. Violet Fagin treated her students well. Many had gone on to become wealthy in their own right, and the Purple Crane was the premier pillow house in the capital, the first place royals turned to for bed servants.

The second turned out to be run by one of Madame Fagin's old students.

The life of a pillow girl might not be perfect, but members of the lower class (from which the Purple Crane culled its pupils) simply couldn't hope to rise as far in other trades.

Satisfied, if a little nervous, Xishi sent a message that she was interested in seeing a contract.

To her astonishment, a floating palanquin came to collect her. Gaudy as a parrot, with bright green curtains and yellow poles, the low-riding chair skirted the edge of the prohibition against rohn flying. Xishi felt terribly flustered as she climbed into it, but also terribly pleased. The matron could make all the dire predictions she liked. Madame Fagin must really want to hire her if she'd sent this.

The palanquin was programmed to take her to the pillow house. All Xishi had to do was lean back against the cushions and give it permission to proceed. Smooth as silver, it let her off at the steps to Madame Fagin's establishment.

The season was spring, and the last of the snow was dripping from the Purple Crane's bird-wing eaves. This was the rural edge of the outer city. The pillow house sat on its own acreage within the embrace of a low brick wall. Other pretty little buildings, of similar color and style, sat behind the main one—classrooms or dormitories, Xishi supposed. Beyond these structures, no more than half a mile distant, rose the capital's outermost ramparts, a barrier so tall alarm towers were required to keep aircars from crashing into it on foggy days.

The towering, snow-streaked crags of the Dragon's Teeth were the only backdrop that could have made the wall look small.

Xishi had never been this close to either wonder, but she was too nervous to indulge her curiosity by staring. Instead, she forced herself up the black granite steps to the glossy indigo door. A silver plaque on the brick beside it, discreetly declaring this to be the "Purple Crane Pillow House," was the only indication that the establishment wasn't a normal residence.

Before Xishi could pull the bell rope, two beautiful black-haired girls, just about her age and sisters by the look of them, swung the door open. Both their eyes were twinkling, though their faces remained politely serious.

"Welcome," they said together. "We're so glad you've come."

They led her down a beautifully appointed hall. The cranes that gave the house its name had been painted on the caramel walls, not in purple but in gold leaf. Many of the furnishings appeared to be antique. Xishi couldn't begin to guess their value, though she did keep her elbows pressed to her sides. The sisters, who had introduced themselves as Lily and Chrysanthemum, gestured her ahead of them through an ebony door.

"All is well," Lily assured her. "You're wanted here."

Behind the door was a large tea green parlor in which three round windows overlooked a winter-tangled strolling garden. Though Madame Fagin was absent, Xishi counted a dozen men and women inside. Four looked young enough to be students. Though she knew they were rohn, not a one was dressed in regulation lower-class gray—or remotely ordinary. Every face she saw was striking, every outfit delightful, every figure mouthwatering. One of the girls was blonder than Violet Fagin. The older ones, who she presumed were actual employees, even had long hair. The madame must have arranged for them to buy a dispensation to grow it out. So healthy and confident did these individuals appear, they easily could have passed for daimyo.

The idea that Xishi had been chosen to stand among them daunted her.

But she didn't have time to dwell on her shortcomings, because "Welcome!" said the little crowd in unison.

They had been lined up across the airy room, a rainbow of silk and velvet and glowing skin. They parted as they called their greeting, revealing the flicker of many candles on a low table. There, on a chased silver platter, sat an array of bite-sized frosted cakes, each holding a small candle. The cakes had been arranged to spell out "Happy Natal Day!" In case Xishi had any doubt this wish was meant for her, the rim of the platter was engraved with her name.

Completely dazed, she blinked at the arrangement. In all her life, no one had given her birthday sweets, much less a traditional birthday plate. Not even Corum had thought of that.

When her eyes began to burn, she covered them in horror.

Chrysanthemum patted her shoulder. "That's all right," she said. "No one minds a few happy teardrops at the Purple Crane."

"We're here to answer your questions," said a young male voice from her other side. "That's why the madame isn't here. You can ask us anything and we'll be honest."

Xishi sensed them moving closer, not crowding her but interested in discovering who she was. She knew they couldn't possibly all end up liking her, but the idea that some of them might was truly wonderful.

She forced herself to wrest her runaway emotions into order.

"Do any of you like made-up stories?" she asked, tentatively lowering her hands.

A delicate doll of a girl stepped forward. Her features were exquisite, her figure slender in the extreme. Since her blue-black hair was only chin length, Xishi assumed she was a student.

"We *love* made-up stories," the girl assured her. "Especially when someone new is telling them."

After that, it didn't matter what any of them said, or what clauses Madame Fagin's contract hid. Xishi knew she had found the home she'd been dreaming of.

The Purple Crane

❧

"All right, boys and girls," said Madame Fagin. "Let's have ourselves a lesson in royal anatomy."

There were seven "boys and girls" in Madame Fagin's class, all around the age of twenty, and everyone sat straighter at her words.

Among her listeners were the dark-haired sisters, Lily and Chrysanthemum, the lemon blonde Amaryllis, and the delicate Tea Rose. Tea Rose was the girl who two years ago had assured Xishi they all liked stories. Now she was the classmate with whom she felt most at home, because she never seemed to judge anyone. The only boys were Mingmar and Jehol. Mingmar was kind and soft-spoken, his face so pretty he could pass for a woman if he painted it. It was he who had given Xishi her flower name, telling her—with the faintest blush—that she ought to be called Buttercup for the kiss of gold in her skin.

The second boy, Jehol, was as good-looking as the rest but built on more intimidating lines. He worked out in the school's resistance machine every morning before dawn, and was so muscular he could have served as a palace guard. The others, especially Amaryllis, liked him—he was full of energy and jokes—but the way he sometimes stared at Xishi wore on her nerves. These looks were neither friendly nor flirtatious. *He* said she ought to be called Buttercup because she was so round.

At Madame Fagin's announcement, he rubbed his hands together gleefully. "Finally! We get to learn what we came here for."

"Now, now," said the madame good-naturedly. "Impatience will get you nowhere when you're in court."

"Yes, but royal anatomy might," Amaryllis interjected just as playfully.

For once Xishi understood their attitude. For the last two years they had been learning everything *but* anatomy. Etiquette, Graceful Movement, Decorative Arts, and Fashion had filled their days. They'd even studied a discipline the madame claimed to have invented called Seductive Speaking, which involved directing the pitch of one's voice like humans did when they sang—an occupation ordinary yama absolutely did not engage in. By human standards, yama were tone deaf. To Xishi's surprise, Seductive Speaking was her favorite subject. As the youngest and shyest student, she'd been eager for any advantage she could get. When her classmates protested they were "melting" at her dulcet tones, Xishi could no longer doubt she belonged.

Today she simply felt excited. Most of the students knew something about sex, but all were ignorant about the specialized sort of sex they were being trained to perform. Madame Fagin had strongly discouraged them from interrogating the working girls, and had ordered them not to experiment on one another—no easy rule to enforce when seven attractive yama were reaching maturity in the same house.

Amaryllis had sighed about it frequently, claiming it was a plot to ratchet up their libidos until they wouldn't balk at anything.

If it was a plot, it was working. Amaryllis exchanged a heated glance with Jehol, whom she'd twice been disciplined for kissing. Xishi suspected the pair had done other things as well, but so far they'd managed to evade detection. The sisters sat next to Amaryllis and were squirming in their hard, wood seats. Tea Rose and Mingmar shared the back row with Xishi. Each was gripping the long table's edge as if they feared an earthquake, and each—inadvertently, she was sure—bumped her feet with one of theirs at the same time.

"Sorry," Mingmar murmured. "Had a little cramp."

Clearly aware of what she'd stirred up, Madame Fagin gave them a demonstration of graceful movement as she strolled in leisurely fashion around the room. The sun struck rainbows off the tiny diamonds sewn into her body-skimming gown. Its material was as richly blue as the sky outside, a perfect foil for her wheat blonde hair.

"Key up your viewplates," she said, her singsong purr as sultry as Xishi's. "Today we're taking a tour of the royal male."

The holographic plates were set into the tables in front of them. Involuntary giggles broke out when the program Madame Fagin had prepared appeared. A small, naked man, no bigger than Xishi's hand, was having . . . well, she could only call it *frantic* intercourse with a naked female on a green divan. The little man's face was distorted, his expression suggesting his life depended on him reaching climax soon. Yama were capable of swift motion, but his hips were moving so quickly the motion blurred. Though this was only a recording, and of nothing she didn't know about, Xishi felt the tips of her ears grow hot.

True to form, Jehol and Amaryllis immediately enlarged and slowed the holofilm.

"Yes, yes," said Madame Fagin, sounding amused. "You will want a good look at everything."

Once all her students had followed their example, Madame Fagin used her controls to start the next segment. This time, a semitransparent figure of the naked man appeared. He was standing in thin air, his arms and legs spread while he rotated above the plate. Various portions of his anatomy were highlighted in glowing colors. Most looked to Xishi like erogenous zones.

"The thing to remember," their teacher said, "is that royals, especially royal males, have more of everything. More glands, more hormones, more *specialized* needs."

"Not more size," Jehol joked, expanding his chest.

Madame Fagin was no stickler for perfect face and did not scold Jehol for his humor. She did, however, correct him.

"Actually," she said, "when aroused, you'll find few rohn, or even daimyo, can match a royal's erectile size."

She must have activated her control, because the transparent man's penis inflated dramatically. Tea Rose gasped, seemingly in alarm, and Xishi felt compelled to pat her hand. Pretending she hadn't noticed either student's lapse, Madame Fagin continued.

"As more of you know than should"—here she narrowed her eyes at Amaryllis—"all yamish males, of any class, have the ability to regulate penis size. Even when aroused, they are able to increase or decrease their erections to suit their partners.

"The same cannot be said for royal males in rut. Every scrap of energy in their body becomes focused on fulfillment. Their erections quickly reach maximum enlargement, whatever that is for each man, and cannot be diminished by anything short of medical intervention until their ultimate goal is reached."

Tea Rose's slender hand shot into the air. "Excuse me, Madame Fagin, but what is rut?"

The madame perched her bottom on the edge of her mother-of-pearl–inlaid desk. "Rut is the height of the royal male's sexual cycle. The cycle covers a period of about four weeks, during which his glands—the extra ones I mentioned—produce increasing amounts of a sexual hormone called kith, unique to their class. The period of rut, which lasts from four to seven days, is the only time royal males are able to ejaculate."

As she gestured with her controller, three of the glands that had been highlighted on the model glowed bright fuchsia. Two were located in his neck, while the third appeared to be piggybacked on his prostate.

"Wait a second," Jehol broke in. "You're saying royal males only come once every four weeks? That can't be true."

He seemed so sure, Xishi found herself looking questioningly toward the madame, too. Madame Fagin smoothed her diamond-studded gown down her long, slim thighs.

"I'm saying nothing of the kind, Jehol. Royal males only ejaculate during the period of rut, but they are able, indeed eager, to do so repeatedly. Rut is rather a mindless state, and you'll find its sufferers interested in little beyond having sex. When they are not in rut, they may enjoy whatever orgasms they please—and they do please, I assure you—but those orgasms are *dry*. During the rest of their cycle, their seed accumulates, as you'll see from the somewhat swollen state of our model's scrotum. As future pillow girls and boys, this dry period is the one you'll usually encounter, but not always. Even if you boys decide you wish to service only royal women, you may, on occasion, be asked to 'help' a wife with her husband."

Xishi fought a flush as she imagined how this might be done. She was glad to see she wasn't the only student affected.

Chrysanthemum spoke up, slightly breathless from these topics. "I don't understand. Why wouldn't we see the royals during rut? Isn't that when they most want a pillow girl?"

"Ah," said Madame Fagin, obviously savoring this. "We come to the heart of the matter, to the mysteries of the royal hormone known as kith.

"You may think of kith as a lock, my dears, which requires the proper key to be opened. This key is a pheromone found in the body fluids of a female, especially those fluids related to arousal. Only royal women have it, but not every royal female can pair with every royal male. When a particular female's genes will combine with a particular male's to produce superior offspring, she is considered his genetic match.

"The man's body recognizes this. Her proximity, her pheromones, spur his kith to rise for the first time. Consequently, if a male doesn't find his mate, he never matures

completely. Once his kith is active, her sexual essence, or
'cream,' to use common parlance, is the necessary catalyst
for the release of seed, thus insuring no one but a prince's
genetically ideal match will bear his child. In this way, the
health of royal bloodlines is guaranteed."

"Excuse me for asking," Lily said, sounding more annoyed than apologetic, "but if royal males can only ejaculate with their wives, why do they need us?"

"For pleasure, Lily, pure and simple. I know we yama
are supposed to be above any need for romance or affection, but imagine, if you will, being dependent for the most
basic of reliefs on a woman you might not respect, a woman
a welter of tiny chemicals in your body has selected to be
your mate. Would you not wish to exercise some personal
choice when you could? Would you not wish to feel like a
master rather than a slave? Do not think for a moment that
you, a mere pillow girl, cannot be as necessary to a prince's
happiness as his wife. I will teach you how to be necessary.
I will give you the power to create pleasures every bit as
deep as the simple spilling of semen. Trust me, girls and
boys, *you* will be important."

Lily sat back in her chair, looking mollified, but her sister had another question.

"What's in it for the wives?" Chrysanthemum asked.
"Besides having their husbands under their thumbs for five
days."

"Under their pussies, you mean," Jehol quipped.

Madame Fagin pursed her mouth at him but not disap-
provingly. "Kith is an aphrodisiac, my dears, and royal
women are no less affected than royal males. They, too, are
slaves to their bodies while their mates are in heat. The
hunger is, so I have heard, sublime. The difference is that
when their mates are not in heat, royal females are capable
of having satisfying orgasms with any man—an advantage
I'm sure you pillow boys will appreciate."

Mingmar appeared thoughtful, but Jehol's expression
approached a sneer. Xishi supposed he thought anyone who
hired a partner must be weak. Whatever the expression's

cause, he wiped it from his face the moment he saw she'd noticed. The chill that came into his eyes before he turned away sent a shiver sliding down her nape. His glance had held more than his usual hauteur. To her perhaps overactive imagination, it had held hate.

"He looks at you like you disgust him," Mingmar murmured, and for the first time Xishi realized she wasn't the only student who had grown wary of Jehol.

Before she could assure Mingmar it didn't matter, Madame Fagin clapped her hands for attention.

"That is all for today," she said. "You are welcome to load the demonstration hologram onto your handhelds. Think over what you've learned, get a good night's rest, and come prepared tomorrow for a hands-on lab."

This announcement could have inspired another hour of questions, but Madame Fagin swept out regally before her "boys and girls" could utter even one.

⟡

The girls' dormitory at the Purple Crane was Xishi's favorite spot on earth. Separated from the main house by a grove of trees, hotboxes of bamboo screened its windows. Inside was the snuggest place imaginable—a long, beamed room with curtained beds, rich golden oak flooring, and soft carpets. Dangerous treats crammed the bookshelves, and the cozy sitting area basked in the charms of a wood fireplace.

Each worn leather chair that faced it had been claimed by one of the girls. Xishi's was nearest the bookshelves, where she could reach out and stroke the spines of the human novels Madame Fagin had bought dispensations for. Some contained the original human text along with a translation. On nights when she couldn't sleep, Xishi worked on building her own Yamish-Human dictionary. It pleased her very much to do it, not only because she enjoyed the stories, but because it proved she was not as stupid as Cor's mother always had assumed.

Though she told no one, sometimes she dreamed of impressing Cor with translating human books for him.

This was as unlikely to happen as her getting the good night's sleep Madame Fagin had recommended. As they often did, the boys had crept through the woods from their sleeping quarters to spend an hour flirting with the girls. Guards were posted at each dormitory, but they were very old rohn retainers, nearing three centuries, and they tended to doze through the intrusion as long as everyone kept quiet. Only twice in two years had they woken up in time to chase out the boys.

Because they had been caught so seldom, everyone was relaxed. Lily had lit a fire since, even in summer, nights in the capital were cool. The lights were off, of course, and the seven of them sprawled around the sitting area in their multicolored silk sleeping robes.

No one suggested anyone put on more clothes.

Per usual, Amaryllis was sitting in Jehol's lap, playing with his stark black hair. In return, Jehol idly petted her sunny locks, now grown to the center of her back. Long hair was still exotic for the students, a slightly forbidden pleasure—though Jehol did not seem pleased tonight. He seemed, to Xishi's wary eye, in a surly mood. Disinclined to coddle Amaryllis's jealousy, his attention roved over the other girls.

The sisters had their noses together over a handheld. They had grown even prettier in the last two years, which a boy like Jehol could not fail to note. Always clever with technology, Lily had enlarged a close-up of the demonstration model's erection until the holographic organ stretched as long as her arm. Chrysanthemum struggled not to giggle as it spun slowly.

Somewhat less interesting to Jehol, Tea Rose and Mingmar had arranged themselves on their backs over ottomans, positioning them so their heads were pillowed on Xishi's thighs.

Given the years she'd spent being avoided like a disease, Xishi didn't mind their presumption. Mingmar and Tea Rose were peaceful company. Like the sisters, their hair epitomized the yamish ideal, blue-black and straight as a die. Draping smoothly across Xishi's robe, it warmed her like a second layer of silk. Every so often, Mingmar would glance over at the giant penis and shift his weight. Tea Rose's eyes stayed closed. Xishi wondered if she realized her partner in relaxation had a monumental erection. Tea Rose was not as oblivious—or as innocent—as people thought. Much to Amaryllis's annoyance, she had slipped away with Jehol a time or two.

As to that, Xishi suspected Tea Rose would not have minded slipping away with *her*.

"What I can't figure out," Lily murmured, barely louder than the crackling fire, "is what this highlighted purple thingie above the urethral slit is. I can't find the label for it anywhere."

"Another kith gland?" Mingmar suggested in a husky tone.

"It doesn't look like a gland. It's curled up inside the head like a little fern. Plus, the index only lists three."

"Show Mingmar where to find the kingmaster," Jehol suggested mockingly. "That's the one he'll need when he's 'helping' those royal wives. That's the one he's spinning fantasies of running his dick over now."

"And what if he is?" Chrysanthemum said crisply. "He'll be that much more popular if he's interested in pleasing both sexes."

"Hear, hear," said Tea Rose without opening her eyes.

"Well, naturally *you'd* think so," jeered Jehol.

"Stop it," snapped Chrysanthemum. "Just because Tea Rose isn't walking out with you anymore is no reason to be snide."

Jehol didn't try to hide his smirk this time, though it was small. "You'd like to think that was her decision, wouldn't you, since you finally convinced her to snuggle up with you. If you had half an eye, though, you'd know you weren't her first choice for girlplay."

"Hey," protested Xishi, because by now he'd managed to set every female in the room fuming.

It went without saying that Jehol wasn't cowed by her.

"What's the matter, Buttercup?" he asked coolly. "Can't stand to see the only family you've got fighting?"

"No, I can't," she admitted, because she had never seen the point in lying when the truth was plain. "And I don't understand why you want to start a fight. There are plenty more interesting things to talk about tonight."

Mingmar squeezed her hand in approval, but Jehol couldn't let the matter lie.

"Oh, yes. Why don't we talk about how royal princes only ejaculate one week in four? Or maybe we should fawn over Madame Fagin. We can marvel at how incredibly in-fallible she is."

Mingmar sat up on his ottoman, clearly feeling that, as the second male, he had an obligation to defend the girls. His gallantry was somewhat undercut by the giant tent at his groin. "What are you talking about, Jehol? As far as I know, Madame Fagin has never been wrong about anything."

"Exactly my point." Jehol pushed Amaryllis to the side so she didn't block his view of Mingmar. "If Madame says it, it must be true. All royal males must be exactly the same. Four-week cycles. Four to seven days of rut. And no way do they reach sexual maturity until some genetically perfect woman has stirred up their kith!"

His voice had risen enough that everyone stared at him. Jehol had never been a model of control, but this outburst was unusual even for him.

"Shh," Amaryllis said soothingly. "You'll wake the guard. Anyway, what do you care? Isn't it enough that you can take your pleasure every day? Why not be grateful *your* seed doesn't get backed up?"

She'd been stroking his broad, hard shoulder, but Jehol didn't want to be pacified. Lifting her off him onto the arm of the chair, he stood and turned his supercilious gaze around the room. "I'm bored," he said. "Who wants to walk with me tonight?"

When Lily immediately dropped her eyes—as if hoping to avoid his notice—he stepped to her. Probably to her dismay, her aura flared.

"You want to," he said, confidence in every line of his imposing body. "And why not? I bet you'd love to learn to kiss better than Lemonhead."

Amaryllis gasped at this less than flattering reference to her hair. Lily started stammering a refusal, but Chrysanthemum stopped her.

"Oh, go ahead," she said. "He is a good teacher."

The admission that she, too, had slipped out with Jehol startled everyone into letting him tug Lily after him with no protest.

"Well," said Xishi into the ensuing silence. "I guess that leaves me and Mingmar as the only students who haven't taken Jehol's 'lessons.'"

Tea Rose's customarily tranquil face assumed a tiny smile. "Don't worry, Buttercup. I'd be happy to pass on to you and Mingmar everything Jehol taught me—preferably at the same time."

Mingmar laughed softly and laid his head back down in Xishi's lap.

"I have a question," he said as he squirmed into a comfortable position, or at least comfortable for him. "What could Madame Fagin have meant by a hands-on lab? Do you suppose she found a prince for us to practice on?"

"She couldn't have." Amaryllis scoffed, doing a reasonably good job of pretending she wasn't smarting from Jehol's behavior. "I'm sure acting as our practice dummy would be beneath his royal dignity."

"Maybe Madame bought an android," Chrysanthemum speculated. "I've heard the latest models are quite advanced."

"Robots with glands," Mingmar mused before nudging Xishi's arm. "You could make up a story about that: the sex-crazed robot who wished he was a man."

Xishi punched his shoulder in response. Of all her classmates, Mingmar appreciated her gift for invention most. Of course, Mingmar seemed to think it was his duty to flatter all the girls. Despite this willingness to please, most of the girls preferred Jehol anyway.

"I wonder," Tea Rose said softly from Xishi's other thigh, "if princes ever fall in love with pillow girls."

"Ugh." Amaryllis tossed her yellow hair. "Who'd want them to?"

"Really," Chrysanthemum agreed. "Can you imagine anything more embarrassing?" With a muffled snort of laughter, she dropped to one knee, pressed both hands to her breast, and squinched up her face like a human in a holovid. The flickering firelight made her expression even more grotesque. "I love you, Amaryllis!" she cried, sotto voce. "If you don't love me back, I shall die!"

Amaryllis had to conceal her smile behind both palms. Xishi was glad to see the other girl forget her anger, though she couldn't help feeling more attuned with Tea Rose. Blockheaded though it was, more than one of her daydreams centered on the possibility of a prince falling in love with her.

Meet Prince Pahndir

❧

The students found something new when they filed into their classroom the next morning, something that had their sleepy eyes widening.

"Boys and girls," said Madame Fagin with an air of suppressed delight. "Meet Prince Pahndir."

Considering last night's talk of androids, it was no wonder Xishi thought the madame had bought one. A man-shaped silver armature stood before Madame Fagin's desk, glinting softly in the sun. Inside it was the naked figure of an adult male. Though tall, he stood upright and unmoving, the straps of metal both supporting and trapping him. Like the demonstration model from the holo, his arms were lifted out from his sides, his legs spread gently to form a V. Despite the light pouring in the windows, his pupils had swollen beyond their normal circumference. His eyes were not blinking that Xishi could see.

He was certainly perfect enough to be the product of technology, but as soon as Xishi drew closer with the others, she knew he was not. The steady vibration of his heart could be seen behind his breastbone, and his energy body definitely wasn't a machine's. Its colors were muddied in a way she'd never encountered, though this was difficult to discern. His aura had drawn unnaturally close to his skin— as if protectively.

This sign of distress should have kept her eyes from sliding over him, but it did not. He was much too fascinating for that. He appeared to have reached his fourth decade, and she understood just by looking at him what Madame Fagin meant by sexual maturity. Broad, muscular shoulders led to a narrow waist, and then on to powerful legs. His body was solid in ways even Jehol's was not. Indeed, compared to this male, Jehol and Mingmar were boys. As was the fashion among the upper circles, the man's torso and legs had been stripped of hair. Bereft of covering, his muscles possessed a harmony that had Xishi swallowing hard.

His cleanly handsome face was also bare. The tail of his neatly braided hair—blue-black and glossy from his royal genes—fell to his hips. Once her gaze had drifted there, the part of his body that he used for pleasure was too magnificent not to admire. His shaft was the color of just opened roses, the skin so smooth she longed to touch it. At the bottom of this thick, smooth length, the helmet-shaped head hung large.

That's more than a mouthful, Xishi thought dazedly. She barely noticed when Chrysanthemum jostled her for a better view.

"Oh, my," the other girl said, leaning so close her nose nearly touched the armature above Prince Pahndir's hips. "Royals *are* bigger."

His finger twitched at her words, causing everyone but Xishi to jump back. *She* had long since realized he was a living being.

"All right," said Madame Fagin, shooing Xishi away with the rest. "That's enough goggling for now. Take your seats. Up front, Buttercup, if you please. I won't have you hiding in the back for this. Amaryllis, you can switch places with her today."

It was hard to tell whether Amaryllis or Xishi was more displeased. Uncomfortable and confused as to the reason for the change, Xishi lowered herself into the empty seat beside Jehol. He was looking particularly haughty today, but thankfully said nothing.

"Now," said Madame Fagin, one hand lifting to rest on the topmost curve of the prince's cage. "As Chrysanthemum noted in her less than elegant way, our practice subject has entered the first stage of rut. You can see this from the enlargement of his pupils, the obvious heaviness of his scrotum, and the greater heft and girth of his as-yet-nonerect penis."

Chrysanthemum jumped as if she'd been pinched. "Oh! Does he have a purple thingie?"

Madame Fagin frowned openly. "Never you mind the purple thingie. That's none of you boys' and girls' business."

Chrysanthemum subsided reluctantly at the scold, and Madame Fagin went on. "As I was saying, fortunately for our purposes, Prince Pahndir is coming into heat. Consequently, as I begin teaching you the thousand and one caresses prescribed for bedplay, you will have no trouble judging their effectiveness."

"Isn't that—" Xishi stopped, surprised to find herself speaking out. She didn't think she'd interrupted in class before.

"Yes, Buttercup?" said Madame Fagin, one elegant pale eyebrow going up.

Xishi didn't want to answer, but her memory of the frantically copulating hologram compelled her to. This prince could have no hope of release during Madame's lessons, not from rohn pillow girls.

"I was just wondering," she said, her face heating, "if the prince . . . I mean, I assume he volunteered for this. Otherwise, practicing on him now sounds cruel."

Xishi was watching the madame's aura for signs of anger, but from the corner of her eye, she saw the prince's head turn slowly toward her in the armature. She didn't dare look at him for fear of blushing even more. Instead, she kept her gaze on the madame's skillfully painted face.

"Prince Pahndir did *not* volunteer," Madame Fagin said, enunciating every word, "and let his story be a lesson to those of you who have allowed your self-control to grow lax within the freedom of this house. Prince Pahndir's family consigned him to my care following the death of his wife. Though eighteen months were allowed to pass, Prince Pahndir was unable to overcome his grief, thus making a public spectacle of himself and his relatives. Finally, and most properly, his family paid me to take him on the condition that I wouldn't release him again. In order to protect the honor of his bloodline, they let it be known that he died in an accident.

"Nor may any of you"—Madame Fagin pointed with a silver fingernail—"disseminate otherwise, as you promised in paragraph sixteen of your signed contracts."

"So this prince is dead," Jehol said, his arms folded in subtle satisfaction across his chest.

"Officially." Madame Fagin looked at him rather more coolly than was her habit. Generally, Jehol was something of her pet. "Let us hope, however, that you will not find him dead to your touch."

Xishi could not help it. She snuck a glance at the prince. Though he must have heard, he showed no reaction to Madame Fagin's tale. His eyes stared straight forward, every bit as machine-like as they'd been when they all trooped in. Whatever the depth of his grief, it wasn't showing now . . . unless he was so humiliated by the treatment he was forced to bear that it had deadened him.

Given that Madame Fagin had told her to sit up front, Xishi really should have expected she'd be called on to practice one of the "thousand and one caresses" first. She hadn't forgotten the madame's comments at their initial meeting about the supposed deliciousness of her chi. All the same, the distracting nature of their practice subject caused her to start with surprise when the madame instructed her to get up.

"Up. Out of your seat," the teacher urged as she hesitated. " 'The last shall be first,' as the humans say. Get her a stool, Jehol. I want her to be able to reach his face."

Jehol fetched the stool, placing it with exaggerated politeness in front of the cage's feet. Xishi stepped onto it nervously. Her eyes were now level with Prince Pahndir's. They looked back at her, the black shining in the silver like pools of ink. What he must think of her—of them all—for using him this way! Seized by an urge to apologize, she pressed her lips together instead.

For the first time since she had arrived at the Purple Crane, Xishi wished she were somewhere else.

"No need to be shy," said Madame Fagin, misinterpreting her delay. "It's not as if he can reach out of that trap to you. Why don't you start by stroking his eyebrows? See if you can soothe him enough to close his eyes."

Xishi had to reach between two bands of silver, but she did as Madame Fagin said. The instant her thumbs pressed the bridge of his nose, the prince sucked a startled breath. The point was an energy center, and it glowed just a little warmer beneath her touch. His eyes glittered with alertness as they met hers. He was looking at her, *seeing* her, in a way he had not before.

"No, no," said Madame Fagin. "*Stroke* the brows, slowly, gently, along the curve of the socket. You want to relax him, not give him a headache."

Nervous again, Xishi obeyed as well as she could. When the prince closed his eyes a few seconds later, she was almost certain it was not because she had relaxed him. Rather, she had the distinct impression that he wanted her gone from him.

"Oh, all right then." Madame Fagin waved her off, seeming disappointed that she hadn't performed better. "That will do. Let the others have a turn."

One by one, her classmates were given the opportunity to caress various portions of the prince's face. The prince looked bored to Xishi, but the madame was sufficiently pleased to remove the portion of the armature that had trapped his head.

"You again," she said to Xishi. "Let's see if you can massage the tightness from his neck."

While Xishi went to look for wherever Jehol had kicked the stool, Madame Fagin addressed the class. "The sternocleidomastoid muscles are a sensitive area for royals, due to the kith glands they lie nearby—which themselves link to the submandibular salivary glands. At this stage of rut, the hormone has built up and wants to be expelled. Naturally, our subject's kith will stay where it is, but were his mate present, it would flow to her through kissing. The genetic markers in her saliva would call it forth. Even without the presence of a mate, caresses in this area are pleasant. Any loosening of the associated muscles will facilitate eventual release. You will endear yourself to your future masters if you don't forget this."

It might have been Xishi's imagination, but the prince seemed tense as she climbed up before him the second time, a possibility that did nothing to dry her sweaty palms. However sorry she felt for him, the last thing she wanted was to fail this most important of subjects.

Because Madame Fagin was still talking, Xishi took her chance to speak to him.

"Your Highness," she whispered, hoping the title would not sound like a mockery. "Perhaps you could blink twice if I do something you don't like. I am sure you know what pleases you as well as anyone."

The prince's mouth fell open at being spoken to, but a second later he smoothed his surprise away. He blinked once to show he understood.

Less nervous then, if not completely confident, Xishi laid her hands against his neck. The long muscles Madame had mentioned were taut indeed. Xishi squeezed them gently, reaching around the back of the prince's neck as well. His skin was warm and smooth—pleasant to touch. Though the prince did not blink as she continued, he seemed to be holding his breath, which did not seem ideal to her. Hoping to inspire a better response, she searched out the swellings of his glands. The increase in temperature told her when she found them. Located near the hinge of his jaw, they were twice the size of almonds and similar in shape. Assuming they'd be tender, she moved her thumbs in gentle circles over them.

A sound broke in the prince's throat, so low and mournful Xishi doubted anyone heard but her. The prince's eyelids drifted down helplessly, a far different reaction than the one he'd feigned before. Xishi felt a thrill course through her as spots of heat bloomed beneath her thumbs. A flush was spreading outward from where she rubbed, a cloud of russet beneath his skin. Evidently, she was not failing at this.

"Ooh," Lily crooned, breaking into Madame Fagin's lecture. "Buttercup must be doing something right. He's getting hard."

Madame Fagin stopped speaking and came to see.

"Oh, dear," she said. "I was hoping that wouldn't happen until tomorrow." She *tsk*ed at the prince's rising organ, but dismissed the worry a breath later. "Nothing we can do about it now. Buttercup, please let Chrysanthemum take your place. We may as well see if the others can bring him up all the way."

Xishi stepped down, somewhat shocked at Madame Fagin's attitude. She seemed to be the only one who felt guilty for tormenting the prince this way. The other students did their utmost to increase his arousal. Xishi supposed this was the point of the lesson, and she couldn't deny having been pleased with her own success, but it troubled her to think of the prince's discomfort. Madame Fagin mentioned that a royal's erection would not subside while he was in rut. He could go forward in arousal but not back.

This appeared to be the case. Though none of the students except for Tea Rose brought him any higher, neither did their inexperience cause his organ to relax. If this was the first day of his heat, the next four or five would be difficult. Xishi winced as the last student stepped away. The prince's penis was bobbing, thick and red, just below parallel to the floor.

Madame Fagin announced the end of the lesson then. To Xishi's surprise, she began unlocking the prince's cage. Apparently, despite his condition, he wasn't expected to attack the students. Maybe rut didn't leave a man as crazed as Madame Fagin claimed. Maybe the prince knew there'd be no point in forcing himself on a rohn.

Curious, she watched the madame help him step from the silver cage. As he did, the grief that had shamed his family became clear. His shoulders were bowed without the armature to hold them straight, his movements awkward and listless.

He must not care about anything, Xishi thought, *except that his wife is dead.*

She understood this concept better than she believed she should. To mourn that deeply struck her as a human extravagance. Surely at some point, he would snap out of it.

"Class is over, Buttercup," Jehol reminded dryly. "Time to go."

Xishi shook herself. She was the only student still in her seat. The edge of hostility in Jehol's voice must have caught the attention of Prince Pahndir. Madame Fagin had been steering him by the arm, but as they reached the door, he looked back. In that instant, his eyes were utterly unguarded, and the sun shone full in his face. His expression was like nothing Xishi had ever seen—certainly nothing like Chrysanthemum's playacting the night before. This was the ruin left by a broken heart. This was how love lost forever looked.

A wintry shadow fell across her spirit. With it came a memory of Cor staring down at her from the window of his tutor's room, trapped by his lessons for the next few hours. He'd been a child, and so had she, but something in his eyes reminded her of this. To her dismay, she couldn't quell the shudder that ran down her spine.

"Careful," Jehol murmured next to her ear. "You wouldn't want that kind of weakness to rub off."

Midnight visitors

～ ～

A shadow slipped between the gauzy curtains of Xishi's bed, followed by a weight creaking on the mattress.

"Shh," said Tea Rose as Xishi bolted up. "It's me."

Xishi pressed her hand to her racing heart. Fortunately, her would-be shriek remained a quiet gasp. Tea Rose was kneeling at the foot of her bed, dressed in her sleeping robe. The light was too dim to make out her face, but her energy sparked with excitement.

"What are you doing here?" Xishi whispered, concluding from Tea Rose's manner that this was not a seduction.

"Answer one question, and I'll tell you."

"Fine." Xishi sighed, seeing she would not be going back to sleep. "What do you want to know?"

"Which sort of pillow girl would you rather be? The kind who gets passed around from prince to prince, or the kind who finds a single master to buy her contract?"

Xishi pushed her hair from her face, stalling for time. This was a little close to being asked to share her dearest dreams. "A single master, I suppose, as long as he isn't aw-ful. That way we might have a chance to be friends."

"Exactly what I thought," Tea Rose murmured approv-ingly. "And how does a pillow girl catch the eye of a good, rich master? I'll tell you: She needs a secret weapon."

Tea Rose dangled something from one finger on a shiny ring. The moonlight caught it as it turned.

"Your secret weapon is an antique key?"

"My secret weapon is Prince Pahndir. This is the key to his secure rooms, stolen and copied for me by my closest friend, the wonderfully sapphic pillow girl, Plum Blossom."

"Plum Blossom likes girls?" Xishi was intrigued in spite of herself.

"Plum Blossom can't get enough of them, especially delicate young flowers like me. Thanks to her predilection, you and I are going to have exclusive access to the Purple Crane's best teaching tool."

Tea Rose's salacious exultation was hard to resist, but Xishi saw the flaw in her plan.

"Why would the prince agree to teach us?"

"Because he *likes* you," Tea Rose said, her mimicry of human simpering far more nuanced than Chrysanthemum's. "Haven't you noticed Madame has been putting you last in all our hands-on labs? If you go first, you get him too ex-cited. The rest of us can't tell if we've done any good."

This was true. Three of the prince's cycles had passed since that first lesson, and each time he came into heat, he seemed more sensitive to her.

"I don't know that he likes me," Xishi said. "I think he just likes my touch."

"Don't be modest. You're the only one he looks at. Everyone else gets his vacant stare. But he watches you when you touch him. He bites his lip. Really, it's too bad he'll never get out of here. I've heard his family is power-ful. He'd be quite a catch for a pillow girl."

Xishi squirmed, uncomfortable thinking along such mer-cenary lines. "I don't know, Tea Rose. Even if he agrees, won't his giving us more lessons make it worse for him?"

Tea Rose took Xishi's face in her hands as if resisting

an urge to shake her. "He's lonely, he's sexually frustrated, and he's male. How much more torment could we put him in?"

"But today was hard for him. I could tell he hardly made it through."

"Why do you think I'm suggesting this? He's already so aroused, no one will notice any difference in him tomorrow. Come on, Buttercup. Join me on this adventure, or I'll go alone."

It wasn't an empty threat. Tea Rose would do it, and Tea Rose wouldn't worry whether she'd asked too much.

"All right," Xishi surrendered. "Give me a minute to throw a cloak over my sleeping robe."

⮌

The prince's quarters were in the basement of the main house. The belowground level was cool enough that Xishi was grateful for her cloak. No one stopped her and Tea Rose as they crept down the dark, red lacquered hall with their glowlights cupped in their hands. The prince's door was black, its brass lock guard a picturesque if less than impenetrable adornment.

"Wait." Xishi pulled Tea Rose back at the last moment. "What if we open the door and he escapes?"

Tea Rose turned to her patiently, her pretty, narrow face serene. "He's not going to escape. Plum Blossom had some good gossip. Prince Pahndir was what they call a solitary, a royal male who only has one mate. His family disowned him, his wife is dead, and he literally can't replace her. There's nothing for him to run to. Why do you think the madame hasn't installed a code lock on his rooms? She knows he's not going anywhere."

Xishi had never thought of this. The idea that he stayed here somewhat voluntarily made her even sorrier for him.

"Who's there?" said a male voice behind the door.

"See?" said Tea Rose. "He knows we're here. It would be rude for us to leave now."

"It's Tea Rose," she said to the prince, "and Buttercup. We have a key. Please step back so we can come in."

There was a pause, and then, "Very well," said the prince.

His quarters were handsome for a prison. There were no windows, but the sitting room the door swung into was rich with dark reds and blues. The prince waited for them in the center of a patterned carpet. He had been awake. He held a glass of brandy in his right hand and a holoprojector in his left—so perhaps he'd been trying to distract himself from his frustration. His robes were green, with rubies set in the lapels. The silk hung lightly from his very upright erection, the thin cloth shivering at each pulsation.

In many ways he was a feast to look at, but what Xishi noticed most was the weary dullness with which he regarded them, as if nothing good had ever come to him from pillow girls, and nothing ever would. She suddenly felt very young and silly to have agreed to this.

"We should go," she said, turning to Tea Rose to take her arm. "The prince doesn't need us bothering him."

"No!" said the prince before Tea Rose could object. He seemed to realize his answer had been too sharp. "That is, I wouldn't mind company."

Tea Rose almost smiled at him. "We're not here to talk," she said quietly.

The prince's face tightened. "Why are you here then?"

"Private lessons. We want good masters, and we need an advantage over the others in our class. As experienced as Madame Fagin is, I suspect only you can tell us what goes on in the royal mind."

"And you?" the prince asked Xishi. "Are you here for that reason, too?"

Xishi pressed her lips together and nodded. "But if you'd rather we didn't stay . . ."

"No," said the prince, slower this time. "Your friend has judged me well. I am hungry for companionship. If that costs me a lesson, I will gladly pay."

He set his holoprojector on a table, then handed Xishi his snifter. "Finish this. Your first lesson is that you are too nervous. Some men find that exciting, but usually it is better if you are relaxed. Your hands will be more supple."

Surprised to hear all these words coming from his mouth, Xishi drank the brandy quickly enough to cough.

"Follow me," he said, leading the way to his bedroom without waiting to see if they followed. As he walked, he dropped his green sleeping robe to the floor, baring what neither girl had seen before: his very muscular and fine back view. A leather thong wrapped his long blue-black hair. With every step, its tail flirted with the crack of his tight buttocks.

Tea Rose wagged her brows at Xishi, her mouth twitching with a suppressed grin.

The prince's bedroom was also blue and red, with walls as dark as a midnight sky. The bed, which was large and square, was set on a carved box platform with corner poles. Curtains hung around it like wisps of smoke. He thrust one panel aside for his entrance, leaving it open as he lay down atop the scarlet coverlet. Though he was graceful, the swollen state of his cock and balls forced his movements to be gingerly. When he was settled, he propped his head on one hand and gestured with the fingers of the other for them to come in.

Oh, this was going to be different from touching him through a cage. Xishi let Tea Rose go ahead of her, then sat on her heels near the prince's feet. His deep, slow breathing filled the space between the sheer hangings. Xishi had a feeling he was controlling it deliberately. She was having trouble breathing evenly herself. The prince seemed much more naked than he had in class.

"You may start," he said to Tea Rose, perhaps for the same reason the madame no longer let Xishi have the first turn. "Take the oil you find in the little cupboard above my head and warm it between your breasts."

Tea Rose retrieved the oil, but before she warmed it, she let her robe fall to her waist. With her hair smoothed behind her shoulders, her breasts were lovely, little apples curving from her chest. Her nipples were flushed and pointed. Prince Pahndir looked at them, but made no comment.

"Take off your cloak," he said to Xishi, without turning his gaze from Tea Rose. "It is not cold in here."

Reluctantly, Xishi doffed the extra covering. Tea Rose watched, then looked back at him.

"Where would you like me to start?" she asked, her hands tucked with the oil between her breasts, her eyes drifting to the throbbing pole of his erection. The prince hardly needed to be telepathic to guess what she wished his answer to be.

"Here is your second lesson," he said. "A man in my stage of rut is not patient. Given his preference, he will ask you to stroke his cock and nothing else. Whatever you do, do not obey him. He will enjoy his orgasm more if it is spread among many nerves. The yama are a tactile race. We love being touched even though—and perhaps because— we so often forbid it to ourselves."

"Here then?" Tea Rose suggested, laying one warmed hand on his chest.

"That would be perfectly pleasant."

Tea Rose's lowered head hid a secret smile. Xishi knew her companion had no intention of settling for "perfectly pleasant." She oiled her hands and began her work, clearly reveling in her access to his uncaged form. Up and over she stroked his beautiful arms and chest, until the prince lay back with a sigh of pleasure and closed his eyes.

"You are skilled," he said grudgingly. "I would not mind if your caresses moved to my groin."

Tea Rose teased his nipples on the way, plucking them with a boldness Xishi could only envy. The prince opened his eyes at this, and shoved a pillow beneath his head. From this new vantage, he had no trouble watching her snake her oiled fingers down his ridged belly.

She paused before grasping his cock. "Is there a special technique I should use?"

Her voice was huskier than the prince's, and Xishi fought an impulse to clear her throat.

"Techniques are for the writers of pillow books. Touch me any way you please. Watch my reactions to see what I like."

"But you are already as hard as you can get."

The prince took her wrist and pulled her hand until it wrapped his shaft. Her slender fingers did not quite close on that rosy flesh, pointing up how very large he was. Tea

Rose shivered at the feel of him in her hold, and the tremor was not dislike. Watching their interaction, Xishi felt like shivering herself. Her nipples were small hot points beneath her sleeping robe, her hands clenching into fists on her thighs. Nothing they'd done in class had been this intense.

"Watch my pupils," he said, lower and softer. "Watch my face and lips to see if they flush. Listen to my breathing to hear if it breaks. If you do not read auras well, learn to do it better. There are feelings so deep no *yama* can prevent his energy body from betraying them."

Tea Rose swallowed. "I need both hands to stroke your erection, but, as you were kind enough to remind us, there is so much else of you to touch. Couldn't Buttercup help me?"

The prince and Tea Rose had been locking gazes all along, but now Xishi sensed something new pass between them, some understanding to which she was not privy. The prince's lips parted for his breath, his eyes darkening a fraction more.

"If she wishes," he said roughly, "she certainly may. Give her the oil that you have warmed."

It was fortunate Xishi did wish, for neither of them was truly waiting for her agreement. She took the oil from Tea Rose and poured it generously over her hands.

"Come closer," said the prince. "Next to your friend."

Still, he did not look at her. Maybe tonight he was afraid to. Tea Rose began spiraling her hold up and down his hardness, using a force that pulled him out from his belly. Perhaps Jehol had taught her to do this, for Xishi would not have dared.

"Good," said the prince. "That is hard enough."

Judging him suitably distracted from her likely ineptitude, Xishi scooted next to Tea Rose and laid her hands on his thighs. The instant she made contact, the heavy muscles jumped as if a shock-gun had jolted them.

"It is all right," the prince said quickly before she drew back. "Your hands were cold."

Her hands were *not* cold. They were hot and a little sweaty from watching him stare at Tea Rose. She didn't bother to contradict him, but slid her oily hold down his upper legs to his knees. Three times she did this, increasing the strength of her grip each time.

She was not prepared for the results.

"Shit," rasped the prince after her third pass. His buttocks tightened hard enough to thrust his hips off the bed. "Move, Buttercup. Move your hands to my balls. Let me feel you squeezing there."

"What is she doing that I am not?" Tea Rose demanded as Xishi shifted to this new place. "Why do her caresses affect you more?"

The prince's head rolled on his scarlet pillow. "It is her chi." He flung one knee sideways so Xishi could reach all of him. "It is very strong. In my current state, I am sensitive to such things." He sucked a breath when she cupped his testicles in her palm, then spoke again shakily. "Do not be concerned, Tea Rose. You will please your master perfectly well."

"Perfectly well is not good enough. I want strong chi, too."

Xishi was not doing anything beyond lightly massaging his swollen scrotum, but this seemed to be too much for the prince. A growl of enjoyment rumbled in his chest.

"You could . . . meditate," he said, clearly fighting not to pant. "If you are . . . familiar with that discipline."

"What?" said Tea Rose. "Sitting still and breathing? How can that old folk practice help?"

The prince could not tell her. He had begun to writhe from side to side. Alarmed, Xishi would have removed her hands, but before she could, he clamped his own on her wrists.

"Release my cock," he commanded, his eyes now burning into Xishi's—perversely, Xishi thought, since he must mean the order for Tea Rose. "Let *her* bring me to climax."

The girls exchanged glances, but Tea Rose nodded for her to go ahead. Xishi didn't bother to warn the prince she'd never done this, as she doubted very much he cared.

Her suspicions were soon confirmed.

He sighed deep in his throat as her hands wrapped his blood-flushed skin. "Yes, move them. Move them up and down *now*."

She moved them, startled by the heat and smoothness of his shaft. She didn't have a chance to ask for instructions. His veins began to pulse more quickly, and then he came, the sudden spasm bowing him off the bed. The orgasm was, as Madame Fagin had predicted, perfectly dry. It seemed to relax him only for a while. Although his organ had throbbed like some frightened forest creature's heart, it did not soften. When his eyes opened and found hers, they were completely black with lust.

Xishi could remember seeing this phenomenon only once before.

"Again," he said, the words a whisper. "Slower and harder this time. Relax into it. Do not allow your fingers to go stiff."

Because he still seemed rational, she did her best. He was very hard and thick, barely giving beneath her squeezes. Her own sex was sultry from feeling it.

"That's it," he said, his neck arching with pleasure. "That's much better. A prince in heat likes a lot of force. Now cup the head in your left hand and rotate. The palm has many small energy centers. You will feed your chi into me."

Privately, Xishi questioned whether this was a good idea, especially when he groaned and gritted his teeth. The way he was shaking, he looked like she was electrocuting him through his penis tip.

"Don't stop," Tea Rose whispered, no doubt sensing she would have. "This is what he needs."

She sounded as lost to reason as the prince, and maybe she was. When Xishi faltered, Tea Rose covered her hand and pressed it back, guiding her in the spiraling up and down grip she'd used earlier. This was indeed effective. The prince cried out, the sound so loud it rang through the room. Sweat glistened on his chest as his hips bucked wildly in her hands, so wildly she was having trouble holding on.

He wanted this release enough to forget any semblance of dignity. Not that Tea Rose cared. She squeezed Xishi's fingers until his penis whitened under their grip. He came again with a choking sound. Though this climax was more

violent than the last, his period of satisfaction lasted no
longer.

"*More,*" he begged a heartbeat later, putting his hand
over Tea Rose's. "I'm almost there."

Xishi knew she couldn't let this continue.

It took all her strength, but she tore her hand away from
theirs. "Enough! Both of you have lost your minds. You'll
never be 'there,' Your Highness. Not with me. Without your
mate, all Tea Rose and I can do is make you feel worse!"

It was not a nice thing to say, but it served its purpose.
The prince groaned softly and pressed his palms to his eyes.
Though she was still worried, Xishi took this as a good sign.
At least he wasn't grabbing for her again.

"Give me a minute," he said. "Please, just move back
from me, and I'll be all right."

He was not all right; he was shuddering intermittently
even after they shifted back—though he did seem saner
once he sat up. His cock was so red it glowed, its stiffness
pressing it against his belly. Xishi and Tea Rose held their
breath, hardly daring to move. After a minute of panting in
this new position, the prince drew up his legs and hugged
his shins. He turned his head to Xishi, his cheek resting on
one knee. He was still shaking, but his eyes had begun to
show a rim of silver.

"Thank you for stopping," he said. "You have exercised
more wisdom than I could. You may go now. I will be fine."

"You will not be fine," Xishi countered. "We have— I
have wound you up worse than when we came. Please, let
us summon help for you."

The prince's face softened. Xishi sensed a bitter amusement behind the change. "If I find I cannot bear my condition, I shall ask Madame Fagin to call the doctor."

"Excuse me, Your Highness, but why not call him now?"

"Because he will draw off my kith with a needle. It is
not painful, but in some ways this is better. When I am in
rut, at least I know I'm alive."

This confession was so personal, Xishi could not think
of a response. Even to say she was sorry seemed improper.
At a loss, she rose awkwardly.

"We will leave you."

Tea Rose came to her feet as well, her mood subdued. Xishi imagined this was due as much to her own loss of control as that of the prince. She expected this to be the end of their adventure, but when they reached the door, the prince called after them.

"Buttercup?" he said, the first time he had used her name. "Will you return?"

"Alone?" she asked, because his gaze was focused on her.

He nodded, the autocratic streak he had displayed before completely gone. He was asking. Politely. And he wanted her, a mere pillow girl in training, to say yes.

"I cannot hurt you like this again."

"Come to talk. When I'm not in rut. I grow weary of having no one to converse with."

"Perhaps that is a sign you are getting better."

"Perhaps." The prince's mouth curved with the faintest smile. "But it will not matter either way. My family has declared me dead, and dead I must remain."

He was feeling sorry for himself. It did not show in his face, but she knew. A tiny flame of anger burst to life inside her. Was his life truly over, or did he simply wish it were? She had not known troubles like his, but she had known some—enough to have learned no one recaptured happiness by giving up.

Hoping she hid her thoughts better than he did, she nodded back. "I will come," she said. "When I can."

The bad pillow boy

Xishi met Prince Pahndir as often as she thought she could get away with. This was less often than Tea Rose would have dared, but the two girls' nerves were wired differently. More persuasive than Xishi's natural caution was the fact that Jehol had begun to watch her suspiciously—or, rather, more suspiciously than before.

She couldn't think why this was. He didn't act as if he were attracted to her sexually, but perhaps his pride couldn't stand any of the girls preferring another male to him.

To Tea Rose's disappointment, Xishi had no carnal secrets to share after her visits. The prince was careful to skirt erotic topics. They spoke of other people in the Purple Crane, of places both had seen in the Forbidden City—from different perspectives, naturally—and sometimes they discussed the weather. Now and then, once Xishi had established that the prince wasn't horrified by the idea, she brought a human novel to share. He particularly enjoyed *The Portrait of Mr. Gray,* the tale of a man who transfers his flaws onto a magical painting. The prince's only complaint was that the author had neglected to put in the sex, which he asserted would have made the story much better.

Neither of them talked about their personal history, though their acquaintance had progressed to the point where that might be allowed. Xishi liked seeing the prince shake off some of his depression. He sat up straighter when he was with her, and did not so often take a gloomy view of things. He spoke of springtime rather than winter.

Also unmentioned was the awkwardness of facing each other in Madame's classroom. The prince's ruts weren't lessening in strength, nor was his sensitivity to Xishi's chi. The opposite was true, in fact. During his last cycle, Madame Fagin had been obliged to call the doctor only two days into his heat, as his extreme state of arousal had been too much for him to tolerate. Recalling what the prince had said about meditation strengthening energy, Xishi was glad she'd dropped the practice young.

Infinity only knew what she would have done to him had she kept it up.

Knowing Madame didn't like to see her investments wasted through missed class time, Xishi suggested she cut back on her visits. Perhaps she was affecting him without knowing how. But the prince would hear none of it.

"It cannot be your fault," he insisted. "We have not touched except to pass a book back and forth. I simply need to get my thoughts concerning sex in better order."

The idea that he was thinking of her in a sexual manner, despite their interactions being so tame, was disconcerting but pleasant. Xishi was training to be a seductress, and this was proof of her progress. The newfound sense of power, however inconvenient, affected both her confidence and looks. Lately, Mingmar hadn't been able to take his eyes off her, and Tea Rose's friend Plum Blossom twice said hello to her in the dining hall.

Tea Rose began to tease her that she must not fall in love with her captive prince, but Xishi didn't think she was at risk of that. It was herself as a woman she was falling in love with, herself as a sensual being.

Perhaps the giddiness inherent in this transformation diminished her good sense. Though it was just one day before Prince Pahndir entered heat, she decided to visit him. Jehol had gone out "walking" with the ever-forgiving Amaryllis, and for once Xishi didn't have to worry about him spying.

When she reached the cellar, she was surprised to find Prince Pahndir's door ajar. A stripe of flickering candlelight stretched into the hall. Xishi supposed the prince had finally exerted himself enough to jimmy the antique lock.

Pleased with his initiative, she stepped into the sitting room. It was empty but for the candles' glowing white columns and the pleasant perfume of beeswax. She drew one scented breath in preparation to announce herself, but then a sound stopped her.

A throaty, pleasured noise—low in timbre and masculine—trailed out from the adjoining bedchamber. Suspicion heated her face. Cocking her ear to be sure, she discerned the wet slap of flesh as well. The prince must be taking his final opportunity for self-pleasure before he went into rut and this indulgence only maddened him. The practice wasn't exactly approved of, but of course people knew it happened.

Xishi hesitated, unsure what she ought to do. The open outer door suggested she was welcome to come watch, perhaps even help. The question was, should she? It would change what had become a comfortable relationship, at least for her. Did she want to risk losing that?

In the end, curiosity decided her. What better way, after all, to learn to please a man than to witness what he did for himself?

She didn't realize she had mistaken what she heard until she pressed her eye to the crack in the bedroom door. The prince was not masturbating. Though he was naked, the prince's hands, both of them, were wrapped around the edge of the carved wood lattice that secured his mattress on its platform. His head hung from his shoulders, wagging slowly in time to his groans. A man in an open black robe stood behind him, bent partially over his back. He was thrusting heavily into the prince's ass, his motions slow and deliberate.

Only when the man tossed back his hair did she recognize him. For a second she couldn't breathe for shock. Jehol wasn't with Amaryllis. He was here, buggering the prince. *He* must have left the outer door open. *He* must have found out what she was doing and broken in. His expression was unguarded—saturnine in the candlelight. He could not mean well, and yet it did not look as if Prince Pahndir had tried to throw him out. Whatever she had mistaken, the prince's physical enjoyment was evident.

It was evident to Jehol as well.

"You like that, don't you?" he gloated, his tone every bit as dark as his eyes. "You love me running my prick over your kingmaster gland, getting the kith you can't let out all warm and itchy. They say the prostate doesn't mind a cock beating, either. How nice for me that she's done half my work. She's got you so hot, you don't care who's bringing you off."

The prince's answer was a moan. Xishi hadn't known her cheeks could get any hotter. The *she* Jehol spoke of had to be her.

"I know," Jehol said, the same as if the prince had spoken. "She's a sweet little piece of pillow-girl ass. Those tits of hers. That juicy bottom. Kind of makes you want to take a bite."

"Leave her . . . alone," Prince Pahndir gasped.

"Oh, now," Jehol said, driving in hard enough to make a slapping sound. "You're just making this more fun." When he repeated the forceful thrust, the prince bit his lip with pleasured agony. In far better shape for talking, Jehol shoved a length of hair from his eyes. "What really amuses me is that none of you suspect what makes the bitch so special. None of you understand how she's different."

"She's kind." The prince's facial muscles twisted as Jehol's cock ground over the buried pleasure spot. "She . . . treats me like a man."

"Well, why wouldn't she?" Jehol said, his sarcasm plain. "A fine, proud prince like you. Say—" He reached around the prince's hip to squeeze his balls, a move that had Prince Pahndir's breath whining in his throat. "Didn't I hear your wife used to like threesomes? So maybe you weren't man enough for her. Maybe she needed two."

"She did that for me," the prince panted out, looking as if he didn't know which delicious torture to squirm toward. "For my pleasure. She loved me enough to try new things."

It was bold of him to speak of love openly, but Jehol was not impressed.

"Really. She loved you. I guess that explains why she killed herself."

Xishi gasped at this revelation. Suicide was rare among the yama, and well hushed up when it occurred. How difficult it must have been for the prince to lose his wife this way! Luckily, her gasp was drowned out by the prince's orgasmic cry. Jehol's rough treatment had led to its inevitable conclusion. To Xishi's surprise, despite Jehol's frequent claims that he preferred women, the climax also affected him.

"Oh, that's good," he said, speeding up toward his own release. "The way your ass clenches around me when you hit your peak. Makes my cock feel big enough to be royal." He leaned farther over Prince Pahndir's back, bringing his sneer closer to his ear. "Bet you wish your hands were free so you could give yourself a few more good ones before I take mine."

The prince growled out a sound of fury even as his hips struggled to meet Jehol's thrusts more fully. When he arched his neck, the twin red streaks that ran down its tendons told Xishi what she should have guessed before. He was in full-blown heat. He must have hit it early. She should have realized this from the way his last climax hadn't calmed his need.

"Hurry," Jehol taunted breathlessly. "I'm almost there." The ornate bed frame rattled as Prince Pahndir's body jerked, no doubt fighting for the orgasm Jehol threatened to withhold. That's when the rest of Xishi's classmate's taunt registered. The prince's hands weren't free. They were tied to the ebony latticework. Xishi had thought he was holding on for support. But this wasn't a flirtation that had gotten out of hand. Jehol was forcing him.

"Stop!" She flung open the bedroom door, unable to stand and watch even if it meant facing Jehol's bullying herself. "Let him go or I'll call the madame."

Jehol stopped for a moment to gape at her appearance. Then he curled his tongue over his upper lip, rudely flickering its dark marking.

"Oh, this is fun," he said, completely without shame as he resumed what he had been doing. "Pillow girl to the rescue."

"Madame Fagin won't stand for this. This . . . this is an abuse of a valuable teaching tool!"

Jehol laughed, the sound startling and harsh. He slapped the prince's butt. "What do you say, Princie? Want me to stop?"

His movements slowed, pulling a groan from the depths of the his victim's chest.

"No," the prince gritted out, clearly hating to admit it, but willing to on the chance that he might obtain the reward he craved. "Please, keep going."

"All right then, Your Highness, I will."

With this, Jehol curved his arms around the prince's chest and shoulders, bracing himself to pound into his anus with all his strength. The prince braced, too, his head thrown back in painful ecstasy, his muscles tightening like a seizure. Tears ran down his face as Jehol brought him to not one but two successive climaxes.

Jehol joined the second as if the ejaculation were being torn from his loins. His big body wrapped the prince's slightly leaner one, an inadvertent intimate embrace.

Xishi's emotions were so confused she could not respond. Anger, arousal, fear for the prince and herself swirled together in a guilty storm. Jehol pulled free, his cock lax and dripping seed. The prince moaned at his withdrawal. Unlike Jehol, he was not satisfied.

"There you go, Buttercup," Jehol said unevenly. "He's all yours. Although, given the state he's in, you might not want to untie him until the doctor has seen to him."

At his continued mockery, Xishi's guilt gave way to anger. "You'll be sorry for this, Jehol."

"Will I? Seems to me you'd have to explain what *you* were doing here if you turned me in. But you keep my secrets, and I'll keep yours."

"This isn't a game. What you've done is cruel."

Jehol shook his hair behind his shoulders and tied his robe. "You don't know what cruelty is, Buttercup. Believe me, though, someday you will."

With this mysterious parting riposte, he sauntered out.

Xishi went immediately to the prince, but hesitated before removing his wrist ties.

"It's all right," he said, though his voice was rough. "I'm not so far gone that I would hurt you."

"It isn't that," she said as she began to work on the knots. Jehol had bound the prince with the narrow leather strips he used to tie his hair. They had left deep grooves where the prince had struggled. Xishi was embarrassed to be seeing them, but knew she couldn't ignore what they implied. "I have to ask. Did you give Jehol permission to do this, or did you say no?"

Prince Pahndir met her eyes. "I said no for as long as I had the will to do so. I regret to admit his method of persuasion had its own brute charm. He is a strong young man, and I have always had a weakness for being overpowered."

Xishi took this in, trying not to judge. To be fair, she had been aroused herself while she was watching them.

"Would you want him to do it again?" she asked carefully. "Because we both know he will try."

The prince released a silent sigh. "Not willingly, no. My pride does not enjoy quite that much battering. But I don't want you to make this your battle. That boy is vindictive. If you get him into trouble, he will do the same and more to you."

"Do you honestly think you can stop Jehol on your own? He forced you, Your Highness. I know some of it felt good, but that doesn't make it right."

The prince winced at her blunt assessment, though she had not used the word she was thinking of. "If you turn him in to the madame, she'll put a code lock on my door. You won't be able to visit again."

"I want you safe!" Xishi's incautious cry was impossible to restrain.

"And I just want you," the prince confessed. His hands now free, he cupped one side of her face. A subtle tremor ran through his fingers, their heat intense. "I want you any way I can have you. Sometimes when you're near me, I feel like a dead man brought back to life. You remind me of being with her, Buttercup. You make me feel like I did when she was alive."

He was only touching her face, but the contact made his breathing quicken again. The sadness she felt at his dilemma, at the knowledge of what she had to do, caused one hot tear to spill down her cheek.

"I cannot help you with that," she said, wiping it away. "Not if it means . . ."

The prince's hand dropped, knowing what she couldn't bring herself to say. "Not if it means allowing Jehol to prove I'm even less worthy of my royal blood than I thought."

"You are worthy. I know you can recover from your troubles if you want to."

The prince shook his head, the self-despising twist deliberately smoothed from his face. "How sweet you are. I almost wish I could fall in love with you. But you don't realize this is the way of things. Nothing humbles a prince so much as his own lust. Your fellow student is simply capitalizing on that truth."

"I can't let this go," she said. "Jehol might do worse next time. I have to inform the madame. Please tell me you understand."

The prince retrieved his crumpled robe from the floor, his movements stiff from what Jehol had done. "I do understand," he said, all coolness now. "I merely caution you to consider the price you'll pay."

⟳

"This is most unfortunate," said the madame from behind the dark gold stone of her desktop. This was not the first time she'd uttered these words since Xishi had come to her private office to tell the tale. Nor was this the first time Xishi had felt her stomach sink on hearing them.

"Can't you send him away?" she asked, still standing uncomfortably on the carpet. "Perhaps to another pillow school?"

"You must be joking." With one bronze nail, Madame Fagin teased back a pale strand of hair. "Jehol is worth a fortune to me—precisely because of his bad temper. You've no idea what some royals will pay for a pillow boy who plays rough."

"But surely the prince is just as valuable. If Jehol continues to torment him, he won't be able to work at all."

"This is true," said the madame, with that same *most unfortunate* purse to her crimson lips. "I wish I could solve the problem by installing better locks on his suite. I suspect, however, that this will only turn Jehol's abuse on you, and your contract is likely to be every bit as lucrative to me as his. Honestly, I don't understand this ill will between you two. Jehol was the one who found you for me in the first place. I never would have thought of recruiting at Infinite Mercy otherwise. Their orphans tend to be awfully dull and spiritless."

"*He* found me?" Xishi asked, taken aback by this information. It was difficult to imagine Jehol recommending her to anyone.

"Yes, yes. He spotted you while you were running errands and thought the royals would like your looks. He earned a handsome finder's fee for doing me that service. When you think about it, you should be grateful to him no matter what. Especially since you are hardly innocent of interfering with the prince yourself!"

This was too much for Xishi to respond to without being rude. Talking to the prince by his own request was hardly the equivalent of raping him. Fortunately, Madame Fagin didn't expect an answer. She had pressed her long-nailed hands together before her mouth and was clearly contemplating her next move.

"I must sell you," she said at last. "It is the only way to salvage *all* my investments."

"Sell me?" Xishi's knees suddenly felt weak. "But I haven't finished my training."

"No, but there are princes who prefer to see to that themselves. You aren't raw, at least, and shall not sully the reputation of the Purple Crane. Yes." She nodded to herself, seemingly unaware of Xishi's shock. "I shall let it be known that I am willing to part with one or two female students early. Buyers will insist on a lineup, but I have no doubt you'll be the one they choose. I've always had an instinct for these things.

"You will not argue with me," she added, pinning Xishi with her dramatically narrowed gaze. "It has been hard enough keeping you on lately, what with the way the prince responds to you."

There seemed no point in reminding Madame Fagin this was not deliberate.

"Yes, Madame," she murmured, in no doubt that she was paying exactly the sort of price Prince Pahndir had warned about.

Sleeping beauty

It was a fact no one could deny. Corum Midarri displayed the elegance only those who didn't care too much could pull off.

He studied himself in his full-length bedroom mirror with an eye both casual and precise. His outer robes were slate, his inner tunic a lustrous navy. His long ornamental belt was wrapped the prescribed three times around his trim waist. The belt was ice blue, its lower edge dangling white sapphires. Though only twenty, Corum had his own wing in his parents' palace, his own business, as well, a moribund weaving center his father had grown tired of, which Corum had transformed into a thriving enterprise. Everything he wore was an advertisement for his workers' skill—and his own high standards.

"Perfect," proclaimed his valet, Habii. "Would you like the silver hair tie or the black?"

"Oh, neither, I think. Everyone is so enamored by the patterns you use to tie them, they'll just be copying them tomorrow. I'll wear my hair down tonight."

"Of course," said Habii. Though he tried to hide his dashed hopes, they showed in the little twitch of his long mustache. The rohn prided himself on his ability to rig out his master well.

"I'll have those navy slippers you designed," Corum said, though he'd been intending to wear gray suede. "We'll see if we can get the other valets emulating your embroidery skills. They'll be pricking their fingers bloody in no time."

"As you desire," said Habii, his manner now collected as he bowed and went to get them.

Corum didn't question why he'd gratified the man. It was simple common sense to keep one's servants placid and at peace.

Satisfied he'd seen all he needed, Corum depressed the section of the mirror's frame that turned it opaque again. He didn't like to admit it—indeed, he didn't admit it to anyone except himself—but the sight of his reflection unsettled him. He felt a stranger to his own face. He was . . . disconnected, he often thought, from the truth that lay at his core.

Not that this was a bad thing. Corum had more reasons than most to turn away from himself.

His flaw was always inside him: impossible to destroy and equally impossible to share. True friends were out of the question. The best he could hope for was to perfect the surface he showed the world.

"Sir," said his valet, returning from the walk-in closet with both the shoes and a paper note. "This came through the message tube. Prince Poll is contacting you."

The hand Corum put out for the formal missive was steady. He applied his thumbprint to the coded sealing wafer and released the folds. The message was brief. His father wanted him to stop by their study before tonight's public dinner—which meant his mother was tired of *her* invitations being ignored.

Corum drew a breath deep into his lungs and reached for the stillness his fighting master had taught him to seek. The ancient martial art known as The Way of the Butterfly had been his salvation, providing him with the tools he needed to control his childhood anger and grief. Not a day went by when he didn't give thanks for it.

The butterfly does not fight the wind, his teacher liked to say. *The butterfly* uses *the wind to carry him where he wants to go.*

Which didn't help a great deal when being alone with his parents was the last place he wished to be.

"Send my acceptance," he said calmly. "And my regards."

"If you are seeing your honored mother . . ." Habii held up the black hair tie.

"No," said Corum, one small twist of emotion tightening his breast. "My hair is fine as it is."

~~⋙~~

His parents' private study, at the head of their suite of rooms, was decorated like a cherry blossom. The frothy pink and white theme had been his mother's choice, and consequently Corum had never felt comfortable here. His mother liked to think she was flower-sweet, but to his mind she more resembled a garden snake: lovely to look at until its little fangs were sunk in one's shin.

It wasn't enough that she'd spent his childhood overprotecting him. She seemed to think she had the right to run the rest of his life, as well.

"Goodness," she said the moment she saw him. "What was Habii thinking? Let me get a tie for your hair."

"No," Corum said with a firmness that made her stop. He knew why she disliked seeing him this way. A streak of pure silver, two fingers wide, ran down his hair from his right temple. It was an unusual feature for a yama his age—and troubling to her especially. Corynna Midarri remembered exactly when and why he had obtained it, and preferred that he minimize the streak by tying back his hair.

Seeing it reminded her too strongly of who she really was.

"Loose hair is unfashionable this season," she tried.

"Tell that to the other princelings," Corum said sedately. "They copy everything I do. Habii tells me they've started calling me the Prince of Ice."

"But—"

"Peace," Corum's father said to his wife. "We did not ask our son here to discuss his hair."

Ah, thought Corum. *Tonight we're having one of those talks.* Resigned to tolerating the usual lecture about embracing his familial obligations, he poured himself a glass of snow water from his father's chased silver bar.

Poll Midarri was something of a mystery to his son. Up until the last five years, Corum and he hadn't spoken much. According to tradition, discourse with children younger than fifteen was considered a waste of time. Many yamish mothers also observed this custom, though on that front Corum's luck hadn't run as gold.

Now he was never certain if his father approved or disapproved of him. If they'd been facing each other in the ring, he would have compared their interaction to opponents who circle and circle but never fight. It didn't seem to matter what he succeeded at. His father would continue to take his measure. The jury was eternally out.

"Our concern can come as no surprise to you," his father began. "You are twenty and have shown no interest in any of the royal females we've arranged for you to meet."

Because they were deadly dull, Corum said to himself on an icy swallow. *Nattering on and on about how much their fathers are worth, and could I believe what some human had done on the vids last night, and—as long as they had my attention—what did I think of their new outfit?*

His silence accomplished nothing. His father required no prompting to go on.

"Now, perhaps those young ladies weren't to your taste, and perhaps you are what the rohn like to call a 'late bloomer,' but it troubles me—yes, I admit it—it troubles me that you seem uninvolved in finding a mate at all. Most young men your age can't wait to reach the next stage of maturation. They're eager to finally find the black of their eye, if only to discover what the fuss is about."

Yes, but they wouldn't rather tear out their hair than find a mate among the princesses hereabouts.

Corum's face showed nothing of his thoughts as he set his empty glass on the bar. "What do you propose I do? I cannot force my body to respond to them."

"No," his father agreed with an alacrity that led Corum to conclude he'd asked the wrong question. "You cannot force your body, but you can coax it. Your mother and I think you ought to purchase a pillow girl."

Corum blinked at them. This at least was new. "You want me to buy a sex slave."

His father flushed faintly. "They are experts," he said, surreptitiously gripping his mother's arm to shush her. "Trained in many erotic skills. Studies have shown that sexual activity with a nonroyal partner can encourage a young man to, to . . ."

"Want more?" Corum suggested helpfully.

"Exactly," his father said with palpable relief. Sex in general did not embarrass the yama, but the matter of kith was personal. "Best of all, you'd be buying a pillow girl from the Purple Crane. Madame Fagin is selling a few of her students' contracts before they graduate. You'd be able to instruct your pillow girl in . . . whatever it is you'd like her to do."

Both Corum's parents looked at him hopefully. Corum wished he hadn't put down his glass. At least he'd have had something to hold onto when he felt like making a fist. If he could have rejected their proposition, he would have. But they were right. Corum was uninterested in finding a mate, perhaps to an unnatural degree. He'd experienced the occasional sexual stirring or carnal dream, but that was all. Nothing like most of his peers had felt as soon as they hit puberty.

"If I agree to this," he said, bracing himself to ignore their excited exchange of glances, "I want no interference. I pick the girl. I pay for the girl. I do with her what I think best. I won't have you engaging in any more attempts to bribe Habii for information." He held up his hand to stop his parents' protestations of innocence. "I know he always declines your offers, but it makes him uncomfortable to be asked. Infinity help him, he thinks highly of both of you."

"It shall be as you wish," his father assured him with a

cautioning glance toward his wife. "We are pleased you have agreed to give this a chance."

"Right," said Corum. "And now that we're done here, I'm going downstairs to greet our guests."

He knew his manner had been more curt than was polite. At the moment, however, with the prospect of who knew what complications this pillow girl might bring, his getting out of there as quickly as he could was best for all of them.

⋙⋘

Two days passed following Xishi's ill-fated interview with Madame Fagin. Then came the news that sent all of the female students—no matter how practiced their self-control—into a flutter.

A prospective buyer had been heard from, an older prince from a respected house. The family name was being held secret, but the girls busied themselves with speculating all the same. They'd heard that Madame Fagin was offering a long-term, exclusive contract. Obtaining one of these without having "made the rounds," as it was called, was considered quite prestigious. Oddly enough, no one seemed reluctant to leave the pillow school early—except the one person Madame claimed was likeliest to go.

Xishi did not divulge this expectation to her classmates, or her inside knowledge of why the sale was happening at all. The other girls assumed the madame had suffered a loss in the market and wanted to recoup; nor would they necessarily have cared had they known the truth. They were eager to stop being students and start being courtesans.

Xishi didn't understand their attitude. She loved the safety and the warmth of the Purple Crane. The people here were her family, just as Jehol had mocked. It was a shock to realize that her "family" didn't feel the same way. Yes, Xishi hoped she'd have a good life as a pillow girl, but hoping wasn't the same as having. If this prince truly did choose her, she feared she'd mortify everyone by bursting into tears.

Since there seemed no one with whom to share her doubts, Xishi did her best to swallow them. As tradition required, on the morning of the day the viewing was scheduled, the older pillow girls escorted the younger to the bathing house, where a small army of maids steamed, scrubbed, depilated, and buffed them within an inch of their lives. They emerged glowing and beautiful, their ambitions shining like candles behind their eyes.

Xishi tried not to think about throwing up.

She didn't often dwell on her murdered mother. Corynna Midarri had once told her Xoushou was good and sweet, but Xishi had no way of knowing if this was true. If her mother had been good and sweet, what would she think of her daughter's choice to be a pillow girl? Not all rohn saw selling oneself into a prince's bed as glamorous. Many preferred the more virtuous path of remaining poor and powerless. Xishi didn't subscribe to that point of view, but suddenly she was unsure if what she was doing was any way to find companionship. Was she trading her soul for security? And could that security be yanked from her as easily as her place at the Purple Crane?

You will make the best of this, she ordered herself. *You will make friends at the palace just as you have here.*

It seemed too much to expect that she would like a man she had never met. In that way, making the rounds had advantages. A clever pillow girl could encourage the partners she was the fondest of.

Her worries must have showed on her face. Though all the girls were being dressed in their formal presentation robes by the maids, Tea Rose came over to comfort her.

"You look beautiful," she assured her. "You need not fear showing poorly next to anyone."

Comparisons would be inevitable. Each girl's garment was identical, and each was fashioned from the finest silk. The white under-gowns were whisper-soft against their nervous bodies, the gray over-robes as smooth and heavy as water. The gray was an acknowledgment of their lower-class origins, but the elaborate flower-patterned weave declared what very special rohn they were.

"You look exquisite," Xishi said in return, thinking Madame Fagin must be wrong about who'd be chosen.

Surely no pillow girl had ever looked as delicately perfect as Tea Rose.

Tea Rose pursed her lips in imitation of one of Madame Fagin's surreptitious smiles, then lifted her arms for the maid to wrap the traditional silver chain around her waist three times. The ends were left to clink and dangle as they walked. Xishi's chain took more maneuvering to put into place, because her robes had to be pulled up and folded in compensation for her shorter height.

"Now we are slaves in truth," Tea Rose teased, giving the end of Xishi's chain a jingling shake. "And it's too eternally bad this prince isn't in the market for a pair."

"Ha," Amaryllis interjected coolly, "as if either of you will be picked."

"We'll have to wait and see," Tea Rose said just as Madame Fagin's personal aide entered the dorm.

"Fifteen minutes," she warned, which set up a chorus of undignified moans. "No exceptions. Madame wants you lined up before the buyer comes. Put on your flowers now."

Xishi's maid had already pinned a spray of enamel buttercups into her intricately braided hair. With nothing left to do, she bit her lip and looked back at the bed that had been hers for the last two years. A canvas bag, tidy but small, sat on its foot. All the girls had been asked to pack in case they were chosen. No prince was expected to wait to take custody of his purchase.

"It's going to be me," Xishi murmured gloomily.

Tea Rose glanced at her in surprise. Understanding flashed into her eyes, more than Xishi expected to see. "Maybe so," she said just as softly, "but maybe it will be a good thing. You'll be away from that idiot, Jehol, at least, and you'll be starting your real life now."

"My real life," Xishi repeated, struggling very hard not to sigh. She felt far too young to be doing anything so dreadful.

※

It was a balmy end-of-summer evening. Beauty veiled the outer city in a riot of trees and flowers. Corum, who had dispensed with his usual driver, piloted himself and his father out to the semi-rural compound of the Purple Crane.

Corum knew his father wouldn't believe his son had truly done this unless he saw it with his own eyes. This was why Corum had allowed him to make the arrangements with Madame Fagin, and why he sat beside him in the aircar now.

When Corum set the vehicle down on the landing site— a quiet click signaling that the antigrav had shut off—he knew he needed to explain his limits. He could not change his father's opinion of him, whatever it was, but that opinion only controlled him if he let it.

Determined not to let it, he turned on his seat.

"Sir," he said, and Poll Midarri took his hand off the door release. "I must clarify my expectations before we go in."

"Yes?" said his father, wariness and surprise mixing in the subtle lift of his brows. The reaction struck Corum as curious. Though he was aware that he had not and probably would never win his father's full approval, that hint of caution positioned him on what his fighting teacher called the power ground. Whether his father knew it or not, Poll Midarri was, in this moment, deferring to his son.

The knowledge released some of the tension tightening Corum's spine. He chose his words carefully.

"Sir, I would prefer that you let me handle the transaction from here. I understand your wish to witness this, but anything that needs to be said to Madame Fagin or the girls can be said by me. I hope you don't take this as disrespectful, but your comments are not required."

His father stared at him, his mouth gaping slightly before he shut it. "I begin to understand why those young men call you the Prince of Ice, and why opponents twice your age fear to face you in tournaments. You claim with self-possession what others have the nerve to reach for only in anger."

"Sir—" said Corum, abruptly fighting a need to apologize.

"No, don't spoil it." Corum's father allowed him a glimpse of his curving mouth as he turned to open the door.

"I rather enjoy seeing you like this. And you may rest assured I'll honor your request."

Centering himself with an effort, Corum released his flight straps and flipped his own door out and up.

The instant he stepped onto the plascrete, he felt a change in the atmosphere. Trees surrounded the landing site, and stars had begun to glint in the sky above. As a soft, warm breeze blew his business robes against his body, he realized that he was excited. His skin tingled with interest, his muscles tensing for some unknown action they wished to take. With his first full breath, his nostrils flared. The air smelled delicious, a whisper of foreign spices riding its currents. Despite his reluctance to be on this errand, every receptor in his body was acting as if his life began anew tonight.

Apparently unmoved by this phenomena, his father was already heading down the neat brick path to the main house. Corum followed with an eagerness he tried to quell even as tiny hairs stood up on his arms. When a servant opened the door, his cock twitched and swelled. By the time they'd been led down the antique-laden hall, it stood so upright the head was brushing his belly.

Luckily, his voluminous outer robes would hide this, the erection being too rigid to betray itself by moving. Corum fought a flush nonetheless. He didn't think his penis had ever been this hard, not even during his erotic dreams. He felt as if a heated poker had lodged between his legs, and his balls were pulsing and hot. The urge to gratify the ache was distracting. To have his sluggish libido rouse itself at this particular moment was simultaneously humorous and annoying. If he were not careful, in his current state, he'd be offering to buy the Purple Crane's entire stable—and fuck them all tonight.

"The girls are ready," said the servant, glancing in silent question from father to son. "Please peruse them at your leisure. Madame Fagin will join you shortly."

Given his private agitation, Corum hoped his father would remain outside. He did not, but at least he was silent as he followed Corum through the door the servant held open.

Behind it was a pretty tea green parlor, lit softly—and flatteringly—by old-fashioned floating globes. No bigger than Corum's fist, the colorfully painted surfaces cast a glow upon the line of five young women. They were dressed identically in gray silk robes. Each head was lowered, each pair of hands clasped demurely before its owner.

They all looked beautiful, but Corum could hardly think for the successive waves of lust now blazing through his body. Sweat had begun to trickle down the small of his back. The air seemed thick, heavily scented with the spice he'd caught a whiff of outside. Was Madame Fagin burning some aphrodisiac perfume? If she was, it was potent. He found himself unconsciously breathing deeper to get more of it. He shook his head, hoping to clear it and concentrate, but the effect simply grew worse. He wanted to growl at someone, to throw them to the floor and ravish them—or possibly just run from the room until these uncomfortable feelings dispersed.

His feet weren't interested in escape. They were leading him down the line of beauties, past two sisters close enough to be twins, past a startling blond girl, and one so slender he winced at the thought of any man covering her. And then he reached the last, at which point his feet refused to move again.

He couldn't have said exactly what stopped him, only that he had to. This girl was shorter than the others and interestingly curved. Her breasts looked as if they would be heavy, and his fingers curled into his palms with a sudden need to test if they were. For the life of him, he could think of nothing sensible to ask her, though he suspected he ought to. Indeed, the only action he could conceive of was crushing her in his arms.

She began to tremble as he stood there staring stupidly, struggling against his body's even stupider urges. Her breath came shallower, and he didn't think she was simply nervous. Her body heat had increased. Beneath the heavy silk of her outer robe, he saw the tightening outline of her nipples. That sight did quite enough to him by itself, but as her temples began to glow with perspiration, finally he knew.

The perfume that had been maddening him was hers. Mixed with her natural scent was pepper and orange and a hint of cloves. On further reflection, he realized it probably wasn't an aphrodisiac. Madame Fagin wouldn't have allowed one of her girls this advantage and not the rest—especially since it would have meant risking her license. It was just his bad luck that he really, *really* liked the scent this girl had chosen.

Before he could stop himself, he filled his lungs. This was a mistake. With the breath, a fresh bolt of arousal stabbed up his cock. His glans actually hurt from how tight it was.

He should have left then, should have known he wasn't thinking clearly, but his slippers might as well have been nailed in place. He was staring so hungrily his eyes teared up. Her beauty was everywhere he turned: the soft curve of her cheek, the full, red mouth that made him want to lick his own, her generous breasts and hourglass waist. He loved the little enamel flowers trembling by her ear. Her hair was wonderful, too, glossy in its elaborate braided arrangement. He wondered how it would look down, that red-kissed black like garnets dipped in ink.

The words shuddered into a memory. *Garnets dipped in ink.* He knew who that description belonged to.

Except it couldn't be. The coincidence would be too great. He dared not even want to hope such a thing.

"This is Buttercup," said Madame Fagin, adding to his confusion. "She is our youngest student. Perhaps you'd like to consider one of the older girls."

He had not heard the madame arrive. For that matter, he had forgotten his father stood behind him. It took a moment for her suggestion to register.

"No," he said as soon as it did.

The sound startled the young woman who could not be Xishi into looking up. At once, the room was too bright. He saw her face through a blur for one heart-stopping instant before she looked down again. Was it her? His gut seemed certain, but his mind questioned. A person changed in twelve years. Memories faded. Could he really project her childhood features into today?

"This one," he said. He suspected it was reckless to be doing this, but he could not stop. In clear defiance of reason, exhilaration flooded him. "I will take this one."

"Very good," said Madame Fagin, pretending his voice had not been overly emphatic. "Shall we go to my office to discuss terms?"

Corum didn't want to leave. He forced his legs to move as his father considerately remained behind, honoring his earlier request. At the door, he simply had to look back. The slimmest girl was hugging the one he'd picked, but his girl barely responded. Over the other's shoulder, her eyes were wide and round on him. Was it recognition he saw there, or simple astonishment? His longing to return to her was appalling, and still he was unconvinced who she was.

This is desire, he thought, awed by the knowledge. *This is the secret to which I was asleep before.*

~≈~

Xishi knew at once the prince was Cor. Despite strict instructions not to raise her eyes, she'd been unable to resist stealing a look at him as he walked the line. The resemblance was unmistakable. This was the same handsome Cor Midarri she'd watched win a holovized all-city tournament through a shop window. She would have known him even without the distinctive silver streak in his hair.

A strange, hot jolt flashed through her body at the recognition. She assumed it was due to the awkwardness of the situation: wondering if he'd know her, what he'd think of her choices, fear he might suspect her of presumptuous thoughts. By the time he paced slowly past Amaryllis, however, she knew embarrassment was not the only cause for her warmth.

The sight of him affected her physically. It was more than his good looks. Prince Pahndir was just as handsome, but Cor possessed a grace above the common run. Every step was perfect, every muscle of his face peaceful. His black and gold robes fell from impressive shoulders in precisely the manner robes should fall. Even his aura was restrained, a muted blue-white glow around his tall outline. He seemed the embodiment of yamish serenity and style, including being unreadable.

The flaming spirit she'd known when they were children appeared extinguished, yet she found this mysterious person he'd grown into just as interesting. She longed to rub against him as if he were a particularly sleek and independent cat. The strength of the desire surprised her. Her lessons had often been exciting, but today the flesh between her legs pulsed with an intensity it had never shown before. Moisture welled and threatened to run down. She wanted to coat his sexual organ in her cream, wanted to drive his hardness in and out of it. Most of all, though, she wanted to caress that unruffled smoothness until it turned ragged.

She wanted to torment him with wanting her.

Shocked at herself, she tried to check her emotions as he approached. She mustn't let him guess the wildness of her reactions. He paused in front of Tea Rose, and she immediately wanted to throw a bag over her best friend's head. She thought she'd die if he didn't choose her, but an instant later she thought she'd die if he did.

If this was what true desire did, she had been too quick to judge Prince Pahndir as weak. He was royal, after all, and his needs would naturally be more keen.

At the thought of *Corum* going into heat, a trickle ran down her thigh.

This, of course, was when he stopped in front of her. She began to shake and could not will the response away. He was just standing there, staring, the warmth of his body increasing hers. It took all her strength not to fidget, for even the sight of his feet in their slippers was enticing. What could he be thinking? Why didn't he speak?

Madame Fagin came over and said something, Xishi's flower name, she thought. When Cor cracked out a sharp no, Xishi positively could not keep herself from looking up.

As she did, a white-gold flash obscured her vision, whether from his aura or hers she couldn't tell. She looked down again, ashamed of her poor control, and heard him say he was choosing her.

Madame Fagin's predictions notwithstanding, she had never been so astounded in her life. She could barely think as Cor and the proprietress moved away, could barely respond when Tea Rose wrapped her in a gentle hug.

"How nice for you," said her friend, seeming to mean it. "He's very rich, you know, and terribly elegant!"

Cor paused at the door, allowing Xishi another glimpse of him. This time no light show interrupted. He *was* elegant, as polished and perfect as a frozen pond before skaters came. Perversely stimulated by his coolness, Xishi's insides throbbed with resurgent fire.

She honestly couldn't say if this was the worst moment of her life or the best.

Changes

Tea Rose bustled Xishi from the parlor before her thoughts could unknot.

"You don't want to speak to them," her friend said of the others. "You should have seen their reactions when Prince Corum stopped in front of you. They're only going to be snide."

Xishi might believe this of Amaryllis, but not of Lily and Chrysanthemum. Still, having nothing lucid to say herself, she let Tea Rose tug her away.

She didn't regain command of herself until she saw a familiar figure slipping across the meeting of two back halls.

"Prince Pahndir," she gasped. "I must speak to him before I leave."

"Honestly," Tea Rose huffed, then relented and released her hand. "Be quick. It creates a bad impression to keep royals waiting. I'll meet you back here with your things."

Xishi was already hurrying in the direction in which she'd seen the prince disappear. The passages in the Purple

Crane's main building twisted like a maze, but after two wrong turns, she caught him opening the door to the cellar stairs.

"Your Highness. Wait. I must speak to you."

Prince Pahndir turned as if he really did not want to. His face was the blankest she had seen it since their early days, as if every emotion that had ever passed behind it had been scoured away. Taken aback, she stammered out her news.

"My . . . my contract has been sold. I'm leaving tonight."

"I know," said the prince. "I was watching from a portrait hole."

Xishi blinked at the utter blandness of his tone, and the rebuff this implied. Then something else struck her. "You have gotten out of your rooms."

"This is true."

Evidently, he had known how. Just as evidently, he did not want to discuss it. She doubted he'd like her next question any better, but she had to ask all the same.

"Are you— Is Madame Fagin putting in new locks?"

"They go in tomorrow. So you see you have accomplished all you hoped. No one will be able to break in and do me harm."

"I regret that your recent liberty will be curtailed."

The prince looked down his nose at her as if this, and she, could not have mattered less.

"Are you *sure* you will be all right?" she felt compelled to ask. "Jehol will still have access to you in class. He may try to cause trouble. I could—" She swallowed, sensing shaky ground. "Perhaps I could ask my new master to intercede for you. He might have the power to get you out of here."

The prince closed his eyes for the space of a long, slow breath. When he opened them, their expression could have frosted window glass. "You overestimate your charms. No prince would embroil himself in my problems for the sake of some pillow girl's paltry bed tricks, especially when that pillow girl isn't fully trained. You'd do better to worry about pleasing him on your own behalf."

"But he is— He seems nice," Xishi whispered despite the hurt tightening her throat.

The prince shook his head at her and turned away. "Good-bye, Buttercup," he said to the cellar door, his hand already grasping the ivory knob. "You have my wishes for a pleasant life."

~~~

She was his. He had paid a fortune for the first three years of her contract, and now this woman who had set his blood ablaze was his.

The words repeated through his head without growing any less surreal.

Corum's father had stayed behind, saying he had a commission to transact with Madame Fagin for a friend. Corum didn't care if this was true or false, nor did he examine his father's face for clues to what story he'd be carrying back to his wife. Corum was too eager to be alone with his new possession to concern himself with what anyone might think.

His sanity, or a portion of it, began to return once he'd put the aircar in flight. Buttercup—as he forced himself to call her—hadn't said a word except to murmur "thank you" or "excuse me." Her satchel of belongings was so humble it shocked him. Of course, it also reminded him she was rohn. However unprepared he'd been for the lust she incited, lust was all it could be. Beautiful or no, childhood friend or no, she could touch him only so deeply and no deeper. She could not be the black of his eye. The pieces of himself he'd worked so hard to bury could not resurrect at her hand.

Everything else, however, evidently could. It was difficult to work the foot controls with such a large erection. He had to spread his knees and rearrange himself beneath the flight harness. This only helped a bit. Every time he caught a whiff of her perfume, his blood surged again.

The moonlit city rolling below them was all that saved him from embarrassment. It held her attention rapt and away from him.

"You have never flown before," he said, pleased to note the steadiness of his voice.

She looked at him just long enough to shake her head. Only then did he realize the question had been foolish. Naturally, she had not flown. The lower classes were forbidden to, for fear they'd get to like looking down on their superiors.

"I'll circle the inner city for you," he said. "You can see the layout of the place where you'll be living."

Again came that quick, shy glance.

"Thank you," she whispered.

Oh, it was wrong of him, deeply wrong, but he loved that shyness, loved that she was less controlled than he. He even loved that she might be frightened. The Xishi he had known as a boy hadn't been frightened of anyone.

The moment he thought this, his body tightened all over, his skin contracting on his muscles, making a mockery of his supposed control. He could smell that she was aroused as well as nervous. When she tangled her hands in her waist chain and squirmed in her seat, he feared his prick would explode. Then and there, he promised himself he would not touch her, would not bare that delectable, curvy body until he had his reactions in better order. Surely the violence of his responses would ease soon. Like all novel feelings, this oversensitivity would fade with time.

Willing this to be true, he did not speak again until they landed on the Midarri palace roof. He exited ahead of her, walking around the car to help her out of her harness—which of course she did not know how to work. Her nearness caused his hands to fumble slightly on the task, and the flush that stained her cheeks made him want to curse.

He saw he wouldn't be able to count on her to help his restraint.

"Thank you, Your Highness," she said, clearly exerting herself to speak in a normal tone. Her not-quite-breathless words had his toes curling.

Her voice was low and pleasing, almost caressing in the gentle rise and fall of its notes. And *caressing* was exactly the word he meant, because the sound of it seemed to stroke the throbbing hardness between his legs. Had he been a fraction less disciplined, he would have taken her on the plascrete in the sight of any- and everyone. Instead, he retrieved her homely little satchel and offered his hand to help her take the long step down. When her palm slid away from his, he had to fight not to rub his fingertips at the loss—one more reminder of how very strange this day was turning out.

Corum knew he lived a privileged existence and that society could not function with everyone on an equal plane, but the lightness of her satchel offended him. That her rohn gray gown did as well he would rather not admit.

She *was* beneath him. That was a reality no one could change.

"You will need more clothes," he said as they stepped onto the lighted path that stretched across the roof. "I'll establish a line of credit so you can buy what you please. I assume you've sufficient schooling in fashion."

Her stare was a weight against his left profile. He longed to see what it held, but kept his eyes facing front.

"Yes," she said after a pause. "Those classes were complete before I left."

"Good. I would rather not interfere in what you wear. If you desire advice, my valet would be glad to help."

"Thank you," she said, murmuring again.

He had the feeling he'd said something wrong, but when he gave in to temptation and glanced at her sidelong, her expression was every bit as placid as he hoped his was.

~∽~

Xishi walked in a dream. She was back in the Forbidden City after all these years, back in the palace she'd been exiled from.

She hadn't remembered it as clearly as she thought. The Midarri residence was only vaguely familiar, but perhaps that was the effect of seeing it from the air at night. It was huge, for one thing, one of the largest in the royal complex, a zigzagging knot of wings and courtyards. The silver leaf on the roof looked magical in the moonlight. In fact, the whole city did. Part of her wanted to beg to be taken up in the sky again. How wonderful flying had been—even with this strange, new Cor Midarri seeming to suck up all the air inside. Her cheeks hadn't stop burning from being in such close quarters, and she wished it were permissible to fan herself.

She also wished she weren't thinking her childhood friend had grown arrogant. The Cor she used to know wouldn't have acted as if she were too backward to pick her own clothes. Then again, he hadn't come out and said he knew who she was.

They walked for a good five minutes along the lighted catwalks. No one else was about, or no one visible. The bird-wing eaves bristled with the bits and bobs of surveillance. Quite possibly, half the house was watching them. Like all yama, Xishi knew princes lived dangerous lives. Threats abounded, often from their own families. The sobering reminder did not fade when they took an elevator down a tall side wing. The conveyance would not move until Cor presented his retinal scan.

"This is my wing," he said as the glassy cylinder sank. "No one comes here without my say-so."

Xishi sensed this was important and nodded at his words, though he wasn't watching her. They exited the elevator into an airy seafoam and gold-leafed hall. Cor strode along two steps ahead, while she worked to keep up and gape at the same time. The Purple Crane had been richly furnished, but this put Madame Fagin's taste to shame. This was grace and lightness. This was perfect, simple touches and harmony. Most of all, this was *modern*, an oasis of restraint compared to the ornate antiques she remembered from his mother's rooms. She could not doubt this decor reflected the preference of the man whose long legs moved ahead of her as if they'd been born to dance.

Maybe he'd been right to question if she knew how to dress. Madame Fagin's penchant for stretchsilk might not be the best example to follow here.

"This will be yours," he said, opening a door and snapping his fingers for the lights to come on.

As she walked into the apartment, her breath caught in awe. These were rooms for a woman far more elegant than she. They were painted seafoam like the hallway and had delicate-looking, lilac silk furniture. The cream-white ceiling moldings were not wood, but some luminescent substance that filled the space with soft, glowing light. A large, plush carpet in a mix of the seafoam, lilac, and cream seemed to float above the highly polished floor. This was a rich black granite with threads of real gold in it. It stretched to a wide, square arch that opened into the bedroom, where glass-paned doors framed a small courtyard. The doors were open, and the pleasant babble of a fountain drifted in.

It was quite the most enchanting place Xishi could have dreamed of living in.

Cor set her bag inside the entrance, drawing her wondering eyes to him. "I will leave you to explore," he said. "You'll be safe wherever you wander in this wing."

She knew better than to balk at the implied restriction. What he asked was within the Imperial Pillow Board's guidelines for the treatment of bed servants. What did distress her was the idea that he meant to leave.

"Wait," she said, struggling to decide what was appropriate to ask. "Don't you wish to come in? You could . . . explain what you expect from me."

"You would like to know that now?"

"Yes."

He took one step inward. "You are not tired?"

"I am yours now. It would not matter if I were."

The answer came to her without thinking. She could not tell from his reaction if it was right or wrong. She had always had a knack for reading auras, most rohn did, but his was singularly uninformative. The only response she could see was a subtle darkening of his eyes.

The lack of cues made her wish she'd had more years of training. Maybe then she'd know what to do.

"I'm very attracted to you," he said, still standing where he was. Though the words held a tinge of warning, all they stirred in her was a wash of heat. She pressed her thighs together to conceal it.

"I assumed you were or you wouldn't have bought my contract."

"I might frighten you if I come to you in my current state."

"You might, but I've never been the sort to run from my fears."

This answer softened the marble stillness of his features, an almost-smile curving his perfect lips. "Did they teach you this at the pillow school, to banter with a royal prince?"

"They tried to. The Art of Conversation wasn't my best class."

He ventured another step inside the room, then turned aside to stroke the trailing crystal dangles of a chandelier. The pendants changed color—violet first, then rose and green—as he ran his long, deft fingers over them. The grace and beauty of his hands enthralled her. She jumped when he spoke again.

"Why don't you tell me what they succeeded in teaching you, and I'll decide what you need to learn."

She found it difficult to think straight enough to answer. The sight of his back cast as strong a spell as his hands. His shoulders were broad enough to carry all of her, his height impressive even for a royal. Both reminded her he wasn't a boy anymore—or the kind and gentle prince of her fantasies. His blue-black hair fell in a braided queue to his waist, the silver streak winding in and out its pattern. Xishi wanted to loose it, to see it spread across his broad back and know how it felt. If he truly was *very attracted*, why was he standing half a room away? What could she say to tempt him closer?

The thought of doing so tightened her ribs. The air should have been plentiful, but as had happened during their flight, she couldn't get enough. She had to fill her lungs slowly before she could speak. Even with this care, her answer came out husky.

"They taught me the many touches princes enjoy."

Cor cast a glance at her over his shoulder. "How did you learn this?"

"A man was there. He belonged to the school. We practiced on him."

A silence fell. Xishi wondered if she should have admitted this. Cor's hands resumed their caress of the color-changing crystal drops. "Did he take your virginity?"

His voice was absolutely normal, as if mere curiosity drove him to ask. "No," she said. "Madame Fagin knows some princes like to do that themselves. He didn't even kiss me."

"Someone must have kissed you."

"One boy offered, but I declined."

"And the girls?"

She almost smiled. Madame Fagin had mentioned some men were interested in such things. "I did not feel that sort of friendship for them."

He turned then, his eyes finding hers, his face intent but unemotional. "Good," he said. "I wish no one to know your kisses but me. It is a good place for us to start."

This was not the answer she'd expected. Apparently, he did not care how adventuresome she was, only that this lesson was exclusively his to give. She waited for him to move, but he did not. Instead, his gaze lowered to her mouth, his tongue curling briefly over his upper lip. He probably did not mean to expose his lamril, but the sight of the marking made her feel as if a fist had clenched on her sex. The pressure squeezed a hot rush of moisture out. Again, she had to fight to fill her lungs. "Do you wish me to come to you, Your Highness?"

"No," he said. "Wait for me."

She waited, barely breathing as he took one step closer, then two. This seemed to break whatever held him back. In three quick strides he was before her. His hold settled on her upper arms, his grip firm enough to seem scolding. The contact felt so wonderful, relaxing and exciting at the same time, that she didn't know how to mind. Something in his face said he knew this. His pupils were very large.

"Do not wear this perfume again," he ordered a second before his mouth came down.

She forgot she wasn't wearing scent the moment his lips touched hers. They were silky, but his mouth was hard. It pushed against hers, a coaxing but insistent pressure against her jaw. She knew what he wanted, at least with her head. Her nerves just weren't up to doing it, not for the first time with him. Cor pulled back without signs of anger, but his breath rushed hotter against her cheek.

"Open to me," he said, putting the request in words. "I want to taste you."

His arms came around her to wrap her close, and at once she needed the support, as if simply being pressed against him could melt her bones. With her tension no longer fighting him, his tongue slid between her lips like liquid satin, long and wet and wonderfully warm. Everything felt so good she hardly knew what to pay attention to. His body was all hardness beneath his robes, every muscle shouting how much stronger than hers it was. When she slid her arms around his waist, he angled his head and kissed her so hard she knew her lips would be bruised.

This was nothing like the sweet, warm fantasies she'd had of him. Instead, this seemed the door to something much better, something unpredictable.

Entirely without her permission, a cry of yearning broke in her throat.

He didn't seem to mind. One arm tightened beneath her backside to lift her higher. Her breasts were crushed to his chest as she clutched his back with her hands, her feet dangling off the floor. She was lucky she didn't want to escape, because she doubted she could have. She remembered Prince Pahndir confessing his weakness for being overpowered, and abruptly understood what he'd meant. No one had ever controlled her physically this way, and Cor didn't even seem to be trying.

I am a prince, said his actions, *and you shall tremble before my power.*

Xishi couldn't find it in her to disagree. Exhilarating tingles rolled through her flesh. Deeper he kissed her and hotter, too. Dizzy, she felt him walking them—to the bed, she hoped—but then a wall pressed behind her and her thigh was being ground against the ridge of a startlingly large erection. That his clothes had hidden it was a marvel. His arousal was impossible to miss now.

It seemed the leverage the wall provided was not enough. Cor squeezed her buttock in a grip of steel. Desire told her to bring her legs around his waist, but he wasn't having that.

"Stay where you are," he ordered, his voice surprisingly rough. "I like the softness of your thigh."

She was glad he did, but would have given her right arm to touch him more closely. "I know better caresses," she offered breathlessly.

His eyes seared into hers, his pupils glittering. "Save them," he said, and crashed his mouth down on hers again.

She'd thought the first kiss was wonderful, but it had only been a warm-up for this. This was positively savage. While his second hand locked the back of her neck in place, he devoured her mouth, plunging in and pulling at her tongue until it was drawn helplessly into his mouth. It was impossible to be sorry. No one had told her kisses were this delicious, that they made one want more and more. Caught up in passion, she pulled at him as boldly as he had her. He tasted faintly spicy, like oranges and cloves. When his groin began to roll against her, she rolled right back, and if her thigh was soft, his was marvelously hard.

She didn't mean to lose control. Every pillow text she'd read advised seeing to one's master first, but when his hand tightened on her bottom, when his long, strong fingers pushed the silk of her robes between the sopping creases of vulva, her desires took on a life of their own. She didn't even have a chance to be embarrassed. She writhed against his thigh, grinding her clitoris against the hard-clenched muscles as he tore from her mouth to press quick, hard kisses along her throat.

He held her so tightly her waist chain dug into her belly through her clothes. If this caused him discomfort, he didn't care. The hitching movements of his hips came faster, the acceleration driving her swiftly to a gasping brink. She tried to hang on, but this was not a cliff she had to fall off of. In truth, it felt more like an ocean of sensation rising up to her. Her sex was coiling, her need for release a piercing ache.

He must have known it. His breath grunted softly beside
her ear, the first explicitly sexual noise she'd heard from him.

The sound slid along some crucial nerve and unraveled
her. Despite how selfish it was to come before him, she
did—a deep, arching spasm she could not have hidden to
save her life. She couldn't shorten it, either, not with him
working against her as hard as she was working him.

He ground his thigh between hers until she simply
couldn't shudder anymore. Then his kisses gentled, sliding
back to her jaw and over her face. He seemed to be forgiv-
ing her, and that might have been his sweetest act of all.

"Oh, Cor." She sighed, grateful from the inside out.

He let her go the instant she said his name. Startled, she
dropped to her feet with a little thunk. Her thighs were
sticky with her own juices. Cor was braced straight-armed
against the wall, no part of him touching her. They breathed
raggedly at each other for a long moment. She had the feeling that if the light had not been so dim, she might have
seen something in his face.

"I wasn't sure you knew me," he said at last.

"And I wasn't sure you knew me."

His neck bowed an inch lower. "I couldn't have forgotten long."

She didn't know how to take his answer. "Did you—"
She laid her hands lightly on his chest, relieved and com-
forted to find his heart pounding. She didn't want to be the
only one affected by what they'd done. "Did you discover I
was staying at the Purple Crane? Is that why you came?"

He shook his head. "In truth, I wasn't certain who you
were when I paid for you."

This left too much unsaid for her. If he had been certain,
would he have chosen someone else? Did the circumstances in which he'd known her make his attraction unwelcome now? Was she regretting having purchased a girl
his mother had once banished from his presence?

None of these questions could be asked politely.

He wagged his head, at what she did not know, and then
pulled his body proudly erect. "You will call yourself by
your flower name while you are here."

This order seemed to confirm her guess. "I understand. Your mother would be upset."

"I don't care about my mother's upsets. I don't want her interfering."

After all his coolness, the heat in his voice surprised her, but it passed quickly enough.

"Forgive me," he said, his dignity intact once more. "You will want to unpack. I'll send my valet, Habii, to you tomorrow. He'll find a maid for you and help you get settled in."

She didn't dare call him back this time, but watched in what she hoped looked like obedient silence as he smoothed his robes and left. The lovely rooms were suddenly empty, and she doubted unpacking her little satchel would take more than two minutes.

Oh, how Jehol would have gloried to see her failure— kissed and forgotten before her lips were cold!

Without warning, emotion threatened to close her throat. The loneliness she felt was deeper and more painful than any she'd experienced at the orphanage. Then she'd had her daydreams. Now she had an awkward and less-than-rosy reality. Why had Cor bought her if this was how he meant to act?

You will make the best of this, she ordered herself. *You will not give in to self-pity.*

This brave vow didn't change the fact that this was not, in any way, shape, or form, the way she'd imagined finding her prince would be.

~~~

Cor sagged back on the wall outside Xishi's rooms and waited for his knees to hold him. The moment he'd escaped her sight, his self-command had collapsed. He was actually shaking, and from a kiss. He had kissed women before—he wasn't that backward—but never had he savaged one like this.

He ran his tongue across his lips, their surface buzzing as he tasted her again.

All he could think of when she came was sinking to his knees and tasting that. He'd forgotten his own release.

Plunging his face into her pussy had become the clarion
call of every cell and shred of consciousness. It was the
most overwhelming impulse he'd ever felt, and it had been
inspired by a pillow girl.

Memory shoved him back to childhood, to the peaks
and troughs of emotion that had too often tossed him
about. He'd been helpless to fight them, a freak who had to
be hidden, an animal who knew no peace.

He could not return there. He gritted his teeth and
straightened, resisting the compulsion to fist his hands.
Standing on his own two feet felt marginally better. He was
not the boy who'd let passion rule him. Nothing and no one
would ever drive him back to that.

The Way of the Butterfly

❦

Feeling in need of exercise to quell his restlessness, soon after dawn the following morning, Corum donned his simple practice robes and went in search of his instructor for the martial arts.

Master Ping lived in an annex attached to the Rhing-Lhing Palace. Most people assumed he was a cousin to the now-departed father of the current prince, but no one knew much about him except that he had instructed many generations of princelings in The Way of the Butterfly. It was whispered that, due to his mastery of the inner teachings, he had found the secret to eternal youth. If this was true, he had chosen to present a grizzled face for it, but Corum couldn't deny his teacher was vigorous enough to trounce any of the present crop of princelings—including himself.

As often was his way, Master Ping leapt out at him from one of the shadowed corners that lined the route to his home. Though Corum had expected this, and was perfectly eager for a fight, it took his wiry old teacher less than five minutes to have him flat on his back and pinned to the lavender-scented cobbles behind the Rhing-Lhing bathhouse.

There were at least a dozen moves Corum might have used to twist out of this. Rather than employ them, he let his head clunk to the stones and sighed.

His teacher snorted in disgust and climbed off him. Barely out of breath, he threw his long gray queue over his shoulder and looked down on his fallen charge. "Still you have not learned. You send your chi to fight inner struggles and do not leave it for outer ones."

Corum mustered the wherewithal to sit up. "I thought the only struggles that mattered were inner ones."

His teacher's mouth twitched. "When you begin throwing my platitudes in my teeth, you have been my student too long."

"Don't," Corum said, suddenly unable to support his head without the help of his knees. He lowered his voice, but it was still shaky. "Don't stop being my teacher."

"Hmm," said Master Ping. "I am thinking perhaps today you would rather I be your friend. Pull yourself together, Prince. I have tea brewing in my rooms."

Corum followed him as soon as his legs felt able, ducking under the low doorway of his teacher's simple post-and-beam home. A steaming cup awaited him on the bamboo table. Corum sat cross-legged on a thin blue cushion and let the tea warm his hands. Master Ping's tame golden finch twittered contentedly on its window perch as something vaguely resembling peace settled into the aching places in Corum's heart.

"I am surprised to see you today," his teacher said once the first small cup was sipped to its bottom and the second poured. "The grapevine has been buzzing over your new purchase."

"I thought you didn't listen to gossip."

"I don't listen *for* gossip," Master Ping corrected. "But sometimes it drifts my way nonetheless."

"I knew her," Corum confessed. "When I was a boy. Before I . . . got better."

Master Ping had known Corum in those days, too. In

one of his rare parental interventions, Corum's father had sent him to the School for Butterflies a few months after Xishi was sent away. Master Ping's seemingly endless patience was a big part of the reason his student wasn't shut up in an institution for studying yama with genetic flaws. Because of this, he could guess why Corum was troubled.

"You are concerned she will wake old ghosts."

There seemed little necessity to say yes. Corum finished his second cup. The brew was delicate and delicious. Despite his humble surroundings, Master Ping always served good tea. With lowered eyes, he poured his student another cup. Corum appreciated his discretion. He knew he could not school his face to the smoothness that was proper.

"The grapevine says your pillow girl is beautiful," his teacher offered after a pause. "And very juicy for one who hasn't finished her training."

Corum nodded glumly into his tea. *I don't have much training myself,* he wanted to confide, but that seemed too much to say even here.

"I think I was too rough with her," he said instead.

"Did this appear to distress her?"

Corum remembered—with an uncomfortable warming of his blood—how she had arched in climax against his thigh. "No, she didn't seem distressed by that."

"Then you have no troubles beyond those you create for yourself."

"I told her I would teach her what she doesn't know."

With no small horror, Corum heard the words blurting from his mouth.

"Ah," said his teacher. The lines around his eyes gathered in what would have been an open smile had his face not been lowered. Corum knew he had surmised what the problem was.

Recovering from his humor, Master Ping set his empty cup on the low table. "I am an old man, of course, but I remember a scrap or two of wisdom from my younger days. First, in matters of love, it is sometimes better to listen than to speak. Second, when a student lets his body become his teacher, he finds he knows more than he believes."

"I don't suppose there's a third scrap of wisdom," Corum said, not seeing how these two were going to help.

Master Ping's chest shook with silent laughter. "Practice," he said. "Practice always makes perfect."

Possibly fearing his laugh would grow if he didn't cut this short, Master Ping rose and slapped Corum on the shoulder. "Let those managers you are so good at giving orders to wait today. Take a run around the city walls. You are not fit for any sort of fight right now."

Recognizing their interview was over, Corum rose and bowed. "Thank you, Master, for your advice."

"Thank *you*, Prince," returned his teacher, his eyes twinkling. "You reminded me of a pleasure I had forgotten."

⟜⟝

A good night's rest worked wonders on Xishi's mood. When she awoke early the next morning, it was much improved. Her rooms were just as nice by daylight, and her huge bed—which was curtained in the same hue-changing crystals as the lamp in her sitting room—was so comfortable it truly would have been a challenge not to fall asleep in it. The Forbidden City lay around her, a place many rohn longed all their lives to see—and here she was living in it a second time! If that was not good fortune, she didn't know what was. Even if Cor was regretting his purchase of her contract, and even if she was restricted to certain areas, there would still be plenty of interesting things to explore.

The thought of Cor's regrets lowered her spirits, but she pushed it from her mind. Figuring out how to work her very automated shower distracted her for a while. That entertainment exhausted, she was delighted to find a sleek computing unit hidden in her bedroom desk. It was, glory of glories, connected to the yamaweb. She sent quick notes to Tea Rose and Mingmar saying she was well.

Within minutes, she received a reply from Mingmar, demanding details and offering gossip. Xishi supplied what answers she could without sounding gloomy, tutted enjoyably over an account of Amaryllis's jealous tantrum because the prince hadn't chosen her, and, over all, finished reading the webmail much more satisfied with her lot.

Her friends were still her friends. She could reach out to them whenever she wished. Now all she needed was a meal.

A tap on her outer door suggested one might be forthcoming. Her heart thumped at the thought that the visitor might be Cor, but her first guess had been correct. A very upright-looking rohn, dressed in what she assumed was Cor's personal ice gray livery, stood behind the door holding a tray of silver-lidded dishes. The man was handsome, as most palace servants were, and not much older than his master. His most striking trait was a long and curving black mustache. Very few yama wore facial hair, and this drew her attention to how daringly dashing he was.

"Oh," he said, seeming surprised that she'd opened the door so quickly. "You are as beautiful as they say."

Xishi knew she was blushing, but the rohn was polite enough to pretend he didn't see. Instead, he busied himself with setting up her rather extravagant-looking breakfast on a small table. There was juice and tea, a pretty arrangement of bread and meats, plus three kinds of fruit carved into flower shapes.

"I am Habii," he said as Xishi tried to pretend she ate this way every morning. "I will be serving you until we find a private maid you like."

"I doubt I need a private maid," she said, not wanting to put Cor to this expense when he'd seemed less than delighted with her last night.

"Of course you need one," Habii contradicted gently. "You are a prince's pillow girl. You must present yourself in the proper style."

This talk of style, coupled with the valet's extremely up-to-date appearance, brought back her previous insecurities. She set down the bread she'd tentatively picked up. "Prince Midarri mentioned you might advise me on my wardrobe."

"It would be my honor." He flipped a napkin neatly into her lap. "I will bring a set of pattern books later this morning if you are free."

"I believe I'll be free," she said slowly, secretly hoping he would mention some plan the prince had for her. The hope was futile. The servant nodded briskly.

"I shall return at nine then and knock again."

"Habii?" she said, knowing she betrayed her doubts by stopping him, but wanting an answer enough not to care.

"Yes, Miss Buttercup?"

"Might I know how the prince is occupying himself today?"

Habii's face grew even more dignified. "The prince is seeing to personal business. He may be busy far into the night."

This was a proper but most unhelpful answer. She could not tell if Cor had instructed him to say this, or if the rohn had invented the excuse himself.

"Thank you, Habii," she surrendered. "You have been kind."

⟨⟨⟨~⟩⟩⟩

Per Master Ping's suggestion, Corum had taken a run around the city walls. Less wisely perhaps, he'd ignored his teacher's advice to meet with his business managers, after which he'd indulged in a supposedly purifying visit to Princes Bath. This he followed by reading sales projections over his dinner, so as not to be obliged to go out in company. The questions he'd faced from his peers in the steam room had been enough:

Was his pillow girl as juicy as rumor claimed?

Had he enjoyed her carnal expertise?

Did he, in fact, have the faintest idea what to do with her?

The last question was solely his own, but no less irksome because of that. Eight o'clock rolled by without an answer, and then nine. Habii padded in at ten to prepare his bed and pretend he was not dying to be told whether his master would be using it.

He let Corum know a maid had been engaged for "Miss Buttercup," and that although she had been "hesitant" to choose a proper wardrobe at first, once Habii succeeded in assuring her it was her obligation to look well for her master's sake, she had displayed a "quirky elegance" of which Habii believed the prince would approve.

That Habii approved was obvious.

"She is a nice, respectful girl," he said, giving Corum's pillow one more punch than it required. "I do not think she will cause trouble."

She might not cause trouble for Habii, but she was definitely causing it for Corum. He lay restless on his back under his smooth, fresh sheets, wondering if "Miss Buttercup" had retired, and if it were remotely possible she could be as obsessed as he was with the thought of him joining her.

With a sigh only he could hear, he threw off his covers on the forlorn chance that the cool night air would ease his raging erection. He wore only light sleeping trousers, but his body was fever hot.

He was tired of this desire business already. It sapped one's energy and confused one's mind, until he hardly knew what his managers had said to him. Xishi was all he could think of: her taste, her smell, the wonderful softness of her haunches as he'd crushed her into his groin. Even now his hand was sliding up and down the muscles of his chest, without his having any memory of when he'd started doing it.

As soon as he noticed, he wished he could have stayed oblivious. Maybe he'd have grabbed what he really wanted before his pride stopped him.

It wasn't the fashion among the upper classes to masturbate. Naturally, some did. During his two-year stint at the Royal Academy of Business, Corum had often heard his classmates taking their private pleasure through the too-thin dormitory walls. He'd done so once or twice himself if he'd had an especially erotic dream. Mostly, though, he'd felt superior to his peers because his needs were more moderate. Oh, it was fine for them to do it, but Corum held himself to high standards.

You're an idiot, he thought, his hands rubbing his hip bones in frustration. He shouldn't be considering pleasuring himself when he had a perfectly good, perfectly affable pillow girl—for whom he'd paid a small fortune—lying in the room directly below his. He didn't have to be an expert in bedsport for this. She knew how to bring a man to release. *I know better caresses* had been her exact words. Wouldn't the sensible course be to see if this was true? He didn't need to make this complicated. He could have her do what he wanted as swiftly as possible and without fuss.

He swallowed back a groan at the abrupt intensification of penile pressure this idea inspired.

It was true the effect she had on him was unsettling, but if he didn't get his hands on her soon—and vice versa—he wouldn't have to worry about uncontrolled emotions. He'd be too busy going insane.

⮞

She was sleeping and she was naked, neither of which he was prepared for.

Corum had slipped down the secret stairway that connected her rooms to his. It opened through an indiscernible door in the wall of her sitting room. When he chose this suite for his future pillow girl, he'd known the passage would allow him to come and go privately—away from servants' prying eyes. Tonight, it allowed him to enter without waking her.

Energy shifted palpably inside him as he watched her sleep, as if the heart of his aura were tightening.

Or girding itself for battle, he thought less romantically.

She had left the lighted ceiling moldings on their lowest setting, perhaps for comfort in this unfamiliar place. Their illumination made it easy to admire her. She lay curled on her side in the crystal-curtained bed, her face turned to the courtyard and her back to him. Her garnet black hair fanned across the pillow, as loose and long as he had always thought it should be. The sheets were pulled over her breasts, and both her hands were tucked beneath her pillow. It was a childlike pose, though her curves were anything but. That rump of hers was too lush for words, its cleavage temptingly delineated by the clinging sheet. He had to grit his teeth against a need to fall on her and bite it.

She must have been hot—*or dreaming*, he thought with another inner tightening—because a sheen of perspiration covered all the skin he could see. He could smell her scent from the doorway, mixed with that spicy-sweet perfume he'd told her not to wear.

He wanted to curse her for disobeying, but could not bring himself to do it even in his mind. It was her job to attract him. Without that, she had no reason for being here.

He moved across the carpet before he could stop himself, as silently as Master Ping had taught. With his heart pounding in his chest, he parted the crystal curtain, lifted the sheet, and slid in behind her. Though his legs were longer, he fit them into the bend of hers.

He might as well have slid his cock into her sex; the effect of snuggling up to her was that strong. He seemed to have no control over his next responses. One hand moved to the dewy small of her back as if magnetized, while the other smoothed her hair off her pillow. His way now clear, he nuzzled from her temple to her neck, instantly enraptured by the softness of her skin. With the sense that he was performing the most voluptuous act of his life, he curled his tongue out to taste her sweat.

His tongue must have been more sensitive than he thought. The moisture tingled on his taste buds.

She stirred in her sleep with a kittenish sound. On hearing it, his cock turned hard enough to pound nails.

"Wake up," he murmured, using his fingertip to draw one warm, salty droplet up and down the lowest curve of her spine. "Wake up, Buttercup."

⇜

In her dream, someone was tickling her serpent energy, the pool of sexual force that resided near her tailbone. Up and down the finger drew the deep red light, reawakening the desire that had barely eased when she fell asleep. Her labia felt swollen, her pussy thick and hot. She'd been dreaming of kissing Cor, of taking him inside her, and now in the dream he was behind her.

He murmured her flower name and licked her neck, his upper leg sliding over hers to bring then closer. He was wearing thin cotton sleeping trousers. When his groin finally fit itself around her bottom, the thickness of his erection throbbed in the crack. His hand drifted up her side to cup her breast. In an instant, both her nipples hardened painfully. With a fingertip, he circled the one his hand was nearest. The caress was so teasingly delicious she had to squirm her hips back at him. It must have been the right thing to do. He pressed her pulsing nipple between his thumb and fingers and pulled firmly.

Xishi gasped and opened her eyes. The little pinch had sent a streak of good, steamy feelings straight to her core.

"Good," Cor said, as her brain fought to comprehend that he was really there. "You are awake."

She pushed herself up and turned to him, gasping when her hand hit his soft chest hair.

He knew at once why she was distracted. "I have not removed my body hair. I wasn't seeing anyone."

His voice held the merest shading of defensiveness. Did he think she would judge him for either of these things?

"I like it," she said, instinct guiding her fingers through the warm black cloud. "If you do not wish to bother, please don't remove it for me."

He winced when she brushed the hardened beads of his nipples, taking her wrists to halt further play. "I want you to pleasure me, to pleasure *this*."

He cast his eyes toward the ridge that was pressed tight to his cotton trousers. Moisture gathered between her legs. His cock pulsed beneath the cloth, its royal glory clearly outlined. A shadow of darker hair surrounded its base, so primally masculine her pussy clenched on itself. With difficulty, she remembered Prince Pahndir's lesson. The wise pillow girl did not head straight for the royal jewels. She took her time with all her master's pleasure spots.

Of course, the wise pillow girl might not have gotten a direct order—one she couldn't help wanting to fulfill.

"The oils I requested have not arrived," she stalled. "My bare hand might feel too rough." Reluctantly, she tore her gaze from his groin. His eyes were burning like silver flames. When she succumbed to nervousness and licked her lips, his pupils swelled.

"You could kiss me there," he suggested, his intonation carefully controlled. "You could suck me. That would not feel too rough."

Xishi's flush of anticipation warmed her whole body. "Do you wish me to remove your sleeping pants?"

Her husky whisper had him pressing his lips together but not, she thought, in annoyance. Perhaps he liked that her control was not as good as his. He nodded, then lifted his narrow hips so she could slide the garment off. He was beautiful naked, tall and lean and powerfully formed. He did not complain when she kissed a gentle trail up the inner surface of one long leg. Instead, he came onto his elbows to watch. The muscles of his belly bunched as his queue fell across his chest. She was gratified to see his calm wasn't perfect. His breath grew shallow the closer she came to his groin, his fingers curling tensely into the sheets.

She reached his erection and bit her lip. Seen from this angle, his organ was a tower of flesh and vein, flushed and shaken by his pumping blood. The head alone looked broad enough to fill her mouth. She couldn't suppress a flutter of worry.

By the time Madame Fagin had reached this lesson, Prince Pahndir had been too sensitized to her to tolerate her practicing on him. She'd watched the others perform oral sex—Amaryllis in particular had been skilled, suggesting she and Jehol had been playing at this on their "walks"—but Xishi had never done it herself.

Caution advised her not to admit this now.

"Do you like it when I cup you?" she asked, wrapping one hand around his testicles. They were warm and firm, already drawing up toward his pubic bone. His knees shifted restlessly up and down.

"Yes," he said, scooting higher on his elbows. "You may do that."

"And shall I steady you?" Demonstrating, she took the solid root of his shaft in her second hand, lifting its heavy length up from his belly. She didn't know if it was right, but his hardness tempted her to squeeze.

"Yes," he gasped as she gave in.

His glans was staring at her now, the narrow slit swollen. The head was redder than his shaft, and the mysterious spot just above the slit, which had always been marked in purple on Madame's charts, was darker yet. Acting purely on impulse, she turned her cheek back and forth across the velvet dome. Cor sighed in reaction, a slow expulsion of pent-up breath.

The sound was thrilling, the sense of power. Whatever he'd felt before, he was glad for her presence now. She rubbed her face across him one more time, then took the pulsing tip of him into her mouth.

~~~

Corum cried out at the assault of pleasure on his nerves, at the first amazing engulfment. He'd asked her to do this to avoid betraying his inexperience, but his prick felt as if it had been waiting all his life to be sucked. He was soon too weak to watch what she was doing; he simply had to lie back again. Sensation was pouring through him in impossibly intense waves—wetness, softness, the raw-silk drag of her agile tongue. His hips rose off the bed to get more, and then the hand she'd used to steady his shaft tightened.

That hand rubbed him where her mouth could not, spreading the enjoyment over his whole cock. It didn't matter that she had no oil. Overcome with pleasure, his fingers tore through the thousand-thread-count sheets as if they were paper. His glans was itching under her saliva, crazed for more wetness, for more pressure.

"Faster," he said, his voice deep and strange. "I want it wet."

She began to suck and lick him at the same time, taking at least half of him into her clinging mouth. An exquisite pain streaked down him at her upward pull. Her lower teeth had caught the tender area beneath his rim. It should have hurt, but it felt sublime. The sheets ripped beneath his hands again, louder this time. His desire to keep his dignity was unavailing. To save his life, he couldn't have controlled himself. He was thrashing slowly on her mattress, his skin prickling all over, every inch of it longing to crawl into her mouth and meet her tongue.

On either side of the bed, the curtains swayed in increasing arcs.

"Yes," he said on the verge of groaning. *Yes, hurt me sweet like that.* "The edge of your teeth is good."

She must not have known she'd caught him, because she hesitated, but then she did that wonderful scrape again. His orgasm rose, the pressure gathering fast and dark. He knew it was too soon for any but a boy to crest, but a much larger, more determined part of him was rushing toward it with all his might.

These new feelings in his body were magical. Aches and buzzes. Delicious itches and coiling heat. How could he fight such unfamiliar enemies? His thighs tensed and eased by turns as each separate pleasure escalated. At last he reached the point where his muscles would only tense. His neck arched back and stayed there. He feared that if he opened his mouth, he'd scream. He didn't dare speak, even to beg her to finish him.

Luckily, she knew what he craved. Suddenly, everything went faster than it had before: the licking, the sucking, the tormenting pleasure-pain of her teeth. She had let go of his shaft and balls, and her hands pressed his thighs down with her full weight. This was all that kept his writhing body anchored to the bed. She settled in to a quick, hard rhythm that brought every feeling rocketing to its peak.

No blue-blooded male could have outlasted that. Cor had just time enough to gulp for air before the spasm broke in a line of electric fire, searing down his spine and shooting out his cock. His back bowed off the bed at the blinding surge of ecstasy. The contractions seemed to last forever, tightening his balls as if to break the laws of physiology and force his seed to burst free.

When he came out the other side, his jaw ached from clamping down on his groans.

She released him slowly, his now-softening organ slipping from her mouth with a quiet pop. She cradled it gently between her hands.

"Thank you," he rasped, his throat sore despite the relative silence he had maintained.

She rubbed her face against his pubic hair, that same catlike gesture that had seemed so sweet to him before. She wasn't simply good at this; she was kind.

He couldn't imagine why she would be. He hadn't been kind to her up till now.

"Come here," he said, knowing he had to hold her.

She crawled up his body and settled against his side, one arm crooking cozily across his chest. She felt right there, like she belonged. That troubled him, but he was too exhausted by pleasure to do more than stroke her hair. Qualms aside, her soft, warm breasts did feel wonderful pressed to his ribs.

"Thank you," he repeated, because once did not seem enough.

She hummed into his shoulder, the sound a bit like human singing. It was as good as one of their lullabies to him. He closed his eyes and drifted dreamlessly.

He had fifteen minutes of blissful floating before his cock rose again.

Forbidden fruit

❧

Xishi knew it was a pillow girl's lot to put her own pleasure last. She did her best not to squirm as Cor sank into sleep, but she knew she'd never wanted to be touched so badly. Her sex hurt with longing, its fluids trickling from it slowly.

Bringing Cor to release had been exciting.

Sighing, she resettled her head on his shoulder and tried not to replay each scorching detail. This turned out to be impossible; the images were too vivid, but at least she couldn't doubt she'd done her job well. He'd cried out when she took that silken hardness into her mouth, and he'd thrashed like he was being tortured when she accidentally used her teeth.

He'd enjoyed that more than she would have imagined, and the memory of his enjoyment had her insides simmering. She began to wonder if she could sneak away to her fancy bathroom without waking him. There was one nozzle in the shower that had struck her as a cleverly disguised sexual aid. She doubted it would take two minutes to achieve the release she craved.

She didn't dare, though. Not on her second night, and not after she'd lost control on the first. It was just too bad her needs wouldn't fade with Cor beside her. He smelled delicious for one thing, and for another he was stark naked. Everything she longed to rub her body over was on display: his hairy chest; his muscle-ridged belly; his long, powerful legs. The sight of his relaxed hands was enough to heat her—and that was before he grumbled in his sleep and rolled to her.

His cock wasn't quite soft. She could feel it firming up as it struck her hip.

"Xishi," he mumbled against her hair, his arm coming around her back. It pulled her waist closer. "I think I want you again."

He kissed her, deep and lazy, and she couldn't hold back a sigh. He drew back at the sound. She tensed, but she'd been right before. He didn't mind her shaky control.

"I'm tasting you," he warned her, his eyes narrowing to slits. "All over."

He pushed her onto her back and began at the crook between her neck and shoulder. Inch by inch, he licked his way across her clavicle. Simple though they were, his kisses left a trail of heightened feeling behind. By the time he reached her breasts, she was wriggling with anticipation—small, jerking motions she could not restrain. When she was ready to die of eagerness, he pushed both breasts upward and rubbed his face across their curves, settling his mouth at last over one peak to suck.

That was perfection. His tongue teased her hardened nipple while his cheeks pulled strongly. Each tug clenched the muscles of her vagina, as if a cord were strung between the two. Her areolae were swollen, the skin afire. Unable to stop herself, she clasped his head and arched closer.

His gaze came up. The look in his eyes was so heated it affected her like a touch.

He shook his queue behind his back and shifted to her second nipple, still watching her. The peak he'd left behind he pinched and rolled between his fingers until her thighs twitched in reaction. The laser sharpness of his gaze was difficult to meet, and yet she couldn't bring herself to look away. Something behind each of their eyes was talking to the other, something she doubted either could have translated into speech.

"Tell me," he said. "Tell me what you want."

She bit her lip in confusion. This was not her job.

He smiled at her with just his eyes. "Then I'll take what *I* want, and you'll have to put up with it."

What he wanted seemed to be to strip her lusts naked. He gave the peak of each breast one long, hard suck, then kissed a path down their lower curves. He was on his hands and knees, crawling backward down her body. When she looked down his chest, his cock wasn't just hanging, it was stiff. His arousal didn't seem to matter. Her pleasure was the goal he was focused on.

Her belly jerked when he licked her navel, the lamril on his tongue exposed openly. This time, the flash of the marking wasn't accidental. Noting her blush, he did it again. Then he gripped her legs above the knees and began to push them apart. She knew it was inappropriate to resist, but she couldn't stop. Her mound was smooth from her last depilation, as bare and unprotected as any woman's sex could be. If he spread her thighs, he'd see what he'd done to her. He'd see her dripping, see her flushed and swollen and desperate. Even with her knees together, he had to smell how aroused she was.

"You're mine," he said, low and feral. "You're not going to hide from me."

He'd been being gentle. When he used his full strength, nothing could keep him from splaying her.

The pleasure she had felt when his kiss controlled her was nothing to what slammed through her bloodstream now. He was taking charge of this. He was going to take care of her.

"Ah," he said, his fingers immediately sliding up her cream-drenched folds. "You *did* like that."

Her moan mixed embarrassment and longing in equal parts. He found the hood of her clitoris, his thumbs rubbing its skin along the swollen rod. She bit her lip against a whimper. From the growing coolness at its tip, she knew

her little organ was peeping out. Indeed, he must have seen it,
because the pad of one thumb moved to brush the unprotected skin. Though it seemed a gesture almost of curiosity,
sensation exploded through her nerves, like an orgasm but
not quite. The feeling was so intense she had to gasp for
breath.

"Now *that*," he said in the same dark tone, "is what I
want."

She could tell he was used to moving other people's
bodies around, perhaps from the wrestling aspect of his
fights. He gave her no warning, but deftly hooked her legs
over his elbows, hitched her hips off the bed, and buried
his face between.

His tongue felt so incredible lapping against her that it
took a moment for her to realize he was groaning. That she
would make such a noise was easy to understand, but that
he would sent heat cascading across her skin. His groan
rumbled into her pussy as he greedily licked and sucked.
Feeling as if she had lost her balance—no hard thing considering how he held her hips off the bed—she gasped with
excitement and clutched his head.

Her own arousal couldn't help but rise when she heard his.

"Oh, *there*," she said as his suction found her clitoris.
She felt odd giving him instructions, but the perfection of
his position virtually propelled the plea from her mouth.
He must have been very practiced. Her little organ buzzed
as if his tongue were painting it in pepper, a delectably
itchy heat. "Oh, please, stay there."

He stayed there, his body jerking strangely as he
growled and suckled her. His tongue rolled over her as
he pulled, so firm and clever that it showed her pleasures
she hadn't known herself capable of. She felt him swallowing, felt the heated dampness of his panting breath against
her bare mound. Softer sounds joined his growls, noises of
pain being wrenched from him. Only then did she understand why his body jerked. Unable to be inside her, his hips
were making love to the air.

The recognition crashed her through her peak. If she
hadn't sunk her teeth into her lower lip, the sound she made

would have been a scream. In truth, it wasn't much more polite, and when Cor moaned into her contractions it got louder. Her cream was running from her, but all he did was curl his tongue inside to taste more.

He set her down before she could succumb to her urge to groan, his body immediately moving over hers. She had no urge to close her legs now. Instead, she spread them wider and writhed with need. Cor's heat was shocking, his breath coming quick and fast. His tongue slid lingeringly over his glistening lips.

When she saw his lamril, that inborn whip to her lust, she knew one orgasm was not enough. She wanted what was coming next.

He cursed, hanging above her on knees and arms. "I didn't mean to do this tonight, but—so help me—I cannot wait. Tell me I should slow down. I know this is your first time."

His voice was shaking with his heartbeat. When she palmed his face, blood rushed up beneath his skin to darken it. Seeing that, feeling her power to move him, she couldn't have the slightest inclination to hide the truth.

"I don't care," she panted. "I can't wait, either."

He nodded, almost grimly, and reached under his body for his prick. His hips came down, and his fingers shifted the head between her labia, both their flesh pulsating with heat and blood. He cursed when he didn't find her opening on his first attempt, prodding her twice before the topmost curve of his crown slid in. His eyes closed in reaction at the clinging fit.

"I'll try to make this good for you," he said hoarsely.

With her pussy weeping around him, she didn't know how he could imagine it would be bad.

"Please," she said, her hands gliding up the muscles of his back. "I need you inside me now."

❧

Xishi's plea was more than Corum could resist. Like most daimyo, he was better at manipulating what his aura said than perceiving those of others. Contrary to expectation, tonight he could feel hers running over him in a rippling flow. Nor was this his only unusual sensitivity. Her sexual fluids burned like brandy fumes in his head. He suspected he should have spent more time reading something besides business texts. If he'd been more interested in royal-specific sex, he might not be so ignorant now. As it was, no one had told him women tasted like this, or maybe only pillow girls did. His mouth was buzzing—as was his cock.

But it was too late to worry. His body was ordering him to go on.

"Brace yourself," he said a second before he shoved in.

His moan of entry was unconscionably loud, but fortunately so was hers. He had taken her virginity in a single thrust, her wetness easing his way, her incredible tightness bringing him to the edge of climax alarmingly fast. He knew he filled every inch of her. He was too hard and large to do any less. If he'd been more experienced, or less aroused, he might have been able to adjust his size to suit her, but that was hopeless now.

Rather than complain, her knees came up around his hips to squeeze. Goaded beyond bearing, all he could bring himself to do was grind in deeper. Her hands were all over him—his chest, his arms, the clenching muscles of his buttocks—as if, in spite of his roughness, she couldn't get enough of touching him.

"Move," she begged him. "I'm going mad."

"Didn't I hurt you?"

"Only a little. Oh, Cor, please, it feels so good."

Her legs climbed higher, one knee pressing his shoulder blade. He slid one heart-stopping fraction further and knew he'd die if he didn't do as she said.

He also knew he wasn't going to be gentle. There wasn't one scrap of his being that wanted to do that.

"Sorry," he gasped as he drew back through the melting clutch of her heat. "Tell me if it gets to be too much."

But she didn't tell him. She was mewling in encouragement.

With nothing to stop him, his first thrust was as hard as he'd feared. His second drove him deeper than he'd known he could go, and every one thereafter raced toward the next. There was no pause between in and out. Movement was what he needed. Movement and speed and the juicy tightness of her sheath fisting over him. His skin began to buzz all over as he hammered into her, and only going faster seemed to soothe the itch. Her fingernails scored his back, but it just felt good.

"Yes," she cried, her neck arching forcefully.

He thought she was coming. Her inner muscles fluttered on his shaft. For a second, he thought he was coming, too. Pleasure catapulted through him in a sudden jump of sensation. But his cock wasn't acting like it had come. It swelled inside her and demanded he pump harder. Xishi met him thrust for thrust, both of them grunting in their efforts to get closer.

He'd pushed his upper body up on his arms. Now he gripped her rump with one hand to help her meet and match his strength. She groaned and her legs shifted, her right foot jerking even higher while the left slid either by accident or design between his buttocks. With every frantic upward push, her heel dug over his anus, a part of his body he'd never thought of as erotic.

He'd been mistaken. Heat flared from the back of him to the front, the pressure exactly what he hadn't known he needed. When her heel slid out of place with another thrust, he reached to shove it back.

"Keep it there," he growled. "That feels good."

She came again as if his order had activated some circuit she could not shut off. She wasn't just juicy then. A sluice of burning wetness washed over him, and every muscle in his body tightened and slung toward her. He came with an almost painful intensity, but the orgasm only made him want to go faster. His body must have known what it was reaching for. A second peak swelled over the first, his cock shuddering inside her as it strove to eject the very substance it was designed to hold on to.

He couldn't think straight enough to make sense of this. Maybe it was all one climax. Maybe this was how all yama came when they were highly excited. Maybe he was going to come all night. He took a third peak with his balls grinding to her body. Infinity knew why, but the tenderness of his scrotum made the pleasure ten times as sweet. He was locked inside her then. Couldn't force himself to draw out for any price. His cock had found the final reach of her passage, and a fourth crescendo rolled like a flood wave over the rest.

She made a noise he didn't recognize as yamish. It sounded more like an animal. From the milking spasms of her pussy, he knew she'd joined him in his last climax. His lungs refilled in a sobbing rush, and he suspected the only reason he hadn't outdone her shriek was that he'd been holding his breath.

His arms wouldn't hold him anymore. He sank down shaking, his exhaustion sweet. Only at the last moment did he remember to roll to the side and spare her his weight. She rolled with him, though whether her hold or his insured this he couldn't say.

Her head was tucked beneath his chin, her mouth pressing delightful, licking kisses against his chest. His cock felt as pummeled as he suspected her cunt must be. His back stung where she'd scratched him and drawn blood. Rather than regret this, he felt pleased for having driven her to it.

He might have lost control completely, but at least he hadn't lost it alone.

⤳

When Xishi woke the next morning, Cor wasn't with her. Soft, rhythmic whistles marked his presence in her small courtyard. She pulled the very rumpled sheet around her and padded to the open doors, her body pleasantly sore, especially between her legs.

She was glad even rohn could heal injuries quickly.

In the sun-dappled ground around her two-tiered fountain, Cor was performing some exercise. It was very graceful, more like a human dance than a model for a yamish fight—though she knew the latter was what it was. The two smooth sticks he held were the source of the whistling sounds. He drew swift arcs in the air with them, and spun them, and stabbed them toward invisible opponents. All this occurred without the slightest sign of strain. His face was more relaxed than she had ever seen it. If he'd had more space, she supposed he would have practiced his flips as well. Even without them, to her dazzled eyes, he was the butterfly of which masters spoke, too light and quick to touch even as he struck.

He was also extremely sexy. His thin cotton sleeping trousers hung low on lean hip bones, leaving no hard-hewn muscle to her imagination—not even the one that was arching up slightly from his groin.

The idea that he could be aroused while exercising immediately had her soreness changing into need.

Xishi wasn't trying to hide; Cor must have seen her watching, but he finished out the sequence before he set down his sticks and stopped.

"I'm sorry if I woke you," he said, coming toward her wiping his face on a white hand towel.

"I'm not. That was beautiful."

The corners of his mouth twitched. "Don't say that to my fellow pupils. They think the Battle of the Sticks is the height of yamish manliness."

To hide her own smile, she looked down at her bare toes—only to discover they had curled in enjoyment while she watched.

"Your chi leaves patterns behind you," she said shyly, wanting to hold the moment, "like a calligrapher painting in the air. That exercise must be good for your energy."

"You must read auras well if you can see that."

Xishi started to hunch her shoulders, then remembered that elegant pillow girls didn't do such things. "I read energy best in the morning, before my brain wakes up and convinces me I cannot."

"Whatever the hour, it is still impressive." He rubbed the towel across his glistening neck and chest. "You . . . did not have a family to teach you to hone your skills."

This was a delicate way to refer to the somewhat disgraceful circumstances of her orphaning. She might have spent more time appreciating his diplomacy, but his musky scent was distracting her.

"No," she agreed, unsure if this answer was appropriate. Giving in to what she really wanted, she looked up and met his eyes.

His breath came faster, the hand that held the towel stopping at his waist. "Do you keep up your practice?"

"My practice?"

"Your meditation. The Golden Breath of Peace, I think you called it."

Xishi's cheeks heated with pleasure. "I cannot believe you remember that. No. I planned to keep it up at the orphanage, but I gave up after a few attempts. I never felt what I had here."

He nodded seriously. The towel was slung around his neck now, his beautiful hands gripping either end. It wasn't the fashion, but he was tanned, his fingernails a lighter color than his skin.

"Sometimes—" He stopped and reached above his head to pull a perfectly good leaf from a trumpet vine. The motion did things to his chest that made her swallow hard. "Sometimes I think I liked my studies with Master Ping because he taught me how to feel what I imagined you did that day."

His voice was steady and soft, and yet she knew this was a confidence: a bit of reaching out for their childhood trust. She was so touched she could not speak.

"You should take it up again," he said, saving her from the silence. "Peace is a good feeling."

"I am glad you found it," she answered in a whisper.

He looked at her, the moment stretching out as they both began to breathe in tandem. Xishi's face felt hot—and grew hotter still as she saw a flush creep up his. When he spoke, he nearly groaned his confession.

"I cannot believe I want you again."

Her heart tripped over itself for two beats. "I can believe I do," she said, emboldened by his example. "You smell good when you're sweaty, and I didn't touch half the parts of you I wanted to last night."

His laugh was soundless, another sort of confidence. "If I strip naked, will you touch them now?"

She flung herself at him and kissed him, not caring a bit how inelegant this seemed to him. He staggered back beneath her onslaught, but thankfully devoured her mouth. Their tongues were soon battling for the right to claim the most ground. Not waiting for him, she tugged the tie to his pants until they fell. He took this as his cue to break their kiss.

"I want you here," he said, yanking off the sheet she'd wrapped around herself. "I want to watch you fuck me in broad daylight."

He caught her hands before she could reach for him, stepping back the length of her arms before descending gracefully to the ground. His legs folded as he sat.

"You do it," he said. "You decide how it goes."

It was not an invitation she'd expected. She looked down at him, wanting to engrave his image in her mind. Sunlight loved him even more than the dark. His cock shuddered in his lap, thick and hard and long enough to give her pause. She didn't care. She wanted him enough to force the room.

She braced her hands on his shoulders to lower herself. The mossy earth was soft beneath her knees. She hovered like someone savoring the unwrapping of a good present.

"Put me in," he said. "I want to feel your hands doing it."

"So do I," she whispered, all the voice she had left.

She grasped his amazing thickness, tilting it so she could press him slowly, luxuriantly where she desired. At once, she realized taking was different from being taken. That she had loved, but this was hers. The tenderness left behind from their previous coupling seemed to have sensitized her nerves. She melted around him as she sank down, enjoying the pang of need inside her, now that she had permission to sate it.

He groaned low in his chest when she'd surrounded all of him, and—oh—it was a lot. She felt positively stuffed by his erection, every throb of his veins quickening hers, every flex of his sexual muscles making hers contract. She so loved the way he filled her that she squirmed to feel it all the more. Her thighs were trembling as his hands came up to fork through her hair. She hardly knew how to handle the force of her desires. She actually feared she might hurt him if she let them loose.

"I never knew," he said, brushing his nose and lips against hers as he held her head. "I never knew sex could feel like this."

His words were oil to the flames inside her.

"Is it all right if I take you fast?" she gasped hopefully.

"Oh, yes," he said, the subtle growl of his agreement soothing her worries. "I'd like that."

The coupling was quick and . . . *violent* was the only word she could use. She did not hurt him, but it truly seemed as if her body tried. Or maybe it was just that he kept demanding she go faster. His grimaces suggested he was wanting something more than speed, but he wouldn't slow down long enough for her to ask. They pounded at each other even harder than the night before. Cor's hands gripped her hips like iron, pulling her down on him every bit as hard as she wished to go. Her head was tossing, her throat racked by hungry sounds. When she came mere minutes later, it felt so good it hurt. When he did, she thought he was going to grind right through her to the other side.

He exhaled slowly when it was over, hugging her loosely with sweaty arms.

She would have been glad for a tighter hold, but she said nothing, running her hands down the length of his braid instead. The silver streak caught the sun like metal. Feeling oddly sad, she pressed her cheek to his shoulder and closed her eyes.

"I need to leave you today," he said, his own hands stroking her back. "I'm flying west to inspect a clothier I may buy."

This seemed genuine, so "Will I see you tonight?" she asked.

"Buttercup, I don't think I'll be able to stop myself."

She didn't like his hint of ruefulness, or his calling her "Buttercup." It turned their relationship into something professional.

Which it is, she reminded herself.

"You don't like me calling you that," he guessed, gripping her hips to keep her from getting up.

"I'm sure you are wise to do so. If you're in the habit, you won't slip in front of your mother."

"It's true I don't enjoy arguing with her, but your feelings concern me most. We will be in company at some point. I don't want her to be able to say anything to anyone that might end up hurting you. If she doesn't know who you are, she cannot put out her claws."

"I am sure she would only do that out of care for you."

"She can keep her care. I am not—" He stopped and calmed himself. "I am not the boy who needed her protection when he was small. It's time she recognized that."

The hold he had on her hips shifted direction until he was easing her off his cock. He was perfectly polite about it, but Xishi couldn't help construing it as a slight.

The kiss he dropped onto her cheek after they had risen was polite, too.

"If you wish to leave the palace, take Habii with you. He knows the places that are safe to go."

"I may leave?"

"Of course you may. I've no intention of keeping you prisoner here, though I do ask that you not go out without an escort. If you like, we will visit the city together some other day. Wherever you wish."

"That would be pleasant," she said, for once answering with correct restraint.

"Good," he responded, seeming vaguely dissatisfied. He rubbed his chin for a moment before he left.

～

Despite his very recent and very vigorous coupling, Corum was tumescent while he dressed for his business trip—not exactly erect, but more swollen than he generally was when relaxed. He gave thanks yet again for the concealing nature of current fashions for yamish men, and reminded himself that the strange effect Xishi had on him was certain to fade soon.

Conceivably, he should have tried reaching more than one orgasm this morning—as he had the previous night. Good though it had been, he couldn't claim to have been completely satisfied. Even during the act, which had been— he paused in the middle of sliding on his shoes—incredibly pleasurable, he had been aware of wanting more.

Nagging twitches in his back passage had distracted him, a restless ache that begged for the kind of friction he could not find a way to request. He'd been seriously tempted to switch positions and ask Xishi to push against his anus as she had before, but he'd sensed even that would not have been enough.

He needed to discover what his pillow girl knew of alternate bedplay. Only then could he approach her for what he was beginning to think he required.

～≈～

Considering Corum's assortment of embarrassing discomforts, it was no wonder he fought a wince as he arrived at the landing pad atop the palace roof. Another prince was conversing casually with his pilot, whom Corum would employ for this formal trip. The prince was Muto Feng, a business ally of Corum's father, and one of the biggest gossips in the whole city. He would know all about Corum's new purchase, and was no doubt hoping to glean a few new tidbits to share around.

As soon as Prince Muto spotted Corum, he stepped from the gleaming aircar toward him. He was only average height and so well fed his figure appeared almost corpulent, a rarity among their race.

"Prince Corum," he said. "How pleasant to see you today."

"Likewise," Corum responded. "Might I inquire how your latest proposal is progressing?"

"Superbly. We believe the emperor will approve it soon."

Prince Muto belonged to a circle of favorites close to the empress. This made him a valuable ally, though not necessarily an honest one. This circle—the Empress's Dozen, as they were called—were proposing the establishment of a special encrypted channel on the holovision, which would be granted a licence to enact and broadcast human fiction. Miss Austen's *Pride and Perspicacity* was the popular choice to receive this treatment first, but Corum doubted it would be as easy a sale as Muto implied.

Though the Empress's Dozen billed their channel as an educational service, guaranteed to impress upon discerning yama what *not* to be, it was widely known that the emperor was uneasy about his wife's previous forays into importing human culture. As Corum understood the deal, much of the licensing fee and nearly all of the income from viewer dispensations would be funneled straight into the pockets of the empress and her friends.

Songyam might not be their nation's brightest imperial light, but he was royal, and that meant he could never be ignorant of the dangers in this arrangement.

"Well, I wish you good fortune," Corum said, thinking to himself that he'd lobby for the new channel if it could guarantee people would spend less time gossiping about him.

Prince Muto bowed his head slightly. "You are kind, but I am wondering if that kindness might extend further."

Corum had been signaling the pilot to open the doors and prepare for takeoff. He paused out of politeness.

Muto gestured toward the car. "Your man tells me you are flying west on business. Perhaps you would be good enough to drop me first. My destination is on your way."

"It would be my honor," Corum said, deciding he might as well get this over with. If he let the Forbidden City's biggest teller of tales corner him, perhaps the others would consider his entertainment value already tapped.

He gestured Muto ahead of him, watching with little pleasure as the older man settled complacently into a leather seat. This was the largest of Corum's aircars, a fine, gleaming machine that would carry eight in comfort. Corum and the prince could sit facing each other in the commodious rear cabin.

"You are as generous as your father," Prince Muto observed once they were aloft.

Not knowing where this gambit was headed, Corum simply hummed. As expected, Muto went on.

"I, too, have made a recent purchase from the Purple Crane, thanks to your father. He has managed to wheedle a pillow boy out of Madame Fagin, one I believe will suit my wife perfectly."

"That was considerate of him," Corum said, privately taking offense at the term "wheedle." Whatever their differences, Corum preferred to think his father had more pride than that.

"It was," said Prince Muto. "We expect his delivery tonight. And now you and I will have something in common. I must admit I am surprised to see you out on business today with such a reputedly lovely distraction to keep you home. Rumor has it you've spent a fortune kitting her out. You had better be careful or she'll grow spoiled."

"I have spent no more on Buttercup than her beauty and skills deserve," Corum said coolly, "and—as I'm sure you are aware—I have the resources to do so."

"Don't you though." Prince Muto seemed more amused than most would have been at Corum's icy manner. "Your father and I marvel at it frequently. No, indeed. No need to worry about you ruining yourself over some pretty pillow girl who's turned your head."

The suggestion that Xishi had done so was a grave insult.

"Quite," said Corum, pointedly activating the computing unit with which the cabin came equipped. It unfolded itself from the lacquered cherry table that stood between them, its screen effectively blocking Corum's view of the other man.

The prince uttered a sound that was dangerously close to a chuckle. "Touched a nerve, did I?"

Corum did not dignify this accusation by looking up. He didn't have to. Even then, knowing Muto was watching him, he had to struggle not to shift uncomfortably in his chair. His cock was growing harder, slowly but surely rising in his clothes. Worse, *things* seemed to pulse inside him, inside his rectum and beneath his glans, hungers he couldn't fathom how to appease. The best he could do was hope they'd wear off.

He heard rather than saw the other man slide into a more lounging posture in his rich brown seat. It went absolutely without saying that his father's ally was enjoying this.

The scent of lies

A package arrived for Xishi, stamped many times to prove that Cor's security had inspected it for dangerous substances. The box was too small to be another of her new gowns, which were piling up with shameful abundance upon her bed—until she became convinced Cor's valet must have tripled her actual order.

But that was neither here nor there. Xishi shook the plain plasboard box to see if it would rattle, then read the sender's name. It rang no bells, but the address did. This delivery came from the Purple Crane. The bed being full, she sat on the floor with it in her lap. Then, feeling like a child at Winter Solstice, she tore open the wrappings.

"Tea Rose!" she exclaimed, recognizing the handwriting on the note that sat on top. The pillow girl had sent the package under her real name.

"Dearest Buttercup," said the note. "I have liberated the enclosed items from Madame's storeroom. Had you stayed another month, they would have been yours automatically, so please do not feel guilty on my behalf.

"I don't know what gossip Mingmar has sent—everything he can think of, most likely—but in case he missed this, I will share: Jehol is leaving the pillow house! Some prince or other has offered a fortune to purchase him for his wife, who it seems is enamored of a good spanking.

"Amaryllis is annoyed, of course (and scrambling to find some way she can leave with him), but the rest of us are hoping Jehol's absence will inspire Prince Pahndir to perk up. He has been useless since you left, barely responding to our increasingly brilliant tricks. It quite puts one out not to be appreciated by the teaching tool!

"But I am sure you are having too much fun to entertain a scrap of pity for us. Enjoy the toys and, please, if you get the chance, send pictures!"

The news about Jehol did surprise her. She hadn't checked her webmail this morning. She supposed if a prince had bought his contract, he'd be moving to the Forbidden City. Xishi didn't like the idea, but of course she needn't necessarily ever see him. With luck, whatever house Jehol now belonged to would not be one that socialized with the Midarri. There were, after all, many factions in the royal city who did not exchange so much as nods.

The news about Prince Pahndir disturbed her more. Was he sinking back into his depression? And what would happen if Madame Fagin decided he was more trouble than he was worth? With his family determined that he remain "dead," Xishi didn't want to think where he might end up.

"He will get better," she told herself. "Jehol's absence will help."

Determined to believe this, she pawed through the protective wrapping to see what Tea Rose had sent. They were toys, as she'd said, but the sort of toys adults played with, the sort that required instruction discs to figure out.

With a cry of pleasure, Xishi spread the contraptions around her on the carpet. She would enjoy learning how to operate these devices. Even better, she would enjoy using them!

~≈~

Contemplating Cor's return and the further erotic explorations they might engage in made her blood run thick in her veins. That life-giving fluid was quick to engorge certain places, and highly reluctant to leave. Even without Tea Rose's delivery, Xishi felt as if she'd spent the day in a steamy dream. The nearer night drew, the more her restlessness increased. Her supper finished, she filled her time with a long, hot shower. Though the self-pleasuring attachment tempted her, she ignored it. She knew her lust, however pressing, was better saved for her new master.

It is good that I want him, she told herself as she watched the maid fold down the fresh bed linens. *Only think how unpleasant this would be if I did not.*

Feeling guilty for her impatience, which she wasn't certain fell within approved limits, she allowed the maid to help her pick a robe and brush her hair. The girl was young and quiet but adept. Xishi's hair hung straight and glossy when she was done. Seen in the mirror in her ice-pink sleeping robe and slippers, Xishi appeared perfectly composed.

"Thank you for your help," Xishi said. "That will be all."

It was disconcerting to be bowed to, but Xishi appreciated how swiftly the girl disappeared.

She was beginning to think Cor had forgotten his promise to visit when the door to her sitting room burst open. The sound of it hitting the wall startled her to her feet. Cor stood in the opening, a strange, wild light shining in his eyes. His normally neat black queue looked windblown.

"Where is it?" he demanded. She realized he was angry. His face was dark with it, his body stiff. It was rare to see any yama openly fuming, and to see Cor this way stunned her. Adrenaline surged through her, a fear reaction that—oddly enough—didn't feel that different from arousal.

"Where is what?" she asked breathlessly.

He ground his teeth and shut the door behind him with deliberate care. "The perfume. The one you used to drug me. The one I ordered you not to wear."

Xishi struggled to shut her mouth. "I'm not wearing perfume."

"Like fuck you're not." He closed the space between them with four tense strides. Taking her arms in a hot, tight grip, he dragged his nose up her neck and inhaled. "There's pepper in it and cloves and some sodding aphrodisiac."

"I don't own perfume," she said, at a loss to understand this and still shivering from being sniffed. "It's too expensive for me to buy."

He drew back from her but did not let go. "Maybe one of Madame Fagin's working girls gave it to you as a gift. Or maybe you have a rich friend I don't know about."

His hold was too strong to shake off. Her confusion began to turn to anger. "You're the only rich friend I have. I promise you, I am not wearing perfume."

His eyes flashed with fury and his nostrils flared. He released her then, but she could not be relieved, because he immediately stalked into her bedroom to search her drawers. He was not harming her new belongings or complaining that there were so many, but he certainly didn't ask permission, or pay attention when she protested. One by one, he dragged out every drawer and pawed through its contents, growing ever more angry as he did not find what he sought.

Finally, he reached the cabinet she'd used to stash the toys from Tea Rose. They *were* expensive, and she expected him to accuse her of lying, but all he did was lift out a dildo and clench his jaw.

When he turned to her, Xishi met his glower with one of her own. She refused to explain that the toy was meant for him. Silence not being satisfying enough, she crossed her arms.

"I do not think the Pillow Board would approve of this behavior," she said. "I assure you there's nothing to find."

He was unimpressed by her hauteur. His narrowed gaze lit on the open door to her bathroom. "Nothing to find, is there? How about something to wash off?"

He was lifting her a second later, was tearing off her sleeping robe and carrying her naked into the bathroom.

Xishi kicked and struggled, but all she accomplished was losing both slippers. With no remorse that she could see— mostly, he just looked grim—Cor pushed her ahead of him into the shower enclosure. She gasped in disbelief when he turned all twelve nozzles to hot and started scrubbing her back with a lathered sponge.

He didn't seem to care that the spray was soaking him. His hands were rough, determined to obliterate whatever phantom scent he thought she was wearing.

"Stop it!" she cried, more plea than anger coming from her now. "I didn't drug you!"

"No?" He pushed up behind her in his wet business robes. The move was so forceful Xishi had to catch herself with her hands on the silver tiles. "Then why was I like this all day? Why was I so hard I couldn't think straight? Why did I feel like a spike was being hammered between my legs every time I remembered you?"

He was grinding his groin against her buttocks. Through all the layers, she felt the stiffness of his huge erection, and through all the dampness, she felt his heat. He was burning like he had a fever, noises breaking in his throat as— despite his complaint that she had unfairly aroused him— he continued to rub himself over her.

"Why can't I stop?" he demanded, the hand that held the sponge clutched between her breasts. "Why can't I think of anything but putting this inside you?"

It shouldn't have been the case, but whatever madness he labored under evidently was affecting her. Her reactions shifted direction, swirls of fear and hurt twisting to desire. Her pussy throbbed the way he'd said his groin did, as if someone had driven a spike into that tender flesh. For her, though, the spike was not inspiring pain. She wanted to turn to him, wanted to lose her confusion in the mindless drive for physical union.

Sadly, the saner part of her wasn't sure this was safe.

Then he dropped the sponge.

"Maybe it is my chi," she gasped as his hand slid down her belly to cup her mound. The hold felt angry but very good, and she began to be a bit alarmed at herself. "Prince Pahndir said it was strong."

The hand on her pussy tightened, two long fingers pressing between her folds. Something about their stiffness made her think his reaction wasn't a good sign.

"*Prince* Pahndir?" he repeated, his voice like shards of glass. "Excuse me, Buttercup, but I was given to understand you had not made the rounds."

"I haven't! I mentioned him before. He was a teaching tool. At the pillow house."

"Of course he was." He shoved his cloth-wrapped cock closer to her buttocks, the jerk of his hips both punishing and delicious. "What better way to train than on a royal prince? And how kind of his wife to loan him out."

Xishi's knees were trembling. Her clitoris was caught between his fingers, pulsing wildly in its eagerness to be squeezed. She wanted to tighten her thighs around his hand more than she wanted her next breath.

"Prince Pahndir was a widower," she said faintly.

"A widower. Yes—" Again came the brutal shove of the hardness beneath his robes. "I can see how that would be more convenient. No messy loyalties to squelch his enthusiasm for serving as a *teaching tool*."

His words were icily calm, but Xishi didn't need to hear sarcasm to know it was there.

"It wasn't his choice," she said, striving to sound more measured herself. "And it did not make him happy. His family sold him to Madame Fagin as if he were a slave. Actually, I . . . I have violated my contract by mentioning his name to you."

"Then I shall pretend I never heard it. The last thing I would want is for my pillow girl to be sued."

"That is kind of you," she said unsurely.

Without warning, Cor pushed away from her. Missing his touch—though it made little sense to do so—she turned to face him. Her jellified legs wouldn't have supported her without her bracing back on the tiles. To her supreme mortification, her sexual fluids were seeping past her swollen folds.

The sight of him glaring at her did not discourage them. He was soaked, his hair straggling from his braid and down the sides of his face—in spite of which he looked absolutely gorgeous. The blood that had risen to his skin in anger magnified his sensuality. His lips were as red and full as if she'd kissed him, his cheeks as flushed as if he'd had an orgasm. The way he was breathing was better suited to a marathon. This was no simple irritation he felt. This was all-out rage.

Aroused by this or not, Xishi eyed him warily. She could tell now was not the time to be pleading Prince Pahndir's case.

Cursing, he peeled off the outer layer of his sodden robes and dropped it to the floor. Without the topmost drape of silk, the jut of his erection was obvious. To her amazement, their holomodel at school could not outdo his size. It was no wonder this prodigy had been a discomfort.

She swallowed past her nervousness. "Do you— Would you like me to see to you now?"

For a second, he just stared at her.

"I accused you of lying," he said, his breath still rough. "And you're offering to *see to me*?"

Was she as crazy as his tone made her sound? It was hard to know while her body burned for his touch.

"I know I'm innocent," she said, "and seeing to you is what you bought me for."

He looked at her, his eyes dark and unreadable. The pause stretched out until she wondered if she should admit she wanted him. Before she could decide, he spoke crisply.

"It's very responsible of you to offer, but as it happens, I believe I'd rather do without tonight. I . . . I accept your declaration of innocence." He held up one hand as she took an automatic step toward him. "No, don't follow me. I know the way."

Despite his words, she found it impossible not to go as far as the arch to her sitting room. From there she watched him open the hidden door. He moved as if his back were encased in metal, no longer dancerlike and fluid. Perhaps it was wishful thinking, but she got the impression that he, too, had been hurt by tonight's exchange. At the least, he must have shocked himself by losing control. And if he assumed her only reaction was fear or anger, how much worse would that shock at himself be?

What had looked like arrogance could have been loneliness. What if he was wishing he could ease it just like she was? What if he was truly sorry but too proud to apologize?

Xishi couldn't bear to let him think she wouldn't forgive him. "Cor—"

He paused without looking back, one hand braced on the frame of the open door. "You know," he said. "It might be more appropriate to call me *Your Highness*. This is a business relationship."

"Cor!" The outrage snapped out before she could pull it back. She pressed her hands to her waist to contain herself. "Your Highness, you admit you accept that I am innocent. I do not see what cause you have to scold me."

He turned his head far enough to show his aquiline profile. "Now I hear the old Xishi."

"She comes with the new one," she found herself saying tartly.

Cor's rigid face softened, but it looked to be with weariness. "Call me what you will then. I do not care."

He continued into the secret stairs, the seam of the entrance disappearing after it swung shut.

"You do care," she whispered to the empty room. "If you didn't, you wouldn't be trying so hard to sabotage our attraction."

The words sounded like something someone wise would say. Unfortunately, Xishi couldn't convince herself she was wise enough for them to be true.

❦

Cor wasn't such a bastard that he didn't know he should apologize. The problem was he couldn't spend another minute in Xishi's presence without treating her even worse than the beast he'd been. What he'd really wanted was to drag her to the floor and take her until she was limp. He'd almost done it when he saw that dildo. In his insanity, he thought she'd guessed what he'd been dreaming of her doing to him. It was illogical, of course, but it didn't matter. He'd carted her into the bathroom as if he were some human marauder. Then, when she'd mentioned that other prince, every cell in his body had seethed with jealousy. Xishi was his. He had bought her, and she was his. He had a right to expect her not to lust after other men, didn't he?

Maybe he did have the right, but, oh, how his chest had wrenched when she'd turned to him in the shower. She'd been trembling, and she'd looked a breath away from tears. He didn't know what he would have done if they'd spilled over.

Fucked her senseless seemed a reasonable guess.

Then again, he'd wanted to do the same thing when she snapped at him.

He flung himself onto his bed and groaned into the pillow. The case was cool against his fevered face. What was happening to him? Was it only his body waking up after a slow start? Did his genetic defect render him incapable of moderating his desires? Or was he readying to find his mate the way his parents hoped?

If that was so, he wasn't sure he'd welcome it. If a pillow girl could crash through his defenses this easily, what effect would his mate have? He'd be her puppet every time he came into heat.

"I'd rather be *her* mate," he muttered to himself.

That appalled him enough to roll onto his back, which led him to realize he'd been humping his still damp hips against the mattress. This final humiliation couldn't prevent him from wresting open his trousers. His erection burst from its confinement like a rabid animal, so hot it seemed unnatural. The relief of fisting it was unbelievably intense. He'd been fighting the urge to do this almost since he'd left Xishi that morning.

"You have really lost it," he panted even as he pumped his hand up and down, "and you will apologize first thing tomorrow."

Tonight, however, he was going to give his tormented prick the treatment it was demanding.

Shadow

He masturbated again as soon as he woke—doing it in the privacy of the shower so as not to offend Habii with his master's lack of control. The second orgasm of the morning helped more than the first, enough that he was able to approach Xishi's door feeling like a sensible yamish being and not a maniac.

The lock was coded to open with his thumbprint, but he knocked for entry, doing his best to conceal the pleasure that jolted through him when she opened the door. Though she was dressed in daytime clothing, her beautiful hair was down. He immediately wanted to bury his face in it.

"Cor," she said, her eyes unsure, her continued use of his childhood name oddly warming. "Do you wish to come in?"

"I wish you to come out. When you're ready. I thought I'd take you around the city today."

"You do not have business to see to?"

"I have put it off."

He hoped she understood he meant this invitation to be his apology. He couldn't tell from her manner if she did. She hesitated before she answered guardedly.

"My maid is dressing my hair. We will be finished in a little while. Perhaps you'd like to wait in the sitting room?"

He'd rather have waited closer, where he could watch, but he knew doing as she suggested showed good intent. To his annoyance, the perfume he truly was convinced did not exist immediately swam up his nose.

Was it possible an ordinary person smelled that good?

With an effort, he managed to remain calm and quiet in the lilac chair while she and her maid finished their primping. True to her word, Xishi emerged a short while later, looking like spring in one of her new gowns. This was pale yellow silk with a light blue over-robe that he recognized as coming from his own weavers. Her gleaming hair was swept atop her head and held with semiprecious gem-studded combs. The "quirky elegance" Habii admired was present in the daring orange sash she'd wrapped around her waist. It was boned velvet and resembled a human corset, neatly showing off the lushness that made her figure unique.

Corum felt his salivary glands activate. He came to his feet.

"No princess ever looked lovelier," he said, which perhaps did not come out as he meant. Xishi had always been as lovely as a princess—however humble her dress.

"Thank you," she said. "Your valet insisted I mustn't bring shame to you."

The twinkle in her eye said she had heard his misstep and forgiven it. Thankful and embarrassed, Corum offered her his arm and escorted her to the door.

"Would you rather walk or fly today?"

"Oh, both!" she exclaimed with artless eagerness. "The weather is lovely, but I did so love being in the air. It is allowed, isn't it?"

"When you are with me, of course it is."

"Then I am glad to be with you," she said, the teasing spark in her eyes again.

He squeezed her elbow in a mute expression of his gratitude for her good humor, and proceeded to have the nicest morning of his adult life. Though Xishi tried to contain her enthusiasm, it was clear that every aspect of this outing delighted her. The city was "amazing," the aircar a "marvel," and his ability to maneuver it "truly impressive."

He began to recognize how many of life's pleasures he had allowed himself to grow numb to in the name of being what a royal should.

Her eyes were wide with wonder as they wandered arm in arm through the public part of the imperial gardens. She especially liked the botanical robots some grant-seeking scientist must have sent to curry favor with the emperor.

"Look how clever!" she exclaimed as one examined her slipper for weeds. "They're no bigger than lapdogs!"

What truly impressed her, however, was the looming rise of Songyam's palace. Every time she looked up at it, her jaw would drop. "It's so large," she kept saying. "How can it be that only two people live there?"

"Only one, much of the time," Corum said. Like most royals, he was aware of the empress's fondness for being anywhere but near her husband. "Unless you count the hundreds of servants."

"I wonder if they like working there," Xishi mused, "or if they'd rather have their own homes."

"I do not know." With a tiny twinge of discomfort, Corum realized he never thought of such things. "I suppose they expect to like it, or the competition for imperial posts wouldn't be so fierce."

"I think I would feel lost. A smaller palace is much nicer."

He pressed his lips together to hide his smile. "If you were a different sort of pillow girl, I'd think you said that just to gratify my pride."

"Oh, no," Xishi demurred. "I haven't forgiven you quite enough for that."

"Shall I take you to lunch then? Work on softening your hard heart?"

"I would like that," she said, a hint of shyness in her lowered eyes.

Loving the reaction as much as he had the first time he saw it, Corum led her along winding silver brick paths to the Sweet Longevity Teahouse. The chrysanthemums were in rich, late-summer bloom, bank rising after bank in every shade from rust to lavender to white. The restaurant was no less attractive, and thankfully empty at this hour. They'd be able to relax free of the usual prying eyes.

It came as no surprise that Xishi pronounced the teahouse "perfect"—and this was before they were seated in the nicest window alcove in the place.

Her appetite was good, which Corum liked to see, her appreciation of the food adding zest to his. He found himself forgetting they shared a past. She could have been any beguiling young female—except he'd never known one he enjoyed being with as much. Despite his legitimate concern about his runaway desire, he relaxed when he was with her. Xishi was different from the royal princesses his parents tried to push on him. She listened to his words without hanging on them, tempered her admiration with teasing, and exhibited an openness of emotion that seemed too natural to be true.

His cock didn't care if it was true or not. It was painfully hard again, throbbing thickly in his covered lap.

"I have a confession to make," she said as they nibbled at a plate of sweet dessert biscuits. Corum thought the way she knelt on her cushion had to be the ultimate in feminine grace.

"A confession," he repeated, ignoring the increase in his temperature.

"About the toy you found in my cabinet. It wasn't meant for me but for you."

"Ah," he said past a sudden raspiness. "I thought it looked a little small."

"You are . . . aware that dildos can be used on men?"

Her reticence had his rectum throbbing like his cock. He fought the need to clear his throat. "Yes, I'm aware of that."

"It is not a skill I have practiced," she admitted, "and of course I would not attempt it if you were uninterested."

He reached across the little table to keep her hand from pulling back into her lap. "I would be. Interested."

His face was warming, but he met Xishi's gaze when she looked up at him. Her maid appeared to have painted her eyelashes. Within this sooty frame, her eyes glowed with rare brilliance. In the illumination from the window, he noticed that their silver bore a mesmerizing hint of blue. He didn't think he'd ever seen a yama with irises that color. Then again, what about her was not singular?

"I'm glad," she said softly. "The instruction disc intrigued me."

This conversation was affecting him a bit too strongly to have in public. Releasing her hand, he shifted on the hard cushion. "Perhaps we should discuss something else."

Xishi bit the inner curve of her lower lip. "The weather perhaps? It has been cooler than normal for this time of year."

It felt sufficiently hot to him. At that moment, a bead of sweat was rolling down his neck. When Xishi licked her upper lip, exposing the flirtatious tip of her lamril, he was pretty sure she'd seen it.

"I believe you're teasing me," he said with a lustful shudder he could not suppress.

"I believe you're right, Your Highness."

The reminder of his previous rudeness hit him hard. "It was inappropriate of me to ask you to call me that. We are friends of a sort, though I have not treated you as a friend deserves."

Xishi lowered her extravagant eyelashes. "Neither of us is used to this arrangement."

"True."

"So we will have to find what feels comfortable as we go along."

Corum took her hand again. "I want *you* to be comfortable. I want you to enjoy being my pillow girl."

"I think I have enjoyed it more than you realize."

She turned her hand until their palms pressed together. Hers was as warm as his, though much softer. When her gaze lifted, he thought he'd go up in flames. She wanted him. It was in the enlargement of her pupils, in the flush of her cheeks and lips. His fingers tightened without him meaning them to.

"I would like to take you home now," he said, his voice unavoidably deep and harsh. "As long as you don't have your heart set on visiting other sights."

"I would like that," she agreed, her eyes truly glowing now. "The sooner the better."

Cor unfolded himself from his cushion and helped her up.

"The bill—" she murmured, but not as if she really cared.

"The proprietress knows who I am. She will charge it to my account."

He could not keep himself from pulling her to his side as they walked out, though this was a display of affection guaranteed to draw eyes. The attention didn't matter. Hugging that tight, boned sash drew his scrotum up toward his cock. Every bone in his body ached to be near her, from his fingers to his ribs to the toes he wanted to dig into her mattress when he plunged inside her. The scent of her arousal made his heart thunder, and the nearby aircar lot seemed miles away. He wanted to kiss her that instant, to suck the lamril she was drawing across her lip deep into his mouth.

His expression must have shown what he was thinking.

"I am hurrying," she said with a nearly silent laugh. "These narrow robes are hard to walk in."

"I love that sash," he breathed, resisting the impulse to pick her up and run.

"And I love the fact that you're going to take it off very soon."

"You are not helping me control myself."

"No?" What should have been a very private dimple appeared in her cheek. "I suppose I must not want to."

"If you don't stop teasing, you and I are going to be intimate in my car."

She wriggled her tongue at him, going from flirtatious to outrageous in one instant. In spite of himself, Corum loved it. His cock surged as strongly as if she'd wrapped it in her hand and pulled.

He didn't know what made him notice the shadow. His thoughts could not have been further from worrying if they had watchers. But maybe it was the years of training with Master Ping. The back of his neck tightened without warning. When he turned to see what had caused the response, he spotted a man ducking suspiciously behind the trailing branches of a willow tree.

Even more suspicious, the man took off running as soon as he realized he'd been seen. To Corum's dismay, he was carrying a small vidcam.

"Return to the teahouse," he ordered Xishi. "Ask their head of security to stay with you."

Corum knew the restaurant had one; Amimam Vasho had worked for him before deciding he was too old for palace work. Corum waited long enough for Xishi to obey, then sprang after their uninvited tail. The man's head start did not daunt him. Corum had been running long distances since the early days of his lessons with Master Ping. No, what worried him was that he'd wring the spy's neck as soon as he caught up.

Chasing after some nosy idiot's employee was not how he'd been hoping to spend the next hour.

If he discovered the idiots were his parents, he might have to wring their necks, as well.

Xishi was mildly embarrassed to be asking aid, but the Sweet Longevity's guard was pleasant and professional. He didn't wait for her to finish stammering out her explanation before bustling her to the protected observation post on top of the teahouse.

Four swiveling long-distance scanners were mounted on poles up there, hidden from the ground by a screen of cedars. The guard, an older man with graying hair who introduced himself as Vasho, immediately went to the scanner that faced the direction she'd seen Cor run.

"Don't worry," he said, his eyes pressed to the viewer. "It's probably just a stringer for the evening vids. You'll be perfectly safe here."

At the moment, she was worried about Cor, but Vasho spotted him soon enough. "Look at him go," he said with more than ordinary admiration. "Stringers can run, but that boy is a cheetah. He's actually catching up to him. Oh, the other one's trying to lose him in the Pavilion of the Four Directions. No, the prince has spotted him. He's cutting around the columns. He's tackling him on the steps! He's got the bastard. He's—"

The guard's excited account broke off. He pulled back from the lenses and rubbed his eyes. Then he refocused the scanner and shook his head somberly.

Xishi's heart threatened to close her throat.

"Come on, miss," he said, whatever he'd seen no longer keeping him transfixed. "I think we'd better rejoin your master."

"What happened? Did Cor get hurt?"

"The prince is fine," Vasho assured her. "But I suspect he's going to need witnesses."

⟋⟍

The man was dead. Despite being the daughter of a notorious murder victim, Xishi had never seen a corpse before. Still, it was obvious that's what he was. He lay on his front sprawled up the pavilion's black granite steps, his neck turned at an awkward angle, his eyes open and staring. His face was an odd, dusky blue, and his left hand lay near his mouth. A cheap cabochon ruby ring was wrenched toward the knuckle of one finger. The stone was cracked down the middle, where a bit of yellow powder clung.

His plain gray robes declared he was rohn.

Cor and the guard looked down at the body with identical stone faces. Cor was holding the corpse's camera. Because neither of the men looked worried, or likely to comfort her, Xishi was reduced to clutching her own hands inside her trailing sleeves.

"Looks like poison," Vasho observed.

"In that ring. He was biting down on it as I tackled him."

"A news stringer wouldn't kill himself over a missed story."

"No," Cor agreed, a flicker of distaste twisting his mouth.

"Maybe a distant cousin?" postulated the guard. "Hoping to supplant you as the main Midarri heir?"

This was when Xishi concluded that Cor and Vasho knew each other. A stranger would not have made this personal a comment. Nor would a stranger—she concluded with a little flush of warmth for Cor's care—have protected her so readily.

Cor hummed a noncommital answer to the guard's suggestion. "Have you seen him around here before?"

"I believe I have, Your Highness, asking for work. Looks like he found it, though maybe not with the right employer."

"If he was so intimidated by whoever hired him that he killed himself rather than face the consequences of failure, I'd say definitely not." Cor looked abstractedly at the sky, his eyes a silver glitter in the sun. "He must have worked in the Forbidden City before he was let go. Otherwise, he'd have had a hard time getting through the gates."

"Which means someone inside the gates probably hired him to shadow you."

Cor turned to the guard, his face carved of something harder than flesh. Xishi shivered at the sight. He looked more dangerous now than he had last night when he'd been shoving her into her shower. She realized she hadn't, until that moment, truly comprehended what being royal meant. Royals had to have nerves of steel. Without them, they didn't survive well or long.

"Ask around," Cor said. "Quietly. I want to know who and what is behind this."

⟞

The imperial police took longer to deal with than Corum would have liked, but Vasho's presence as a witness helped. The emperor's men promised to relay whatever they discovered about the dead man—a promise Corum put absolutely no faith in. The emperor's men were the *emperor's* men. Any intelligence they gleaned belonged to him.

He was glad he'd had time to conceal the dead man's camera before they arrived. Once he erased the recording of him and Xishi, his security might be able to trace where it had been bought.

Through all the imperial police's questions, he could sense Xishi's fear. Corum didn't like seeing her frightened. He wasn't embarrassed for her; he simply didn't want her to feel this way. As soon as they reached the privacy of his car, he pulled her hand onto his thigh. Her fingers stopped shaking almost at once, though she remained pale.

"Don't worry," he said. "I'm not going to let this happen again."

Though he regretted the interruption of their afternoon, he was glad his arousal had receded to a more manageable state. He had an investigation to set in motion, and having half his mind on her could only be a distraction.

He left her safely in her rooms, then crossed to his parents' section of the palace. His father was out, but he found his mother closeted with her cook in her noxious cherry blossom study. She was flipping through upcoming menus on her handheld. Apparently, this was crucially important. She barely glanced up when the maid announced him. She did, however, speak.

"What excellent timing you have. I was going to send a messenger to ask if we'd be seeing you at meals this week."

"I doubt it," he said with a bit too much bluntness.

The cook took one look at the *keep-your-distance* jags in his aura and bowed hastily from the room. At this, his mother gave him her attention. Her brows drew a trifle closer above her nose.

"What is wrong with you today? You're all disarrayed. And your face is flushed."

He imagined it was, given the morning he'd had— though it annoyed him to have this pointed out by her. He drew a deep, slow breath to quiet his mind. He needed to see her energy as clearly as he was able when he asked his next question.

"Did you or Father arrange to have me followed?"

"Cor!" she gasped, pushing up from behind her pink mother-of-pearl desk. "You were followed?"

For a moment he said nothing, just watched her aura swell in distress. "My pillow girl and I were."

"Goodness. This is serious." His mother reached for her handheld again. "I'll inform your father's security right away."

Corum caught her wrist before she could touch the keys. "Don't."

"But you might be in danger."

"Mother." Hearing how angrily that word scraped out, he gritted his teeth. "I have security of my own—very good security, as it happens—and if they catch one whiff of your or Father's men sticking their noses in this investigation, it will be a very hot day on Mount Excelsior Glacier before you see me at your table again. Now answer the question. Did you have me and Buttercup followed?"

"No!" she said. "And, believe me, I was tempted. Your father ordered me not to, and that valet of yours refuses to answer the most innocuous questions. I had to hear her name from Prince Muto."

Her air of aggrievement seemed genuine. Corum hadn't thought she was guilty; neither she nor his father was ruthless enough to inspire their employees to suicide . . . at least, he didn't think they were.

"Thank you for your honesty," he said, turning to leave.

"Corum, wait."

He didn't want to, but he paused. His mother twisted her hands together before composing herself.

"Prince Muto has invited all of us to his natal day celebration. I would like to tell him you are coming. I know you don't approve of him, but it would show respect to your father, and it seems likely the empress will be there."

Which meant the empress and whatever royal princesses his parents were hoping to see his eyes go black for this week.

"Muto does have a wide social circle," his mother added. "You might be able to make a business contact or two."

Corum suppressed a frown and decided. "Forward the particulars to my calendar. And thank you for your attention to my concerns."

"Always," murmured his mother, her hand to her throat.

Corum bowed himself out before she could say more.

Heat

~~❧~~

Corum had never gone out of his way to make enemies. Oh, he knew he had them. Any financially successful royal did. For that matter, any royal who possessed something another royal wanted might have a few. Despite the unavoidable nature of his world, it was depressing to spend a beautiful summer evening compiling lists of people who wished him ill.

"Your pillow girl could have been the target," his chief of security pointed out.

Corum shook his head. "Buttercup wouldn't have been embarrassed by the publication of that recording."

Apart from some footage he'd shot of the dead man before the imperial police arrived, Corum hadn't shared the contents of the vidcam with his men. The segment with him and Xishi he'd watched alone. For a pillow girl to have a prince hanging over her the way he'd been was more coup than embarrassment.

"Maybe he, or they, are after more than embarrassment."

"The dead man wasn't armed," Corum said, "except for the poison he used on himself."

"Maybe they wanted a record of your usual habits, to set up a later attack."

Just because Corum paid the man to think this way didn't make it pleasant to hear. He pushed back from his chief's state-of-the-art surveillance desk. "We'll know more after we trace that camera. Or after Vasho picks up something about the man."

"Right," said his chief, who'd worked with Vasho when he was on Corum's staff. "And in the meantime, neither you nor Miss Buttercup should leave the palace without one of us."

Corum agreed reluctantly. At this present juncture of his life, he hardly wanted extra company. What he wanted even less, though, was any harm to come to Xishi because of him.

By the time he was able to return to her rooms, he felt like he'd been cycled through a laundry sterilizer.

She must have been listening for his approach. She opened the door before he could knock. Right there in the hallway, where any servant could see, she threw her arms around him.

The tight embrace felt so wonderful, so bone-deep warming that he couldn't bring himself to push away. Instead, he hugged her back and rubbed his cheek in her hair. She had changed into her sleeping robes. Her sweet, lush curves were all the easier to appreciate beneath the silk. When she released him, his cock had remembered every single thing it had been wanting to do to her this afternoon.

A few other parts of him chimed in as well.

"You're all right," she said, holding his face in both hands.

"Of course I am." He let himself smile at her. "But I'd rather be having this reunion inside."

She blushed and smiled herself. "So would I."

Lust seemed to have stripped him of all politeness. The door had barely swung shut behind them before he pushed her robe off her silken shoulders and took her mouth.

His kiss was deep and hungry, probing, sucking, claiming every inch of her hot, wet mouth. Greedy to make up for the hours he'd had to wait to do this, he ran his hands over her. Her glorious rump enticed them, the graceful curve of her spine, the full, firm globes of her breasts. Her nipples were deliciously engorged with blood. She trembled when he ran the pads of his thumbs around them, and shuddered when he pulled their rosy centers out.

He knew the shudder was for desire. The scent of her arousal was intoxicating. He began to breathe like an antique steam train, his hands on fire with the pleasure of touching her.

Finally, he had to stop kissing her to catch his breath.

"Ah, Xishi, can you imagine what it's like to have you welcome me this way? To know you can forgive me for last night? When I think of what I did to you, that I could have touched this beautiful skin roughly, I could almost cut off my hands."

"Well, I hope you won't do that." Her cheeks were pink and glowing. "As I tried to tell you earlier, it doesn't make what you did right, but you didn't hurt me." Her voice fell to the pitch of a confession. "The way you were in my shower was exciting. When I saw how much you wanted me, when I felt that same intensity inside myself, it . . . wound me up."

Cor wanted to groan at the savage longing her words inspired. "Don't tell me that. I'll never be able to hold back."

"Maybe I don't want you to. Maybe I want you to tell me everything you've been dreaming of. And maybe I want most of all to give it to you. Isn't that why I'm here? Isn't that what pillow girls are for?"

His fingers had tightened on her shoulders as she spoke, but Xishi wasn't pulling away.

"I don't want to hurt you," he pleaded.

"Then put yourself in my care. Let me show you how much I want to pleasure you."

His brain stopped functioning. He let her lead him by the hand to her bedroom, though he knew this mild-mannered obedience couldn't last. His body felt like it was coiling to attack, and his emotions were in such turmoil his eyes teared up. Since her room was too bright for comfort, he ordered the lights to dim. Then, as his vision cleared, he saw what was lying in the center of her crystal-curtained bed.

It was the slim jade dildo he had pulled out of her cabinet last night. With attachments. And a bottle of lubricating oil. Corum shuffled to a stupefied halt, his rectum pulsing with anticipation at this perfect offering to its desires.

"I'm going to fuck you until you can't walk," he growled, for once speaking from the heart.

Xishi licked her lips and swung his hand in hers. "You're welcome to do that, *Your Highness*. But first I think you should lie on my bed so I can relax you. The instruction disc was very clear about that step."

No matter how good this sounded, he didn't have the patience. He grabbed her to him and kissed her, lifting her off her feet before sliding two fingers into the heated softness between her legs. She was so juicy he had no trouble pushing in to the last knuckle.

"Oh!" she said, squirming helplessly off the ground and seeming to enjoy it. Her face was bright pink now, twisting just a little with her desire. "I thought—"

"Shh." He nuzzled her flaming cheek. "I just had to know you really wanted to do this."

"I want to do everything, Cor. Everything you can think of."

He believed her, but he stroked her for the pleasure of hearing her moan. Her cleft overflowed with cream.

"Let go," she whispered, her body countermanding her words by grinding down on him. "I'll never remember what I'm supposed to do to relax you."

"Screw relaxing." With undiluted determination, he set her down. "Just oil that thing and put it in me."

"You'll want the attachments," she cautioned. "From what I've read, you really will."

The attachments were electrified. They consisted of a power pack which fit into the flaring base of the little dildo, three wireless moldable metal patches, and a sleek black remote. Once he'd torn off his clothes, Xishi affixed two of the silver patches to his jerking balls. His scrotum was heavy and tender, but the quickly warming metal wrapped it in an odd comfort. The third patch required him to brace his arms on the wall, spread his legs, and bend over. She pressed it snugly over the ridge of flesh behind his sac.

One day, when he was mated, his kingmaster gland would awaken there, but it was hard to imagine this part of his body feeling better than it did now. The brush of her fingers smoothing down the patch was so incredibly pleasant he couldn't be self-conscious about the indignity of his posture.

"I think that's right," she said, patting his ass in friendly satisfaction. "Now all we need is the oil."

"Do it," he said, bending his elbows until his sweaty forehead rested on the wall. He was shaking with need, his buttocks clenching in an effort to create the stimulation he'd been dying for. "Hurry."

He supposed she did, because she came back soon.

"Relax," she crooned, kissing his shoulder.

Somehow he managed to do so well enough to let the dildo in.

The sensation was instantly enchanting. Nerves that had been itching with frustration suddenly blossomed with intense pleasure. Corum didn't even try to contain his moan. When she pulled the toy out and pushed again, it felt so good he had to laugh.

"I think I'm in love." He sighed.

Xishi kissed his shoulder again. "You've never done this before."

"I've never done any of it before." His spine arched and stretched with bliss. "You're the first woman I've been with. Oh, no, don't stop because I told you that. Take it as a—oh, yes, do that again—take it as a compliment that you've robbed me of my embarrassment."

He couldn't speak after that because she was running the little mushroom head of the dildo over a spot whose stimulation felt like a mini-orgasm. Chills broke out over his body. What she was doing affected more than the nerves she touched. From the straining tip of his penis to the heavy swing of his balls, he could swear he felt the toy moving. It was as if his every nerve connected to it, the receptive filaments all taking orders from Xishi's hand. Sweat rolled down his body as the amazing sensations built. He was either going to come just from this or melt into a puddle of ecstasy.

"Does that feel good?" she asked. "Because I can program the device to repeat any motion you enjoy."

His only answer was a delirious groan. At once, he saw the possibilities in her having her hands free. His cock saw them as well. It jolted against his belly, demanding its share of pleasure. Then again, her hands weren't really what it wanted.

Her cream was the drug it had been dreaming of all day long.

"I want to fuck you," he croaked out. "I want to take you with this thing inside me."

"I don't know if that's wise. The instructions said—"

He turned and kissed her until she gasped for air. Again she spoke worriedly.

"I haven't activated the attachments yet. Don't you—"

The kiss had worked so well the first time, he shut her up that way again. When she started climbing his thigh and clutching his back, he decided it was safe to release her mouth.

She blinked at him starry-eyed.

"Bed," he said, backing her toward it. One impatient sweep of his arm slid the crystal curtain out of the way.

She fell onto the mattress when her legs hit the edge.

"Bed," she agreed, her knees already lolling.

Corum pushed them further apart. Despite his impatience, she was too gorgeous for him not to stare. Her pussy twitched in invitation, glistening with the evidence of her need. He wasn't thinking about appropriate behavior then. He was too desperate for relief. He fisted his cock and stroked it even as he steered it toward her.

Xishi's eyes widened as she watched him touch himself. He didn't apologize.

"I'm going to take you while I'm standing," he said, his second hand planted by her shoulder. "I'm going to give us both so many orgasms we'll lose count."

He nearly cried when the swollen head of him eased inside her little clinging mouth. How could this act keep getting better? How could simple yamish nerves hold so much pleasure?

"Oh, yes," she moaned, her knees climbing his sides. "Oh, please, give me all of you."

He gave her all of him and more, working firmly in and out until her inner muscles made way for him. Reaching full penetration felt like coming home for the first time. His eyes were stinging, and his throat ached from choking up. Her scent was headier than ever. It seemed as if he could taste its peppery-orange sweetness on his tongue. He had to kiss her. Needed it as much as he'd needed to get inside her, as much as he needed those warm hands of hers on his chest. His skin was tingling everywhere she touched, his head positively spinning from how much he wanted her. He closed his eyes to make it stop.

Or maybe he just closed them to feel it more.

"Cor," she said, her voice coming from a distance. "Cor, your neck!"

She was touching it where it ached and then, suddenly, astoundingly, she was trying to scramble out from under him.

That opened his eyes again.

"No," he said, pinning her more firmly with his hips and cock. "What are you doing?"

She gripped his face between her hands. "Cor, you're in heat."

He nuzzled her palm hungrily. "That's not possible."

"No? Look in the mirror if you doubt me."

He refused to let her go. His cock was far too happy where it was. Instead, he hefted her up and walked her with him to the mirrored section of her wall.

He didn't believe it even when he saw the streaks of red blazing on his neck.

"My collar must have chafed me."

"Cor, those are your kith glands. Trust me, I've seen this before. You must have—" She paused and lowered her eyes. "You must have met someone."

"I've met no one!" he exclaimed, not trying to hide his

anger. Sensing how hurt she was by this idea, he hugged her closer to his body. Off in its own world, his cock flexed with enjoyment. "I told you. You're the only woman I've been with."

"Maybe you met your mate without realizing it."

Corum let out a snort and didn't care. "If you knew how closely those princesses—and their parents—watch me when we meet, you'd know I couldn't have found the black of my eye without *someone* noticing."

"But you must have. Only a royal female can bring you into heat."

Her face was hidden in his shoulder. He kissed the crown of her head. In that moment, he didn't understand why he'd been afraid of his emotions. This tenderness welling up for her was wonderful. "I promise you, I haven't gone into heat. Something else must be wrong with me."

Of course, being in heat would explain what he'd been going through these past few days. His sudden obsession with sex. His sensitivity to her scent. Why he'd been needing more and more orgasms for relief. Even the stinging in his eyes would make sense. The light would seem too bright if his eyes had gone momentarily black. Once he'd found his mate, they could do this from any strong pleasure stimulus, but that didn't necessarily mean his mate wasn't in this room.

Caught by this new idea, he began to pace with Xishi clinging to him like he was a tree. The dildo was an awkward but arousing pressure inside of him, reminding him that this window of relatively clear thinking was destined to be short.

If he was in heat, it wouldn't be long before he could think of nothing but continuing their coupling.

"You should let me go," Xishi murmured plaintively. "If you're in heat, making love with me won't help at all."

"Won't it?" He wrapped his arm more firmly around her bottom so he could tip her back and look into her face. "Do you remember when we were little how much trouble I had controlling my emotions?"

"You weren't so bad," she said protectively.

"I was awful and you know it." He took a breath and let it out, but strangely enough, he had no need to seek calm. He was giddy at the idea of sharing his secret with her. When he opened his mouth, the words flowed easily. "I have a rare genetic defect. My mother did her best to hide it, but that's what affected my emotions. And now I'm thinking, maybe, it's causing my body to single you out as my mate."

"But I'm rohn. My mother was a maid. There's never been any doubt about who I am."

"I know that. It's just—" He shook his head, the wonder of his conclusions unexpectedly delighting him. "Xishi, if you're not my mate, I don't think any woman can be. I didn't care about sex until I brought you here. My own parents were starting to worry I'd never mature. You were the only person who could wake me up."

Xishi's mouth fell open, and he knew she was beginning to believe. "It can't be," she breathed. "What would people say?"

"Truly, I'm not convinced I care."

"You have to care. You're a prince! Anyway, how can you be certain *what* you think with all those hormones flooding through you. As to that, I'm not certain what *I* think!"

Since she was, at that moment, rolling her hips in restless surges against his cock, he suspected one part of her was quite decided in its opinion. His face stretched into a grin. Enjoying what *he* was thinking, he walked her back to her bed.

"There is one way to prove my theory."

"No," she moaned, but her pussy went swiftly hot. She had guessed what he meant.

"Yes," he contradicted, laying her down under him, loving the sound of her juices as the descent hilted him. As before, he pulled her hips to the edge of the mattress, with him standing between her thighs. Leverage was key, and this position would provide it. He knew very well how vigorously he was going to want to thrust. "Raising my kith for the first time isn't the only thing my mate could do.

She's also the only one who could get me to spill my seed. I think we're going to have to finish what we started and see what happens."

"If you're wrong . . ." She gasped as he pulled his hips back for his first stroke.

"Then I'll die of frustration while you expire from too many orgasms."

"This isn't funny. Dry orgasms aren't enough when you're in heat. You might go mad if you can't ejaculate."

He knew that wasn't going to happen. The clarity he felt was extraordinary, the ebullience. He was in heat, and he absolutely knew he was in heat for her. Joy ran through him with his arousal, and he gave thanks for every ache and throb.

He suspected she was already inebriated from kissing him, but that didn't stop him from wanting to help her share his certainty.

"If you're my mate," he said, the words so husky her flush deepened. "My kith will arouse you, too."

"*You* arouse me," she said, wriggling half in protest and half in need. "I don't need your kith to do that."

He smiled and slid his arm under her back to arch it until one nipple pointed up at him. When his mouth inevitably watered, he didn't swallow, but let the fluid drip down his tongue.

"Cor," she gasped as the droplet hit her. "You're not thinking straight!"

The nipple his kith had rolled down was now twice as red as the other. With a surge of triumph, he bent down to suck it. Her genetic triggers weren't only in her cream. At his first taste of the perspiration on her skin, his neck pulsed and the glands flooded her again.

"Ohh." Her tone changed as anxiety became pure arousal. "Oh *Cor*." Her hands clutched his head, her pussy squirming desperately up his cock. "Oh, Cor, do the other one."

He did the other one only when he was done tormenting the first. He loved how wild she grew beneath him, how he had to use his weight to hold her down. His little Buttercup was stronger than she looked. Struggling with her was exciting, and—given what she'd confessed about his use of force in her shower—he didn't have to feel guilty for enjoying it.

Not that he had any shortage of reasons to be aroused. His kingmaster had been aching all along, but with the dildo to clench it against and so many other delights to explore, he hadn't paid it much mind. That changed when a violent cramp deep beneath his penis brought his head snapping up. He'd never felt anything like it—a knotting muscle where no muscle was supposed to be. He had a second to be alarmed before the gland convulsed.

The contraction was a hard one, shooting a rush of kith straight up his urethra. It was a pleasure tightly twined with pain, as if there were no difference between relief and urgency. Involuntary responses took control as the rush repeated, locking his hips against her and leaving him unable to do anything but gulp for air.

What the kith did to Xishi's pussy he could only guess. She said his name and clutched his backside hard enough that her nails bit into his skin. She sounded frightened, but the aptly named kith gland was his master. It wasn't letting him pull out. Indeed, it was all he could do not to grind in harder. Already, his heavy scrotum ached from the pressure. Unable to stop these primal impulses, he was flooding her with the most powerful aphrodisiac known to their kind. His body must have been compensating for his late start. He shot so much it ran out of her.

She moaned when she felt it, her hand squeezing frantically between their groins to rub where it trickled.

"I'm sorry," she said, groaning as she caught her lip between her teeth. "I can't help it. It itches so good I have to touch myself."

Corum couldn't be sorry. Growling in approval, he found some unsuspected strength of will to drag his shaft out of her. He was just in time to deliver one long spurt of fluid to her clit.

She arched as if he'd electrified her, then ground the suddenly supersensitized organ against his crown. They

both cried out at that, but neither could stand more than
seconds apart.

"Come back," she urged, her hand grasping his where it
steered his shaft. "Cor, come inside me and take me hard."

To save his life, he couldn't have done anything else. He
slammed inside her and began thrusting, his hips rotating
faster and faster until the only thing that kept their skin
from igniting at the friction was how wet they were. Corum
had thought he could run fast, but that was nothing compared to how fast he now discovered he could fuck. The
sound of their pelvises colliding blurred together. He lost
count of Xishi's cries of climax—or his own groans of
frustration as a new sort of pressure built.

His scrotum felt like it was weighted with smoldering
lead.

He knew he was going to spill his seed. Every sign he'd
seen said she could pull it from him. His kith had stopped
shooting, but every ripple of her pussy, every sluice of her
cream felt as if it dragged him closer. Her chi had flared so
high that rubbing his chest against her was like bathing in
rainbows. Bursts of sweetness broke against his skin without rhyme or reason. For one irrational moment, he entertained the possibility that the ecstasy he felt was hers—the
important difference being that she climaxed from it and
he did not.

He tried stroking her in new directions, putting pressure
on different areas of his cock. While she seemed to like it,
it wasn't really helping him. Apparently, until his swollen
testicles released their load, he wasn't going to have more
orgasms.

"Fuck," he finally gasped, loving every second of the
rising tension while at the same time not sure how much
more he could stand. "How long can it take to ejaculate?"

"C-Cor!" she said, her voice broken by her current,
who-knew-how-many climax. Sighing at the ending glow,
she brushed a fallen strand of hair from his eyes. "I forgot
to massage your scrotum. I'm sure that's supposed to
help."

"Well, I'm not pulling out so you can do it now."

"No," she agreed as her neck arched with rapture. "I don't— Oh, my, that angle's nice. I don't think you have to stop what you're doing. Just see if you can find where I threw that remote."

Determined not to lose his mooring, he floundered around the covers until his hand hit the control.

"Here," he said, thrusting it at her.

Between groans of pleasure, she peered at it owlishly. "Oh, here's the repeat key."

If he hadn't been inside her, he would have jumped a foot in the air. The flaring base of the dildo whirred as four tentacle-like arms unfolded and attached themselves to his butt.

"What the—" he gasped, but then the toy began to move.

His eyes couldn't decide whether to cross or just roll up inside his head. The dildo was repeating the last motion Xishi had performed, the very motion that had sent chills winging up his prick. He realized the thing was rubbing directly over his kingmaster gland.

Xishi giggled, a sound he couldn't remember ever hearing a yama make. "I guess that's good. Let me see if I can remember the sequence for the electrical massaging disks."

He gabbled out a word that made no sense in any of the world's languages.

"I think this is it," she said, and then pressed the keys.

The moldable metal disks began to writhe and vibrate where they'd wrapped his balls. For the space of three gasping breaths all he could see was stars.

Xishi touched his shoulder. "Is that all right? You look very strange."

"It's good," he groaned. "Oh, fuck, it's good."

It felt so good he'd stopped thrusting. The second he realized he'd done it, he began again. This time, when he drove himself inside her, he went so deep his glans knocked her womb.

"Oh . . . *my*," said Xishi, her eyes screwing shut. Obviously wanting more of this, she grabbed her thighs under her knees and pulled them up. "Oh, Cor, please keep doing that."

It was a good thing she wanted him to, because he honestly didn't think he could stop. His body was roaring toward its goal, the rise as sure as death this time. His balls were tightening, his skin crawling with waves of unbelievable pleasure. In he slung himself, and in again. The pulsations of the disks intensified. Xishi's fingers were creeping back to her clit, though her pussy was already spasming. She really must have wanted to rub herself.

"Let me," he gasped, working his thumb over the bursting fruit.

She screamed the second he pressed down, at which point everything inside him cut loose.

His seed might as well have been lava; it burned that fiercely, that forcefully through his cock. The question of pain or pleasure lost all meaning. This was transformation. This was worlds crashing down and being born anew. His entire body seized with an ecstasy beyond the physical. His consciousness narrowed to a wordless flame.

I love her, he thought—except it seemed to be the universe that said the words. *I love everything.*

He hung there in that mindless bliss—for minutes or hours, he couldn't say.

Xishi, he thought, and then he came back.

She was holding him, her arms and legs tight around his back. Her muscles were trembling, her vagina twitching with aftershocks. Behind him, the dildo was still sliding mechanically in and out. The pleasure of that was nothing to his climax. He wanted to swear to God like the humans did. Only a deity could understand what he'd felt.

For that matter, only a deity could understand him now.

He was at peace. Every part of him. Mind. Heart. Body. Warm and peaceful, inside and out. Master Ping had tried to teach him this for years, but now he knew. Peace didn't come from locking his emotions inside a box. It came from allowing himself to be who he was.

He buried his face in Xishi's hair, afraid to ask if she felt it, too. He wasn't certain he was ready to hear.

"Cor," she sighed, the bliss in her voice enough to stiffen up his penis. "Do you think we could do that again?"

~~~

They did it again for the next four days, stopping only to shower and eat and sleep. Whatever hormone Cor had in his kith, it made Xishi as crazed for him as he was for her. She should have been too sore to move, but the hormone must have had healing properties. She was only tender—and impossibly sensitized.

They didn't leave her rooms except to test the carnal possibilities of the various grassy corners of her courtyard. One by one, Tea Rose's toys got a tryout.

After the first awkward appearance of Xishi's maid, Corum dismissed her. She was a new employee, and perhaps not a witness they wanted. Habii brought them all their meals from then on.

Though the valet couldn't hide his shock at what his beloved master had gotten up to, neither Cor nor Xishi could find it in them to be concerned. Getting their body parts hooked up was all that mattered now: quenching the erotic fire that never seemed to abate for long. Each time Habii's elegant mustache twitched with disapproval, the best they could do was muffle their giggles.

"I'm never leaving you," Cor swore sometime on the third day. "I'm going to fuck you until the last snowfall."

Since Xishi's ankles were around his ears, and Corum's fingers were tugging her clitoris, she really didn't have the breath to comment.

She'd gotten so used to coming, it barely took a heavy sigh from him to set her off.

All in all, going through heat with him was marvelous—freeing, as if pleasure were what life was about. She grew to know his body as well as her own, and to feel comfortable with every inch of both. He loved the way she was made, and was only too pleased to prove it. In the face of that, she couldn't worry about not matching the usual standards for beauty.

When he smiled at her, his eyes as warm as winter fire, her joy was a bell ringing through the air, the note penetrating everything it touched. Best of all, she didn't have to hide her feelings. The only person who might have judged them was as happy as she was.

Cor cared about her. More than a prince about his pillow girl. More than a lonely boy about his long-lost friend. She didn't need to hear him say the words to know it was true.

"I love this," she sighed, flinging her arms wide on the evening of the fourth day. They were in her garden, enjoying the rising moon among other things. Cor lifted his head from between her legs.

"Really?" he teased, rearing up on his knees to squeeze his fingers up and down his hugely erect cock. Any shyness they might have felt about touching themselves was gone. They knew how pressing their urges got. Now Cor stroked and wagged his hungry phallus at the same time. "Why don't we turn around head to toe, and I can see if you love this, too."

She did love it. Loved how the taste of her pussy could bring it up. Loved how a good, wet tonguing could draw its kith. Most of all, she loved how it filled her when he grew too lost in rut to do anything but pump insanely until he came.

With all this lubricious activity, her entire apartment reeked of sex. To her, his kith smelled like he'd said she did—like oranges and cloves and a hint of cayenne pepper. She was convinced it was the best perfume in the world.

"I could stay here forever," she murmured into his chest just past midnight. They lay on their sides on her sitting room carpet, too exhausted to move to her bed.

"Forever," Cor agreed dozily as he lifted her upper leg and slid thickly into her.

His heat kept him in a near constant state of hardness, but he had found they could sleep this way—at least until his arousal became too insistent and his body woke him up to thrust.

That, she had decided, was the perfect wake-up call from a dream come true.

Muto's natal day

~⊗~

The minute Corum opened his eyes he knew his heat was over. He also knew he'd spent the last four days drugged out of his mind by his own hormones. The things he'd said, the things he'd done and felt, slapped him with a hot shock of shame.

He'd exposed himself to the person he least wanted to be vulnerable to.

His cock was still inside her body, almost soft but held in place by the possessive clutch of their limbs. Even free of the influence of his kith, her skin felt wonderful to him: smooth, warm velvet humming with energy. Careful not to hurt her, he eased away.

They had fallen asleep beneath a rumpled sheet on the carpet of her sitting room. Autumn's cool kissed the morning. Missing his warmth, Xishi made a sound and curled closer on herself. She looked like a child with her hands tucked between her knees.

How many nights did you sleep like this after my mother

*sent you away? How many nights did you know no warmth
but your own?*

It had been years since he'd contemplated these questions. He'd forced himself not to ask about her, not to give
his mother the chance to refuse to say, but now and then
he'd wondered.

Was she all right? Was she missing him?

He found his hand against her cheek, betraying himself
just a bit to stroke that soft skin. His eyes were stinging
again, and he knew they had not gone black.

He felt empty rather than calm. He might not be in rut
anymore, but he was not quite the Prince of Ice, either.

Her sooty lashes lifted as he drew back his hand. "Cor?"
she asked, stretching a little straighter on the lush carpet.

"It's over," he said. "The heat is gone."

"Oh." She clutched the sheet to her breasts and sat up
like him. Her gaze searched his face. "Are you all right?"

"I am well."

And he was well. Apart from a lingering sexual bruise or
two, apart from the ringing emptiness in his head, his body
felt as good, as alive, as it had in all his twenty years of life.

Xishi's fingers pressed her kiss-chafed lips. "What are
you going to say?"

He knew she meant about her being his mate. Drugged
out of his mind or not, that truth was undeniable.

"Nothing," he said, then softened the answer when she
flinched. "I don't know what to say yet. I need time to think."

Her nod was gentle. "I understand it won't be easy—
whether you tell someone or put if off."

He wondered if he understood how hard it would be
himself. He was the House of Midarri's sole direct heir.
Their line had bred with emperors. More things would
change because of the last four days' events than his own
place in the yamish world.

"I should return to my rooms," he said. "Habii will be
worried."

She nodded at that as well, watching—a little forlornly,
he couldn't help but think—as he looked back at her from
the secret stairs. For all he knew, he looked forlorn as well.

The pang that tightened his chest as he left did not strike him as a good sign.

~~~

"You must dress very simply for this party," Habii said once he'd dragged his master into his dressing room. "Everyone will be trying to outdo Prince Muto, which is not only stylistically risky, but also impossible. That man doesn't know the meaning of moderation. Your Highness, of course, is too wise to fall into such a trap."

Corum didn't feel particularly wise just then, but simple sounded fine to him. He had no desire to outdo Muto Feng or anyone else tonight. If he got through this celebration without incident, that would be accomplishment enough.

He was sorrier than he could say that he'd told his mother he would go.

"Ah-ha!" said Habii, snagging a set of robes from the rotating rack. "This white will be perfect."

The snowy cloth was the finest patterned silk from Corum's factory, its surface enhanced with the invisible, stain shedding barrier that made it a best seller. It draped perfectly, which treated fabric didn't always do.

Habii held the hanger against his master and examined the effect in the freestanding mirror. "Yes, this shows off your golden skin."

Corum felt one eyebrow tick up a notch. "I thought you disapproved of my tan."

"You are an original," Habii sniffed. "You can be any color you like." He turned again to the racks of clothes, his finger to his chin. "The black trousers will be best, I think, and the silver sash with the three diamonds. I have been thinking lately that fringes are on their way out."

The diamonds were the size of pigeon's eggs, but since the rest of the outfit was unjeweled, Corum supposed this counted as moderate.

"Those black trousers are too snug," he said when he saw the ones Habii meant.

"I do not think so, Your Highness. You have lost weight in the last few days."

This clipped remark was Habii's first allusion to his time with Xishi—though Corum was certain it had been on his mind all along. Knowing this, Corum's slow exhale of resignation came out louder than he intended.

"Forgive me, Master," Habii said, his head hanging. "But how can it be that you and that pillow girl . . . She is rohn!"

This left Corum in no doubt as to how much his servant had figured out. Knowing Habii's pride was very much tied up with his master's, Corum put his hand on his shoulder.

"It is a mystery," he said, "which time alone may solve."

As far as it went, the answer was honest, but Corum knew the effect it would have on his drama-loving employee. Habii's eyes went round. Behind them, he was probably spinning tales of Xishi being a long-lost princess, cast out cruelly from her family into who knew what suffering, only to be rescued by his wise and brave master. Perhaps it wasn't right to let Habii think this, but it had to be preferable to knowing his perfect master was in truth a perfect freak. Habii had never been around Corum when he was anything less than controlled.

"My lips are sealed," the valet promised. "No one shall learn the truth from any mouth but yours."

"Thank you." Corum squelched his guilt at the gratification shining in his servant's eyes. "I knew I could count on you."

⁓

In honor of his natal day celebration, Muto Feng had transformed his ballroom into an enchanted wood. Full-grown trees, their branches strung with fairy lights, stretched toward the barrel ceiling from convincing mounds of earth and moss. Between these built-up mounds wound the ballroom's actual floor, its shining hardwood surface obscured by countless clusters of guests dressed in garish clothes. The wealth of jewels that encrusted their shoes and garments sparkled like a news stringer's flashbulbs.

Habii had been right about the attendees trying to outdo Muto.

Corum looked around for his parents, but couldn't spot them in the crush. The empress was here, looking bored and regal among her clique, her restless eyes dimming just a fraction of her beauty. She was exquisite nonetheless, a perfect statue of a yamish queen. Corum could see why the emperor was besotted, though he had no urge to mingle with her crowd himself, even in the name of business.

He eased into the room, nodding at those he knew, accepting a glass of wine from a passing tray. The illusion of being in a forest deepened as he progressed. A stream had been carved out of the central mound and was being used to cool drinks. A young female servant in an extraordinarily flimsy gown was tucking new bottles between the stones as he watched. She was joined by a man who was just as scantily clad, with the added singularity of having his legs tricked out to look like a goat's.

"Figures from human myth," said Muto Feng, appearing at Corum's elbow. He *chinged* his glass of wine against Corum's. "We're thinking that after Miss Austen has her airing, we'll try adapting fairy tales."

"So the negotiations for the new holochannel are going well."

Muto's eyes twinkled. "Thought I was lying, didn't you? That's all right. We've been obliged to bend on the money angle, but I always knew the old man would want his cut."

Corum didn't think of himself as stodgy, but hearing the emperor of all the yama referred to as "the old man" shocked even him. At a loss for words, he allowed himself to be distracted by the squawk of a parrot in the transplanted trees. Its plumage was nearly as brilliant as Muto's fuchsia and orange robes. As it took flight, its wings made an unnatural whirring sound.

"They're cybernetic," Muto said, noting his gaze. "Invented by a family of clever daimyo who live up north. Friends of the science minister. I thought artificial birds would be better than risking my guests' nice outfits with the real thing."

"I'll give you this," Corum said, impressed in spite of himself. "You know how to set a stage."

"Don't I, though." Muto chuckled softly. "I was thinking of bringing in genuine humans to play the naiads, but Her Illustriousness"—he nodded at the empress—"drew the line at that. 'What if they start touching people,' she says, 'and everyone goes mad from imbibing their etheric force?'"

"And you wouldn't have been concerned?" Corum asked. Given his history of struggles with self-control, the topic of human energy and its effect on yama had always caught his interest—if in an uneasy way.

"Well, my guests are going to get drunk tonight regardless. What do I care if they get drunk on that?"

"But the humans would be transferring emotions as well as etheric force."

"Oh, pooh," Muto scoffed, an expression Corum had never heard. "We yama make such monsters of emotions you'd think we didn't know what they were. But it's not as if we're rohn. We royals would never become addicted to human energy, so why shouldn't we have fun with something new?"

His face a picture of satisfaction with himself, Muto balanced his drink atop his stocky belly. "It's just as well, I suppose. The security I would have needed to ship humans in and out of the Forbidden City would have cost the moon. Fortunately, it wasn't as expensive to pull all this together as you might think. Nothing like my mother's diamond-theme Winter Solstice bash."

Corum had managed to evade that invitation. With the death of Muto's father, the Feng family matriarch had grown increasingly extravagant. He vaguely remembered some legal wrangle surrounding Muto's succession to head of house. As he recalled, the elder Feng had wanted to put a cousin in his son's place. Corum didn't remember how the attempt was thwarted, but felt sorry for anyone who got in Muto's way. Muto's mother couldn't be mistaken for anything other than a dragon, but her son was twice as devious. As tonight was proving, he was well able to hide his teeth behind a mask of affability.

Unsettled on a number of different fronts, Corum was relieved when a lovely young woman—not Muto's wife—tripped up to them. She was dressed in a filmy, flower-patterned gown like the bottle girl, her breasts and depilated pubis visible behind the cloth. Her labia and nipples had been painted red.

"Muti," she complained in a childish voice, "the centaur won't let me ride him."

Muto tweaked her nose between two knuckles, a familiarity that sent an uncomfortable yearning through Corum's chest. "We'll see about that. And in the meantime, how would you like to meet the famed Prince of Ice?"

"Ooh," said the girl, turning big eyes to Corum. "That's you, isn't it? I can tell because you're so elegant. I love your hair down like that. But where is *your* pillow girl? We've heard so much about how beautiful she is."

As was polite, Corum bowed to the girl. "I wasn't aware this was a mixed party. Otherwise, I would have brought her."

Oddly enough, this was true. Corum remembered Xishi's love of magical tales too well to have deprived her of seeing this.

"You should have told him, Muti," scolded the girl. "I wanted to meet Buttercup."

"It must have slipped my mind," her master said smoothly. "Or possibly it slipped his mother's. Prince Corum is, as you know, an unmated prince. She may have wanted him to attend undistracted by those who cannot alter that fact."

The girl rolled her eyes at this, obviously not seeing why this mattered compared to having—from her perspective—a more entertaining complement of guests.

Muto bent closer to her ear. "Tell the centaur I told him to give you whatever rides you wish, and I'll meet you in my rooms later."

This satisfied his pillow girl. With a brief backward wave for Corum, she scampered off.

"What children rohn are," Muto mused, watching her bottom jiggle in the transparent dress. "Though, by all reports, that isn't bothering you. Do me a favor and come greet my wife. She's been after me to have you over."

Since Corum was here to offer respect to his father's ally, he had no reason to refuse.

Erymita Feng was something of an anomaly—an unlovely yamish female. As occasionally happened when royal genes combined, her tallness was exaggerated, resulting in limbs and features that were disquietingly thin and long. She was as elegant as pride and Muto's money could make her, but Corum knew her lot was not an easy one. He forgave some of her trademark vitriol on this account—though he suspected forgiveness, or sympathy, was not what she wanted from anyone.

She certainly wasn't worried about public displays of affection. No more inhibited than her husband, she sat beneath a tree with her pillow boy curled against her side like a large and dangerous house pet—more sharp-clawed panther than cute kitty. His large, rather brutal-looking hand was stroking familiarly down her thigh. She patted it before she stood. As she shook her robes into their proper folds, Corum saw they were a vivid mix of blue and yellow.

"Corum Midarri!" she exclaimed, inclining her head gracefully. A miniature jeweled garden had been pinned into her elaborately braided hair. "How wonderful to see you here." The pillow boy stood as well, and Erymita regarded him fondly. "This is Jehol, who knows your Buttercup *very* well."

Corum dismissed her emphasis as an attempt to make trouble and regarded the pillow boy. Despite his abbreviated dress—a flowered cloth wrapped around his loins—he fit the royal ideal better than his mistress. He was taller than most rohn and powerfully built, his perfectly aristocratic face blessed with slanting cheekbones and a narrow nose. He scanned Corum's body with the arrogance of a rohn who'd never faced a royal on the fighting mat. Size didn't matter there, only coolheadedness and the power advantage inherent in royal genes. Elitism wasn't what barred rohn from competing—or, not only that. There wasn't one rohn in a thousand who could provide a royal an equal fight.

Corum concluded this particular rohn was choosing not to acknowledge that. He bowed to Corum a beat too late for strict politeness.

Well, Corum thought, mildly amused, *he's certainly full enough of himself to give Erymita a good spanking.*

"I hope you are enjoying your new position," he said, not about to say he was honored to meet him.

The pillow boy's lips tightened. "Very much. I must admit I was surprised, and pleased, to hear our dear Buttercup is enjoying hers."

His frigid eyes said that pleasure was the least of his reactions.

"Yes," agreed Erymita, stroking the boy's bare shoulder with a long-nailed hand. "Four days without leaving her rooms! Even Jehol and I come up for air more than that."

"You are to be congratulated," Jehol continued, still addressing Corum as if they were peers. "I was certain Buttercup would pine when she left pillow school."

"Over you perhaps?" Corum suggested softly, sensing where this was going and straining to contain a laugh. Handsome or not, a crude boy like this could never have interested Xishi.

"Oh, not over me," the boy demurred, surprising Corum. "It was our teaching tool who caught her eye. The prince was taken with her as well. They met in secret at night. Bit of a scandal. But I suppose women are fickle. How can a captive, if tragic, figure compete with the romance of a rich, free prince?"

"Well, he can't!" Erymita said with a silent laugh. "Which goes to show the students at the Purple Crane have a lot of sense."

"Sense and skill," Jehol purred, clearly enjoying himself.

Corum's face felt stiff and cold. He knew Erymita and the boy were being catty, but that didn't guarantee the accusation wasn't true. Xishi had mentioned the prince already, and she had seemed to view him in a romantic light. Was the scandal the reason Madame Fagin had parted with her early? Could Xishi have lost her heart to another man? Corum hated to think so, for this would mean the last four days had been no more than a pleasant professional fiction. Worse, her attraction to him might only have been the product of his personal genetic flaw.

Men weren't the only ones who went out of their heads while under the influence of kith.

"Excuse me," he said, offering Erymita an automatic bow. "I see a business associate I must greet."

Erymita looked annoyed at this brush-off, but Corum couldn't regret cutting her entertainment short. He saw no point in staying another moment with this pair's eyes on him.

It isn't true, he told himself as he strode through the glittering crowd. Xishi hadn't spent all her time dosed on his kith. She cared for him, not this Prince Pahndir. No matter what house had trained her, no pillow girl was that expert at deceit.

In his anger at the possibility that she was, he forgot how embarrassed—and unsure—he'd been about his own feelings.

That was then

~~

Xishi's rooms echoed with silence now that Cor was gone. She paced them back and forth from the lantern-lit courtyard to the secure door. She had no books in which to lose herself, no maid, and when the valet, Habii, stopped in briefly to leave her meal, he acted strangely—miming shushing motions on his own mouth rather than chatting with her in his previous friendly way.

Xishi guessed he was too stunned by her being his master's mate to talk anymore.

Of course, he wasn't the only one who was stunned. She had wanted to be Cor's lover, his cherished pillow girl and friend. Instead, her body had somehow tricked his into this other bond. Adjusting would have been easier if he'd seemed happy about it, but he did not. As soon as his rut was over, he hadn't been able to get away from her fast enough.

With no one to judge her for being visibly upset, she stopped in the arch between her two rooms and pressed both hands to her mouth. What was going to happen to her?

To them? Cor's mother would have an aneurysm when she found out. She'd be convinced she'd been right to banish Xishi all those years ago.

The Corynna Midarri of her memories had adored her son beyond anything. It wasn't impossible to imagine that she'd try to have Xishi killed; these were royals she was dealing with, the most scheming set of people known to yama. But what would happen to Cor if his mother succeeded? Would he sink into depression like Prince Pahndir? Or would he shrug off the loss of her in relief?

No matter what Cor believed about her being the only female who could arouse him, it might be possible for him to find another match. Few royals were like Prince Pahndir. Most had a handful of potential mates; though, from what she'd read at school, once a pair was bonded, another mate couldn't activate until the first black of a prince's eye had died. If that was true for Cor, maybe she should begin considering escape.

"Stop it," she whispered to the empty rooms. "You're jumping at shadows you've cast yourself."

Corynna probably wasn't going to kill her, and certainly not tonight because she didn't know what had happened yet. Cor had implied he was going to keep their mating secret for a while. They had time to sort this out somehow. Xishi didn't need to plan on fleeing for her life . . . unless Cor's mother had guessed the truth and hired the man who'd followed them to confirm it.

"She couldn't have," she told herself. No one in their right mind would have thought she could be Cor's mate, even if Corynna had discovered "Buttercup's" true identity.

One thing was certain: This mating business had been more enjoyable when her sole concern was how Cor would take her next.

When he knocked on the door and called her name, she had to force her legs not to run to him.

This turned out to be the last of her restraint. He offered her a crooked smile, and she flung her arms around him and burst into tears. She'd been afraid she wouldn't see him at all.

"Shh," he said against her hair as he eased her into the room. "It's all right. I'm here. I brought a bottle of wine. I thought we could share a glass and talk."

His warmth was wonderful, but Xishi pushed back from him and dried her face. "I'm sorry, Cor, for everything."

"Why should you be sorry? None of this is your fault. Help me move this little table, and we'll sit in your courtyard."

Xishi helped him, suddenly aware of how intensely—and inappropriately—elated she was. Cor was here and he was not icy, just calm and kind. Her happiness forced her to admit that part of her had been dreaming of this. Part of her wasn't sorry she'd never have to share him with a wife—no matter how uncomfortable being his mate would be.

Inappropriate or not, part of her had always been in love with him.

The realization made her shy as they pulled two chairs up to the table. Because the night was cool, she activated the heating element under the paved area. While she did this, Cor popped the cork and poured glasses.

"It's human wine," he said. "I hope you don't mind."

Though she'd never had it, Xishi shook her head.

The first sip was smoky and exotic, and her hands stopped trembling. Cor reached across the table to cover one. The gesture was so sweet, so welcome, Xishi's tears almost spilled again. His face looked serious in the lantern light.

"I want to keep this development to ourselves," he began. "At least until I can consult my lawyers."

"Your lawyers?" Her eyes widened. She didn't know what lawyers had to do with this.

"My parents might want to disown me."

Xishi gasped. "Your mother would never stand for that!"

"Maybe not, but she and my father value family honor. However blameless both of us may be, a match between us cannot enhance that. I need to know what it would take to fight such an action and, if I choose not to, which of my assets would be mine to take away."

"To take away," Xishi repeated. "You mean you might have to give up the businesses you've built?"

Cor turned his wineglass in a circle, though his manner was composed otherwise. "Giving you up is not an option. Living without you would be torture."

This was a statement of biological fact and not romance. Consequently, she was surprised to see his eyes drop shyly.

"You would be free to leave me once your contract is up."

"Cor!" she exclaimed, squeezing the hand that had been covering hers. "I wouldn't do that."

When he looked up, his gaze was worried. "I would understand if you wanted to. Your body is only bound to mine because of my kith, and that effect wears off. If you left me, you would be free to pursue . . . other affections."

"You are my affection," she said gently, hardly able to believe he needed this assurance. But he must have, because his shoulders relaxed.

"I *have* grown more attached to you than I expected."

Xishi's smile was soft but irrepressible. "You mean besides being addicted to the way I smell."

"Yes." He brought her hands to his mouth to kiss. "I've discovered I want us to be more comfortable with each other. I want us to have a relationship outside the bedroom. I want to know everything there is to know about you."

This declaration held a hint of defiance, as if he knew how deeply those of his class would disapprove. Xishi wasn't offended. She sensed what an adjustment this was for him, and she admired him for putting as brave a face on it as he could—even if she would rather he felt something warmer than "attachment." Some would say she should be grateful he was too kind a royal to consider getting rid of her himself. Instead, he was giving them a chance to be happy, and that was more than she'd thought they had an hour ago.

"Ask me anything," she said, the love she felt for him a tinder flaring in her chest. "I'll do my best to answer."

~⊛~

Though he'd requested it, her openness took him aback. Or maybe it just made him nervous. He was much calmer now that his heat was gone. His ability to think clearly had been restored, and yet he could not regard *her* coolly. He knew he didn't like the idea of her having fallen for someone else, but was he truly ready to know her now that he could see her through unclouded eyes? Was he ready to feel more of a bond between them than he already did? When she'd flung herself at him at the door, he'd savored her embrace every bit as much as when his hormones had been driving him. While he wanted their relationship to be good and friendly, life had taught him to be careful.

His emotions had betrayed him before.

He drew one hand back from hers to pick up his wine. The fortifying swallow gave him the courage to ask the question he most wanted the answer to. "Tell me about the orphanage."

Her face fell into darkness as she lowered it. "They didn't hurt us, if that's what you mean."

In spite of himself, he leaned forward. "What do you mean they did not hurt you? Were they cruel in some other way?"

She shook her head. "They did what they thought was right, but there were rules, and they didn't always suit me."

"What rules?"

She pulled a face at her glass. "Rule-rules. Infinite Mercy wanted their orphans to be perfect yama, to increase the chances for adoption. Since I was never perfect, they didn't want the other children being friends with me. They'd warn them to keep away. I suppose they thought I was going to infect them with my strangeness."

"You weren't strange. You were different. And never as out of control as I was."

Xishi hitched one shoulder and let it fall. Cor's anger rose. An image came to him, as if it had been dragged bumping on a string behind her words. In his mind, he saw a child cringing away from her, big-eyed and frightened, no more than four or five, and Xishi's throat so tight with hurt she couldn't swallow. They'd made her think she was a monster when nothing could have been further from the truth.

"You were *wonderful*," he said more strongly. "And, what's more, you used to know that."

Her eyes swam with tears as they came up. "You're right. I did used to know that. I thought I'd hung onto myself all these years, thought I'd kept my spirit strong, but coming back here reminds me how confident I used to be. When I was little, I believed I was magic. I never cared what people thought. I was the heroine in those stories I used to tell. I was the giant and the witch and the genie who smashed his bottle."

"And then my mother sent you away."

"Your nurse, Matreya, told me you'd never get over your problems unless I left. And you have gotten over them, so maybe she was right. Maybe it would have been better for both of us if I'd stayed away."

He couldn't help himself. He pulled her up from her chair and hugged her. Her head fit naturally beneath his chin. "It wouldn't be better, it would just be different. I'd spend my life mate-less, and you'd be the most sought after pillow girl in yamish lands."

She laughed through her sniffles. "You're not the Prince of Ice, you're a flatterer."

"I speak only truth," he intoned, then tipped her head back to stroke her cheek with his thumb.

Corum didn't know if she was magic, but that chi of hers surely was. He still loved touching her, still felt the tingle of her energy on his skin. If human chi felt anything like this, he understood how the rohn who lived among them could become addicted. His cock began to thicken, the process slower than it had been when he was in rut but all the more sensual. Their gazes locked without him quite deciding they ought to.

"Your hair looks nice tonight," she murmured, her hands smoothing down its unbound length. "You've never worn it this way for me."

"Haven't I?" His voice was as soft as hers.

She shook her head shyly, her stroke stopping at his hips. "I wanted you to. I wanted to see it on my naked body, to feel it sliding over my skin."

Even with no heat to goad him, her words were enough to engorge the tissues of his penis with what felt like half of his blood volume.

"Would you like to feel it on you now?" he asked huskily.

Her fingertips brushed electricity across his mouth. "I want so many things it would take a lifetime to do them all."

He bit the finger that was tracing his lower lip, holding it captive for the teasing flick of his tongue. Her blush sent a fresh wave of heat rolling through his groin.

"When you lick me like that," she whispered, "I can feel it between my legs."

He didn't care if the pillow school had taught her to talk this way. He groaned and lifted her for his kiss, savaging her mouth as if he were still in rut. Xishi clung to him just as eagerly, tugging at his silver sash with an absolute disregard for the fortune in diamonds its mountings held.

"Please help," she said between hungry kisses. "I really want you unclothed."

"I'm not rushing this," he swore, even as he tore the sleeves from his arms. "It's been too long since I had the patience to take my time."

"No," she agreed, her hand immediately sliding between his black-trousered thighs. "No rushing."

He sucked a breath as her fingers compressed his balls in a swath of silk.

"Does that still feel good?" she asked, though he couldn't imagine why she needed to. He'd moved his feet wider the moment she began. "The manuals say keeping your testicles and perineum well massaged will facilitate ejaculation during your next heat."

He laughed, too happy to hold it in. "I love it when you talk dirty."

He swung her up into his arms so quickly she let out a squeak. Her hands tightened pleasurably behind his neck. He loved the sensation of her holding onto him this way, of him being her sole support.

The soft curves of her body weren't bad, either.

"Are you taking me to bed?" she asked.

"Yes, I am, Buttercup. What's more, I might not let you out for a while."

⟞⟝

When he turned that molten silver gaze on her, it was difficult to remember that any trouble remained between them. They were too obviously of one mind about what they wanted this minute. Cor's proud face was flushed with arousal, his hands as sure as steel. Xishi was buzzing with anticipation as he set her down beside her bed. He tugged off her robe and gently turned her around.

For one sweet, melting minute, he pulled her against him, her naked back to his trousered front, his arms wrapped snugly beneath her breasts. The silk-covered hump of his erection was hot and hard as he rubbed it slowly across her spine.

Then he nudged her away from him.

"Climb onto the bed," he said, his tone so dark it made her shiver. "Facedown. You'll want that bolster under your hips."

Her body pulsed from head to toe at his order. Evidently, her fondness for his lovemaking wasn't going to lessen just because she hadn't tasted his kith tonight.

"That's it," he said as she clambered up and lay down with the hard, round pillow beneath her hips. The bolster was large, and it shoved her bottom into the air. The breeze from the courtyard cooled the moisture running from her sex. She arched her spine at the sensation, unable to stop herself from shifting her knees wider.

The sound of Cor hastily divesting himself of his trousers made her glad she had. Presumably naked, he braced his hands on either side of her thighs, leaning close enough that the heat of his next exhalation washed across her pussy.

"Oh, yes," he said even more softly. "That's exactly what I want to see."

She sensed he didn't want her to look at him. Having sex under no influence but their own was different: more intimate and naked. His mouth brushed what she'd bared for him, a tease of lips and tongue that left reluctantly. She closed her eyes as his weight depressed the mattress, then bit her lip as his big, warm hands ran over the halves of her uplifted rear. They slid the length of her back up to her shoulders. There they smoothed her hair aside.

"You're so beautiful," he murmured, squeezing muscles that had grown taut. "It's going to be hard to wait even now."

She was tempted to beg him not to, but the first whispering sweep of his long black hair changed her mind. He had gathered it into a tail and was teasing its silken thickness in winding patterns across her spine. She sighed his name with pleasure and was rewarded by a licking kiss on her vertebrae.

"You like this," he said, "even without my kith."

She squirmed in answer, the curves of her bottom bumping his erection. She couldn't doubt he liked what they were doing. His breath caught at the contact, and he slid one hand between the covers and her chest. The soft flesh of her breast spilled over his grip. When he found the hardness of her nipple, his fingers scissored together to pinch it tight.

This was enough to make her cry out softly, but then that sensation was joined by his cock head delving through her folds. His mouth came down to nip her ear.

"I'll never tire of this," he said, the fat, smooth head pushing with tormenting slowness along her cleft. "You dripping down my prick like you can't wait for me to slide in."

"It's hard to wait," she admitted with another wriggle she could not control. Determined to make the waiting just as hard for him, she stretched one hand under her belly and through her legs. She could touch him then, could rub the slippery crest of him with her fingertips.

A more forceful roll of his pelvis said he liked that.

Curious, and for once clearheaded enough to recall her lessons, she dipped one finger into her juices before running it gently over the spot she remembered as the mysterious unnamed "purple thingie."

That drew a ragged moan from him.

"Oh, yes," he said, the words throaty. "I'm very sensitive there."

It was difficult to be sure, but she thought she felt an extra bit of firmness beneath the taut, hot skin, perhaps another gland, one too secret for pillow girls to know about. Whatever the truth, he enjoyed the added pressure—and enjoyed it even more when she circled the spot with her thumb. He began to writhe slowly against her, the tension in his body ratcheting up.

"I have to get inside you," he warned, though she was more than agreeable. "You're making this feel too good."

As soon as he nudged her entrance, she realized another difference from being under the influence of his kith. She was wet and eager, but her sheath was nowhere near as relaxed. He felt absolutely huge pushing into her, deliciously huge, but a little alarming, too.

He cursed as he registered her constriction. "I'm sorry, Xishi. I can try to make myself smaller."

He grunted as he worked to do it, his girth changing inside her in a series of sharp pulses. This allowed him to push deeper, but obviously it wasn't easy. The strain of maintaining the smaller size wound him so tight his body was shaking.

"Okay," he huffed when he was halfway in, "this is a little harder than I expected."

"Cor?" she said, feeling how fiercely he had to concentrate to stay as he was. "I think I liked it better the other way."

That was all it took to fray his control. His cock throbbed once, and he was huge again. He groaned with pleasure and tried to push, but now it was as difficult as before.

"Sorry," he panted. "I need more practice at this."

She could only moan in encouragement. Her hand was still between her legs, and she couldn't resist touching him where his shaft stretched her pussy's mouth.

"Shit," he breathed, his frustration a kind of praise. "Hold on. I'm going to get us past this."

With another grunt of determination, he swung his right foot flat onto the mattress and gripped her hip with his left hand. This gave him the leverage he needed for penetration, and the bliss of that long possession dragged sounds of pleasure from both their throats.

From that point forward, each push and pull seemed a gift. Slowly, surely they rose toward culmination, their bodies coiling and relaxing, rubbing and arching, as the excitement grew.

Cor's hold on her hip and breast tightened by degrees, his formerly smooth breathing shredding to pieces.

"It's so good," he gasped in marvel. "Xishi, it's so good."

She couldn't have seen his face even if she tried, but he was hiding it against her shoulder. His grunts of entry vibrated there every time he pushed. His hair pooled around her like a cloak of silk. With her free hand, she reached up and held the back of his head. The way they were wrapped together felt so tender she could have cried.

"Cor," she moaned a second before her sensitivity increased.

And then it was more than sensitivity. She was coming as slowly as they were making love, each flutter of her inner muscles clear. Heat expanded from her center like a newborn sun, her chi radiating outward with the orgasm. All beings' energy spiked at climax, but she had never known hers to swell like this. Though the peak didn't have the violence of the last four days, it was the most comforting orgasm she'd ever known. The energy didn't even feel like chi, but like pure well-being.

The effect must have pleased Cor as well. He made a low, rough sound and shoved up against her even tighter, every possible inch of him pressed to her. His cock throbbed inside her, and though he could no longer ejaculate, she knew he was coming, too.

Twice more the incredible slow-motion climax ebbed and crested, after which they both sagged onto her bed like overcooked noodles. Cor's cock slid from her in relaxation. For one long, contented minute, he did nothing but nuzzle her cheek.

"You're amazing," he said. "However they taught you to do that, you're amazing."

She wriggled around beneath him until they were face to face. She laid her hand against his jaw. "They couldn't teach me that. It's you who brings it out in me. It's us together."

He looked at her, his expression sleepy and relaxed. She couldn't tell if he was convinced. "Ask me for a favor. I want to do something nice for you."

"You have, Cor. I loved what we did tonight."

"Then I want to give you more. Please. It would make me happy." He pretended to bite her nose. "Diamonds, maybe. Or a special license to ride in an aircar anytime you want."

The special license appealed to her more than the diamonds, but she knew she might never get a better chance to ask the favor that had been shadowing the back of her mind.

She drew a circle with one fingertip on his chest.

"You could help my friend," she said. "If it's possible. The one I mentioned from the pillow house."

His body stiffened.

"He's being treated like a slave," she said hastily, compelled to try in spite of this less than auspicious reaction. "A prince just like you. His wife died, and he loved her, and she was his only match. When he couldn't get over losing her, his family had him shut away and told everyone he'd died. He doesn't deserve that, Cor. He's a good man."

Cor's face was as smooth as a frozen pond. "And what, exactly, do you propose I do?"

"Maybe you could buy out his contract. I know it would be expensive, but Madame Fagin likes money. I promise I'd try to find a way to pay you back."

Cor pulled away from her and sat up. "Perhaps you could pay me back by making the rounds."

The words were spoken so calmly, they took a moment to sink in. "Cor!"

"Well, really, Buttercup, how else could a pillow girl expect to reimburse a debt like that?"

"I know it's a lot to ask." Cautious, but needing to touch him, she laid a hand on his thigh. "I just hate to think of him trapped there for his whole life."

Cor looked at her, then let out a roar of rage and pain

she'd never thought to hear from a yamish being. When this primal scream failed to exorcize his fury, he took a handful of her crystal curtains and wrenched it so hard he pulled half the metal track out of the ceiling.

"Fuck!" he shouted like a madman. "Fuck!"

Without realizing she had moved, Xishi found herself shrunk back against the headboard with her arms wrapped around her knees.

"Tell me," he demanded, his attention targeting her once more. "Why did Madame Fagin have an early sale this year?"

He was panting from his outburst, his eyes as hot and angry as they'd been cool before. Xishi willed her teeth to stop chattering. "P-people said she had some losses on the stock market."

"*People* said. But you knew different. It was you she was hoping to cut her losses on. Because you and this Prince Pahndir became involved."

He had spit the words out. "Not exactly," Xishi replied.

"Not exactly isn't a no."

"It was more complicated than that. There was another student who—"

Cor cut her off. "Just tell me if you have feelings for this prince. And so help you, do not lie again."

His hands were curled into fists. Xishi forced herself to release her knees. She had lied the first time because she was afraid, but she wouldn't insult her pride that way again. She lifted her chin. "Prince Pahndir is a good man. He doesn't deserve to be a prisoner."

Cor's mouth twisted. "I'll take that as a yes."

"What do you want me to say?" she said, her temper bristling. "That I hate him? That I'm madly in love with you while you stand there berating me?"

A muscle bunched in his jaw as he gritted it.

"I liked him," she said. "He stirred my sympathy."

"You were more than sympathetic. You were attracted."

"What if I was? I'm a woman, Cor, not a stone. And, yes, if you really want to know, at this particular moment I'm thinking I am fonder of him than you."

He blanched at that, but she wouldn't apologize. He'd abused her enough since he'd brought her here, accusing her of drugging him, blowing hot and cold for who knew what reason, and now this. Caring about a fellow yamish being was not a crime!

A second later she was sorry. He drew back from the bed, pulling his dignity around him like a mantle of snow.

"Forgive me, Buttercup. I had no idea my company was so distasteful. I will spare you from it at once."

"Cor—"

He ignored her, bending gracefully to retrieve his robes from the floor. He shrugged them on and tied them, apparently satisfied with leaving his trousers where they lay. Xishi scrambled after him to the sitting room.

"Your Highness," she tried before he could close the secret door behind him. Her use of his title simply narrowed his eyes.

"I expect I'll see you next month," he said.

His upper lip was just barely curled, a perfectly respectable royal sneer. Seeing him regain his control, and in such an insulting manner, caused her to lose hers completely.

"Not if I see you first," she snapped and slammed the stupid hidden passageway in his face.

A sob caught in her throat, but she refused to release it. Crying would not help her—or Prince Pahndir. In fact, chances seemed very good that nothing was going to help either one of them.

"Fuck," she said, taking a page from Cor's tantrum.

Faintly, behind the wall, she heard his feet stomping up the stairs.

⤸

Given his preference, Corum would have spent the next ten years in a cave, trying to forget his humiliation at the scene he'd just enacted. Unfortunately, a sound in his private office warned him he was not alone. He found his valet polishing the holoplate on his desk.

"Habii," he said, his voice odd and disconnected in the dim-lit room. "What are you doing here at this hour?"

Habii turned and gaped at him. "I did not expect you back from the party yet." He paused uncertainly. "Forgive me for asking, Master, but are you well?"

Only then did Cor remember his legs were bare. Suspecting this wasn't the only oddity in his appearance, he raked his tousled hair back distractedly. As he did, the silver streak caught his eye. *My mark of shame,* he thought with an inner bark of laughter, experiencing a sudden longing to yank it out by the roots. Knowing how deeply his valet admired him, he suppressed the urge.

"I am well," he said as evenly as he could.

"And Miss Buttercup?"

Miss Buttercup had proven herself to be the nightmare every royal male dreaded: the mate who inspired one to fall in love while giving her heart elsewhere. Outwardly, Corum's peers might pity the emperor his plight. Inwardly, they prayed they'd be immune.

"Miss Buttercup is well," Corum said, the answer grating unnaturally.

Habii's mustache twitched in worry. "Her situation has not changed?"

His valet truly had been charmed. Whatever tale he'd spun to account for Xishi being his master's mate, it allowed him to continue thinking well of her.

Abruptly exhausted, Corum sank into one of his silver-blue yokeback chairs, barely noticing when the automated back realigned itself to support his spine. He was drowning in lies tonight—the ones he'd told, the ones he'd heard, the ones that were sure to unravel without bringing joy to a single soul. Worse than the lies was the awful truth. The woman he'd just realized he loved, the woman his flawed genetics had bound him to, loved another man.

I am fonder of him than you, she'd said, which—for a yama—amounted to a vow of undying devotion.

"I'll bring you some wine," Habii said, no doubt reading the turmoil in his energy.

He returned almost before Corum noticed he had gone. He set the flask of traditional heated rice wine in its warmer on an inlaid table, then poured a small steaming cup and placed it in Corum's hands. Corum drank it in a single swallow, but refused a second cup. The first had caused his eyes to well up with tears, and he did not wish them to overflow.

"It's all right," Habii said gently, crouched before his master's chair. "Matters of the heart can trouble any man."

At that point, Corum had no recourse but to hide his face in his hands.

Estranged

The next three miserable weeks had few bright spots. The weather was as gloomy as Xishi's mood—fall having fallen with an especially wet vengeance. The first storm had stripped every leaf from her courtyard trees, but she'd refused to remain cooped indoors. Screwing up her nerve, she'd had one of Cor's private guards escort her out each day. They were too serious about their jobs to make conversation, and their insistence on her carrying defensive weapons made her uneasy, but their silent company was a fraction better than brooding in her rooms.

Listening to the endless patter on their floating rainshields created at least the illusion that every person in the world wasn't bent on avoiding her.

She'd returned from her latest outing with her robes soaked through by a gusting wind the rainshield had not been able to defend against. Her escort couldn't have been any drier than she was, though her apologies seemed to offend him.

"This is my job," he'd finally said. "It is my honor to protect the prince's pillow girl."

Xishi was sure the tears that sprang to her eyes weren't the appropriate response to his words. She'd turned away before he could see them, but not before they'd warned her how shaky her control was. Now she wanted a steaming shower, a hot meal, and a thick, warm blanket to hide under while she recovered from the crying jag she intended to indulge in while she washed up.

In light of these wishes—though she'd been missing her friends more than ever—finding one curled up on her bed was almost unwelcome.

"Tea Rose!" Xishi exclaimed, hoping the redness of her nose and eyes could be mistaken for a product of the cold outside. She wondered how the girl had gotten in, then decided she must have charmed Habii. "What are you doing here?"

Tea Rose, who appeared to have been drowsing, unfolded her slender body and stretched like a cat. "One of the regular working girls at the Purple Crane has been engaged by your master's head of staff. I asked if I could tag along and give him a surprise." The creamy satisfaction in her expression said this surprise had been well received. "I'm glad you finally came back. My pass expires in three hours."

"I went for a walk." Xishi turned to the console table where her yamaweb unit was concealed. The natal day plate the students at the Purple Crane had chipped in to buy for her sat there as well. Reminded of other, very different times, she busied herself with peeling off her damp outer robes. When she hung them on the back of a chair, the little charge-knife she'd shoved in the pocket clinked on the wood. The guard had said she could keep it, that she should always carry it.

With an effort, Xishi turned her focus back to her guest. "I'm sorry I didn't know you were here."

Tea Rose came to her side and put one hand on her shoulder. "What's the matter, Buttercup? You seem troubled."

She considered lying, but she'd had no one to talk to

for so long that the implicit offer of sympathy tempted her too much.

"Cor and I had a fight."

" 'Cor,' is it?" said Tea Rose. She sat on the edge of the console table. "I wasn't aware pillow girls were allowed to fight with their masters, but if you're on a first-name basis, I suppose you can."

"He's been avoiding me. We haven't seen each other in weeks."

"Well, that's not good." Tea Rose wrapped her hands around one knee, her examination of Xishi's face too close for comfort. "If you're not holding up your end of the contract, he might decide to send you back."

"He won't," Xishi said, though the certainty caused no joy.

She had been running her hands around the border of the birthday plate. Tea Rose covered it and stopped her. "You can't be sure of that," she said. "I know, compared to most people, you're a little sun everyone wants to get closer to, but it doesn't pay to be overconfident."

"He won't send me back. He can't."

"Can't?" Tea Rose had both brows raised.

Xishi pulled out the chair and sat. Tea Rose's expression was curious but mild. Xishi trusted her for the most part. She wasn't the gossip Mingmar was, though Xishi had observed that Tea Rose was more practical in her priorities. And maybe that was for the best. Right then she felt in need of practical advice.

"How good are you at keeping secrets?"

"Please." Tea Rose waved a graceful hand. "I'm the queen of the secret keepers—which you have reason to know, given how quiet I kept your meetings with Prince Pahndir."

"I know, but this is big."

Tea Rose took her hand and squeezed it. "I'm your friend, Buttercup, and—though you may not know it—there aren't many yama who are more loyal, or more useful, to have at your back. You can tell me anything."

"I believe you," Xishi said, then filled her lungs with air and let it out. "My master and I are mates."

"Mates?" Tea Rose goggled. "You mean black-of-his-eye, genetic-match mates?"

"I know. It seems impossible, but it's true. His . . . his kith rose and everything."

"Well," said Tea Rose, clearly at a loss for words. "That's extraordinary. But that means you must have royal blood!"

"Hardly." Xishi spread her hands to indicate her atypically curved figure. "I can barely pass for a decent rohn."

"You still could be some royal's illegitimate daughter. Your mother might have kept your parentage secret, and of course she was killed before you were old enough to hear the truth."

Tea Rose's familiarity with how her mother died made Xishi uncomfortable. They'd never talked about the past, but considering Tea Rose's talent for snooping, the pillow girl probably knew all the gory details.

Now Tea Rose gasped as an idea hit. "Maybe your mother was murdered to keep her quiet!"

"Then why was I left alive?"

"I don't know. But maybe your father has been waiting all these years to find a way to acknowledge you."

"Now who's being romantic?" Xishi teased ruefully. "I'm sure it's just some freak mutation in my genes, something no one could have predicted."

"Maybe." Tea Rose peered at her sideways. "But now that I look at you more closely, your nose does resemble the emperor's."

Xishi welcomed her attempt at humor, even if she couldn't quite join in. She knew whose mutation was responsible for her and Cor's bond, but that was a secret she wouldn't share with anyone. With a gusty sigh, she leaned forward on her knees.

"The problem is Cor thinks I'm in love with Prince Pahndir, and now he won't talk to me."

"Tell him you're not," Tea Rose advised instantly.

"I'm not sure he'll believe me. He was a beast about it. I'm afraid I implied I did like the prince better than him."

Tea Rose smiled unexpectedly. "You're angry at him."

"Of course I am."

"And he's feeling possessive because of all those hormones."

Xishi didn't like the idea that Cor's possessiveness was only hormones, but she had to admit that probably was the case. "I'm just not sure I can say I'm sorry and mean it. I thought I'd wait until he came into heat again and hope our differences sorted out themselves."

This seemed rather ineffectual said out loud, especially when Tea Rose gave her a dubious look.

"You can't wait," she said. "What if he hires another pillow girl, and you lose all this lovely power? The fact that he's jealous says you have a chance to make him fall in love with you. If you ask me, no amount of pride is too much to swallow in return for that."

"I can't be that sensible!" Xishi cried. "Sometimes I wish I could, but I can't. I don't think asking him to help Prince Pahndir was wrong, and I'm not sure I want his love if I can only get it by being someone I'm not. Am I supposed to never speak well of another man? Never have a friend he doesn't approve of? I want him to trust me, and accept me, as I am!"

This speech rang out more passionately than she'd meant. Tea Rose's mouth formed a startled O.

"You're in love with him," she whispered, then put out her hand. "Oh, Buttercup, I'm sorry."

Her tone made Xishi even grumpier. You'd have thought she'd told the other girl she was dying.

"Let's talk about something else," she said. "Tell me what you and Mingmar have been up to."

"Nothing but trouble," Tea Rose assured her, but the pity shone as clear as ever in her almond eyes.

⤚⤙

The fourth week of her isolation dawned too foul for Xishi to go out. Still on edge from her less than satisfying visit with Tea Rose, she tried to meditate—to recapture the Golden Breath of Peace she'd tasted as a child. Sadly, her mood could not reach serenity from where it was. Memories of all the reasons she was furious, and had a right to be, kept interrupting her attempts to quiet her mind.

Giving up, she decided to walk indoors.

Her wanderings were limited to Cor's wing of the palace, not only to avoid any chance meetings with his mother, but because her retinal pattern was not approved for access elsewhere.

Luckily, the Hall of Records was a neutral zone between Cor's part of the palace and the larger portion controlled by his parents. From its dozen data stations, any topic regarding the Midarri family—and, indeed, most topics involving the Forbidden City—could be researched. The ceiling was a coffered cavern faced in rich, dark wood, the carrels cozy niches where one could curl up on cushions to view the evening vids from centuries ago. Hardly anyone came here, but for some reason, the automated vat of coffee—a human drink Xishi's people had not been able to resist adopting—supplied a more delicious brew than any that was prepared by the staffed kitchens.

In the lonely, rainy days since Cor had stomped from her room, the Hall of Records had become a sanctuary for Xishi. It had no books of the kind she liked, but the endless collection of historical recordings did provide welcome distractions.

This being so, she could hardly be happy to round the corner to her favorite carrel and find Jehol lounging there.

The bulk of his muscle notwithstanding, she could not deny he was a handsome beast. He was sprawled on his side on a heap of pillows, lazily fast-forwarding a crackled holovid. Tiny figures darted around the Plaza of Justice. Jehol must have been replaying an old trial, though she marveled that he seemed to be enjoying it so much. He was positively smirking as he watched. Curious, she thought she recognized the emperor's formal blue, green, and crimson robes on one of the figures.

When her shadow fell across the projection, Jehol pulled out his earphones and sat up. To her surprise, he immediately shut off what he'd been viewing.

"Well, well, well," he said in a drawl that was more

insulting than his usual. "If it isn't Miss Buttercup. I thought I was fated to die of boredom while my mistress dissected every detail of her latest shopping expedition with Corynna Midarri. How delightful that you've come to brighten my wait."

Xishi knew she didn't look bright or even calm. Seeing him, remembering how abominably he'd treated Prince Pahndir, had her fuming for a new reason.

"Forgive me," she said stiffly. "I do not wish to interrupt. I'll leave you to your entertainment."

Before she could withdraw, Jehol caught her wrist.

"Nonsense," he said, the mocking light in his eye daring her to try to tug away. "You must keep me company, old schoolmates that we are. After all, it's not as if you have other calls on your time right now."

Xishi caught her breath involuntarily.

"Yes," he said, his other hand now playing with her fingers. "Everyone has heard about the unfortunate rift between Miss Buttercup and her formerly doting master. Princes can be so fickle. But please accept my sympathy."

A crocodile had more sympathy. Xishi yanked her wrist from his hold, but not before he'd gripped it tightly enough to leave a friction burn. Then and there, she jumped to a conclusion.

"You said something to Cor," she accused, refusing to clutch the abraded skin. "About me and Prince Pahndir."

"Did I?" Jehol examined his fingernails. "That would have been most unkind."

She didn't buy his mock innocent manner, nor did she think he meant her to. He wanted her to know he'd sabotaged her happiness, if only to add relish to his gloating.

"What did I ever do to you?" she asked in exasperation. "What possible reason could you have to wish me harm?"

Jehol's face turned dark and cold. "You were born, Buttercup. One piece of gutter trash whelped by another."

For a moment the unexpected answer, and the icy contempt with which it was uttered, simply confused her. Then a barrier inside her crumbled, and a well of rage she hadn't known was in her broke free.

"Take it back," she demanded, her entire body hot with anger. To her amazement, she had his throat in one hand and her charge-knife in the other. Though she couldn't remember keying up the blade, it was not retracted. Its sharp, shock-dealing tip pressed beneath his ear. It didn't seem to matter how outrageous this behavior was. She didn't hesitate more than a second before she pressed harder. "Take it back, Jehol. My mother was an honest maid. It wasn't her fault she was murdered."

Jehol's eyes had turned to circles at her attack, but her words enabled him to recover his air of superiority.

"My, oh, my," he said. "Look at the pillow girl's little stinger. I guess the apple doesn't fall too far from the tree."

"What are you talking about?" she hissed, more tempted than ever to depress the button that released the charge. The zap wouldn't kill him, just put him out. If he hadn't sounded so insufferably knowing, she was certain she would have. "What do you think you know about my mother?"

She was digging in harder with the knife, forcing Jehol to lean back on the pile of cushions or be nicked. In spite of this, he didn't seem to be taking the threat she posed seriously. She supposed he didn't have reason to. He could probably overpower her and take the weapon anytime he chose. Knowing this, she wished she were unhinged enough to open his vein.

"What could I know?" he said with that same deliberately unconvincing innocence. "Your mother's death is a mystery. Now are you going to prick me, or is this little drama strictly for fun?"

He licked his upper lip suggestively, his lamril dark and shining. His pupils were dilated. It seemed his mistress wasn't the only one who liked a bit of pain.

Xishi flung away from him in disgust, but the trickle of red running down his neck startled her enough to freeze her in her tracks. To her relief, the cut wasn't deep. It stopped bleeding almost as soon as he put his hand over it.

"Well, would you look at that," he said softly, turning his red-stained palm to her. "Miss Buttercup has drawn first blood."

❧

She had lost her mind.

It was the only explanation she could think of as she strode faster and faster down the palace halls. She was not stopped or questioned. All Cor's guards recognized her now, though a few did regard her strangely.

She was glad they hadn't seen her wipe her bloodied charge-knife on a nice curtain.

Xishi would never be an unemotional yama. She'd accepted that long ago. But discovering she had murderous tendencies was a bigger revelation than she could easily process.

I guess the apple doesn't fall too far from the tree.

Jehol's words returned with such unnerving clarity she had to duck into an alcove and close her eyes. The events of the last quarter hour caught up to her all at once. With one hand pressed to her breast, she tried to calm her galloping heart.

Jehol knew something about her mother, something to contradict the wistful, shadowy image of an honest maid. He knew, or thought he knew, she'd been involved in some scheme that had brought her murder on herself.

Xishi had always realized this was a possibility. Murders were uncommon among the lower class, and violent, bloody murders rarer yet. The whiff of shame that attached to them might not be fair, but occasionally it was warranted.

"What did you do?" she whispered to the twelfth-dynasty hanging with which she shared the alcove. "What sort of genetic legacy did you leave me?"

Naturally, no one answered, nor could she hope to force Jehol to be forthcoming. He'd gain far more joy from sitting on what she wished to know.

I don't need to know, she told herself. She straightened her shoulders. Her hand still clenched the charge-knife in her pocket, but she didn't force herself to let it go.

The past was past. She was the person she made herself.

Which, at the moment, was a slightly mad and murderous pillow girl.

She pressed her lips together with grim humor. She

hadn't realized it before, but being this angry was like being drunk. The thought occurred to her that if her normal self-control was going to be impaired, she might as well use this recklessness to her benefit. To do any less would only give Jehol more reasons to exult in her misfortune.

~~~~~

Corum tried to pretend his life hadn't changed. He conducted business and visited friends and continued his practice sessions with Master Ping. Outwardly, he succeeded. Inwardly, he was a wreck.

Sleep evaded him, socializing seemed a bore, and Habii was threatening to force-feed him if he had to call the tailor to take in his clothes again.

"Miss Buttercup eats," he said behind Corum now. The valet was combing his master's hair a bit too briskly into its evening braid. "Miss Buttercup enjoys her friends and takes nice walks."

He shifted in the styling chair, trying not to grimace as Habii yanked his scalp again. He presumed Xishi's example was meant to prick his pride, and it did—just not the way Habii hoped.

Corum's heart was broken. Hers seemed perfectly fine.

He hadn't been able to bring himself to consult his lawyers. Explaining what had happened would involve too much that depressed him. The only portion of his person that still seemed alive was his sex organs. They were counting off the hours to his next heat, to the moment he'd have no choice but to face the source of his shame again.

That shame intensified at knowing he was looking forward to being forced into her company. Then he wouldn't be depressed. Then he'd barely have to think at all.

A pounding on the outer door stopped Habii's comb mid-tug.

"Who could that be?" He sniffed before going off to see.

A dangerous joy

Corum had missed many things about Xishi. Her softness haunted him most, and her delicious smell, but her voice was definitely on the list. The added warmth she could put into the simplest phrase was a pleasure he hadn't known it would be so difficult to do without.

When he heard her voice ordering Habii to reveal where his master was, he did not at first register its wildness, only his deep, visceral relief that his mate was there.

His heart was pounding too hard for comfort as he came to the door of his dressing room. It opened into his formal entryway, which was clad from floor to ceiling in stainless steel panels. The ambience was different from the one he'd created for Xishi's rooms, but she did not appear intimidated. Looking furious, she pushed past Habii's halfhearted attempt to block her path. When she caught sight of him, she stopped.

"You," she said, the syllable accusative.

Corum folded his arms, wondering—despite his unavoidable enjoyment of her presence—what cause she had to be mad at *him*.

"Don't give me that look," she said. "I'm done waiting for you to come to your senses. Done waiting for you to save me. I'm taking charge of getting what I want."

Corum had the sensation that his brows had crawled onto his scalp. "You're taking charge? Excuse me, but you must be drunk."

She stalked across the brushed steel floor to where he stood, the low heels of her slippers echoing. She poked her index finger into his breastbone. "I'm not drunk. I'm angry and fed up. And you're going to hear me out."

She was showing the manners of a child, but it didn't matter. His cock began to swell the second she came toe to toe with him—which didn't mean his pride couldn't do the same.

"You are free to speak anytime," he said coolly.

Her scowl darkened at his tone. "I love you," she said, "not Prince Pahndir. I'm sorry if you have trouble believing that, or if you're uncomfortable hearing the words, but you left me little choice but to speak the truth."

Corum stared at her, temporarily unable to get his mental footing. She loved him? She loved *him* and not Prince Pahndir? What sort of yama said such things out loud? His face heated with a mixture of embarrassment, disbelief, and nearly violent hope.

Habii cleared his throat. "Forgive me, Master. I find I must return to my chambers now."

Corum didn't look away from Xishi to watch him flee, though he did wait until the door shut to speak again.

"You love me," he said, aiming for skepticism but not calm enough to succeed.

Xishi folded her arms to match his, a gesture distinctly altered by the generous swell of her breasts. "I do, but I'm not going to tolerate you treating me badly on that account. I asked you to help a friend, not a lover."

Corum's head felt like it was floating—though that could have been the effect of the blood rerouting to his groin. She had not retracted her declaration. He hadn't been mistaken in what he heard. The degree to which he wanted to believe her was alarming. He must not let her make a fool of him this easily. "Why are you telling me this now?"

Her jaw clenched mutinously. "Because I don't want you hiring another pillow girl!"

The thought of doing this had not crossed his mind. Knowing it had crossed hers had his face stretching in response.

"Don't you grin at me," she said. "I'm not just your pillow girl anymore. *You're* the one who said I was wonderful, and I'm damn well going to be enough for you by myself."

"I don't know." He pretended to shake his head doubtfully. "Most princes have wives *and* pillow girls. You'd be taking on quite a burden to handle me alone, not to mention undercutting my dignity. People would say I had no standards."

Her shriek of feminine fury was a sound he'd never suspected could fill him with elation—though that emotion muted when he saw she was fighting tears.

"Shh," he said, taking hold of her before she could pummel him. "I love you, too."

Her eyes were wide as she craned her head to look at him.

"Yes," he assured her a little hoarsely. "So help me, I really do."

"It's not just hormones making you say that?"

"Well, I've had three whole weeks without them to learn the difference."

"You're not going to hire another pillow girl?"

"That idea never occurred to me. You—" He paused to steady his voice. "For many reasons besides the physical, you are the only woman I want to be with."

His confession, which contained no extravagant assertions, calmed them both—though, perversely, he did have to fight an urge to express his admiration in more detail.

She saved him by biting her lip. "Cor," she said. "I'm sorry I lost control."

"I'm not." He stroked her hair to settle her head against him. "Seeing you in a fury was as exciting as you claimed my shoving you in your shower was."

"I haven't forgotten that," she said, but the warning wasn't all anger. Her arms hugged his waist meaningfully. Encouraged by the pressure, Corum's cock lifted even more.

"Want to balance the scales by shoving me in mine?"

One corner of her mouth tilted. "That would be fair. Then you'd be as wet as I am."

~~~

Oh, she did love watching his eyes go black as her words sank in. Cor took a second to catch his breath.

"I'm two days off yet," he rasped, his fingers tightening unconsciously on her arms. "At least I think I am."

Using his most princely manner as her model, Xishi pushed him backward into his dressing room. "I don't care if you're two *weeks* off, Your Highness. I'm ready enough for both of us."

She was ready, and readier yet when he flushed. Cor stumbled back at her unexpected assertiveness, the grin he rarely let out starting to crack. Despite being caught off balance, his next words were exultant. "You really didn't like doing without me."

The growl that issued from her throat was unintentional. "As soon as I get your clothes off, you're going to show me how much you didn't like it, too."

When he immediately dropped his robes and shucked his trousers, they almost didn't make it to his shower. Those robes of his hid such marvels—the golden skin that stretched over his shoulders, the haze of hair she still found so exotically male. His navel was a graceful interruption to its final plunge. She had to press her thighs together at what the last thin line arrowed to. His cock was thick, all veins and shudders, and it thrust out straight enough that she wanted to test its hardness without delay.

"No," he said when her hand came out to touch its quivering tip. "I know which part of you I want on me first."

"If it isn't the same part I want, we may have to negotiate."

Rather than argue, he stripped her as naked as he was, his hands swift and businesslike except for their heat. All the same, she knew he liked what he uncovered. His eyes stayed black as he carried her into his bathing room, where their sensitivity obliged him to order the lights on low.

More steel abounded here, continuing into the wrap-around shower. When he pushed her backward into its shining wall, the metal made a soft booming sound. He loomed all around her: his body, his breath, his heat. He seemed to have forgotten she was supposed to be manhandling him. His hands slid up her sides, catching her breasts with wonderful firmness before reluctantly releasing them.

"Which part," he asked as he caged her between his arms, "were you thinking of putting on me?"

Xishi licked her upper lip, delighting in the way his eyes followed the tip of her tongue around. His face hardened with lust as he guessed what she was telling him.

"You can have five minutes with your mouth on me. And then I'm taking you properly."

"Oh," she said soft as silk, "I think I can get you to beg for more than five."

More confident of her power than she'd ever been, she trailed her hands down his ribs while sinking to her knees. It was so good to touch him again, to smooth her hands over the tight-packed muscles of his stomach, to give those powerful thighs a squeeze. Loving every inch of him, she breathed against the pulsing head of his cock.

"Turn on the spray," she said when he shivered. "This steel floor is cold."

"My lady's wish—" he began, then moaned with pleasure as her lips engulfed his crest.

He fumbled for a good ten seconds before he found the shower controls.

She took this as a compliment. Cor was so easy to please—and so pleasing to please, what with all his sensitive spots. His testicles overspilled her massaging palm, their fullness exaggerated by the tightening of their skin. When she slid her fingers farther, to his perineum, the pounding of the spray could not drown out his groans.

Though the steam rose quickly, she didn't miss the growing redness of his three kith glands. Knowing what was happening to him was a warm, soft hook tugging at her sex. He was coming into heat sooner than he'd thought, perhaps for no better reason than that she was there. As she sank up and down his shaft, she began to taste the first slight seepage of his kith from his penile slit. The hint of spice was enough to make her body tighten on itself.

Naturally, neither of them was counting, but she suspected his five minutes had long since passed before he admitted she'd proved her point.

"You win," he gasped as she dug her tongue into the slightly firmer spot above his opening. "That feels too good to stop."

After all their time apart, she didn't think she could have stopped. She was obsessed with making this silken hardness hers again, with forcing it to give up its last secret.

It seemed it would do so. The patch of skin on which she was focused grew hotter beneath her laving. With a moan of pleasure, Cor's hold tightened on her ears, his palms blocking out the sound of the pelting shower. She could hear her own racing heartbeat, her own ragged breathing. She tried to soothe him by running her hands over his clenching legs, but the jerk and push of his pelvis didn't calm. He was too big now, too long and thick to risk losing control while he was in her mouth. Knowing there was no way he could shift his size smaller now, she wrapped one hand around his base to ensure he could not choke her.

He cried out suddenly and hunched over. She thought she must have gripped him too hard, but when she tried to pull away in concern, she found he had her trapped by the hair.

"Please," he said, panting it. His head was braced against the metal wall above her, his face contorted in pain. He could barely get breath to speak. "Lick it. Keep licking it."

"It" was a tiny seam in the drum-tight skin of his glans, which she hadn't noticed until that moment. It was opening like a magic trick beneath her tongue. Within its smooth pink edges lay the crimson curve of Something Else.

"Cor," she breathed.

He wrapped more hair around his fist, obviously struggling against a compulsion to force her back. "Please, don't stop. Your saliva is coaxing it out."

Xishi stared at his glazed black eyes. Did he know what this part of him was, or was he acting on sheer instinct? She wasn't sure it mattered. Fear and desire had mixed a heady cocktail within her veins. She returned to licking him, to drowning him in the fluids of her mouth. He began to shudder rhythmically—an orgasm, she thought—one he didn't seem to want to end.

As he moaned hoarsely with pleasure, the thing began to unfurl.

～

Corum knew he'd die if she stopped, though it felt as if his glans were being split in two. No pain had ever been this ecstatically sexual. He climaxed through the lancing burn of the emergence, emissionless but intense, wanting to push and push and *push* until this new thing inside him won its freedom.

The next time she said his name, it held a note of fear.

He had to release her then, despite his wrench of regret. With a sense of inevitability, he opened his eyes and looked down.

His vision was blurred by arousal, but this change was hard to miss. An extra finger of flesh had uncoiled from his penis. Bright red with blood, it was an inch-and-a-half, no more, but something about the way it pulsed and wavered suggested it could stretch. When Xishi touched it lightly with one knuckle, the thing was so sensitive, it might have been all nerve.

"Do you know what this is?" she asked.

Memory struggled to surface: private royal archives idly paged through when he was too young to be anything but apathetic about the knowledge. Some of it had sunk in regardless: more than he knew.

The royal flagellum, he thought. *The little whip.*

"Explanations don't matter," he said, his voice unnaturally deep. "What matters is getting it where it's supposed to go."

He lifted her as if she weighed nothing, her breasts and body sleek from the spray. He had never felt so strong, so sure of what he wanted and what to do. He kissed her as his cock and its addition breached her juicy sex, both penetrations deep and thorough and slow. Her tongue was honey stroking his. With a sigh of profound relief, he pressed her into the shower wall, in and in and in until he was home. This was what he'd been waiting for. His kith began releasing with a vengeance. Into her mouth. Into her pussy. She moaned at the influx of the natural aphrodisiac, kissing him back so recklessly that at last she had to break for air.

"I can feel it," she panted, "moving inside me."

He rubbed his cheek against hers, feeling it, too. The whip was stretching, seeking. Every brush against her velvet walls jagged through him like a lightning bolt. This was a pleasure to rob a man of sense, but it wasn't the particular pleasure the little appendage was reaching for. That prize she was getting in the way of without even knowing it.

"Don't wriggle," he managed to grit out.

"I need to," she moaned, doing it again. "Your kith is burning me."

"Don't." He pressed her harder into the steel, using his weight to hold her still. "The flagellum is trying to find its lock."

"Its lock?"

He groaned as the thing stretched longer and whipped wildly; he was helpless to answer until it slowed. "The place in you it needs to fasten onto. The place in you that it's made for."

The place was in her womb, just inside the mouth, a tender spot as sharp with sensation as the flagellum. She stiffened in surprise as the tip of his extension brushed it and skidded by.

"Oh," she squeaked, her fingers digging into his shoulders as she suddenly tried *not* to move. "Oh, please, do that again."

He couldn't have refrained. With his body to remind him, the details of his old reading were coming back. The whip would keep searching until it hooked what it sought, truly a sexual organ with a mind of its own. Compelled by its instincts, he pushed deeper into her, straining to give the whip more play. The sweat of extreme erotic need broke out on his forehead. He knew the angle had to be just right for the two surfaces to engage.

And then they were engaged. Their bodies jolted at the sweetness of the puzzle finding its fit. The whip was humming strongly where it had latched onto her, who knew what chemical messages transferring. Though he expected her to be frightened, when Xishi's eyes rose to his they were sheened with love.

His heart tightened at the sight. He couldn't doubt her fondness any longer, no more than he could feel that he was worthy of receiving it.

"They didn't teach us this at pillow school," she breathed.

He kissed her, unable to speak with so much emotion welling in his breast. He pulled back and swallowed hard.

"This isn't going to take long."

"How do you know?" she asked, her calves hitched tight behind his buttocks.

"Can't you feel how good this is? How close we are to climax?"

"Yes, but don't we have to move?"

It will move, he began to say, but before he could get the words out, the whip began to vibrate. The pleasure of that was blinding, running in shivering jolts from the tip of the flagellum to his heavy balls. When he could open his eyes again, Xishi's face was twisted with ecstasy.

"Forget I said that," she gasped. "I—oh, my—I don't think I ever want to move again."

He would have laughed if he'd been able, but his body was preparing to spill in her. This was the job of the flagellum: to sense when she was fertile and increase the chance that she would conceive. Like a secret weapon for procreation, the whip produced a catalyst to facilitate impregnation. It ensured she would have an orgasm no matter what, and—if that weren't enough—it held the mouth to her womb ajar for his semen's jets. Corum could feel it swelling thicker to do just that. Eager to fulfill its role, his heavy scrotum lurched upward.

Sensation ran through him like chills—too strong to bear, too good to evade. He grunted. Clutched her. Heard her cry out and blaze like fire.

When her sheath contracted and sucked him, his seed seemed to explode from him all at once.

It wasn't all at once, though, because the instant the hard spurting stopped, the flagellum restarted its vibration and made them both come again. Twice more the process repeated, causing him to shoot a seeming ocean of ejaculate. Only when he was emptied out did the violent spasms of pleasure end.

They'd fallen to their knees without him noticing. In fact, he might have lost a few seconds in the aftermath.

"Cor," Xishi moaned, her mouth soft on his shoulder. "You're still hard."

He was more than hard, he was so distended her vagina fit him like a second skin. He suspected this was his body's way of ensuring that his semen did not flow out, but he dared not move for fear of hurting her. He wasn't sure he could move, in any case. Every muscle he had was shaking. Giving in to necessity, he sat on his heels with her on his lap.

The shower pounded around them like steaming rain.

"Lights dim," he said, bringing the illumination even lower.

She must have been tired, but she kissed him like a butterfly on his mouth, her little smile reassuring him she was all right. "That was amazing," she said. "I never imagined—"

Suddenly she stopped speaking and looked upward, an expression of childlike wonder upon her face. Corum followed her gaze and gaped himself.

Two spheres of transparent golden light, the size of ripe apricots, were dancing in a circle in the shower mist above their heads. Rainbows shot out from their edges, their color so pure and bright he had to squint. There was lighting that could mimic these behaviors, but Corum had installed none here, and he was sure he knew of no light globes that could feel so much like they were made of joy.

Tears pricked his eyes without his knowing why.

"Cor," she marveled, reaching up for them, "they're giggling."

He heard a high, quick chiming that could have been that sound. Certainly, these lights looked like things that could laugh. They bounced to Xishi like rambunctious puppies eager to lick her face. She was used to seeing energy effects, but this clarity was unprecedented for him. When one light veered from her to nuzzle his nose, he began to cry as he hadn't since he was a boy.

"Oh, God," he said, unable to stop the words any more than he could stop the tears. "Say yes, Xishi. Say you want them to stay with you."

But she didn't need to. They already knew. With one last chiming giggle, they darted into her belly and disappeared.

Xishi gasped and covered her abdomen.

Their eyes met with matching expressions of shock and awe. That neither had ever heard of this phenomenon didn't matter; they knew what had happened. Xishi was pregnant. With twins.

"One boy, one girl," he whispered, and she nodded.

Corum didn't need his lawyers to tell him this changed everything.

The truth will out

Though they'd only made love once, Corum's heat appeared to be over, maybe because its purpose had so obviously been achieved. His strength recovered, he laid Xishi and her precious cargo on his bed. Feeling as if he'd been given a treasure he could never earn, he pulled the down-filled covers up to her chin.

If the gleam in her eyes was anything to go by, she found this amusing.

Not about to be inhibited from his urge to cosset his pregnant mate, he sat on the mattress and took her hand. "I want you to stay here while I talk to my parents."

"Now?" Her sweet lower lip pushed out. "I thought it might be nice to cuddle for a while."

"It would be nice, but I won't relax until I've settled this with them."

"I could come with you."

He shook his head. "They won't react well. I don't want them near you until they've calmed down."

"I'm not fragile."

He couldn't help but smile. "Neither am I, Buttercup. You can trust me to handle this."

"I guess you can always put on your Prince of Ice mask."

He kissed the tip of her crinkled nose. "Master Ping insists I can do anything I set my mind to, so please try not to worry. Whatever happens, you and I and these little folks will be safe."

She covered the hand he'd laid on her belly, biting her lip with a consternation she could not conceal. "I hate that this is bringing trouble to you."

"Only for a little while. Once the dust of the uproar settles, I promise you, we're going to be happy."

He wasn't sure how this miracle would be accomplished, but his determination would not let him dwell on his doubts. That her fear seemed mainly for him relieved him. How far his parents' outrage would go he honestly couldn't say, but he preferred that she not realize they might pose a threat to her safety. If nothing else, he'd make it clear he wouldn't stand for that.

Reading something in his expression, she touched the side of his jaw.

"I love you," she whispered shyly.

"I love *you*," he whispered back.

He had a feeling the forbidden thrill of saying that would take a while to wear off.

～

As Corum stepped into the corridor, a maid was busily pretending to dust a dustless spot on the wall. He suspected that hadn't been what she was doing before he came out. Whispering rumors into her handheld was more like.

"Off with you," he scolded. "There's nothing to gawk at here."

The girl scurried away guiltily, but the worst response he could muster was a gusty sigh. Servants gossiped. It was the nature of the beast. Little did this one suspect there would soon be far greater matters for tongues to wag at than her master's latest reconciliation with his pillow girl.

He caught his parents at the Midarri Palace's grand front door. Their formal dress suggested they were on their way to an evening out, but when he hailed them, they turned with perceptible expressions of pleasure.

These, he knew, weren't destined to last.

"Forgive me for keeping you from your engagement," he apologized. "I need to speak to you about a private matter."

"Of course," said his father, waving off the two liveried men who'd been escorting them. "Why don't we duck in here?"

Ironically, "here" was the same hideous dragon-theme parlor in which his mother had told his younger self she was sending Xishi away. The room hadn't changed much in the intervening years, though at the moment the dust was clear.

His parents sat side by side on the gilded dragon divan, but Corum's nerves would only permit standing. Knowing that the outcome of this interview depended most on his father, Corum forced himself to meet Poll's eyes.

"I don't know what Mother has told you about my genetic anomaly."

Nothing to judge by her muffled intake of breath. His father, by contrast, barely blinked.

"Less than I guessed," he said. "I don't think there's much you need to explain—unless there have been new developments?"

"An unexpected side effect. I have found a mate. It is my pillow girl."

His father had been sitting back casually, the picture of royal calm. At this blunt pronouncement, he uncrossed his legs and leaned forward. "Your pillow girl?"

"No," said his mother, shaking her head a bit too forcefully. "You must be mistaken."

"I am not mistaken. I've spilled my seed for her. She is my mate."

His mother fell back as if he'd slapped her. His father laid a comforting hand on her thigh, though he looked nearly as pale.

"There is more," Corum said, "which I shall not be able to hide once we are married. My pillow girl is someone you know. Her birth name is Xishi, whom you raised with me until we were eight."

"No," said his mother, rising slowly from the divan. "You are not doing this, not after all I sacrificed to keep your secret, after all I did to ensure your place would be waiting when you came of age. You are not making that . . . that scheming servant girl your mate!"

"My genes have seen to that already. It is not a matter for debate."

His mother drew herself straight. "You can get rid of her, like any decent royal would."

He had known it might come to this, had braced himself, and still the words came as a cold, hard blow. It was no strain at all to pull on what Xishi called his Prince of Ice mask.

"I hope you are not saying what I think you are, because, believe me, Mother, harming Xishi would be a mistake."

His father caught her arm before she could retort. "Of course she's not suggesting that. Your mother only means you should consider sending the girl away. With sufficient time and distance, the biochemical bond might fade."

His mother's face was red with anger, her muscles working as she fought for control. Cor was convinced he hadn't mistaken her meaning.

"I love her," he said softly, knowing that these, of all words, would impress his father as being true. "I have loved her since I was a boy. I consider it . . . the deepest of honors that she is going to bear my children."

"No!" his mother screamed, effectively distracting his father from taking this in. "No, no, no, *no*!"

She lashed out at the nearest table, sending three priceless ancient vases crashing to the floor.

"You were safe!" she screamed. "I made you safe!"

It was only through the echo of the broken porcelain that they heard the pounding on the door.

"Imperial police," said a harsh, male voice. "Open up!"

Corum's father was the first to regain control. "Pull yourself together," he said sharply to his wife. "I'll take care of this."

Four tall guards in uniform awaited behind the door. "Poll Midarri?" their leader asked, though he had to have been familiar with the visage of every head of house. "By order of the empress, we have come to arrest your son."

Corum gave his father credit: His royal hauteur didn't waver in response to this. Instead, he held out his hand. "I presume you have a warrant."

The officer removed it from his inner breast pocket. "The warrant authorizes deadly force," he said as he passed it over, "should your son choose to resist."

"We will treat that information with the seriousness it deserves," his father answered drily. "Now please wait outside while we go over this."

The officer's displeasure showed in a frown, but he knew the special consideration senior princes were due. With a glance around the room to check for means of escape, he bowed stiffly and withdrew.

Cor strode instantly to his father's side.

His father's gasp after he broke the seal to the warrant wasn't a good sign. "You're being charged with treason. It says you have been consorting with a human in secret. That you have endangered the imperial bloodline by cohabitating with Xishi Huon. Son, how can this be?"

"It's a mistake," he said, taking the densely printed document from his father's hands. "They must have confused her with someone else."

He didn't have to read far to see they hadn't. The document included embedded holos, not only of his mate, but of her mother, Xoushou, and her grandmother, Xasha. It described how Xasha Huon, a former royal, had been exiled for having sexual relations with a human while at a diplomatic posting within their lands. According to the testimony on which the warrant was based, Xasha had given birth to a child, who later gave birth to Xishi, who had been insinuated into the Midarri household under the pretense of being rohn. By yamish law, Xishi was one-quarter human and thus unclean. The warrant claimed that Corum had consorted with her knowingly and was therefore guilty of treason.

Of all the charges he read, the last was the only one he could swear was false.

Reluctant, but wanting to be sure, he showed the holo of Xoushou Huon to his mother. "Was this the maid who brought Xishi to the palace when she was a child?"

Corynna was trembling, bloodless fingers pressed to bloodless lips. "Yes. But she did not say her family name was Huon. I would have recognized that from the old scandal."

Corum closed his eyes, knowing then—if he hadn't already—that the seemingly wild assertions were true. Xishi was part-human. That was why she looked and sounded different. Why she'd never been as cold as ordinary yama. Why her energy was sweeter than any drug. Her chi might even be the reason they were mated. Their bond might have nothing to do with his genetic flaw.

I don't care why we're together, he thought, the realization unexpectedly freeing. *I only care that we are.*

"It's true then," said his father, reading his reaction. "This girl is part-human."

"Yes," said Corum. "I believe it is."

His father nodded, shaken, but trying not to be. He pulled his handheld from his pocket. "I'll call Muto. This warrant came from the empress's court. Maybe he can sweet-talk her out of it."

"Father." Corum's tone of caution stopped him before he pressed the keys. "I can't be sure, but Prince Muto may have had a hand in this. The signatory witness, this Jehol, is Muto's wife's pillow boy."

"They're taking the word of a *pillow boy*?"

"Apparently, and since the charge is treason, it seems likely he has someone high-placed to vouch for him. And look here. The date says the accusation was only entered this afternoon. No pillow boy acting alone could get the courts to move that fast."

"But why would Muto involve himself?"

"Probably because the opportunity came up. He knows I don't trust him. If he manages to discredit me, which this certainly will, you might feel obliged to name another heir.

However long it is before you step down, I'm sure Muto would prefer to deal with a successor he can charm."

"Muto," said his father, shaking his head.

Corum gripped him gently by the shoulder. "Call my lawyers. And my chief of security. They may be able to find some ammunition with which I can fight."

"With which *we* can fight," said his father, a steely light glinting in his eye. "I'm not letting that two-faced bastard maneuver me into disinheriting my son. I know you didn't do this on purpose."

Corum inclined his head in thanks, but his father wasn't finished yet.

"This girl," he said, a hint of hesitance creeping in. "This Xishi. Are you sure you want to stick by her now?"

Corum sensed that his father was as willing as his mother to take drastic measures, the difference being that he would wait for Corum to give the word.

"I'm sure," he said in his quietest, firmest tone.

"She may have known what she was," his father cautioned.

"Even so," Corum responded.

"Then I'll have our lawyers see to her defense as well."

A wash of fear swept Corum's skin with ice. It had not occurred to him before now, but it made sense that he wouldn't be alone in facing arrest.

"The firm will treat her like a daughter," his father assured him, while in the background his disappointed mother wept bitterly.

⌒

Xishi's head was spinning so dizzily from what she'd learned that being taken into imperial custody scarcely seemed real.

It became real once they locked her in the cell. Then she had plenty of time to tug her rattled brain back into place.

She was one-quarter human. And her mother had been half-royal. Xishi wasn't sure what it said about her that being even a quarter royal seemed as strange as being part-human. She'd always known she was different, but she'd never thought of herself as anything but a maid's daughter.

The guards were probably convinced she was different, too. They'd been careful not to touch her more than they had to, and they'd stared at her like she was demented when she'd begged to keep a copy of the warrant in her cell.

Those embedded holos were the only glimpse she'd ever had of her family. Each time she clicked them on, her eyes overflowed. She didn't even care that the electronic eyes in the cell's black ceiling saw every tear.

In addition to being fitted out with more surveillance than a diamond shop, the cell they'd taken her to was clean and stark. Black plascrete walls and floor. Black cot. Black bars. Black shower cubicle and toilet. Xishi paced the space back and forth until her shaking knees forced her to sit.

She was glad there were no other cells nearby, but this was the extent of her special treatment. The empress's police hadn't asked her if she wished to call anyone. She supposed her human blood robbed her of that right. She expected Cor would hear what had happened soon . . . unless he'd been arrested himself.

At this thought, it took all her will not to press her palm to her abdomen. She knew the gesture would betray her, and the last thing she needed was to let whoever was behind this know she was carrying mixed-blood children.

She could feel the babies' energy just a bit, a glow she could only see if she closed her eyes. The impression she received from them wasn't fear, but their consciousness might not have been attuned to outward things. Possibly it was all taken up by the job of growing into little people.

When she remembered how easily—and how unquestioningly—Cor had accepted them, she wanted to cry.

I will protect you, she promised them in her mind. *Cor and I will protect you.*

⤙

"Where are they holding her?" Corum demanded the moment his lawyer arrived.

He'd been pacing the solitary cell for what seemed like hours, desperate to hear news. Despite his anxiety, he noticed that the firm had sent its highest-ranking counsel, the young but brilliant Tsewang Krptlt. Because his specialty was trials and not business law, Corum hadn't dealt with him before.

With a bland but quelling glance at Corum's agitated state, the lawyer set his bulging alligator briefcase on the plascrete outside the bars.

"Miss Buttercup is—"

"Princess Xishi," Corum all but snarled.

Tsewang blinked at him. "You are correct," he said slowly, as if reassessing his new client. "Our defense is likelier to go smoothly if we accord your mate her proper rank. Princess Xishi is being held in the women's wing of this prison—a private cell, from what I hear. Before I continue, however, I would like to deactivate these listening devices. We are entitled to a private consultation, no matter how susceptible some authorities are to forgetting that."

With an expression of mild distaste, the lawyer swept a magnetic pulse wand over their surroundings until the tip glowed green. "There. Now we may speak freely."

"She is well?"

"She is well, Your Highness. There has been a slight delay in obtaining approval for counsel to visit her face to face, but we have been able to ascertain her well-being. I fully expect we'll have the interview soon as well."

"Who have you assigned to her?"

"My partner, Rom Shrestha."

Corum knew the yama well. "That is good. He is older and has a reassuring manner. She will feel safe talking to him."

"It was Prince Poll's suggestion. He thought she might welcome a fatherly figure."

Corum nodded and gripped the bars, finding himself able to breathe more fully even if his mind didn't yet qualify as sharp. "Have you had an opportunity to speak with my chief of security?"

"Yes. We've been able to establish a link between the pillow boy, Jehol, and the rohn who shadowed you and Princess Xishi through the imperial gardens. The pair were seen together on two occasions, and sums of cash sufficient to have paid the rohn's fee were withdrawn from the pillow boy's personal account."

"And no doubt he received those sums as 'gifts' from his new mistress."

"Quite," Tsewang said crisply. "Unfortunately, giving gifts to one's bedmate is no more illegal than vouching for his honesty before a judge—which Princess Erymita was also kind enough to do."

"Leaving her husband, the empress's close, personal friend, conveniently out of it."

"Precisely." Tsewang sounded more satisfied than daunted. The lawyer had a reputation for enjoying challenges. "Prince Muto's probable involvement may also explain why the rohn chose to kill himself rather than be questioned. Our defense will have to be a bit more circuitous than our usual. Naturally, we'll dig into this Jehol's background. If his skeletons are dirty enough, Prince Muto may decide to withdraw his support. If not, we may need to find some way to engage the emperor's interest. He can overrule his wife's decisions, if he's adequately motivated to do so."

The lawyer's eyes were alight with enthusiasm, but Corum had to swallow back a groan. The emotional and political webs that bound the current emperor and empress were a tangle others rarely found it pleasant, or healthy, to step into. With Muto's proposed holochannel likely to pad both their imperial highness's purses, the emperor's motivation would have to be great indeed.

"My mother may be a problem," Corum said.

Tsewang nodded soberly. "The firm has set someone to watch her, with your father's permission. She will not easily be able to compromise your wishes for the defense of Princess Xishi."

Tsewang's eyes met his. Suddenly, they were not lawyer and client, but simply two young men who understood the need—and the occasional difficulty—of establishing a place in the world independent of one's parents' will.

"Xishi is important to me," Corum said softly. "Everything else I am willing to sacrifice as long as I know she's safe."

The lawyer's lips took on the subtlest curve. "Understood. But let us hope something less than *everything* is required."

~~~~~

Two days had passed since Xishi's arrest, with no word from anyone except the guard who brought her meals and told her to "eat up" in a scornful tone. Tired of being afraid, and even more tired of having no idea what was going on, today she was lying on the cot, trying to meditate for the babies' sake.

The serenity she sought escaped her, but in its place came a memory. It must have been from before Corynna sent her to the tiny closet in the servants' hall, because she and Cor were snuggled under his blankets, telling stories past his bedtime as they often did. Xishi guessed they were no more than five.

"And then the prince saves the princess from the dragon with his mighty sword," Cor declared dramatically—or as dramatically as one could when speaking in a whisper.

"*I'm* the dragon," Xishi corrected. "And I'm going to bite the princess's head off."

"You're the dragon?"

"I am."

"I thought we liked the princess."

"Only because she's tasty."

Cor giggled, a sound he only made when they were alone. "We'll roll her in flour and put her in the fryer. Then she'll be crispy, too."

Rather than giggle herself, Xishi began tickling him. "Better watch out, Prince, or I'll decide you're dessert!"

"Stop!" he said, his laughter rising uncontrollably. "You'll get us both in trouble with Matreya."

Xishi couldn't recall whether trouble had come then or later, but the memory of those muffled shrieks of delight were clear as a bell. She wanted the freedom to be joyful for Cor again. She wanted it for them all.

She experienced the desire so strongly, so pointedly, that—in the garbled logic of her weary mind—it seemed as if the universe had no choice but to deliver it. They would survive this difficulty. She would hear her children laughing. She and Cor would hide under their covers and tell them all the stories her unsuspected human heritage had inspired.

Maybe it was the sweetness of the daydream, or maybe she was simply too exhausted to be unhappy anymore, but in that moment, as she imagined their twins' laughter, her long-lost Golden Breath of Peace washed over her. It was like reuniting with an old friend, a glorious sense of connectedness enfolding her. All was well. All was peaceful. All was exactly as it was meant to be. Her chi ran over her like sparkling water, so warm she broke into a light sweat.

I am a dragon, she thought from that delightfully altered state. *If I put my foot down, it will shake the world.*

The belief was so powerful it barely wavered when a tall male person in long bronze robes came to stand before her cell bars. Xishi sat up and looked at him. He was slim and gray-haired, with an air of quiet confidence. He held up a finger, signaling her to be quiet, then waved some sort of surveillance-canceling wand in all directions. This taken care of, he pressed a button on his black and silver briefcase. The case turned out to be the Traveling Office model that had been all the rage a few years back. In less than thirty seconds, a small desk and attached chair unfolded itself. With a smile so natural it startled her, the man slid his narrow hips into the chair and pulled out his handheld.

"Forgive my delay in coming to see you. I am Rom Shrestha, from the firm of Krptlt and Shrestha. Your husband has engaged me to defend you against these charges."

"My husband," Xishi said, nonplussed.

"We're claiming you are Prince Corum's common law wife. The law is a bit muddied regarding the topic of interspecies marriages, there having been so few, but we believe this will entitle you to the same rights and protections as any yamish citizen."

He keyed his handheld to record.

"I need to ask you some questions, if you don't mind. Anything you tell me will be confidential, and—needless to say—the franker you are, the better we can strategize. First, were you aware of your unusual background?"

Unusual was one way of putting it. Xishi rose from the bed and went to stand before him. "Until two days ago, I thought I was a rohn orphan."

The lawyer nodded, but not in a manner that let her know if he believed her. "And are you acquainted with a prince named Muto Feng?"

"I think Corum's father is. Why do you ask?"

"Because the Throne's main witness is his wife's pillow boy."

"*Jehol,*" she said, unable to hide her loathing.

The lawyer looked up. "Him I see you know. Do you know why he would bring these charges against you and Prince Corum?"

"No. Except he seemed to dislike me from the day we met."

"As students at the Purple Crane."

"Yes."

Again the lawyer smiled kindly. He must have thought her human blood would find it reassuring. "Can you share your observations of his character? Any knowledge of his background?"

"I really only know he liked to hurt people. He was always being cruel to his girlfriend and . . . another man at the pillow school." Xishi wasn't sure if she should bring up Prince Pahndir's name. "Madame Fagin could tell you about that."

The lawyer's face grew somber. "Madame Fagin is claiming she disclosed your mixed heritage to Prince Corum before he bought your contract."

"That's outrageous!" Xishi cried. "Cor had no idea what I was! Nor did Madame Fagin, as far as I know."

The lawyer watched her outburst without reacting himself. "She may have been paid to say she did, or she may be worried she'll be sued for malpractice if she does not."

"But it's a lie!" Xishi gripped the bars in plea.

"Sadly, court cases are often built of lies." He spread his hands on the little desk. "Princess Xishi, what I'm about to ask you is delicate, so I hope you won't take offense. If you have, in your previous capacity as a pillow girl, made any powerful friends, now might be the time to ask them for favors."

Xishi was reeling a bit from being called *Princess*. She took a moment to answer. "Cor— Prince Corum was my first partner."

"And you have no idea how to contact your grandmother?"

"Is she alive?" Xishi's pulse jumped into her throat.

"I have never heard otherwise. Naturally, as a law-abiding corporation, Krptlt and Shrestha could not establish communication with a banished royal. If *you* were able to reach her, however, she would be a good ally. Before she went into hiding, Xasha Huon was a force to be reckoned with."

She did not at first understand his suggestive tone. "You think I lied to you," she said, finally comprehending. "That I knew all along who and what I was."

"It's my job to think such things."

He seemed both unoffended and unrepentant. Somewhat at a loss, she rubbed her hands up and down the bars. "At this moment, I wish I were lying, but I never heard of her before I read the charges."

"And the identity of your father?"

She shrugged helplessly.

"Very well," he said, beginning to twist himself out of his traveling desk. "Thank you for your time. Krptlt and Shrestha will do our very best for you."

"Wait!" She reached through bars to catch his hand. It was terrible manners to do so, but Xishi didn't care much about that now. "I might have a not-so-powerful friend who could help find my grandmother, assuming you could contact her without getting her in trouble."

Rom Shrestha returned to his seat and lifted his gaze to hers, his pupils widening with interest. "I believe we could assure you of discretion."

"Could you . . . Could you also tell me how Cor is doing?"

"The prince is well. Worried for you, but well." He hesitated, clearly mulling over some decision. After a moment, he put his second hand over hers. "Your Highness, I have concluded your ignorance of your background is genuine. Consequently, it might take longer to find Xasha Huon than we'd like. I'm wondering . . . would you be willing to speak to the one person who seems to know more about your family than you do?"

"Jehol would never speak to me!"

The lawyer grinned broadly. "Oh, I think he would. He's been trying to bribe the guards to get in to see you. Thus far, we've blocked his attempts, but perhaps we ought to allow our vigilance to lapse. One never knows what a young man might reveal when he is gloating to a pretty girl."

The lawyer's voice was oddly cheery, almost as if he were drunk. Twice he tried to extricate himself from his desk before he stood swaying on his feet. Xishi feared he was ill, but this was not the case.

"Goodness," he said, looking down at her hand, which he was still clasping in both of his. "I am daimyo, and you are only a quarter human, but I really do not want to let go. Human chi really is as seductive as people say."

"Oh, forgive me," Xishi said, tugging back her hand, mortified. "I was meditating before you came. My energy doesn't usually have this strong an effect."

The lawyer's face was slightly flushed, and she didn't want to think what other parts of him had been affected. He laughed openly. "It's a shame you were found out. You could have ruled the world as a pillow girl."

"That was never my ambition. Only to be safe and loved."

The mention of love sobered her counsel.

"Yes," he said, smoothing his hair around his head. It was already neat, a long, gray, upper-class queue hanging down his spine. "Well, just remember, if you can do this to a daimyo, your energy will put a rohn out of his head. Not a bad advantage to have when you get your chance to deal with that pillow boy."

Xishi didn't think it was a bad advantage, either. She just wished the lawyer didn't seem to be counting quite so heavily on her efforts.

Treason was, after all, a capital offense.

Left to her own devices

Jehol came to her in the night—the better to avoid Krptlt &
Shrestha's "vigilance," she supposed. She'd been sleeping,
though not deeply, and it took a breath or two to remember
how she'd decided she was going to handle this—or try to
handle it. She didn't have a lot of faith that her plan would
work. The simple fact that she was in jail suggested Jehol
was more cunning.

On the bright side, her groan of disgust at seeing him
was convincing.

"You wound me," he said, his hand pressed mockingly
to his breast. The single light in the corridor outside her
cell, the one that never turned off, cast a cone of brilliance
around his tall, handsome frame. "I was hoping for a shriek
of horror, or possibly a plea for leniency."

"Like that would do me any good."

"True," he said as she sat up.

She wanted to wrap her blanket around her sleeping
robes, but decided it would only get in her way. Her visitor
didn't seem to feel the prison's seeping cold. His robe and

trousers were black, the same simple cotton style fighters practiced in. The clothes weren't new, and he looked comfortable in them. Xishi would rather have seen him wearing something pretentious. Then she might have convinced herself he was a fool.

That being hopeless, she put her hands on her hips. "Just tell me why you take such pleasure in ruining my life."

"Oh, I hope I've done more than ruin it. I hope I've done my best to see it taken away."

"Fine. Don't tell me."

"I might tell you for the price of a kiss. As I recall, you never did try me out at school."

For a second, she thought of doing it, but she realized he'd never believe she would and would guess she was tricking him. Instead, she flung herself from the bed, stalked the two strides to the bars, and spat in his face. He dodged the missile easily, but grabbed her wrist before she could pull back. Knowing he'd hold on as long as she seemed not to want him to, she tugged away ferociously.

He held her without effort. Now that she knew she was part-royal, his strength impressed her more. The mornings he'd spent on the Purple Crane's resistance trainers had paid off.

"Such passion," he said as she struggled. "How I used to marvel that anyone could miss what you are."

"It's all lies," she said, her fury coming out easily. "Lies you invented out of jealousy!"

"Jealousy!" His contempt was not as icy as he would have liked.

"Because Prince Pahndir liked me best. Because I was the first to leave the house!"

He wrenched her wrist until she feared it would break. It took all her concentration to call on the peace she'd found when she meditated, to will her human-tainted energy to rise and spill over him. She wasn't sure how successful her effort was. The air above her skin did seem to vibrate, and his pupils were swelling, but that response might have been the effect of rage.

"Your bloody grandmother," he clipped out, "is the reason I'm not a prince myself!"

"You, a prince? When pigs sit on the throne!"

"I am Huon," he said. "Just like you. Your grandmother's disgusting lack of control led to my branch of the family being barred from the court as well. We are cousins, little Xishi, averse as I am to admit we share anything."

This admission shocked her speechless. "You cannot be royal," she retorted a moment later. "You spill your seed for anyone like a common rohn!"

He broke her smallest finger with a nasty snap, then followed her to the floor as she sank to her knees moaning.

"You have human blood, you loathsome little bitch. My father was at least yama."

She gasped in pain from the pressure he was putting on the broken joint, but as long as he maintained contact it was worth it. She tried to will her chi to flow faster into him. The more he took, the more incautious he would become.

"Your father wasn't royal yama," she taunted, "and probably not upper class, either."

His face flushed with fury, evidence that she'd hit the mark. She remembered how surly he'd been after discovering how royal males differed from ordinary men. It must have lashed his pride to discover he could never pass for what he aspired to be.

"Too bad," she mocked, determined to rub it in. "I guess your mother didn't have a lot of men to choose from after the emperor kicked her out."

Pushed past all his limits, Jehol stuck his arm through the bars, grabbed the back of her neck, and yanked her face to him. To her amazement, he kissed her, his tongue thrusting thick and forceful into her mouth. She didn't think the kiss was about attraction, though she could have been wrong. When she finally managed to wrench away, his eyes were nearly black. An eery ring of silver was all that remained around his pupils.

"You're the reason my parents died," he panted. "Your grandmother hired an assassin to have them killed. She waited years to do it, until she knew no one would suspect her. She would have killed me, too, if my mother hadn't hidden my existence. Instead, she let me have just long enough with them to learn to hate you."

He had released his grip. Xishi's injured hand slid down to rest on his knee, where he seemed not to notice it.

"She had them killed because they killed my mother," she deduced.

"She would have killed mine first. She had the poison in her pocket when my father slit her throat."

"I don't believe you," she said, though in that moment she absolutely did.

"They were allies until Xoushou betrayed her," Jehol insisted, taking her wounded hand into his again. He was swaying on his knees, not unlike the lawyer had. "My mother helped yours conceive you."

"Then she knew who my father was."

Jehol shook his finger teasingly. "You'd love to know that, I bet. But it wouldn't help you. It would only drive the nails in deeper." He leaned close enough for her to smell the tea on his breath. "It was their plan all along, that you seduce a prince of the realm, preferably a prince of the Midarri, where you and your children could sit so comfortably near the throne. Maybe even breed into it."

"My grandmother planned this?"

He didn't seem to mind answering. He was playing with her broken finger, stroking the throbbing swell of it up and down. "You were going to help her win back her place in the Forbidden City. My mother's, too, though that was probably a lie."

"I want to hear this from her," Xishi said, unable to think of a guileful way to lead up to it. "I want my grandmother to admit it to my face."

Jehol stuck her finger in his mouth and sucked it. This was hard to sit still for, but he seemed unaware of how strangely he was acting.

"She can't admit it to your face," he laughed around the digit. "The old emperor banished her."

This must have been the trial she'd caught him watching with such enjoyment in the library.

"I could write her," she said, scrambling for an opening. "I could demand she tell me the truth."

This time Jehol collapsed with laughter, the sound high and giddy. Clearly, her focused chi was heady stuff. "I know better than that," he giggled. "You're hoping if I tell you how to reach her, the old dragon will find some way to get you off."

"She wouldn't dare come here. She'd be breaking the terms of her exile. The new emperor might throw her into prison, too."

Jehol straightened and blinked. "Yes," he said slowly. "That he might. Might kill her, as well, even if she is full royal. Not that she'd be easy to find. All I've ever tracked is a ghost address on the yamaweb. You'd have to beg her, Buttercup, and pray she cares enough about her old plots to save your neck."

"Give me the address," she demanded. "I'll take my chances."

"Take *her* chances, you mean." Jehol snickered. "I almost admire you, risking your dear grandmother's life like that. But I suppose I can't lose either way. I can revel in watching her disappoint you, or I can revel in watching you all be executed. One big, happy, doomed family."

He licked her throbbing little finger, then used it to smudge a yamaweb address onto the black plascrete.

Ignoring her pain, Xishi memorized it before it could fade.

Jehol stood with a regretful sigh. "You know," he said, seeming almost fond as he gazed down at her, "I enjoyed our time together at the Purple Crane, after I told Madame Fagin she ought to recruit you. It gave me such pleasure to imagine the would-be princess working as a whore. I would have waited longer to savor my revenge if you and Prince Corum hadn't looked like you'd be happy. You should have kept fighting. I'd have allowed you years of unmolested misery with him."

Xishi said nothing, just cradled her hand against her breast. She'd gotten more from him than she'd dared hope. Tea Rose would know exactly the sort of letter a devious royal grandmother was likely to respond to. The risk to Xasha Huon's safety concerned her, but Krptlt & Shrestha seemed to think the banished royal could take care of herself. Xishi's only job would be to wait for an answer and hope they were right.

Well, that and hope the old dragon cared enough to interfere. Given how few people in Xishi's life had, that might turn out to be the hardest part of all.

The dragon rises

Xasha Huon had flourished in her exile.

Oh, now and then, she thrashed around in her head over the wrongs the world had done her, but for the most part she was content. She had a lover of whom she was fond, her publically cuckolded husband had left an eon ago, and her estate in the northern mountains was comfortable. Though the far-flung province in which she lived was not exciting, she had left her need for storm and thunder behind.

She had her just-in-case hobbies, of course, should she require defending against some threat. They were hobbies, however, and not the driving passions they'd once been. Because of this, when she checked her handheld for mail at the breakfast table, she was surprised rather than pleased to receive a communication through one of her untraceable ghost addresses. She'd used these for information gathering, and the information that was coming through today was quite enough to widen her eyes.

"My granddaughter has been arrested," she said to no one in particular.

Her lover, an even-tempered upper-class widower whose lands bordered hers, looked up from his eggs. "I didn't know you had a granddaughter."

"I do." Her eyes pricked at their very backs as she remembered her daughter, Xoushou, lost and revenged in the effort to produce this child. Xoushou had had spirit, though maybe not the best judgment. "She has married a prince of the Midarri, wrapped him around her finger, apparently, and—Infinity take me—Jela Huon's son has gotten her arrested as an accessory to treason simply because she has a little human blood."

This had her lover setting down his fork. "The old rumors were true then."

Xasha shot him a sharp look. "They were, and it's far too late to expect me to feel ashamed. I never understood why, just because you're royal, sleeping with someone from another race is treated as a threat to the Throne."

Then again, maybe she did understand, considering what she'd learned over the years from her just-in-case inquiries.

"Well, I don't care," said her lover. "That sort of imperial prissiness rarely makes it to the provinces."

Xasha heard him with no more than half an ear. She was too busy tapping her teeth with a fingernail.

"You going to get her out of it?" he asked.

"That crowd in the Forbidden City will think I wouldn't dare."

Her lover snorted, a rusticity she tolerated because he was so warm in bed. "That means you'll go. Just let me know how big an escort you want to take."

She didn't need his men; she had her own, a far better trained cadre. She'd accept the loan of a few, though, to let him think he was helping.

Yes, she thought, the blood flowing faster within her veins. She'd lost her heart for scheming after her daughter died, but maybe it was time she drew a line through the last few entries in her old ledgers.

And, really, it would be too bad to let the emperor kill his own daughter.

━━∽━━

A handful of the finest forged ivory passes finagled Xasha Huon and three of her men through the inner city gates. The men were killers, all, and she was traveling light. When one knew as many secrets as she did, one didn't have to rely on force of numbers.

A generous roll of cash—a rarity in the capital, appreciated for its ability to go unreported—procured a lovely corner suite at an inn. She sat before a large window now, tired from traveling, but satisfied with herself. She pulled a page of creamy green notepaper closer to her on the desk, selected a gold-nibbed pen, and wrote a brief message.

"Genesis 521," it said. Under that, she signed herself "Xasha H."

She didn't fear identifying herself to the note's recipient. The words it contained were their own guarantee of safety, a code only the emperor and one other were supposed to know.

She sealed the note and handed it to the most experienced of her guards. "See this gets to Songyam personally. He'll want an interview when he reads it. Wait for his response and relay my terms."

She also gave the guard a packet of money, which he accepted without comment. He knew precisely how to manage the various bribes that would be required to carry out her wishes.

She was almost smiling as she watched him go.

She had made the best of her long exile, but it was also good to be back. She had missed being in the center of everything.

━━∽━━

Xishi hadn't seen her lawyer since she'd conveyed the information she'd tricked from Jehol. The only other news she'd had was disheartening. The guard who brought her food had informed her, with no particular effort to hide his glee, that a date for the trial was being discussed. This wasn't a good sign. Trials in royal court rarely lasted long. Even more rarely were they settled in favor of the accused. She'd known their best hope had been a dismissal. As a result, her awareness that she and Cor could actually lose their lives was sinking in.

But this reality was too much to face. She kept her sanity by filling her mind with the pleasures she planned to share with Cor when they were free. For hours on end, she lived in her imagination: braiding his hair, holding his hand, or simply sitting in his presence and being at peace. Each night, she fell asleep with her head on his phantom chest and dreamed of chasing toddlers into his arms. They were always squealing with laughter, healthy, chubby babies loved by both parents.

Fantasies though these visions were, they felt like the most important stories she'd ever spun—anything to keep the unpleasant present and the possibly intolerable future at bay.

Considering how she'd been occupied, she was more than a little disoriented when four strange guards came to her cell early one morning and unlocked the door.

"Wash your face and tidy up," they said. "It's time to go."

"Is it the trial?" she asked. "Will I meet my lawyer outside?"

They said nothing, just waved her toward the toilet cubicle.

Only when she was safe from view did she press her hands to her abdomen. She didn't know who to pray to, only that she was.

Once she was presentable, the guards escorted her up a private staircase in the prison, then into a windowless black aircar. She saw no one along the way. Clearly, she was being transported, but she had no idea where. Even when the aircar landed, it was in a covered, empty garage. The guards hurried her along another unpeopled corridor—a service corridor, from what she saw of its blank gray walls. At last they reached an unmarked door, and the lead guard shoved it open.

"Here," he said. "Mind your manners."

To her amazement, the guards pushed her through and stayed behind. Xishi found herself in a palace, in a lofty, snow white, diamond-spangled hall. A regal-looking older woman awaited her in front of an immense white-lacquered double door. She was robed in crimson edged with black-spotted fur, a perfect match for the white streaks in her tall coiffure. The grand surroundings could not diminish her. She was the most elegant woman Xishi had ever seen, her cheekbones sharp and slanting, her lips as red as if they'd been painted. Her face was hard and proud, her eyes as still as polished crystal.

She looked naggingly familiar.

With a heart-thumping shock of comprehension, Xishi realized this had to be her grandmother. Tea Rose's efforts to reach her must have borne fruit. One glance at her supremely autocratic bearing made it easy to believe she'd had Jehol's parents killed. This was a woman who would let no one step in her way.

Willing herself to show no fear, Xishi offered as graceful a curtsy as Madame Fagin had ever taught. She felt shorter than usual when she rose. This paragon was over six feet tall.

"Well, you're no imposter," the woman said, her voice as cool as her eyes. "You look more like him than your own mother."

"Him?" Xishi was relieved to find the word steady.

"Your grandfather. He was a good man, in case that concerns you. No idiot, but sweet in the way only humans seem able to be. Of course, you'd be better off leaving that legacy behind you."

Xishi could say nothing. She was working too hard to breathe. Luckily, Xasha Huon seemed to take her silence as a sign of strength. "No comment? Well, keep your own counsel then. I've done a few things for love I've learned not to be sorry for."

This was hard to imagine. "Why are we here?" Xishi asked, realizing she had better not assume anything.

"*I'm* here to save your neck," said her grandmother.

"You're here to keep your mouth shut and your ears open. Until you've amassed my power, speaking up in an emperor's presence is a chancy business at best."

An emperor? Xishi repeated, but no sound issued from her lips.

Being in the company of the emperor was extremely strange. He was beautiful, of course, in a slightly otherworldly way. As far as Xishi knew, all the members of his line—which had ruled for many, many generations—had shared this ethereal handsomeness. With looks like his, the monstrous quartz crystal throne from which he stared down at them was perfectly appropriate. What surprised Xishi was that, despite his physical perfection, he seemed like a real person. His eyes were weary, the pull of his mouth just a trifle sad. He looked as if he'd seen more of life, and of himself, than he'd wanted to.

The trailing sleeves of his official blue, green, and scarlet robes bore creases where he must have been in the habit of rolling them up. They were down now, and the fingers of his right hand, just visible beneath the sapphire-studded border, gripped a small green note.

"I don't know what you think I can do about your situation," he said once their obeisance was complete. "This trial is my wife's affair. More to the point, there can be no question about the charges being valid. Certainly, *you* can have none."

This reference to her grandmother's legal troubles did not cause a ripple to cross Xasha's smooth features. "I notice you didn't invite the empress to witness this adjunct to 'her' affair. Dismiss the guards as well and I'll explain my position."

"Your Magnificence!" protested the behemoth who stood on the platform beside their ruler. The guard's scarlet bandolier bristled like a hedgehog with high-tech weapons.

Clearly piqued, the emperor pressed his handsome lips together. "Oh, go." He gave the guards a tiny shooing motion. "They're not here to kill me, just drive me mad."

"They've been searched," assured the guard who'd admitted them to the throne room.

"I would hope so," said the emperor. "Now, please leave us."

The guards marched out in blank-faced formation, somehow conveying their disapproval with every step.

"Well?" said the emperor after they were gone. "Why have you left the safety of your exile to speak to me?"

"You have my note." Her grandmother gestured toward the paper half-hidden by his sleeve. "Or were you hoping I was just fishing?" The twitch of the emperor's mouth seemed to confirm this jab. Xasha smoothed the rich, spotted fur that circled her neck. "Why don't you let my granddaughter read it? I think it's important that she understand why you're going to pardon her."

The emperor's eyes narrowed down to slits, but to Xishi's surprise, he stood, took one step down the crystal dais and extended the note to her.

When she opened it, the words meant nothing. Rather than say so, she folded it again and handed it back. If she had to be a pawn in this particular game of chess, she decided she'd prefer to be a silent one.

"Such an interesting entity the law is," her grandmother mused. "It decides to punish one or two individuals for an act so many are guilty of."

The emperor clenched his teeth and slid back in his chair. Evidently, Xishi wasn't the only one who'd decided to let her grandmother do the talking.

"Genesis 521," she continued complacently, "is the name of a project only you and the minister of genetics are supposed to know about. A project so old it qualifies as ancient history."

"How did you—"

"Find out about it? Well, Your Magnificence, after I was banished, I had a great deal of time on my hands. Given the crime I was accused of—"

"Convicted of," the emperor interjected, causing Xasha Huon to nod graciously.

"Given the crime I was convicted of by your honorable

father, naturally I was interested in the topic of blood and race, in the origins of yamishkind. How very fascinated I was to discover humans and yama share the same root stock, that they are not—as so many like to believe—different species. I'm sure you were shocked yourself, Your Brilliance, when you learned the truth upon taking the throne."

Xishi didn't get a chance to see his reaction, because her grandmother turned to her.

"Yama come from humans," she explained, her strong hand heavy on Xishi's shoulder. "During a time so far in the past no human record of it exists—and precious few yamish ones—scientists began tweaking the genes of those who had the power and the money to pay for it. When that civilization fell, as civilizations inevitably do, the survivors separated into two groups. Those who'd had their strengths genetically enhanced went into isolation as a means of protecting their advantage. Those who had not, sank into a dark age, evolving much more slowly into the race we know as humans.

"For millennia, our culture has been ruled by our belief that we are superior and must not mix with them, but the truth is that our blood flows from theirs. It is natural for human chi to seduce us. The attraction is our wilder roots calling out to us. Only imagine what would happen to our lovely, self-worshipping society if every yama knew he owed his existence to the creatures he loves to scorn."

Xishi knew her mouth was hanging open, but the emperor had heard this tale before. He drew himself up sternly.

"The Throne will not be blackmailed," he said. "I have only to call my guards and neither you nor your granddaughter will leave this room alive."

"Songyam," Xishi's grandmother scolded, not the least put out. "You must know I have prepared for that. At this moment, a hundred packages containing this assertion, and the documents to back it up, are scattered about the country waiting to be delivered to a hundred human news editors. You know how humans love a scandal. They will print what I send them whether they believe or not, and sometime, somewhere—probably sooner rather than later—the truth will trickle back into yamish lands. If you kill me or my granddaughter, I won't be able to give the hundred secret signals I've set up to prevent this from happening."

The emperor's face had turned a mottled red, and he was breathing harder than any yama who had not run a race around the city should. The hands that gripped the arms of his crystal throne were white-knuckled claws.

"Poor Songyam," her grandmother crooned archly. "Perhaps you'll feel better when I explain just how close *you* are to a yama with 'tainted' blood."

⤚⤙

The emperor didn't appear to feel better once he'd heard about Xishi's mother's theft of his seed. Nor did the prods his memory required to recall the incident improve matters. Xishi could see he would much rather have forgotten that night of weakness when he, the leader of all the yama, succumbed to a half-human. That his weakness had come in part from a loneliness he still suffered under could only re-salt the wound.

By the time Xasha finished speaking, both his eyes and lips were pinched.

"I will pardon her," he said with a single, dark glance at Xishi. "After which you will remove her from my lands."

"You will pardon her prince as well," Xasha said before Xishi could. "And you will promise to do their line no harm."

"Their *line*!" the emperor barked derisively.

"Their children will bear your blood," she reminded him. "And the blood of the Midarri. The time may come when your issue cannot find the black of their eye anywhere else."

"And thus you shall win," the emperor said bitterly.

"Your descendants may win as well. We are an inbred class. Any geneticist can tell you the occasional infusion of fresh blood benefits the pool as a whole."

The emperor shook his sleeves over his hands. "You'll forgive me if I express my wish that neither you nor I shall live to see that day."

This seemed to be their dismissal. Xishi's grandmother bowed, but her own spine felt too apt to topple over to try. Her entire body was shaking from what she'd learned. The place where her grandmother gripped her elbow was her sole point of steadiness.

Evidently, what people had always whispered was true. Her mother had brought her death upon herself.

Knowing this affected her differently than she'd anticipated. She felt sad for Xoushou, but she could not make her mother's drama real to herself. It was removed, not only by time but by temperament. Emperor's daughter or not, Xishi couldn't think like one. The treasures she was willing to fight for had nothing to do with pride.

Her relative did not speak until they emerged from the palace and stood in the bright, cold sun. Xishi turned her face to its lemon rays. A haze of frost from the night before sparkled on the grounds. They were in the imperial gardens, where she and Cor had walked a lifetime ago.

"You did well," her grandmother said. "I realize that could not have been pleasant."

Xishi wondered if she meant discovering the truth about her conception, or that her father's sole response consisted of a desire that she be sent away.

"Will he do what he promised?" she asked instead. "Will he let Cor and me go free?"

Her grandmother nodded. "Songyam is an honest man for an emperor—even a kind one, from what I hear. His other children rather follow their mother's pattern. He may find he's not as ready to cut his ties to you as he believes."

Xishi wasn't sure how she felt about this idea, but it was not the last startling speech Xasha Huon would make.

"Come sit with me," she said, leading Xishi to a sheltered marble bench. A guard dressed all in crimson stood nearby—Xasha's guard, she was sure. When they were seated, Xishi's grandmother patted her knee.

"I owe you an apology. I left you to languish after your mother died. Her death took something out of me, something I could not replace. I thought I was invincible until then, but when I lost her, I wondered why I'd ever thought my ambitions were important."

"And was that all I was to you?" Xishi found herself compelled to ask. "Another of your ambitions?"

Her grandmother touched her hair so gently Xishi barely felt the contact. "You were a symbol of them, certainly. At the time, I convinced myself you'd be better off on your own. You were with the Midarri, where we'd meant you to be. You had a chance to make something of yourself without my old scandals to drag you down. But I should have followed your progress. I should have made certain you remained well."

It was the first apology anyone had ever given her for the challenges she'd faced. Xishi discovered that it meant more to her than she'd thought mere words could. Her grandmother was confirming what she'd always tried to believe: Like any child, she'd deserved better.

"You came when it counted," she said softly. "That is what matters now."

Her grandmother's eyes glittered. She covered her mouth in what looked to be a combination of embarrassment and humor at her own emotion.

"Oh," she said, the little sound verging on a laugh. "Your heart is so very like his—your grandfather's. I should be sorry, but, at this moment, I am forced to admit I'm not!"

A dish best eaten

❦

Corum's circumstances changed so quickly it made his head hurt. One minute he was locked in a cell, racking his brains for some new stratagem they might try, and the next minute he was free.

And not just free: He was pardoned, banished, and escorted by a squadron of Midarri guards to Thousand Plum Tree Square, where those of his staff who'd chosen to join him in exile were waiting. To his surprise, he saw quite a crowd outside the palace, though some might only have been there to gawk. Above the square, behind the swooping eaves of his home, a line of aircars were being loaded with belongings.

Banished he might be, but not empty-handed. As part of Xasha Huon's agreement with the emperor, he would keep his holdings. He could continue to run his businesses, just not from yamish lands.

Corum pressed his hand to his forehead, having trouble taking it all in. He was almost afraid to look around for Xishi. She'd been released earlier than he, but surely she

was here somewhere. He ached to hold her after their
time apart. He wasn't used to thinking about his actions
from a woman's perspective. Would she be disappointed he
had not passed more messages between their lawyers? He
had wanted to, but everything he'd longed to say was personal. Now his dearest wish was to kiss her, to pull her into
his arms and assure himself no imprisonment could change
the strength of their connection.

At this point, he didn't think he cared if he caused a
scene.

He'd given in to his temptation to scan the crowd when
Habii pushed to him through a line of guards. Luckily for
Habii, they recognized him.

"Master!" he said, his mustache quivering. "You are all
right! I am coming with you, and I don't even know where
we're going!"

This prospect had so clearly frazzled the valet that Corum had to fight a smile. Hoping to calm him, he braced
Habii's shoulders between his hands.

"I am glad," he said. "As long as you're there to look out
for us, I know wherever we go will be fine."

Habii's face threatened to crumple at the praise, but he
mastered himself. "It will be more than fine, Your Highness. I am certain you will choose well for all of us."

"I'll do my best. And now *I* am certain I must let you go.
There seems to be much to organize."

"Yes," said Habii, clearly feeling he was the only man
for the job.

Corum literally bumped into his mother as he craned
around a cluster of servants for what he thought had been a
glimpse of one of Xishi's gowns. Reluctantly, he stopped
for Corynna.

"Son," she said, gripping both his sleeves. "You're home."

Her eyes were pleading and bright with tears, her robes
and hair not quite as tidy as usual. He felt her love for him,
her desperation to be forgiven. She seemed fragile of a
sudden, an object of pity rather than anger. Despite his impatience to be elsewhere, he laid the back of his fingers
against her cheek.

"Mother," he said, "thank you for greeting me."

"It will be all right," she whispered, her manner conspiratorial and a little odd. "If we wait long enough, people will forget you mated with that girl. You'll be able to come back and marry a real princess."

He didn't drop his hand from her cheek, though as he turned its palm to her skin, it felt as cold and heavy as a hand of lead. Even now, she refused to accept the choice he'd made.

He knew why that was. She'd been raised to think of humans—of everyone—as less than she was. Her tolerance of difference had extended to her own blood, but no farther—and only if that difference could be hidden. Corum had aped such attitudes himself, and yet, when it came down to it, he wasn't sure he'd believed. It had been all too easy to cast off his prejudices when he fell in love.

"Mother," he said, "the only way I'll ever come back here is with Xishi."

She blanched and backed away from him, the crowd immediately moving to swallow her. "I only ever tried to love you," he thought she said.

He sighed from deep in his belly as he watched her disappear. Though they'd been at odds for years, he hadn't truly expected it to come to this. Maybe they would find a way to be civil or maybe not, but the ties that had so tightly bound them—the anger, the obligation, and the regret—had finally been cut. His soul had registered the snap. What Corynna Midarri thought and felt about his decisions would never matter to him again.

"The butterfly does not fear the changing wind," said a familiar voice behind his shoulder. "Though sometimes he does miss his former companions."

"Master Ping!" Corum cried, spinning around to face him. The old man was beaming with pleasure, and Corum could not stop himself from pulling him into a tight embrace.

This man he would miss. This man had been the best parent anyone could have.

"Ach!" Master Ping exclaimed even as he slapped Corum's back. "Let your teacher breathe."

"I cannot believe you're here."

"And where else would I be? Are you not the student of whom I am proudest?"

Corum had to snort through his nose because he was, in that moment, obliged to wipe a bit of moisture from beneath his eyes.

Master Ping shook his finger. "Do not be ashamed of your feelings. And do not neglect your practice after you leave here. You are closer to learning everything I tried to teach you than you imagine."

Corum dried his face with his sleeve. "And what would the butterfly do in my shoes?"

"The butterfly would fly, my prince. Far away with his butter-wife. And they would both do their best to live a happy life." The fondness did not leave Master Ping's expression as he glanced over Corum's shoulder. "I see your father. I will leave you two to your words with my best wishes."

The crowd was getting thicker by the minute. Corum had trouble spotting his father, though he must have been close. Half the Forbidden City seemed to have turned out to see the latest scandal's conclusion. Long-lens vidcams glinted from windows and balconies, the reporters kept at a distance by his guards. When Corum's view was clear, he saw that Poll Midarri had a companion—a tall older woman with dramatic white streaks winding through her high, lacquered hair. Her face was lovely and proud . . . and hard enough to have been chiseled out of granite.

The muscles at the back of Corum's neck tightened. This woman didn't resemble Xishi, but he knew at once who it was. He also knew he and Xishi had been lucky she was on their side.

Wary, he bowed to her deeply.

"This is Xasha Huon," his father said, sounding slightly wary himself, "whom we all owe a debt."

"The boy knows who I am."

Her tone was curt enough to bring Corum stiffly out of his bow. She measured him up and down with her gaze. When her cool eyes returned to his, he was prepared to meet ice with ice. "Xishi and I thank you for your intervention on our behalf."

Something flickered behind Xasha's proud, still face. When she spoke, he realized it was amusement. "Your great-grandfather used to stare people down that way. Merciless as the dead of winter. It quite terrified me when I was a girl."

"I did not mean to insult you—" he began, but Xasha cut him off.

"No insult taken. I'm glad my girl fell for a prince with spine. If there's anything you need, you've only to ask."

Corum hesitated. There was a matter he wanted help with, but he wondered what the help might cost. He needn't have debated. Xasha read him easily enough.

"There *is* something you want," she said, delighted in her dry, dragonish way. "Do tell me what. It's been so long since I had anyone to do favors for."

Corum spared a glance for his father. "I'm only reluctant to ask because you've done so much for us already."

"I did what I did for my granddaughter," Xasha said. "For you I have done nothing."

"In that case," Corum said, appreciating her bluntness, "it would be a comfort to me if you would help my father with a commission. It may be more than he can safely see to on his own."

His father looked mildly offended and Xasha intrigued. Corum steadied his breathing. He had thought this through while he was imprisoned, and had planned to handle it himself, but the swiftness with which the emperor pronounced their sentence had precluded that. He considered a moment longer and then decided. Deepening the debt he owed Xasha Huon didn't matter any more than the last jagged edges of his jealousy.

For Xishi's sake, this was a wrong he must try to right.

"My wife made a friend at the Purple Crane," he said. "A man named Prince Pahndir who was sold into servitude to the madame against his will."

"Oh, that's a bit of fiction," his father said dismissively. "No doubt, some down-on-his-luck royal took the name to save his own family's pride. The real Prince Pahndir is dead. He died in an aircar crash, a year or so after his wife committed suicide. I remember because people were saying the crash wasn't an accident, that Prince Pahndir killed himself out of grief."

Corum shook his head. "I've had time to remember the old stories. Prince Pahndir's family is related to the Fengs. He was the cousin Muto's father tried to supplant him with. The court disqualified Pahndir for being unsound of mind, after which his family announced his 'death.' Having seen the way Muto works, I suspect he may have nudged the wife into suicide, trusting that her loss would send his rival around the bend." Corum cleared his throat. "Rumor had it that Prince Pahndir was a solitary. His wife was the only match he would ever have."

Corum's father found something fascinating on his slippers' pointed toes, no doubt aware that his son likely shared the trait.

"That is a sad fate for anyone," he said slowly, "but I don't think we could fight Muto in court and win—even if we had evidence."

"I wasn't thinking of fighting," Corum said, making sure his voice was low. "I was thinking of breaking Pahndir out and transporting him somewhere hard to find."

"Oh," said his father, taken aback.

Xasha's mouth quirked up at the corners. "You do owe that Madame Fagin a slap for saying she gave your son full disclosure about my granddaughter's human blood. Stealing the cornerstone to her pillow house's success might be an appropriate punishment."

Corum's father rubbed his chin thoughtfully.

"My men can handle it," Xasha offered, "if you feel uneasy breaking the law."

"No," his father said. "In this particular instance, I believe I feel fine. I was merely thinking it would be best to do this fast, before it occurs to anyone that we might strike back."

"Excellent." Xasha purred softly in approval, a disconcerting sound coming from her. "My poor, bored men are going to be happy we came here."

The crowd behind the conspirators parted momentarily, allowing Corum a glimpse of shining garnet-black hair. Only one person he knew had hair that color. His heart gave a leap that drove every other thought from his mind.

"Excuse me," he said, shouldering past his father. "I must leave you now."

Xasha Huon's knowing hum bothered him not at all.

⁓

By some means Xishi didn't want to inquire into too closely, Tea Rose and Mingmar had obtained a day-leave from pillow school to say good-bye. Tea Rose seemed to understand the immensity of what Xishi had escaped, but Mingmar was mostly upset that she would no longer be a convenient friend. The possibility that she might have died appeared not to have crossed his mind, or that Madame Fagin had a hand in putting her in danger. Xishi couldn't imagine what he'd say if he knew she was the emperor's daughter.

"*Must* you go to some horrid human city?" he was asking.

"Those were the emperor's terms," Xishi confirmed, refraining from pointing out that she was, in part, a horrid human herself. This aspect of the pardoned charges had made the news. "Cor and I are required to leave yamish lands."

"Well, at least you'll be with your husband," he conceded, his face betraying some confusion as to how her marriage to her master had come about. Tea Rose must have kept her lips sealed on that. "I suppose he'll still be a prince to humans."

"And rich," Tea Rose added softly, rolling mischievous eyes toward the aircars being loaded on the roof.

"But how will you let us know how you are?" Mingmar asked worriedly. "If you're in human territory, you won't be able to use banned technology. You'll be cut off from the yamaweb!"

"I suspect we'll still have access to that," Xishi said, suppressing her amusement at the horror in his voice. "My grandmother mentioned we can have whatever conveniences are easily hidden. Plus, I think she's planning to buy us a few exemptions as a wedding gift."

Mingmar shivered at the mention of Xasha Huon, the formidable old woman having frightened him down to his aqua slippers during their brief meeting. Tea Rose had been intrigued, perhaps seeing in her the matriarch qualities she aspired to.

Before Mingmar could express his condolences over Xishi's newly discovered relative, Tea Rose put her hand on his arm. She tipped her head meaningfully toward someone behind Xishi. "Come away, Mingmar. I believe we're about to lose our friend's attention."

Xishi turned and saw Cor pushing through the crush to her. His height made him stand out, and the intensity of the emotion blazing in his face. Her heart pounded with excitement. He was thinner than when she'd last seen him and had dark circles under his eyes, but he was still the most beautiful sight in the world.

He stopped before her, his hands rising to her shoulders and then her face. His thumbs stroked gently over her cheekbones.

"Xishi," he said in a throaty rasp.

She went on her tiptoes to catch his lips.

The second their mouths touched, his breath rushed out. His tongue pushed deep inside with a little moan, restraint impossible then. The slide and pull of their tongues was immediately sexual—not that Cor seemed to mind. He kissed her as if no one were there to see it, as if he loved her too much to care if someone was. Xishi clung to his shoulders and pressed her body to his full length—eager, tender, *home* in a way no set of rooms would ever re-create.

With a soft utterance of pleasure, he rubbed his hands along her back, molding her lower body against his arousal's rise.

It was a long, long time before he let her go.

"You're all right?" he asked huskily, his eyes shining.

She nodded through her tears.

"And the babies?"

She touched the warmth of his face. "I don't think they

even noticed anything was wrong. They were off in tiny baby land—wherever that is."

"With the fairies," he said softly, "like you used to tell me stories about."

She smiled. "With the fairies and the good dragons."

He put his hand between them shyly, covering the place their children were growing. "I can feel that glow of theirs just a bit. I'll kiss them, too, when we're alone."

She kissed him for them, gently on the lips. What she felt in that moment was sweeter than peace; it was pure joy.

She didn't know whose energy was rising—hers, his, the babies'—but she felt it humming through her, stretching like rays of sunshine until everything around her seemed to have a ringing, diamond clarity.

She heard the voice as if it spoke in her ear, one note out of place in the symphony.

It isn't going to end this way. You aren't going to be happy.

Cor's head came up. "Did you hear that?" he said, looking this way and that.

She couldn't answer. The air had turned to molasses. She turned her head through the strange resistance. The sun flashed off something shiny on the Midarri roof.

Camera, she thought even as Cor shoved her behind him.

"Down!" he shouted. "Gun!" Blood sprayed out from his arm a instant before she heard a muffled report.

The world returned to normal speed as abruptly as if time had punched her in the heart. People around them screamed and crouched down. Horrified, Xishi stared at the spreading red spot on Cor's sleeve.

"It's just a scratch," Cor said, squeezing her arm hard enough to penetrate her terror. "It barely hit me."

Xishi checked for Tea Rose and Mingmar, and heaved a sigh to see both were fine. Mingmar's gallant side had come out; he was shielding the slender pillow girl with his body.

She and Cor had plenty of shielding. They were on their knees, guards flanking them on every side with their weapons drawn. One gestured to a projectile half-buried in the paver beside Xishi's knee. The thing was thicker than her thumb.

"That'll kill anyone it hits," Cor said. "And in this crowd, it's bound to hit someone. We've got to get that shooter."

"I can send some men around the back. Sneak up on him."

"Do it, and radio whoever's inside to get the house defenses down. We don't want the system targeting our own people. Shit. He must have taken out whoever we posted on the roof. I'll take three men through the front and up the elevator from inside."

"Sir . . ."

"I can move through the palace faster. You organize the rest to protect the crowd. Maybe someone can pick off the shooter from the windows across the way. And get the princess to safety!"

Cor wasn't waiting for the guard's permission. He took off like a gazelle for the palace steps, leaping over the bodies hunkered in the plaza. The gun barked again and someone near Cor screamed.

The sound shook the guard out of his stupefaction. He started spitting information into his mouthpiece. "Get the princess out of here," he ordered the guards next to him.

Two men picked her up and started running, her feet no longer touching the ground. "Go with the prince," she pleaded, but neither paid her any mind.

One grunted and nearly fell as something hit him.

"Faster," said the other. "He'll stop shooting once he can't see her."

They pushed through the panicked crowd until they reached the farther corner of the next palace. Getting her to safety seemed to give the guard who'd been struck a license to collapse. He pitched face forward into the shadow and began to jerk. The same projectile she'd seen before was sticking out of his shoulder blade. The blood that welled around it was smoking.

"Fuck," said his companion. "That bullet carried a charge. I think he's having a heart attack."

Xishi could see that the fallen man's aura was going crazy, its normal rhythms desynchronized.

"I can help him," she said, rolling him over and tearing his uniform open over his chest. Her mind was too full of fear for Cor to question why she thought this. It was instinct, or maybe insanity. But human etheric-force did more than get yama drunk; it was supposed to have health-enhancing effects as well. She pressed her hands flat atop his heart, willing her energy to entrain his back into harmony. Her chi swelled so strongly—like a bright, white flame roaring up her spine—that her brain seemed to be swooping inside her head.

The wounded man's eyes fluttered.

"Shh," she said, hoping he could hear her. She recognized him as one of the quiet guards who had escorted her on her walks. "It's all right. Just relax."

His body went completely still.

No, she thought, fearing the worst, but a moment later he quivered and drew a breath.

The guard beside her whispered something in relief, then keyed on his mouthpiece. "Tell Prince Corum the princess is safe."

Xishi was glad Cor would know this. She just wished someone could give her the same assurance.

There wasn't a doubt in his mind who the sniper was. Jehol must have found a blind spot in the house defenses. Corum knew he'd been to Midarri Palace before—as had his master and mistress.

"Don't underestimate this man," he said to the guards who'd accompanied him. "He has royal blood and possibly some martial arts training. His reflexes may be as good as mine."

The three guards, all daimyo, nodded grimly. They'd followed Corum's exploits in tournaments and didn't take his skills lightly—probably the only reason they'd allowed him to lead them through the house. Together, they'd taken the elevator to the floor just beneath the roof. From here, they would split up, so as not to present a single target when they emerged. They could hear the shooter firing intermittently, so they knew he was still up there.

"You're sure it's this Jehol?" asked one.

"I'm sure. Revenge may be a dish best eaten cold, but he'll eat it any way he can at this point. With luck, he'll be furious enough to make mistakes."

"All right then," said the team leader, with an air of gathering himself. "Let's make sure we don't give him the same advantage."

None of the men let Corum take the elevator to the landing pad. This was the area the shots were coming from, and Jehol was sure to be watching it. They understood why Corum felt he had to be here, but that didn't mean they'd let him be killed.

He was relegated to a distant staircase instead, where he'd have to run across the maze-like network of catwalks to be any use at all.

Or possibly not. As fate would have it, the chase was coming toward him when he reached the roof. Jehol was running flat out, doing his best to escape his pursuers by leaping from catwalk to catwalk over the gulfs between. He was fast for a man his size, and either fearless or desperate. The roofs of the Midarri Palace rose and fell like a silver sea, as steep and slippery as if they'd been oiled. Even as Corum watched, one of the guards misjudged the distance of a leap and ended up sliding down the roof tiles. All that saved him from the final drop was being impaled through the thigh by one of the house's disarmed security devices.

Corum hissed through his teeth, knowing the man could bleed to death if he wasn't helped. He hoped the other two guards had the sense to stop and do it. Corum could take care of Jehol. Corum would be happy to.

For that matter, he might have to. As fast as he was, Jehol would soon leave the heavily armored men behind.

He felt his own determination, the simmer of rage that powered his muscles as he leapt from his current walk to one that would bring him closer to Jehol's path. The arm the pillow boy had creased with his bullet only burned a little as he ran.

Watch your control, he told himself, flying across another chasm without a thought. *Let him be the one whose emotions get the best of him.*

Jehol heard Corum's weight clang down on the metal walkway, which prompted him to stop long enough to turn and shoot. Corum ducked, cursing the lack of cover, but the gutter the projectile shattered wasn't even close. Apparently, Jehol hadn't expected to hit him. The pillow boy laughed and shook the gun above his head.

"Come and get me," he shouted. "I'd love to kill that Huon bitch's precious prince face to face!"

Corum literally saw red, fury goading him to attempt a jump so wide it was beyond even his fully royal strength. Falling short of his goal, he had to catch himself on the walk's railing. This left him swinging dizzily above the gulf below, but he didn't waste time berating himself or let the near miss steal his nerve. Instead, he grunted with effort and swung himself up. His bicep twinged, warning him its numbness from the strafing was wearing off. Corum ignored it. He was on the same path as Jehol now.

Breaking back into his run, he drew the weapon the senior guard had forced on him—a lightweight, plasmabolt handgun. Corum might not be a marksman, but he could make Jehol think twice before he tried to shoot him again.

Someone shouted a ways behind him, probably a guard wanting him to stop. Corum just increased his speed. He was closing the distance between him and Jehol. He could see the sweat staining the man's simple fighting robes, could almost smell his loss of hope . . .

And then Jehol vaulted over the catwalk railing, propelling himself into space. It was a beautiful, insane leap, taking him over the nearest roofline. He disappeared behind the other side, where Corum heard him land and slide. What he didn't hear was the sound of a body hitting the ground.

Corum couldn't hesitate. If he gave Jehol a chance to settle into this sheltered spot, he'd be in the best possible position to pluck off his pursuers. Even if they waited him out and scrambled an aircar, that rifle of his was powerful enough to take one down. Rather than let Jehol claim another life, Corum found the nearest launching spot and flung himself toward the same roof.

He landed with a bone-jarring rattle on the nearer side, the slippery, silver-coated tiles almost defeating his attempts to get purchase. His breath was nearly but not quite knocked out of him. Fortunately, no shots rang out. When he finally clawed his way up to the top and peered briefly over, he didn't see what he expected.

Jehol, the pillow boy, was dangling by both hands from a roof ornament, the gilded bronze dragon all that spared him from a five-storey plunge into a courtyard. His overdeveloped muscles bulged against the seams of his plain black robes.

"Help me," he said weakly, his face red with strain. "My arms are ready to give out."

Corum swung up to straddle the roofline, his brain struggling to adjust to this turning of tables.

"That bitch's grandmother killed my parents," Jehol pleaded. "I was only trying to even the scales."

Corum had stuffed his gun into the back of his trousers before he jumped. Now he pulled it out, aimed, and steadied the butt with his other hand. His arm was throbbing where he'd been shot, but even he couldn't miss at this distance. Seeing what he'd done, Jehol's eyes widened.

"Please," he said. "You understand family honor. You can't kill me in cold blood."

It was hardly cold. Corum's body seethed with anger. This man had tried to kill his beloved, once through the empress and once by his own hand. Loyal guards lay dead because of him, and probably more than one bystander.

Corum could have lost his unborn children because of this man's vendetta against his wife.

His muscles shook with fury as he clicked off the handgun's safety and curled his finger through the trigger guard. Fuck trying to act like the Prince of Ice. Peace didn't come from locking his emotions inside a box. It came from allowing himself to be who he was.

The words sparked a memory. He had thought them before, drunk on kith from making love to Xishi when he was in heat. He'd dismissed the revelation as inebriated nonsense, but now it cleared his mind unexpectedly.

He stopped trying to push himself in any direction and turned his attention inward. The knowledge came that his emotions held the answer. They would tell him which way to go.

Without question, they were strong—vengefulness, fear for his family's safety, the aching love he felt for Xishi. When he let his feelings be, neither fighting nor denying them, he saw they were not the poison he'd always feared. To his surprise, beneath them lay a pool of quiet—the very quiet he'd thought could only exist in his deepest meditative state. But it had been there all along. It was a deeper part of him than fear or anger. Those would pass. His peaceful center was forever.

The epiphany didn't distract him from the choice he faced. Jehol was weeping, one hand reaching for him beseechingly. Then, as if this effort was too much for his flagging strength, the arm he'd lifted to plead with dropped beneath the edge of the roof.

Metal scraped metal, and from the silence within Corum a sense of something not right emerged. His gaze flicked to the courtyard below. Jehol's charge-bolt rifle wasn't lying there.

Jehol's head exploded in a hot red cloud almost before Corum knew he'd shot him. The decision seemed to have taken no time at all. What remained of the body immediately plummeted, its right hand wrapped around the weapon Jehol must have stashed under the overhang. So desperate was the grip that his fingers didn't release the stock until impact.

Jehol's seeming helplessness, his appeal to Corum's mercy, had been a ruse to get Corum to let down his guard. In the end, the pillow boy had proved his royal blood ran true.

Corum didn't know how long he sat there staring at Jehol's headless body, every muscle he possessed quivering with shock. He'd never taken a life before, and had scarcely had a chance to realize he'd had no choice but to take this one.

He came to himself when a guard in a safety harness clambered up the slope of the roof.

"He's dead, Your Highness," assured the man. "You got him."

Corum fought a surge of nausea. "The princess?"

"Safe, Your Highness. We wanted to tell you, but you didn't have an earpiece. I hear she saved one of the guards' lives."

"Glad to hear it." Corum's state of mind was so peculiar that this news came as no surprise. Why shouldn't Xishi save a life? Had she not, in her way, saved his? "Maybe now people will see she's just as good as anyone."

"Yes, sir," said the guard, buckling him into a second harness. Another guard waited on the catwalk to haul them up. Corum needed the help. His knees had turned to jelly. "We guards have been thinking for some time that Princess Buttercup is better than most. Very polite she is, no matter who she's dealing with."

Cor couldn't help but smile at both the name and the compliment. They might be going into exile, but it seemed they would be leaving friends behind.

free at last

❦

Cor pushed halfway inside her with a quiet groan, his phallus thick and pulsing, his eyes shuttered with delight.

Apart from a wall of crates lashed with shockproof webbing to hooks in the floor, Cor and Xishi had the cabin of the largest aircar to themselves. Once Cor assured her the door between them and the pilots locked on their side, it took less than two minutes for her to tear off her clothes. Cor was even faster, and took advantage of his lead to unroll a sleeping cushion on the carpet. Xishi practically flung herself onto it and spread her legs, a boldness she didn't get a chance to be embarrassed about. Her mate had followed her quickly down, his right hand aiming his erection before his left hit the floor.

They'd been too long apart to bother with foreplay.

Now, as the aircar's liftoff slung him a little deeper, they both made small, appreciative noises.

"I missed this," he said, the light fur on his chest brushing her breasts. "Every night in that prison, I fell asleep dreaming of you."

Xishi stretched under him, her hands running up the smoothness of his muscled back beneath the even sweeter silk of his hair. Despite their mutual impatience, he had unbound his braid for her. She drew her fingers through the long black strands and hummed with pleasure. Cor's eyes darkened at her enjoyment of his assets. He ducked his head until his lips met her ear.

"You know what else I missed?" he whispered. "How fucking wonderful you smell."

His words were candy for her sex, melting in the heat they raised. She hitched her knees higher on his waist, trying to coax his huge erection in farther. He wasn't in heat, so the fit was tight. He grunted, constrained his size enough to penetrate all the way, and then let his girth relax.

"That's what *I* missed," she cooed, wriggling helplessly at the delicious pressure against her walls. "Nothing feels as good as you completely inside me."

He nipped her earlobe. "I want to stay like this for a while."

She moaned at the idea of waiting, but she understood his need just to enjoy being connected.

"Here," he said, his hand slipping under her buttock. "Turn on your side and sling your leg over my hip."

Xishi rolled with his help, the pressure they both exerted keeping the joining tight. Once they were settled in this new position, he circled his hips against her, a tight, pleasurable movement, testing how much scope his hardness had to move.

Just enough, she thought with an inner sigh. His lips curved softly. Perhaps he'd guessed what she was thinking.

"Now I have my brain back," he said. "I really couldn't think until I was inside you."

"Why do you need to think?" she teased, drawing an X across his right nipple.

He sucked in an interested breath but caught her hand. "I thought you might like to hear where we're going."

"I would," she agreed.

To increase her comfort while she listened, he tucked an upholstered pillow beneath her head. "We can change our minds if we don't like it," he assured her, "but I thought we'd try our luck in Bhamjran."

"Isn't that in the desert?"

"Near it. It's very hot, but I thought we might like the change. For a human city it's quite cosmopolitan—a melting pot. I know a few yama who do business there. I don't think we'd have trouble fitting in. The Bhamjrishi have a reputation for open-mindedness."

The wag of his brows told her they weren't just open-minded about commerce.

"That sounds nice." She pressed her hips more strongly into his groin. "It will be strange living among, well, sort of my own people. I hope I get a chance to use the dialect I know."

"You speak human?"

"Avvarian. I taught myself at pillow school." She laughed at the unwitting irony. "In my daydreams, I always found some way to meet you and impress you with how smart I was for a rohn."

"And instead we discover you're a royal . . . who happens to read auras unusually well."

"I don't know why that is. Unless I simply convinced myself I ought to be able to."

"Mm," Cor hummed, his hand smoothing up her breast to mold it higher on her ribs. "I suspect your human quarter makes you a wild card. Who knows what else we'll find you can do?"

He bent to suck her nipple with distracting strength, the pull of his cheeks tugging at nerves that rooted much lower. Xishi's already slippery pussy began to liquefy.

"I think—" she said, her thought processes abruptly more disjointed than before. She gasped for breath as he switched his suckling to the other breast. "I was always curious about humans. I think I'm looking forward to the adventure."

"What about this adventure?" He growled the question, sexy and low, rolling her under him again.

His weight was lovely, especially when he put it all behind his first slow thrust.

"My grandmother wants to visit us," she panted before she could forget.

Cor stopped moving. "She's welcome," he said. "As long as she leases her own house."

"Will your parents want to visit?" she asked shyly.

Cor released his breath on a sigh. "I don't know. I may never want my mother to come."

Xishi nodded, not wanting to push him to explain. He would when he was ready. She'd learned for herself that parents could be complicated, especially royal ones. Wanting to soothe him, she ran one finger down the distinctive silver streak in his hair.

"You know when I got that?" he asked, shifting his weight onto his elbows.

Xishi shook her head.

"It was the night my mother sent you from the palace. I woke up the next morning and it was there. When I was younger, I liked to call it her badge of shame. Now I think it was my true self's way of never letting me forget you."

"I never forgot you, either. So many times I dreamed of meeting up with you, even when it seemed foolish to."

"You were waiting for me to save you."

Her mouth fell open at his unexpectedly pointed guess.

"You told me yourself," he said, his voice very quiet and serious. "That day you stormed into my rooms. You said you were tired of waiting for me to save you."

"I didn't mean—"

"Yes, you did." His hands stroked her hair gently from her brow. "And you were right. I should have tried to find you years ago. You were more my responsibility than anyone's."

She could have made a thousand protests—that she'd only been a childhood friend, that his mother's reasons hadn't been without validity. She didn't want to argue any of these things. She wanted him to know she absolved him completely.

"Do you like who I am?" she asked.

"I love who you are" was his rough answer.

"And I love who you are, so I think we both have to

accept the journey we took to get here, without blaming anyone. Including me."

"Who could blame you?"

She smiled at the anger coloring his voice, loving that she didn't have to guard her face with him. Chances were this freedom would only grow. Certainly, living among humans would do nothing to discourage it.

"Some might blame me," she said, "for allowing Matreya to convince me to leave. Some might blame me for never trying to contact you. But I am going to forgive me, and I think you should do the same. We found each other, and we were fortunate enough to be able to fall in love when we did. As far as I'm concerned, that's no small blessing."

Blessing was a human concept, but Corum decided he could live with it.

"We'll start anew," he said, "with a clean, fresh slate."

He loved the grin with which she greeted this—and the suggestive undulation of her hips. The first came from the renegade child she'd been, the second from the woman she had become.

"I'll tell you what you could start," she said, her hands sliding to his rear to squeeze. He knew she was inviting him to begin thrusting.

"Ah," he said, joy rising in him like the sun. "You always did like flying."

The other prince

〰️

Eavesdropping hadn't been Prince Pahndir's intent.

He hadn't known what was happening when the guards slipped into his rooms at the Purple Crane. Breaking into a pillow house was no great feat, but these men were professionals. Silent as the grave, they'd worn no livery, their all-black outfits bearing no identifying mark. Prince Pahndir's first thought was that his family had finally decided to validate their lie.

His second was whether he minded.

But it wasn't his day to die. The guards informed him he was coming with them, then led him—without explanation—to an aircar that had been fitted out to look like a food delivery airvan. It set down on the roof of Midarri Palace, a place he'd only ever seen from outside. His family hadn't been as high on the royal ladder as that of Buttercup's prince.

The thought of her tightened the muscles above his breastbone. Buttercup must have had something to do with his removal from the pillow house, and he was far from sure that was a good thing. He'd heard the other students talking about her arrest, but had only gotten pieces of the story. Madame Fagin had been uncustomarily nervous since the event, snapping at her students and working girls alike. It was as if she were hoping her former pupil would be executed, and—for some unfathomable reason—feared the consequences if she were not. Pahndir supposed his liberation from the madame's care meant the trial had gone Buttercup's way.

Somehow, he doubted the silent guards would confirm this if he asked.

Before he could attempt it, they were transferring him from the delivery vehicle to a private aircar that was emblazoned with the Midarri crest. Normally, it would have seated eight in luxury, but the seats had been removed to make room for a pile of plastic packing crates. The guards withdrew once he was inside, with the exception of the youngest one.

"We'll move you to another flyer for liftoff," he said. "Some of the other cars were compromised during an incident this afternoon, but the security systems in this one are fine. You'll be safe as long as you don't unlock the door."

Safe from what? Pahndir thought as the door slid shut behind his last companion. *And safe* for *what?*

He could have cursed Buttercup for involving herself in his affairs. What happened to him hadn't mattered in a long time. His body's reactions to her were nothing more than a stirring of physical urges that hadn't had the decency to die with his heart. He cared about her just enough to wish her far away from him.

That night in Madame Fagin's parlor, watching through the hidden portrait hole as the girls lined up, he'd seen Prince Corum's eyes go black. He hadn't been certain he and Buttercup would be mates, but he had sensed their relationship would be rare. He'd wanted Buttercup to have that. Only she, out of all of Madame Fagin's classes of students, had treated him like a man. She shouldn't be jeopardizing her future by championing his cause. If he'd wanted it championed, he'd have fought for himself. As it was, he'd discouraged her as cuttingly as he could from giving him a second thought after she left.

It had been the only act he'd been proud of in years. And now it seemed it hadn't worked.

He pressed his temples between the heels of his palms. Couldn't she see his family had been right to do what they did? Thallah's death had exposed his fatal weakness, had made it obvious to anyone who met him that he'd never survive the cutthroat world of royal life. He was damaged. He couldn't lead his own second-tier family, much less a powerful one like the Fengs.

If Buttercup had ruined her chance for happiness by helping him, he'd never forgive himself.

He didn't know how long he stood there, wondering what in creation he could do that wouldn't make matters worse. As much as an hour might have passed. Though the aircar's cabin windows were opaqued for privacy, the change in the light told him winter's early dusk had descended.

It occurred to him that the guards had not come back to move him to another car. Had something happened to rob them of the chance? They'd seemed too professional to forget, but maybe his disappearance had been noticed, and they didn't want to risk discovery with more contact. He hoped they'd warned whoever's vehicle this was that he was here . . . unless they'd decided to give the owners deniability about their stowaway.

With this possibility uppermost in his mind, he heard footsteps coming up the outside ramp.

He moved with the quickness any royal prince could call upon. Mere seconds were required to lift the stretchy web that secured the crates and make a cave for himself between them. He was well concealed, if not comfortable, by the time Prince Corum and Buttercup walked in.

It was immediately obvious they had no idea he was there. The sound of their openmouthed kisses was a plague he could have done without. Robes were torn off and thrown, endearments exchanged, then overtaken by sighs and moans. He knew the instant the prince slid inside his partner. That groan of relieved entry was one he'd made himself countless times.

To judge by the ensuing, breathless conversation, they were mates after all, and joyous ones. Though Pahndir had wanted a future like this for Buttercup, knowing she had it hurt all the same.

He remembered being that much in love, remembered needing so deeply to connect that it was agony. Thallah had been the perfect playmate for his erotic adventuring, a lover and confidante. He'd thought he'd known her better than any living creature until she killed herself.

That had been a breach of trust he still didn't understand.

His body woke at the memories, but even more at Buttercup's extremely aroused nearness. He knew she was part-human; that bit of news had reached him. He supposed this was why her chi had been so intoxicating, why it had made him feel he could almost come when she stroked him. Her energy teased him now. His heat was days away, but— as had happened so many times at the pillow school—he felt her presence spur it on early.

He lifted within his clothing, thickening, stretching, growing heavy with blood and lust. Images clawed unbidden through his mind. Tearing Prince Corum off his beloved. Taking his place between her legs. Plunging himself into Buttercup so hard she screamed.

In the end, the desperate pounding of his cock was too much to bear. He'd been deprived of true release for too long—through every heat since Thallah died, through every class of students who tried to devise new ways to "get a rise" from him. No matter that the drive for sex wasn't that different from the drive for life; some dark and bestial corner of his soul was perfectly ready to betray his one great love. His soul was exhausted with just surviving. It wanted to mate again.

He shoved his hand into his trousers and gripped himself. Up and down he rubbed his aching erection, his fist so tight the pressure burned his skin. He didn't care. The moans outside the boxes increased in volume, the eager slapping of flesh to flesh. If he couldn't join them, by Infinity, he could lose himself in their lust. At the least, he knew his orgasm would be good. All living beings radiated extra etheric force at climax, and from what he'd tasted of it already, Buttercup's was sure to be sweet.

He timed his strokes to match their excitement—faster, tighter, and then their mutual peak was there. The prince and Buttercup cried out hoarsely, the energy of their orgasm rolling over him like hot, moist wind—a palpable shock wave of ecstasy.

He was not prepared for the intensity of the effect. His sensations peaked beyond any he could recall, his balls contracting as if a large, strong hand had slapped them forcefully to his root.

He gasped for air, throttling back a scream. This couldn't be happening. This was too much. Too good.

His body overruled his mind's objections. Deep in his groin, gates which had been tightly shut fibrillated wildly and flew open. His own sexual essences flooded him too quickly for him to muster the least defense. Heat rushed through his cock and burst violently over his hand. For the first time in seven years, Prince Pahndir spilled his semen.

When it was over, he gulped for air as quietly as he could, his relief as momentous as his shock. However this miracle had happened, he knew what it meant. His curse was broken. He was alive again.

And he didn't have the faintest concept what to do about that.

Turn the page for a special preview of
Emma Holly's novel

Fairyville

Coming soon from Berkley Sensation!

Chapter One

Zoe Clare saw dead people.

This wouldn't have been bad if dead people were all she saw. In this day and age, a person could make a decent living talking to ghosts. But Zoe's gift had come with an eccentric extra—an tiny, annoying extra that was, even now, tugging at the covers she'd pulled so determinedly over her head.

"I need my sleep," she said, her eyes screwed shut against the bright Arizona morning. "It's important for a medium to recharge her batteries."

The tugging changed to a weighted prickle on her scalp, between the corkscrew curls of her long black hair. One of the fairies who'd been her constant companion since childhood—much to her parents' dismay—was standing on Zoe's head.

"Wakey-wakey," it said like a DJ on helium. "It's a beautiful day in Fairyville, and your batteries are as charged as they're going to get."

"Your mother was a toadstool," Zoe retorted, her eyes still closed.

The avoidance was ineffective. Her tormentor shone clearly in her mind's eye, complete with a diaphanous gown and dragonfly wings. Like many mediums, Zoe saw the other world better without her physical sight. While the different fairies' voices sounded the same to her, this one's iridescent purple wings and gaudy yellow tiara proclaimed that she was Rajel, queen of Zoe's personal flock. She flashed her tiny white teeth in a blinding grin, Zoe's insult having slid right off her.

Serious fairies, apparently, had little hope of rising through the ranks. Only the most persistently positive could be queen.

"It's time to rise and shine," Rajel cooed. "You know you hate to be late to work."

This was usually true, but today was the day after the full moon. Spiritually, this affected her not at all. Personally, it made her stomach sink to her toes.

The full moon was when her landlord-slash-manager, the painfully scrumptious Magnus Monroe, indulged in his monthly sexual debauch. The day after the full moon was when she had to watch him stroll into their office, all loose-hipped and jovial, and know that—yet again—she wasn't the woman who'd put that smile on his face.

She wondered who his partner had been this time. Every month was different, and he didn't seem to have a type except female and breathing. She suspected the lucky lady was Sheri Yost. Magnus had been flirting with the waitress at Zoe's favorite steak house over the last week, which meant Zoe's lunch would be as hard to stomach as going in to work. The women who slept with her manager always had a glow afterward, an I've-been-screwed-six-ways-to-Sunday-and-I-loved-it glow.

Just remembering how many times she'd seen that sensual female smirk made Zoe sit up growling in disgust. She shoved her tangle of long black curls away from her face. Now that her physical eyes were open, Rajel was a sparkly purple sphere, no bigger than a penny, hanging in the air in front of her. Most people wouldn't have seen her, but Zoe could see her and more. Rajel's fairy court bobbed behind her, a cloud of at least a dozen snickering rainbow glows.

It was a larger gathering than usual.

"Well, well," Zoe said. "The gang's all here. Must have been a slow night for parties."

The fairies giggled in agreement and whizzed off in different directions.

"Dibs on helping Zoe with her hair!" cried one.

"I'm picking her jewelry!" said another.

"I'll talk to the toaster!" announced a third.

"No!" Zoe whipped out her hand to grab the last fairy, but the little bugger was too fast. "No talking to the toaster! You guys keep shorting it out."

The darting rose-pink sparkle paid her no mind. "Stop her," Zoe begged Rajel. "I'm tired of cold cereal."

"Oh, I couldn't discourage Florabel." Rajel brushed a bit of fairy dust from her gown. "She's only trying to communicate with the machinery. It does have a primitive form of consciousness, you know."

"Great," Zoe mumbled, throwing off the covers and stumping toward the shower. "I guess until Florabel figures out the toaster's 'primitive consciousness,' I can kiss my morning bagel good-bye."

⸻

Cold cereal aside, if a person had to go to work, Fairyville, Arizona, was a pretty place to do it, especially on a cool, bright morning in July. The sky was a deep, saturated blue barely brushed by clouds, and while the temperature might climb toward ungodly as the day went on, for now it was as pleasant as baby's smile.

Zoe's fairies swooped off, somersaulting into the ethers, chasing bees, or showing off. Zoe couldn't begrudge them their high spirits—or their abandonment of her. No matter how many times she'd seen the local red-rock cliffs against that deep blue sky, the sight never failed to catch at her breath.

You just couldn't forget the power of Mother Nature here.

A definite beneficiary of that power, Fairyville lay north of its more famous sister, Sedona, but shared the same awe-inspiring landscape of buttes and spires—and the same reputation for mystical oddities. Zoe's home had been a virtual ghost town fifty years ago, a copper mine gone bust in the Great Depression. Revived by a carefully calculated tourist scheme, Fairyville was now divided into two camps—the "real" Fairyvillers and the "normals." Being a real Fairyviller had nothing to do with how long you'd lived there. You became one by having a psychic gift, by treating those who had psychic gifts with respect, or by being so looney tunes everyone figured you had to be touched by *some*thing.

Normals were the folks who thought the real Fairyvillers were "colorful."

Zoe grimaced at just how much local color she herself represented and parked her classic white VW bug at the end of Canyon Way, well beyond the spots the tourists would be fighting over once they rolled out of their B&Bs. Even at this distance, her walk would not be long. Fairyville's carefully restored historic district was, at most, a ten-minute stroll from end to end. Zoe knew every inch of it, from the mix of Old West storefronts to the rock shops to the Spanish adobe architecture.

She'd lived in or around Fairyville all her life, and considered herself lucky this was the case. Her parents, normals down to their toes, had tolerated her claims of being visited by dead relatives. This was, after all, a mainstream sort of weirdness. When she refused to outgrow her fairies, however, they'd drawn a line. Dead people existed. Fairies were delusions. It was time Zoe admitted she'd made them up.

Fortunately, the psychologist they'd insisted she see while she was in high school was a real Fairyviller, too. Dr. Gordon ended up being—unbeknownst to Zoe's parents—her spiritual mentor. In truth, it would have been hard for Catherine Gordon to avoid it, seeing as how *she* liked to call in angels for consults. She'd guided Zoe to the best teachers to hone her gifts, even covered for her when she went to workshops.

"Thank you, Doc," Zoe murmured as she forced her

reluctant sandals past the Navajo rug store. She felt in need
of counting her blessings. The gallery in which she did her
readings was only a few doors down, a restored two-story
brick building from 1910. She could see the potted prickly
pear cactus that guarded the entrance from where she
stood, the last of its lush hot-pink flowers drooping off.
Magnus loved that cactus. He called it "Gorgeous" and
said hello to it every morning. The first time Zoe had heard
him do it, her heart had clenched.

Magnus was sweet to women no matter what their
species.

You can handle this, she told herself. *Every month you
see him do the same thing, and every month you survive.*

But the pep talk didn't do much good. The Open sign in
her gallery window sent her pulse into a panic. Magnus
was already there, probably lazing back in her chair with
his long, strong legs propped on the desk she used for pa-
perwork. He looked good in cowboy boots, Magnus did, a
man's man with a sensually handsome face. The memory
of the way his faded Levi's cupped his basket made her
whole body flush. He always looked mellow the morning
after, as if he'd just lie back and let a woman ride.

Chickening out at the last moment, Zoe ducked into the
Fairyville Café, one door short of her own storefront. Her
first client wasn't due for fifteen minutes. She didn't have
to torture herself by spending every one of those minutes
pining after her well-screwed landlord.

Metaphysically speaking, that wouldn't do anyone any
good.

The café's owner was Teresa Smallfoot. A mix of Na-
tive American, Anglo, and six-foot-tall goddess, she'd
been a friend of Zoe's from the day she opened, trading
free coffee for the occasional free reading. Since Teresa's
troubles were of the mild romantic sort and the coffee was
hot and strong, Zoe considered the exchange a fair one.
Plus, Teresa's departed relatives were well behaved. Not a
pesterer in the bunch. Considering some of her clients'
connections showed up hours ahead of schedule to jabber
inanities, Zoe valued the ones with restraint.

Teresa was watching her customers from behind the coffee bar today. The decor was Western Victorian, with little round antique tables and sepia photos of long-dead people hanging on the walls. Teresa leaned forward as soon as she saw Zoe.

"Girlfriend," she said in a low, excited tone. "You should have heard the ruckus from next door last night! There was such a caterwauling coming out of Sheri's bedroom windows, you'd have thought a pair of cougars had been locked inside!"

Zoe fought a wince. She'd forgotten Sheri Yost was Teresa's next door neighbor.

"Great," she said, pouring herself some coffee from the carafe of dark roast on the counter. Teresa used real cups, mismatched china she picked up in junk stores. "Just what I was hoping to hear."

"I know, honey," Teresa crooned sympathetically. That lasted about two seconds, or until Teresa's love of good gossip had her grinning again. "I'll be surprised if Sheri comes to work today. In fact, I'll be surprised if she can walk. That manager of yours is a *luvv* machine. Every time I thought he must be wrung dry, they started up again. If I didn't know you had a thing for him, I'd be tempted to throw myself in his path out of sheer curiosity."

Zoe took such a big swig of coffee, she nearly scalded her throat. "Don't let me stop you," she said through her coughs.

"Oh, right. Like you wouldn't want to gouge out my eyes if I slept with him. I know the girlfriend rules."

"At least I could see why he'd go for you. Sheri Yost is a whiny bore."

Teresa flipped her long black locks behind her shoulders, her expression pleased by the compliment. "Sheri Yost is a whiny bore who isn't smart enough to make change. You, on the other hand, are beautiful, sweet, and wise. Clearly, Magnus has no sense."

"Unfortunately, you can't force people to have sense— as I've learned from my many years of giving advice." Zoe turned her cup between her hands. "I just don't understand him. Why would a guy with his looks and charisma restrict himself to having sex once a month? And why does it have to be a new woman every time?"

"Maybe that's the secret to his stamina. Abstinence plus variety. I mean, he can't be the only man who'd like to be able to perform like that. Without Viagra, I mean."

With a rueful cluck, Teresa interrupted the conversation to serve another customer.

"He's a freak," Zoe said when her friend returned, though she probably should have let it go. "I have no idea why I like him."

"How about because he's a hunka hunka burning love, and you've got eyes. Plus, he's nice."

Magnus was more than nice. Magnus was considerate, charming, funny, and had the sunniest disposition of any human being she knew. Nothing got him down—not hundred-degree weather, not dents in his SUV, or the evening news. His only flaw (and, to be fair, it was only a flaw to Zoe) was his refusal to look at her in a sexual way.

Teresa set her elbows on the counter. "Couldn't you ask your little friends what his story is?"

Zoe's mouth quirked. Teresa was open-minded, but she never liked to say the word *fairy*. "I have asked them. They're keeping mum."

Weirdly mum, in fact. Zoe's fairies tended to air their opinions about everything.

"Well, what good are they then?"

"They aren't my slaves, Ter. They hang with me because they think I'm fun."

"Fun on every topic but one."

This tease was a bit too close to the mark. Some days Zoe thought that if she didn't get over her crush on Magnus, she'd turn into a lifelong grump.

"I don't know what's wrong with me," she grumbled into her empty cup. "I never used to like guys that tall."

Teresa reached out to pat her arm. "Oh, face it, honey. It's not the height you like, it's him."

It is *him,* Zoe admitted, though she only pulled a face at her friend.

She was debating buying a chocolate muffin as consolation when a flicker of gray in her peripheral vision reminded her of the time. The ghost was one she knew: Mrs. Darling's late husband, Leo. Once he'd finished materializing, Leo nodded to her and smiled. He was one of her favorites, as gentle in death as he'd been in life. In spite of her sour mood, it cheered her to know he'd be her first job.

"Gotta go," she said to Teresa. "My special guests are starting to line up."

"Brr," Teresa responded, pretending to shiver as she hugged her arms.

Leo tipped his Stetson to Teresa, but Zoe was the only living being who saw.

Zoe gave her readings in the front room of the gallery. The furnishings were as homey as she could make them—secondhand chairs and sofas, for the most part, with nicked tables set between. A beautiful Navajo rug hung on one wall, her biggest decorating splurge. The light from the wide front window filled the space with gold, glinting pleasantly off her assortment of crystals and stones.

The fairies had insisted she buy them to "cleanse the atmosphere." They were her only mystical bric-a-brac. Most of her clients felt more comfortable without too much woo-woo stuff, though tourists sometimes asked why she didn't use tarot cards. Zoe knew such touchstones worked for others, but she'd never wanted to be dependent on objects. She needed nothing to jump start her gift except an open heart and a focused mind.

Even that seemed unnecessary with a contact as clear-spoken as Leo Darling. As usual, Ada Darling's weekly appointment went smoothly. She liked to share her news with her disincarnate spouse, to get his advice on the decisions of daily life. Her husband was always patient with her concerns, letting her know which handymen she could trust, reminding her that she didn't need his permission for anything.

Mrs. Darling never seemed to doubt the authenticity of

these interactions, but she also never seemed to realize they might inspire deeper thoughts. The soul survived death, and the dead still loved those they left behind. That was Big, as far as Zoe was concerned; that was a message she suspected she'd never tire of delivering. While Mrs. Darling was a sweet old lady, sometimes Zoe wanted to shake her out of her mundane world.

Heaven loves you, she longed to say. *What does it matter if your best friend cheats at bingo?*

When her hour was up, Mrs. Darling counted out her payment in cash like she always did. Her old, arthritic hands made each bill seem as heavy as *War and Peace*. Each time Zoe watched her do it, she had to bite her tongue against telling her to keep her money. Zoe performed a service, and she performed it well. This was her sole source of income. Even more important, if she didn't charge Ada Darling, Zoe suspected the woman would be in here every day.

Mrs. Darling sighed with satisfaction once the painstaking ritual was complete. "Thank you, dear," she said, handing over the fee. "You've put this aching old heart to rest."

Zoe smiled in spite of her impatience. "That's why I'm here."

Mrs. Darling nodded, her usual reluctance to go showing itself. She really didn't like facing her life without "dear old Leo" to hold her hand.

"You'll be fine," Zoe said, reaching out to squeeze her plump but fragile arm. "Leo watches over you all the time, not just when you talk to him here."

"But you're the one who makes me feel him," said Mrs. Darling. Her faded blue eyes teared up, though she waved off the tissue Zoe offered her. "You're a good girl, Zoe. I hope you find a man like Leo yourself someday."

"So do I," Zoe admitted, and then had to clear her throat.

Without warning, Mrs. Darling cackled out a laugh. "Ask those fairies of yours to fix you up. Then you'll be set!"

"You hear that?" Zoe said to the apparently empty air above her head.

No piping voices answered, even after Mrs. Darling left. A prickle at the back of Zoe's neck told her why. Magnus was standing in the open door behind her, the one that led to her office.

From their first meeting, Magnus had struck her as more man than most. He was tall, for one thing, at least six five—though you didn't notice how big the various parts of him were until you stood up close. With half a room between them, he simply looked in proportion. At five foot six Zoe was no pygmy, but she wasn't fooled by the distance. Toe to toe, Magnus could make an Amazon feel delicate. His looks were as dramatic as his size. He had dark, beautiful hair—not long but a little shaggy—smooth, high-colored skin; full, kissable lips; and eyes as green and clear as a mountain stream. If he hadn't exuded masculinity, he'd have been pretty. Instead, he came off as unbelievably sensual. Zoe had known him for two years, but she still had to swallow at the sight of him.

No matter how cool she wanted to act, he was hard to look away from.

Now his face held something uncertain, something she hadn't expected to see on this of all days. She wondered how much he'd heard of her conversation with Mrs. Darling. She could only hope it wasn't much. Zoe might be psychic, but she wasn't a mind reader. She caught images from people now and then, but they weren't conscious thoughts. They came, she was almost certain, from the part of them that shared the same non-physical territory as the deceased: the high, wise angel of their better selves.

As far as she could tell, Magnus's high, wise angel didn't have a peep to say to her.

"Your hair looks nice today," he said, waving one hand in its direction. "Glossy."

Zoe couldn't help touching it self-consciously. Left to itself, her hair had a tendency to devolve into a long black snarl. "I had help this morning."

He nodded without his usual trademark smile. Like most of the locals, Magnus knew about her fairies. He also knew, because she hadn't figured out how to keep it from

him, that they avoided him like the plague. She only had to
think hard about Magnus and they'd disappear into whatever dimension fairies hung out in when they weren't in
hers. Zoe had no idea why they did this—unless they simply didn't like his effect on her moods.

In all her life, only one other man had provoked a similar reaction, but that was a ghost Zoe preferred not to resurrect.

"I don't suppose they're still around," he said with an
uncustomary tinge of wistfulness. His Western-style shirt
hugged his chest just right, and his big, tanned hands were
thrust into the front pockets of his jeans. The faded patches
in the denim, where his cock and balls continually rubbed,
pointed out how very well hung he was. Sadly, none of
these things were encouraging Zoe's eyes to stay where she
wanted them.

"I think the fairies are outside playing," she said. She
shifted from foot to foot, caught off guard by his strange
mood. "I didn't expect to see you here this late."

Magnus owned a number of properties in Fairyville,
where he also acted in a managerial capacity. From the day
he'd invited Zoe to set up shop here, she was always his
first stop, though half an hour was generally as long as he
stayed.

He didn't respond right away, and she was soon sorry
she'd forced her gaze to his face. He was looking at her
steadily, as if whatever he was thinking was serious. She
would have given her right arm to have him look at her like
that in bed. Unable to stop the reaction, Zoe felt a bead of
sweat trickle down the small of her back. If he'd figured
out she had a yen for him, she was absolutely going to die.

"You got some more requests to speak," he said at last.
"I was trying to see if I could organize them into a tour."

"A tour?" she repeated, praying the words wouldn't
strangle on their way out her throat. He *had* figured it out.
He was trying to get rid of her.

"You could go in August. Get your name better known.
You deserve that, you know. You're a princess, Zoe, not a
girl wrapped in a donkey skin."

Zoe blinked at this odd reference. Then, realizing her traitorous eyes were threatening to overflow, she dropped her gaze to her feet. The sight of his shoes momentarily blanked her mind. He wasn't wearing his usual cowboy boots, but a pair of high-topped yellow sneakers with Wile E. Coyote painted on the side. With an effort, she pulled her concentration back.

"I'm not sure I want to travel. My friends are here. I . . . I feel more comfortable at home."

Her voice was low and husky, and all the curses in the world wouldn't erase the emotion that gave away. Magnus crossed the room before she could step back. He didn't touch her, but the heat from his body was distracting. Magnus's appeal was based on more than his looks. His energy always seemed twice as high as other men's.

"Zoe . . ." he began.

Zoe knew she had to stop whatever he was going to say. "I hope you're not unhappy with what I'm earning," she interrupted hurriedly. "I could advertise for more clients. Maybe put a site on the internet."

"Zoe." He gripped her shoulders between his hands, the tingling warmth of his hold like hot molasses running down her skin. She struggled not to shudder with enjoyment as it sank in. "I am not unhappy with what you make. I want this for you. Because you deserve it. You can't imagine I'm looking forward to you being gone?"

She did cry then, horrible, sniffly sobs that had her gasping into the tissue Mrs. Darling had refused. Completely mortified, she tried to struggle out of Magnus's hold, but he wasn't having that. He pulled her close instead, tucking her head under his and enfolding her in his arms.

Zoe used all her self control to stiffen instead of melt.

"Shh," he said, then swore softly into her hair. "Zoe, Zoe, Zoe. You had to go and make this even harder than it was."

"Oh, God," she cried. "You're turning me out!"

"Zoe." He sounded exasperated, but he tipped her head back and held her face. "Listen to me. I like you. I'm not turning you out. I'm not trying to get rid of you. I enjoy having you around."

She mopped the last of her crying jag from her nose. She was light-headed from her outburst, and probably not thinking straight, but she knew she'd never find the nerve to ask this again.

"If you *like* me," she said as deliberately as he'd been addressing her, "why haven't you ever made a move on me? Aren't I as interesting as the other women you go for?"

His green eyes darkened a second before his face followed suit, a flush washing up his lean, hard cheeks. She'd thought his smile could knock a woman flat, but the intensity of this expression stole her power to think. His hands tightened on either side of her jaw, and his gaze burned down at her from his greater height. He looked like he was angry, but she was pretty sure that wasn't it.

She was certain when his lips covered hers.

His kiss might have been soft, but it sure wasn't wasting time. She felt his tongue push into her mouth and heard her own knee-jerk moan of excitement. The rest of the world disappeared as that hot, wet flesh speared deep. His heat, his scent, his pounding heart became her universe. Suddenly, his arms were wrapped hard around her, one hand forking through her hair to cradle her head. He angled it to suit his pleasure while his second hand crushed her left butt cheek. She was wearing a gauzy, printed skirt, and he gripped that buttock like he owned it. His long, hot fingers stretched farther forward than she let most men get on a third date.

She had no urge to stop Magnus, and it wasn't just because it had been longer then she could count since she'd had any date at all. At first contact of his finger, her body jolted with an erotic shock so powerful it surprised her—even with the time she'd spent hankering after him. No wonder women dropped like ripe cherries around this man. His hands conveyed an energy that fairly buzzed. A flood of moisture ran into the folds he'd brushed with his fingertips, then overflowed them in a heated rush. If the mewls she kept spilling into his mouth hadn't clued him in already, Magnus had to know what he'd done to her.

Right that moment, it didn't seem to bother him. Feeling the evidence of her arousal against his hand, he made a low, rough noise and kissed her harder, his hunger a savage, delicious thing. His body moved in one slow undulation, his erection grinding against her belly.

God, it was big. Big and hot and—

Magnus tore his mouth away from hers.

"This is . . . not the plan," he gasped.

Dizzy, Zoe stroked the pulse throbbing in his neck. She had to touch him, had to feel his skin against her palms. His tendons were tight, his skin dark with the blood rushing under it. Going on tiptoe, she tipped her head up for another kiss.

"No," he said, very firm but still breathless. "You're not thinking like yourself."

Zoe's head cleared reluctantly. If thinking like herself meant stopping, she didn't think she wanted to. Magnus had kissed her. Magnus had eaten at her mouth like he wanted to swallow her, like he'd been lusting after her every bit as much as she'd been lusting after him. His big, broad chest went up and down with his ragged breathing. Then he let his hands slide to her elbows and stepped back.

Zoe dropped onto her heels like a balloon with the air let out.

"I'm sorry," he said. "This isn't how I want it to be with you."

Hurt and anger had her eyes sliding to his groin. She might not be the queen of the sex parade—her oddball calling saw to that—but she knew the difference between a man who wanted her and one who didn't. Magnus's erection shoved starkly against his jeans, almost too thick and long to be real.

"This isn't how you want it?" she repeated in disbelief. "Excuse me, but I'd say a part of you would beg to differ."

"I'm easily aroused," he said with an odd, defensive dignity.

Zoe folded her arms across her breasts, uncomfortably aware of how sensitized they were. "Well, that explains why you only fuck once a month."

Her sarcasm called a shade of purple into his face. The contrast made his eyes blaze like emeralds; in spite of which, his voice was calm.

"Don't be crude, Zoe. It doesn't suit you."

Her temper, which she almost always had under control, abruptly snapped. "How about this? Is this too crude to suit me?"

She slapped her hand around the bulge of his big erection, squeezing hard enough to feel the juicy give of his balls through the worn denim. Part of her brain forgot to be angry in her enchantment. She might have taken hold of a python; his cock felt that substantial, that alive. Magnus moaned, pain and pleasure mixing in the sound. His hand jammed over hers, completely covering it.

It took a second to register that he wasn't trying to pull her away.

"Don't do this," he said through gritted teeth, his hips beginning to circle into the cup their locked hands had formed.

Zoe's jaw dropped as she watched him writhe. Maybe he *was* easy to arouse. He did seem to be having trouble controlling himself. He was pushing at her so hard her fingers were going numb. When he spoke again, he sounded desperate.

"You know you won't appreciate being the next notch on my bedpost. You know you're too good for that."

She looked at him, her soul gone cold. "You're saying I wouldn't be any different than the others?"

"I'm saying you *couldn't* be."

Failing to see the distinction, she wrenched her hand out from under his. She would have stepped away, would have salved her pride somehow, but he brushed her cheek with his fingertips, and the tenderness of the gesture arrested her.

It was pathetic, really, how badly she wanted to believe he cared.

"Be my friend," he said. "Be the friend I've always hoped you would be."

His tone was gentle, his expression genuinely fond. She didn't say she couldn't be his friend, that she cared too much in a different way. That would have been a lie. Magnus meant so much to her, she suspected she could be his friend even if her heart cracked in two.

She did, however, have too much self-respect to admit it.

She blew out her breath instead. "You're even weirder than I am."

That inspired one of his dazzling smiles. "High praise," he said, "coming from a real Fairyviller."

She should have been grateful he was still comfortable with her. Unfortunately, she was too busy fighting memories. The sad truth was that Magnus wasn't the first man she'd loved who'd pulled a number like this on her.